#1 *NEW YORK TIMES* BESTSELLING AUTHOR
KRESLEY COLE

LOTHAIRE

"I think this is one of the few series that is actually getting better as it progresses. . . . My favorite thing about these books is that Cole lets the characters act like immortals. They are so violent, so cunning and evil. And yet they are hilarious and smart and, of course, amazing in bed." —*USA Today*

"How do you make the crazy, arrogant, and ruthless archvillain of a series a hero? With great difficulty! Yet Cole pulls it off splendidly." —*RT Book Reviews* (Top Pick)

DREAMS OF A DARK WARRIOR

"Fast-paced, engaging, and captivating. . . . The perfect getaway." —Examiner.com

"Sex scenes so hot there is a danger the pages could spontaneously combust. . . . Still fresh, still thrilling. . . . Phenomenally awesome!" —*LoveVampires*

DEMON FROM THE DARK

"A dangerously sexy story infused with pathos and hard-edged passion!" —*RT Book Reviews*

"Intense danger mixes with insatiable desire to create a scorching hot romance that plays out against a fast-paced backdrop of thrilling supernatural adventure. Addictively good reading." —*LoveVampires*

PLEASURE OF A DARK PRINCE

"Consistent excellence is a Cole standard!"

—*RT Book Reviews*

"There are few authors that can move me to tears. Kresley Cole is one of them."

—*Book Binge*

KISS OF A DEMON KING

"Kresley Cole knows what paranormal romance readers crave and superbly delivers on every page."

—*Single Titles*

"Cole deftly blends danger and desire into a brilliantly original contemporary paranormal romance. She neatly tempers the scorchingly sexy romance with a generous measure of sharp humor . . . simply irresistible."

—*Reader to Reader*

DARK DESIRES AFTER DUSK

"Cole outdoes herself. . . . A gem."

—*RT Book Reviews*

"A gifted author with a knack for witty dialogue, smart heroines, fantastic alpha males, and yes, it has to be said, some of the hottest loves scenes you'll read in mainstream romance. . . . You're in for a treat."

—RomanceNovel.tv

DARK NEEDS AT NIGHT'S EDGE

"Poignant and daring. You can trust Cole to always deliver sizzling sexy interludes within a darkly passionate romance."

—*RT Book Reviews*

"The evolution of this romance is among the most believable and engrossing I've ever read. Cole's Immortals After Dark series continues stronger than ever."

—*Fresh Fiction*

BOOKS BY KRESLEY COLE

The Immortals After Dark Series

The Warlord Wants Forever
A Hunger Like No Other
No Rest for the Wicked
Wicked Deeds on a Winter's Night
Dark Needs at Night's Edge
Dark Desires After Dusk
Kiss of a Demon King
Deep Kiss of Winter
Pleasure of a Dark Prince
Demon from the Dark
Dreams of a Dark Warrior
Lothaire

The Sutherland Series

The Captain of All Pleasures
The Price of Pleasure

The MacCarrick Brothers Series

If You Dare
If You Desire
If You Deceive

The Arcana Chronicles

Poison Princess

KRESLEY COLE

shadow's claim

**SIMON &
SCHUSTER**

London · New York · Sydney · Toronto · New Delhi

A CBS COMPANY

First published in Great Britain in 2012 by Simon & Schuster UK Ltd
A CBS COMPANY

1 3 5 7 9 10 8 6 4 2

Simon & Schuster UK Ltd
1st Floor
222 Gray's Inn Road
London
WC1X 8HB

www.simonandschuster.co.uk

Simon & Schuster Australia, Sydney
Simon & Schuster India, New Delhi

A CIP catalogue copy for this book is available
from the British Library.

Paperback ISBN: 978-1-47111-390-1
Ebook ISBN: 978-1-47111-391-8

Printed and bound by CPI Group (UK) Ltd, Croydon, CR0 4YY

Warmly dedicated to Lauren "The Rock" McKenna.

Nineteen books down, one hundred to go . . .

ACKNOWLEDGMENTS

My deepest appreciation goes out to Louisa Edwards, Beth Kendrick, Kristen Painter, Gena Showalter, and Roxanne St. Claire, all fabulous friends who happen to be incredible writers (keep doing like you do).

GLOSSARY OF TERMS FROM
THE LIVING BOOK OF LORE...

The Lore

"*. . . and those sentient creatures that are not human shall be united in one stratum, coexisting with—yet secret from—man's.*"

- Most are immortal, can regenerate from injuries, and can only be killed by mystical fire or beheading.
- Their eyes change to a breed-specific color with intense emotion.

The Vampires

"*In the first chaos of the Lore, a brotherhood of vampires dominated by relying on their worship of logic and absence of mercy. They sprang from the harsh steppes of Dacia and migrated to Russia, though some say a secret enclave, the Daci, live in Dacia still.*"

- Each adult male vampire seeks his *Bride,* his eternal wife, and walks as the living dead until he finds her.
- A Bride will render his body fully alive, giving him breath and making his heart beat, a process known as *blooding.*
- *Tracing* is teleporting. A vampire can only trace to destinations he's previously been or to those he can see.
- Three vampire factions exist: the Forbearer Army (turned humans), the Horde (flesh-takers), and the Dacians . . .

The Dacians

"Whispered to have vast intellects and stony hearts, the vampires of mist and legend observe the Lore with dispassionate eyes. Cursed with unending strife until the House of Old rises. . . ."

- Dacia's closed kingdom, the Realm of Blood and Mist, is said to be hidden within a hollowed-out mountain range.
- Do not drink blood from the flesh.
- The Daciano royal family consisted of five arms, each with a sacred duty to the realm.
- Upon the old king's death, and the rightful heir's disappearance, the family fractured into warring houses.

The Sept of Sorceri

"The Sept forever seek and covet others' powers, challenging and dueling to seize more—or, more darkly, stealing another's sorcery. . . ."

- Born with one innate power, their *root power*.
- One of the physically weaker species in the Lore, they used elaborate armors to protect their bodies. Eventually they held metals—and especially gold—sacred.

The Demonarchies

"The demons are as varied as the bands of man. . . ."

- A collection of demon dynasties.
- Most demon breeds can teleport to places they've previously been.
- A male demon must have intercourse with a potential mate to ascertain if she's truly his—a process known as *attempting*.

The Death Demons

"Violent, warlike, and ruthless, they constantly hunger for their next kill—and the strength it brings. . . ."

- A demonarchy located in the plane of Abaddon, once famed for its blood sport tournaments.
- Harvest power with each kill they make.

The Vrekeners

"Death descends on swift wings. The righteous reckoning of the Lore, they strike like a plague from the heavens, their wings blocking out the light of the sun, casting the land in shadow."

- Mortal enemies of the Sept of Sorceri, who they consider wicked and unclean.
- They live in the air territories. Their royal seat is Skye Hall.

The Accession

"And a time shall come to pass when all immortal beings in the Lore, from the Valkyrie, vampire, Lykae, and demon factions to the phantoms, shifters, fey, and sirens . . . must fight and destroy each other."

- A kind of mystical checks-and-balances system for an ever-growing population of immortals.
- Two major alliances: the Pravus Rule and the Vertas League.
- Occurs every five hundred years. Or right now . . .

"Wrong an assassin's woman—and he will make you pay."

—TREHAN CRISTIAN DACIANO,
PRINCE OF DACIA,
LAST SCION OF THE HOUSE OF SHADOW

"I thought gold was the most precious and beautiful thing on earth. Until I met him.*"*

—PRINCESS BETTINA OF ABADDON,
KINGDOM OF THE DEATHLY ONES

1

A savage kick to Princess Bettina of Abaddon's back severed her spinal cord.

A blessing.

The searing pain that had been clawing through her entire being faded below her waist to pinpoints of pressure, then tingles, then . . .

Nothing.

Blessing. She'd long since stopped begging for her life, knew she'd never leave this field of poppies alive.

The four winged monsters who'd dragged her here had plans for her: as much agony as possible before her death.

Just as their kind had delivered to her sorceress mother twenty years before.

Though half demon, Bettina was weak in body, hopeless at fighting. She'd depended on her Sorceri power for protection—the one that these Vrekeners had siphoned from her as easily as they'd snatched the clothes from her body.

No longer could she open her swollen eyes. Her last sight? The leader standing over her, brandishing a scythe, his eyes frenzied. His claw-tipped wings had blocked the light of a low yellow moon. The scythe's blade wasn't fashioned out of metal, but of black flame. . . .

Yet Bettina could still hear, was still aware. In the distance, a new age band played in an outdoor arena. Young mortals danced and sang—

The force of one kick jostled her over onto her belly. Her mauled face shoved against crushed poppies. The leader played with her as a hawk would a mouse, ravaging the meat from its bones. His followers jeered and doused her with bottles of spirits.

Menacing yells, steel-toed boots, the blistering sting of alcohol.

Ah, gods, she was *too* aware. She tried desperately to lose herself in memories of a boy with smiling blue eyes and sun-kissed hair.

He doesn't know how much I love him. So many things I wish I'd done—

Her upper body exploded with even more pain, as if to compensate for the numbness in her fractured legs. She could perceive her broken ribs jutting from her skin. Her mangled arms draped limply across the ground where they'd fallen when she'd last tried to protect her head. . . . Anguish multiplied.

Or perhaps the Vrekeners' blows rained down more swiftly. The kill was near.

All she'd wanted was to go to a party with her mortal college friends. She'd been excited, happy to fit in with them, or to appear to—as a halfling, she'd never *fit in* before. Little did she know that she'd already drawn her enemy's notice with her sorcery. She'd never intentionally used it—

Over all other pain, she perceived the heat of that burning scythe descending ever closer to her. Hotter, hotter, *scorching*.

Alcohol on her skin, the black flame . . .

Bettina choked on a sob. They planned to burn her?

Suddenly she felt weightless. *This is what dying feels like?*

No, she was traveling. *Summoned?* Dear gods, yes, the demon in her had been summoned across realms. Naked, powerless, sightless, she slipped from that field in the mortal world to her home plane of Abaddon.

In a flash, the poppies were replaced by cold marble, a balm on what was left of her skin. That awareness returned. *I'm lying on the floor of my castle's court, broken, wearing only my blood and the Vrekeners' rank liquor. The courtiers still gossip and laugh. Can't they see me?*

She tried to scream for help; blood bubbled up over her lips. *Can't scream, can't move.* She could only listen. A conversation between her godfather Raum—the Grand Duke of the Deathly Ones—and another was already under way.

"Now you've done it, Raum." It was Caspion the Tracker. The demon she secretly loved. "Tina hates being summoned with that medallion." *Not at present!* "She considers it a leash."

Her guardians had insisted on it, a condition of her leaving Abaddon.

"Ha! It probably makes her feel more like a demon," Raum said in a gruff tone, knowing that wasn't true. They'd had words over his use of the mystical medallion. "Besides, she told me she was coming home from college by month's end."

"You know time moves differently in the mortal realm," Caspion said, amusement lacing his words. "And more, she said she was very busy but would *try* to visit—"

Bettina heard a courtier gasp. *They've seen me.* Murmurs rose to a furor.

From the front of the court, Caspion demanded, "What is it?" Closer by, he asked, "Who *is* this pitiful creature? No, no, this isn't *Tina.* It can't be!" A touch on her forehead . . . a sucked in breath of recognition . . . a roar of grief. *"Bettina!"*

Raum bellowed, "What has happened?"

"Tina, wake up!" Caspion commanded her. "Ah, gods, stay with me. *Stay.*"

For him, she managed to slit open one eye. His curling blond hair hung over his harried face. His own eyes had gone from midnight blue to black, signaling his emotion. They even started watering as he gazed over her injuries.

She saw a shining hero of old. Her beloved Cas.

He yanked off his warm coat, covering her. "A physic!" he yelled into the crowd. *"Now!"*

Others gathered around her. She heard Raum stomping closer. "Who's done this to my little Tina?" Something broke directly. No doubt from his fist. "Damn you, tell me! Who's hurt her?"

She tried to answer, parting her lips. . . . Her jaw must be broken.

Another anguished roar. *Oh, Cas.*

Visibly making an effort to control himself, he said, "You hang on and *stay* with me."

There's nowhere else I'd rather be than with you.

"I'll get you through this, Tina. I swear it. You're going to be all right," he said, his voice thick. "Don't leave me."

Bettina felt the tiniest sliver of hope, something to fight for. Surely Cas returned her feelings, saw her as more than a little sister.

"Will she live?" Raum bit out. "She's not hardy like a demoness, not strong like we are."

She hadn't been a true demon before. Now she was no longer a true sorceress. *They took my root power. My soul.*

A male she didn't recognize asked, "Has she frozen into her immortality?" The physic?

Cas answered, "She was on the cusp. Maybe by now . . ."

"We need a Sorceri healer. If we act quickly, the princess could recover," the physic said, but hastily qualified his statement: "Her *body* could recover from this."

What did that mean?

Raum ordered, "Find Tina's godmother! Don't return from the Sorceri plane without Morgana!" Coming into Bettina's line of vision, Raum yelled to Cas, "I should never have let her go! I was too lenient! Things will change in Abaddon!" His eyes were glinting, his voice choked up. The crusty old warrior was at a loss. He began ramming his horns against a stone wall, roaring to everyone, "Heed my words! We return to olden ways!"

Free of the attack, Bettina's body started trying to regenerate, nerves sparking to life once more. Pain erupted all over her, blistering waves of it.

Even in the midst of her escalating agony and lingering horror, the words *olden ways* struck fear in her heart.

Prince Trehan Daciano shot awake in the middle of the day, bolting upright from his pallet of furs.

He gazed around in confusion, seeing his usual surroundings—shelves of books, weapons, his sideboard with carafes of mead-laced blood.

Though he'd experienced no nightmare, sleep had been snatched from him, replaced by a marked unease. With each moment, he grew even more on edge, a feeling like . . . like *emptiness* settling in his chest.

Like *dread*. So different from his usual numbness.

Brows drawn, he rose, tracing across the spacious room to one of the curtained balconies.

These grand apartments had once been the royal library. Centuries ago, he'd moved in and never moved out, haunting this place until no other member of the family would enter.

Time and history seeped from these familiar stones. He knew every crag and groove as well as he knew his own grim reflection. *Like these stones, I quietly endure the ages.*

Drawing back the thick curtain, he gazed outside. From this height, Trehan could survey far into the Realm of Blood and Mist, the secreted lands of the mighty Dacians.

The royal city below was still at this hour. Only the sound of Dacia's bubbling blood fountains could be heard.

Across from his residence stood the majestic black stone castle, the heart of the realm—abandoned without a king. How many of his kinsmen had perished trying to seize that keep? How much deceit and murder surrounded it?

The warring houses of the royal family had once boasted hundreds of members each—now dwindled down to a handful.

For an immortal family, they knew death so well.

Trehan was the last born to the House of Shadow, the assassin arm of the family. Though he was a potential contender for the crown—along with four of his lethal cousins—he had no real aspiration to seize it. A quiet loner by nature, he loathed spectacle and attention, was content to blend into the shadows.

He only wanted to perform his duty. For nearly a millennium, he'd been the enforcer of law, a merciless assassin.

As his long-dead father had oft told him, "You are the *sword of the kingdom,* Trehan. Dacia will be your family, your friend, your mistress, the grand love of your life. That is your lot, Son. Want for nothing else. And you will never be disappointed."

Trehan had once foolishly entertained secret hopes, but he'd eventually embraced his father's teachings. As was logical.

I want for nothing. This *was* his lot, to await down here in the earth until Mother Dacia needed his sword. To strike, execute, then return.

So why this unaccountable restlessness? This sudden . . . frustration?

It was similar to that niggling feeling of some task forgotten. Except this feeling had teeth, gnawing at his chest.

And why should Trehan have a sense of something left undone? He *always* did everything that was expected of him. Ever cold, ever rational Trehan couldn't explain this.

What have I left undone? Rubbing a palm over his chest, Trehan crossed to one of countless bookshelves. He selected a recently acquired explorer's narrative, adjourning to his favorite seat before the fire, planning to lose himself in tales of life outside this mountain, of emotions he never felt, and interactions he never experienced.

Not on this day.

After rereading the same page a dozen times, he closed the tome, staring into the flames as he struggled to identify the hollow ache in his dormant heart.

His fingers tightened on the book, sinking into the cover. *Gods damn it, what have I left undone?*

Yet the dread only mounted. Then came one word, a whisper in his mind. . . .

Protect.

2

The Plane of Abaddon,
Demonarchy of the Deathly Ones
THREE MONTHS LATER

"Bettina, you don't understand," Caspion muttered as he gazed out into the night. He clutched the balcony rail with one hand and a silver mug of demon brew with the other. "I've done something that I can't undo, something that even *I* can't talk my way out of."

Bettina stood beside him at the rail, drink in hand as well. "Oh, for gold's sake, what could possibly be so bad?"

Bad was recovering for months from a savage beating, then returning to "olden ways."

Bad was being offered up as a tournament prize by one's godparents.

"Can you not relax, Cas? Enjoy the night and tell me what worries you." Though her apartments in one of Castle Rune's great spires were now a sort of jail, the view couldn't be beaten.

Her balcony circled the entire spire and was elevated above the fog that swathed the medieval town of Rune below. From here, she and Caspion could see the tops of the giant moonraker trees that stretched from the marsh five hundred feet into the air. Bats jagged in front of the waxing moon.

The setting was as romantic as she could have hoped. Sidling closer to Cas, she basked in the warmth emanating from his big warrior's body. But he exhaled wearily, taking a drink from his mug, his troubled gaze fixed below him.

As an adult death demon, Cas could see in the dark, could even penetrate Rune's infamous fog bank. What was he watching for? Why was he nervous?

She hated seeing her soon-to-be lover in this condition. His eyes were bloodshot, his golden hair disheveled. Fatigue was etched into his normally flawless face.

"Surely my predicament must be worse than yours." She was about to be married off to whichever "suitor" prevailed in the upcoming tournament for her hand. *Unless I seduce Cas tonight* . . . "Did you get caught bedding another nobleman's daughter?" she asked, biting back her jealousy. Caspion was legendary for his conquests.

"If only that was all." He downed his brew.

So Bettina drained her mug as well, coughing as she finished. She'd never had more than a few sips of this potent concoction before tonight, preferring lighter Sorceri wines. But she was on a mission, would do anything to achieve it.

"Easy, girl," Cas said with a ghost of his usual heartbreaking grin. "That drink gains on you with each drop."

Eyes watering, she forced a smile. "It tastes so . . . different." *Like fermented ghoul urine, I imagine.*

Bettina knew that this brew left one relatively sober

up to a tipping point, beyond which sudden drunkenness ensued. Then one became *tore up from the floor up*, as her snarky new servant would say.

Hey, as long as Cas was drunk with her. "I'd love some more, darling. Let's go back inside." *Back to my softly lit apartments and cozy settee.*

"A final cup, then," he muttered, turning toward her sitting area.

Inside her spire, all twelve rooms were filled with imported silks and antiques, adorned with flame chandeliers of the finest crystal. Everything was luxurious, polished splendor.

Well, everything except the small, dented copper bell on her coffee table. . . .

After pouring them another round, Cas sank down on the settee, raking his fingers through his curling hair.

She joined him there, gazing at his handsome visage and muscled frame with a sigh of appreciation.

Standing more than six and a half feet tall, he towered over her five-and-a-half-foot height. His eyes were a hypnotic blue, turning stormy black with strong emotions. His proud horns were the ideal size, curving back along his fair head like a Grecian wreath. He kept them polished; they glinted like amber in the candlelight of her room.

He had sublime features—a strong chin, broad cheekbones, and full, kissable lips. She could only *imagine* how incredible those lips would feel against her own. They'd never kissed, had never touched beyond a hug.

She'd fallen for Caspion from the moment she'd first seen him ten years ago, when she'd been only twelve. Her beloved sire, King Mathar, had just died, and she and Raum had been presiding over Abaddon's royal court. Or at least Raum had been presiding, reluctantly.

Just three years older than Bettina, Cas had come striding into the chamber, dashing in his armor. All conversation had stopped, the crowd parting as he'd offered a bound bounty—one of her realm's most feared foes.

He didn't present it to Raum. But to her.

She'd still been in the depths of grief, feeling all alone, like a hornless Sorceri imposter who would never belong among the martial Abaddonae. But then a ray of sun had caught Caspion, highlighting those blond locks, setting his eyes aglow. Like a sign.

And she'd known that her life would never be the same.

Besides the fact that they were both orphans, they'd had little in common. She'd been a wealthy royal, treated like a fragile porcelain doll; he'd been found in an alley as a downy-horned toddler and had grown up begging in the streets. She'd been filled with self-doubt, wondering how a peculiar halfling like her could ever be queen; he'd been bold and brash, determined to make his mark, to earn the respect of the Abaddonae.

And yet the unlikeliest of friendships had blossomed. After that first day, she'd followed Caspion everywhere.

In the years to come, he'd routinely sneaked her off-plane, teleporting her to the world of mortals so they could discover those new lands together. He'd eventually taken her on his less dangerous bounty hunts, while she'd marveled at his talent in tracking his prey.

They'd shared each other's secrets: his continual sexual dalliances; her modern ideals and fears about assuming the crown once she came of age and was wed.

Yet after all they'd been through together, Cas still considered her his best friend and nothing more. Perhaps this was because her looks weren't on par with his—or demonic in the least. Her features were most often described as "elfin." One problem: she wasn't an elf.

Maybe her breasts were just too small. She glanced down, briefly glaring at them.

Didn't matter. For all her physical shortcomings, tonight she would attempt to change her friendship with Cas, to *elevate* it.

In preparation, she'd extinguished the chandeliers and lit a few candles throughout the rooms. She'd procured several jugs of demon brew, then dismissed the guards stationed outside her door.

And she'd dressed for the occasion.

"Won't you tell me what's going on, my darling?" she asked, edging closer. "You always trust me with your secrets. You know I'll keep them forever."

"My problem doesn't concern you," he said, absently rubbing his throat. "It mustn't."

"Hmm. Very well." She'd try another tack. "You haven't complimented me on my outfit." Bettina had grown accustomed to the jeans, sandals, and T-shirts she'd worn during her two-semester stint at college, but in Abaddon, she'd returned to dressing as her foremothers had.

In other words, she'd clad herself in provocative clothes, plaited her dark hair into wild, disordered braids, and donned as much gold jewelry as her body could carry.

As was the Sorceri way, she also wore a mask. The scarlet silk was a thin band around her eyes, making their color stand out—champagne-brown irises circled with a ring of black. According to her godmother, Morgana, her wide eyes were her best feature.

But now Cas barely spared a glance at her red lace-up bodice or her skimpy black skirt with slits up to her hips. The thigh-high boots encasing her legs in soft leather evoked no reaction. He said nothing about the gold armlets winding up each arm, the matching collar around her neck, or the diadem perched upon her head.

A master goldsmith, Bettina had created each of the pieces in her workshop—adding a surprise *design modification.* She was secretly proud of her skill.

"Very pretty," he said in a distracted tone, glancing in her direction. "You grow prettier with each year."

She'd read in a women's magazine that a male who liked you wanted to watch you all the time. You'd catch his eyes on you constantly.

Sometimes Cas didn't look at her at all. When he did, sometimes he didn't seem to *see* her.

No, I must snare his attention! One of two fates awaited her, depending on the outcome of her mission tonight.

If she succeeded in seducing Cas, she would wed her heart's desire and be forever protected by the only male she'd ever loved. They would become king and queen of the Deathly Ones and live out their eternal lives together.

If she failed with her demon, a tournament would begin for her hand—and for the crown of Abaddon. Bettina had seen the caliber of contestants beginning to file into Rune.

Swilling demon lords who already had dozens of brutalized wives.

Snakelike Cerunnos who would expect her to feed their spawn—with her flesh.

A troll that wasn't an anatomical match for her.

She knew none of them desired her; they only wanted the throne. Reminded of her prospects, she laid her hand on Cas's thigh, saying in a breathy murmur, "It's been so *lonely* without you here these past few weeks." She edged even closer. "You still won't confess where in the Lore you went off to?"

"Doesn't concern you," he said, but she'd known him long enough to know she was wearing him down.

"Please talk to me, Cas." She twirled the ends of her bodice laces, trying to draw his attention to her diminutive—but expertly displayed—breasts. "Take my mind off my fate."

"And that is another worry I contend with." He clenched his mug until the handle bent. "How could your godparents do this to you?"

Though Raum and Morgana, the Queen of Sorceri, were lifelong foes of each other, they agreed on one thing: Bettina's need for a husband/protector/king. But since they couldn't agree on a particular male—or even a particular species—they'd decided to host this tournament.

Searching only for the strongest champion in the Lore, they'd opened it to *all* creatures.

Olden ways. Abaddon had once been known for blood sport within its notorious Iron Ring—and for virgins offered up as prizes.

Bettina knew her two guardians loved her; they *meant* well. She also knew how fortunate she was to have them in her life. Halflings born of two hostile species were often shunned by both.

"I agreed to all their terms, Cas." She remembered that fateful conversation. She'd been sobbing, telling them, "Yes, yes, I'll do *anything*. Just get me my power back!" Sinister and destructive as it might be.

Cas scoffed. "*Agreed*? You mean they *manipulated* you."

If Bettina ever got famous enough in the Lore to earn a trailing name—like Maksimillia the Butcher or Lothaire the Enemy of Old—it would probably be Bettina the Pushover. Maybe Bettina the Easy Mark.

"Always, they get their way with you!"

Not *always*. Last year, she'd stunned everyone—including herself—and defied her guardians in order to attend a mortal design college. Ever since she was young, she'd been obsessed with fashion and jewelry creation, the Sorceri love of gold and garb running deep in her. She'd consumed every book on the subject and had been hungry to learn more and hone her craft.

Far from the prying eyes of Castle Rune, Bettina had been a carefree Lorean, blending with humans, enjoying freedom, new friends, and even her own flat with electricity and modern amenities! No longer had she been a halfling freak among hardy demons—she'd been a design geek, immersed in a tribe of them.

One night had changed her entire life. She swallowed, tamping down that memory. "I wasn't exactly in a position to resist my guardians again."

The first—and last—time she'd defied them, she'd been punished to within an inch of her life.

It'd taken her two months to convalesce; being part Sorceri and on the cusp of immortality meant she had healed fully—but *slowly*. The only thing that had gotten her through it?

Caspion.

Each day, he'd sat at her bedside, entertaining her with tales of his debauched companions, a randy pack of young demon males.

And each night he'd hunted her attackers relentlessly. Sixty days of hardly eating or sleeping.

But a month ago, Raum had ordered an exhausted Cas off the trail, promising that a cadre of soldiers would take over. Bitterly disappointed, Cas had vanished, returning only last night.

Now he took another drink. "Why in the gods' names didn't you wait for me to come back before you agreed to something like this tournament?"

Because my godparents pushed so hard. Because I feel unwhole without my power. Because they withheld the worst details of this medieval fiasco.

"I had little recourse." And even less now. In fact, Bettina had only one move available to her: seduce Caspion. Only a virgin could be offered up for the tournament. "And besides, I had no idea when you would return since you left me no word." Over the years, he'd disappeared from time to time, going on his more perilous hunts—or benders or attending orgies or whatever else he and his wild friends did.

"What's done is done, Cas. The fact remains that unless I come up with a way out of this tournament before the start tomorrow night, I'm going to be married off to a stranger by the end of next week."

His voice barely above a whisper, he said, "I'm going to be dead by the end of the night."

Chills raced over her. "You can't say something like that, then not explain. Aren't we friends?"

"So many things I've wanted to do," Cas said, his eyes distant. "So many things I've never even begun."

She'd felt the exact same way in that field of poppies.

He finally faced her. "Remember when we were going to travel the rest of the worlds? See every single demonic plane in the Lore?"

"We can *still* do that."

"No, Tina." He ran a palm down the leg of his black pants. "I've broken one of their laws. They will send *him*. Straight from the Realm of Blood and Mist."

"Who?" Bettina demanded. She'd never heard of this realm. "Who do you think will hurt you?"

Who *could*? Caspion was an adult demon male, now fully immortal. He was also a talented swordsman. She'd watched him train for countless hours. Even now his ever-present sword glinted proudly from the sheath at his side.

So why was his expression one of obvious dread? She'd never seen the stalwart Cas like this.

He suddenly looked his age: a young twenty-five. "They have a secret kingdom, hidden from the Lore. . . ."

Oh, yes, he was on the verge of telling all. "Go on, darling."

"Their people rarely leave—and then only in a cloaking mist that makes them invisible. Though most 'otherlanders' are forbidden within, I had a powerful friend, a sponsor of sorts, so I was allowed inside." He paused for a long drink. "But once an otherlander enters, he can't ever leave—except upon pain of death. Yet I did. I couldn't stay in that place any longer, one just as primitive as Abaddon. Here, at least I'm free to roam where I will! And my sponsor . . . he changed. Drastically. So I escaped, never thinking their killer could find me on our plane, but I sense him. Already I sense him in Abaddon."

"Tell me who is looking for you!"

Staring past her, he muttered, "The Prince of Shadow. The most soulless bastard I've ever met. He comes in the mist, an assassin without equal. To be targeted by him is to be as good as dead."

"No! We'll fight this male. I'll sic the entire army on him, place a bounty on his head! What type of Lorean is he?"

"The kind our army can't fight. Ah, Tina, I shouldn't have left here, should never have gone there to begin with! I was just so godsdamned frustrated, after failing over and over. . . . Now the last thing I'll see is a crescent moon."

"My darling, you're not making any sense," she said, desperate to stop this assassin. She would gut any foe of his with her new blade—the secret one she'd designed to slip into her gold collar. "Let me repay all your kindness to me, Cas. I can help you now."

"Without your power?"

How matter-of-factly he spoke about that, while she suffered chills. "Then Salem can help." Salem, her new "servant."

Once a phantom warrior, able to solidify his body at will, he'd been cursed to be a sylph—an invisible spirit, an air elemental. He could possess just about anything—a raven, a pillow, a clock. She would order him to keep an eye out for this mysterious assassin.

Instead of always spying on me. Did Morgana and Raum actually expect her to believe that Salem was a mere domestic? She'd barely shooed the sylph out of her rooms before Cas had arrived tonight. "Salem's telekinesis is surprisingly powerful—"

"No one can help me." Cas stood unsteadily, unfolding his tall form. "I must go, meet with some friends. Settle my accounts. Tell no one of this, Tina, or you betray my trust."

Shooting to her feet, she cried, "*Please* don't leave." He could be going to his death!

"My cards have been dealt. At least no one can say I didn't pay what I owed." He gave a bitter laugh, as if at an inside joke.

She grabbed his brawny arm. "Then return here tonight."

He shrugged. "Maybe."

"No, not *maybe*." Recalling his many conquests and his love of females, she glanced up at him from under her lashes, licking her lips. "Come back to me, and I'll welcome you with open arms, Caspion."

He groaned. "You're still a virgin, and the future queen of Abaddon. I'd have to wed you to bed you."

"Okay! You'd make an incredible king."

"Really? The Abaddonae welcoming the guttersnipe orphan as ruler?"

Some of the old guard Deathly Ones held him in low esteem because he'd been a foundling with no land or family name, but . . . "You've been making such strides, Cas."

She alone knew how much he yearned for acceptance. Though he reveled hard—he worked harder, accumulating wealth with each bounty.

He gave her a sad smile. "You know I can't have you."

For half a decade, she'd assured herself that he hesitated because of the difference in their stations. All she had to do was help him see his own worth.

Or maybe he simply needed to sow his wild oats before settling down.

After all, who could possibly adore him more than she did? Though he must have guessed her feelings long before now, she finally confessed to his face, "But I . . . I love you, Cas."

He chucked her under her chin. "I love you too."

"Don't be obtuse." She laid one hand on his muscular chest. "I am *in* love with you. I want you above all others." She'd tried to forget him—her stint offplane hadn't been only for school—but Caspion remained firmly in her heart.

"You only feel this way because of what awaits you tomorrow," he said. "You're desperate for an escape. I understand why you're doing this, but you aren't my mate."

"You can't know that for certain, not until you 'attempt' me. *In the throes, you know*; isn't that what you demon males say?"

He gripped her hand, pulling it off his chest. "You shouldn't be musing about such things, Bettina!"

Sometimes Cas could be as medieval in his thinking as the rest of the denizens of this plane. He might admit his conquests to her—but he withheld all details. "I'm not a child. I know simple biology."

A male death demon—like the males of many demon species—couldn't produce semen unless he was with his mate. He could enjoy sex up until then, could attempt a bevy of females and take release in a way, but the pleasure paled in comparison to what could be found with his fated one.

"Take me, Cas, and let's find out once and for all."

"If you're not mine, I'd still be honor-bound to wed you. Would you deprive me of my future mate? I'd grow to hate you." He pinched his forehead. "Ah, none of this matters anyway! I am done. I brought their killer down on my head."

"*Whose* killer? If you tell me, we can figure out a way to defeat him, or hide you. Just talk to me. *Please*."

Cas faced her, cupping her cheek with a callused palm. "Good-bye, Tina."

"Wait!"

He'd already traced away, teleporting from her apartments. But she couldn't follow, or search for him. Even if she were demon enough to trace, Bettina was unable to leave this cursed spire alone.

Her . . . *condition* made it impossible. Sure enough, her body had healed.

But not the rest of me.

She rushed to her circular balcony. During the day she could see the central market, but at night that fog rolled in. She squinted, straining to spy Cas; no use. She had the sight of the Sorceri, nearly as bad as a human's!

Can't go to him, can't watch over him.

Hastening inside, she called out, "Salem! Come here!" Nothing.

With great reluctance, she grabbed that copper bell—one that would summon Salem to her. *A medallion controls me; a bell controls him.*

She was well aware of how demeaning this could be, but seeing no other choice, she rang it.

A moment later, the grandfather clock spoke in a deep baritone voice: "You booted me out, and now you're ringing me back in? Somebody needs to make up her bloody mind!"

"Salem, I want you to guard Caspion tonight."

"What's doing wiv the demon?" he asked with his thick accent—exactly how a grown-up Oliver Twist would sound, Bettina often thought.

"Will you just follow my order for once?"

"Let me guess," Salem began in a surly tone, "he's hacked off the wrong sort yet again. Went cherry-picking wiv a lord's daughter? Played slip the pickle wiv a warrior's wife?"

"Aren't you supposed to follow my every command?" Salem's services had been a get-well-soon gift from Raum after the incident. Clearly, Raum had no idea that Salem was a rogue whose hobbies included spying on her bathing.

"Fiiine," Salem said begrudgingly. "Caspion'll be at his usual haunts?"

"Yes. Meeting with friends."

"Then by all means, I go to the closest cat-house forthwith," he said, the last word sounding like *forfwif*. The air around the clock seemed to ripple, and then Salem was gone.

Alone, she paced. If anything happened to Caspion . . . No, no, Salem would watch over him. Not that Caspion even *needed* watching over, she reminded herself.

And what foreign assassin would dare target a Deathly One in Abaddon?

Thirty minutes passed.

An hour.

She gnawed her fingernails, but they kept growing back, her immortal regeneration finally at its peak. The grandfather clock ticked ominously.

Oh, why wouldn't Cas return? To remind him that she awaited, she hung a lantern in her window. No, she couldn't see the town, but Cas could see her spire. A lingering light might beckon him.

Suddenly, a wave of vertigo hit Bettina. Her vision blurred.

Realization dawned. "Oh, no," she whispered, her tongue heavy in her mouth.

The demon brew had just caught up with her.

She shook her head against its effects, needing to

think. *I've been so despairing about Cas's safety . . . that I forgot my mission to seduce him failed.*

One of two outcomes. *Tomorrow, I am doomed.*

She rocked on her feet as more dizziness followed. Light-headed, she blundered into her bedroom, crawling past the curtains of her canopy bed. Falling back atop the silken sheets, she closed her eyes as the room spun.

Perhaps Cas might come back this night. If she could just get one more shot at him, she wouldn't let him out of her clutches so easily. Bettina wasn't exactly known as a fiery fighter. *But desperate times . . .*

She would strike fast and hard.

Her last thought before she passed out: *Please come back to me, Caspion.*

3

So this is where the demon hides. . . .

Sword at his hip, cloaked in a mist of his own making, Trehan surveyed an imposing castle and surrounding town. Both had been built on a plateau inundated with fog. On three sides lay swampy jungle with small rivers forking out. Gargantuan trees twenty feet in diameter soared from murky waters.

Though Trehan had never seen such a jungle, he turned without interest, crossing an ancient-looking drawbridge into the town. A weathered sign read: *Welcome to Rune, Royal Seat of Abaddon. Might Maketh Right.* The words had been carved between two dragon heads.

Abaddon. He vaguely remembered hearing of it, knew it to be a demonic, backwater plane, closed off from most of the Lore. Yet Rune was bustling this eve. Merchants hawked their wares along winding cobblestone streets. Banners hung in shop windows. Many in the crowd peered around with the open curiosity of tourists.

As Trehan moved unseen through the throngs, he heard snippets of conversations, gleaning that a tournament was beginning tomorrow night for the hand of this demonarchy's orphaned princess. The throne of this plane was up for grabs as well.

Already competitors of various species were encamping near a large iron combat ring.

A change in regime? Despite his interest in politics, Trehan ignored his spark of curiosity, concentrating on the task at hand.

The Prince of Shadow had a sanctioned kill to make.

Just moments ago, he'd used his scry talisman—a priceless crystal passed down through his house for generations—to locate his target here.

He normally wore it on a leather tie around his neck, but now held it aloft; the four-faceted crystal emitted a red light, casting a flare to indicate the location of this night's prey: Caspion the Tracker.

That demon had broken the laws of Dacia and was now marked for death.

The crystal's flare appeared directly above what sounded like a brothel, filled with boisterous laughter and tinny music. Not surprising—Caspion was a wastrel with a penchant for drinking and whoring. He'd done plenty of that in Dacia.

A public place was not a favorable hunting ground for Trehan. He had to remain unseen, as was the Dacian way.

Deciding to lie in wait in the alley alongside the tavern, he retied the crystal's leather around his neck. *Knowing Caspion's predilections, I fear I'm in for a long delay.*

There'd be no reading before the fire in his lonely rooms this eve. No polishing the weapons in his meticulous collection. Resigned, he started toward the alley.

He scanned his surroundings, not to admire or explore—but to be prepared for any threat. Dacians were a breed of observers, watchers from the mist. *Forever to observe, never to engage.*

Though Trehan had traced to hundreds of different Lorean planes, each with its own attractions and wonders, he'd never enjoyed them.

Trehan rarely enjoyed *anything*. He drank blood, but didn't taste it. If he slept, he woke unrefreshed. He performed his duties for Dacia, but the satisfaction he'd once derived from his job had . . . ebbed.

One of Trehan's cousins, Viktor, had recently told him, "You must've been punished by the gods to live the most stupefyingly boring existence imaginable—with the added curse that you can't even recognize how onerous and aimless it is."

"I live a life of service," Trehan had corrected him. "And I have pastimes I enjoy. I read by the fire—"

"Because your only alternative is to stare mindlessly at the flames."

I do that as well. Trehan had heard the whispers about him. Some Dacians likened him to a ghost, calling him a *shade*—a play on his Shadow title—because his life consisted of nothing but silent, grinding toil, devoid of goals or plans. They conjectured that he had no desires—secret or otherwise.

He'd been taught early *not* to desire, and certainly not to aspire to more than service to his kingdom.

Yet three months ago, an old longing had resurfaced, one he'd thought he'd been rid of after all this time—

Trehan halted, his senses on alert. He peered around through the mist. He spied no threat, yet his inexplicable tension did not ease.

Then his gaze was drawn up far above him to one of the half dozen spires in the castle, the highest one, well beyond the fog's reach. In a swampy region like this, an elevated floor probably contained royal apartments.

One window in particular held his attention. A lone lantern glimmered inside, like a beacon. For some reason, he felt nigh *compelled* to investigate it. Which didn't make sense. No rational Dacian would court unnecessary exposure.

Focus on the mission. A target roamed free; Dacia was at risk so long as Caspion lived. Because the demon knew the way back to Trehan's kingdom.

Though the Dacians had mystically hidden their realm, no cloaking was foolproof forever. As an added security measure, they'd outlawed anyone from leaving without a special exemption. Disobey—and *die.*

That was where Trehan came in. As Dacia's master assassin, he stalked these lawbreakers across the ends of the Lore, locating them with the scry crystal and striking them down before they could lead anyone back.

That was his sacred duty—and he would complete it this eve.

With a determined shake of his head, he dragged his sights toward the talisman's flare over the tavern.

Yet just as quickly, his traitorous gaze slid back to the lantern. Why leave one lit in the window? What would Trehan find inside those apartments? What story was even now playing out within those walls?

Is my life truly stupefying?

Glancing from the flare . . . to the lantern . . . back to the flare . . .

Damn it, he was the last Dacian who should risk expulsion. No one loved his home more than Trehan.

When the lantern guttered out, he hissed a curse. *And* still *I go to investigate?*

Although such a move was completely unwarranted—and unprecedented—he teleported to the balcony outside the apartments. A warding spell was in place to bar his entry, a security measure that he easily circumvented.

Over the years, how many had surrounded themselves with spells to keep Trehan's sword from their neck? Breaching such magics was a particular talent of his.

He made himself into mist, ghosting past the glass doors into a spacious sitting room. The chamber was now pitch black, but he could see perfectly, noting the lavish—and feminine—decorations.

Instead of furs, woven rugs covered the stone floors. Precious silks in myriad shades of purple streamed over the windows and draped a settee.

Purple meant royal. So what demoness resided here? He wasn't familiar with the line of this demonarchy. Was she the princess about to be wed?

Shelves of well-worn books lined a gallery, tomes on design, fashion, ancient art, weapon history, and . . . goldsmithing? All had pages flagged.

Trehan was someone who revered weapons—and books; the specific focus of this collection intrigued him.

But before he could explore the shelves, he found himself following the scent of a light perfume down a corridor.

Sketches lined the walls, the subjects as unusual as the books. A talented hand had rendered the inner workings of an antique clock. The mechanisms of various spring traps. A three-dimensional diagram of a bolt-action crossbow. They were all signed simply *B.A.*

The level of detail and the unique style were fascinating. To Trehan, this was unparalleled art. He wanted to possess these pieces, to closet himself with them in his solitary quarters; they wouldn't be the first he'd "liberated" back to Dacia.

Only the sound of soft, even breaths coming from an adjoining bedroom could pry Trehan from his discovery. Inside, he stalked closer to a sizable canopy bed, easing back the curtain . . . to find a small female sleeping.

Shining braids of dark brown hair fanned out around the top of her head, while the rest of her mane lay loose about her slim shoulders. She looked as if she'd fallen back on the bed and hadn't moved since.

He canted his head, taking in her delicate appearance. This was no demoness—she had neither claws nor horns.

She was trim, with a tiny waist. Young-looking.

Most Loreans were frozen into their immortality when they were physically strongest, never aging past that point. She couldn't have been more than twenty when she'd transitioned. He'd turned at age thirty-one. As with all male vampires, his heart had gradually stopped beating and his lungs had ceased taking air. His sexual drive—and sexual ability—had vanished.

That had been nearly a millennium ago. . . .

Over that endless span, Trehan had made a study of the various species of the Lore, and he recognized this one's clothing. She was dressed as a sorceress of old in a scanty outfit designed to reveal as much skin as possible, several pieces of gold jewelry, and a red mask.

One of the Sorceri. Here in Abaddon?

She was a long, long way from home. Perhaps she was a companion of the demon princess soon to be given away.

He wondered what her power was. He'd heard of Sorceri who could move mountains and boil oceans.

Her mask was slim enough that he could see most of her pixieish features: high, defined cheekbones, an elegant jawline, and a gracefully pointed chin.

Yet her carnally red lips seemed out of place on her finely-boned face, more suited to a siren.

He couldn't tell if she'd be an incomparable beauty, not until she opened her eyes and removed her mask. No matter. For a male who enjoyed little, he was liking this inspection *very* well.

His gaze dipped to the delectable swell of her breasts in that revealing top, and lingered. He noticed his hands were opening and closing of their own accord, as if he was imagining fondling those little mounds.

Touching her? A frown creased his brow. He shouldn't be reacting like this. He was unblooded, the walking dead—until he encountered his fated Bride.

At that time, his body would wake for her.

For centuries, Trehan had awaited a daughter of Dacia for himself. As his father had told him: "If it's meant to be, Mother Dacia will give you a Bride. Within our stone borders, you will find her. Until then, want for nothing and embrace the shadows."

Trehan had done that. *I extinguished any foolish hopes.* He'd all but put a Bride out of his mind.

So why was his gaze rapt on this otherlander's breasts . . . ?

I must leave this place, complete my kill. Trehan had never missed a target. Besides, if she woke and saw him, he couldn't return home—unless he dispatched her. He had permission to leave and return, but only if he was unseen *by any he left living*.

There was one exception to the rule, but it was so ridiculous that it didn't warrant consideration.

Even as he mused these things, he inched closer to the bed. Before, he'd thought the beacon in the window had drawn him; now he wondered if this female had somehow been the draw.

Remember the mission! He finally pried his gaze away, only to realize he'd been so spellbound by her that he'd allowed his mist to fade. The carelessness! With a flare of unease, he turned back—

Her eyes flashed open, met his.

I am . . . seen. But *zeii mea,* my gods, what eyes she possessed! The irises were the lightest brown, ringed with stark black. He could stare into them for lifetimes.

Where had a thought like that come from?

She blinked thick black lashes up at him. "Oh! You scared me," she murmured in English.

Seen. Why hadn't he disappeared before she'd awakened? Why hadn't he remained invisible to her? Now he would be forced to kill her, or else never return home.

"You've come at last." Her lips curled into a grin that would've stolen his breath. If he still breathed. She raised her arms over her head, stretching sensually.

At last? Who did she think he was? She gazed up at him as if they knew each other. She gazed at him . . . with desire.

All at once, he understood why he hadn't disappeared, why he'd let his mist fade.

Because deep down, he'd *wanted* this creature to see him.

As she rose to a sitting position, her exotic braids and lustrous, wavy hair cascaded over her shoulders. Her locks were chestnut brown, threaded with strands of black, the colors complementing her distinctive eyes.

She reached for him, boldly laying her hands on his torso. When he perceived the warmth from her palms, he shuddered like a young vampire, unschooled with women—

Boom! . . . Boom! . . . Boom!

The floor seemed to quake beneath his feet, the walls to shake with deafening tremors.

Yet Trehan knew what was actually happening. The sound was his heart awakening for her, a drum beginning to thunder in his chest.

Beating again and again, faster, *harder*.

This ethereal creature had roused his body! Soon his lungs would fill with breath, his shaft with blood.

An otherlander belongs to me? A sorceress? He'd heard of worse pairings. Considering where he'd found her, she could have been a demoness.

Then he remembered a critical fact. To return home, Trehan had to eliminate all who witnessed him—*except* for his Bride. The far-fetched loophole that was too ridiculous to consider had happened tonight!

Thoughts of witnesses and ancient laws faded, replaced by an instinctive protectiveness.

Could she feel the same pull toward him? She was born of a different species. From the tales he'd heard of otherlander Brides, he knew she wouldn't automatically want him with the same ferocity with which he desired her.

"So happy you've come to me," she whispered in a slurred tone, eyeing him with such a proprietary glance that he was taken aback. "To my bed." She was looking him dead in the face, but acting as if they'd met before.

Then comprehension struck. She was of the Sorceri; it was likely that she—or one of her kind—had foreseen her mate. Of course!

"Been waiting for you, darling."

At her words, excitement soared inside him. A shade with a stupefyingly boring existence? No longer.

He merely needed to complete this blooding, then take his new Bride back to his underworld realm. His target could wait until she was safely ensconced in Dacia.

Then this delicate sorceress would grace his home—and his bed—for all eternity.

He knew of other males who'd felt panic at this realization; Trehan experienced only satisfaction. Secret longings resurfaced, at last to be appeased.

I am ready *for her.*

At that moment, his lungs started to expand. He inhaled deeply, until they felt too big for his chest. Blood rushed to his shaft, hardening it. He groaned as it distended against the confining fabric of his pants.

His gaze raked from her pert breasts to her waist, dropping to the titillating skirt that bared most of her gently flaring hips and her long, shapely legs.

Her Sorceri adornments—the collar around her neck and the gold climbing her pale arms—now struck him as unbearably erotic.

A sexy, delicate sorceress. Apparently I've been waiting for you as well.

Long-dormant drives came roaring back to life—to mate, to claim, to *bite*? After eons, he *hungered.*

No, *not* hunger! Dacians didn't pierce the flesh of others. He wanted only to possess and master her.

But first, he had questions. *What is the name of my pretty Bride? Why are you so drunk? What is your connection to this demon realm?*

He'd gone the better part of a millennium without bedding a female. *Will you forgive how out of practice I am with all this?*

She gazed up at him from under her lashes. "I won't disappoint you, I swear it."

Disappoint *him*? "I am—"

She raised her fingertips to cover his lips. "Shh. Don't say a word. *Please.* You're in my bedroom for a reason. Let me show you how right you were to come here." She began unlacing her bodice, shimmying from the material. With a shy grin, she tossed it aside to bare the most exquisite little breasts he'd ever seen.

At the sight of her rosy nipples tightening before his eyes, Trehan's powerful, rational mind went blank, his questions forgotten.

4

Bettina had awakened to a darkened room.

All her candles had burned out, but she'd sensed a male's presence, an awareness that made her skin tingle. She'd barely been able to discern the outline of his towering form.

Cas! He'd returned. *How to get him to stay?* she'd thought in a drunken panic. *How to get him into my bed?*

So she'd taken off her top. His response: a sharp intake of breath. Which told her he either liked the view—or was merely surprised by her daring.

Talk to him; don't let him get away! "I'm going to make you so glad you've come to me, darling," she said, but she could *hear* herself slurring. *You've got one shot at this, one shot at a future worth having!*

Strike fast and hard? She would seduce him yet. When she piled her hair atop her head and arched her back in invitation, he gave a not-so-subtle growl. A growl of appreciation? Or frustration that he couldn't have what he wanted?

She fretted her bottom lip, letting down her hair. But as soon as the locks concealed her breasts, she felt two wisps of air as he swiftly swept her hair back over her shoulders.

When she could *feel* him staring once more, Bettina couldn't suppress a buzzed sense of accomplishment.

This was actually happening. Caspion. Here in her bedroom. Admiring her breasts. He was finally *looking* at her—because he wanted her!

Cas was going to be hers tonight, and then he'd understand what she'd always known. She was *his* as well. Their fates would intertwine. There'd be no tournament for the "unchaste" Bettina.

She was giddy—and drunk, but mainly giddy. She imagined walking hand in hand with Caspion the Tracker, announcing their betrothal to all.

Yet he still hadn't caressed her or kissed her. With another spike of alarm, she rose, swaying until his callused hands gripped her shoulders to steady her. Ah, contact!

A lifetime of swordplay had roughened his palms. *Because my Cas is a warrior, none finer, none braver. . . .*

She laid her hands on his chest, lids growing heavy at the feel of his mighty body. But this was just a tease; she needed to trace his skin, to explore him.

She reached for his coat, working it over his bulging shoulder muscles. He shrugged from it, and she heard it land over the foot of the bed.

For years, she'd been beset with curiosity about sex, about the masculine form. Yet she'd never touched a male before. Would nights of fantasizing at last come to fruition?

When she attempted the top button on his shirt, her normally agile fingers were clumsy. She made a sound of frustration. "I'm impatient to touch you—"

The material of his shirt disappeared with a single rip, joining his coat.

"Thank you. I-I just need to feel you for the first time." Bettina worked with metal every day, engraving, forging, casting. To check for the slightest imperfections, she would often close her eyes and trace her sensitive fingertips over her work, as if seeing with them.

Now she smoothed the pads of her fingers over Cas's naked torso, holding her breath . . .

The reality was so much better than fantasy! "My gods, I love your body."

Her words made him groan. Light grazes over the hard planes of his pec muscles made them tense for her, made his heart thud louder. And oh, how his flat nipples hardened. When she dragged her forefingers across them, he hissed between his teeth.

She dipped her hands, savoring each rise and fall of his rigid stomach muscles as they contracted. His body was honed like unyielding iron, his skin flawless.

Initially he'd felt cool, but now he ran hot as a forge.

Any shyness she might have felt disappeared. Every caress deepened her desire, until even her breasts felt heavy. His scent washed over her—normally pleasing, it had now grown *intoxicating*.

Inside, she felt like molten gold . . . smoldering, awaiting a chance to be made whole.

Her nipples stiffened so much they ached, and he must have noticed; his hands tightened on her shoulders, as if he didn't trust himself to touch any other part of her body.

He was such a ruthless demon warrior, and yet he was being patient with her, letting her explore him.

Was he *too* patient? He should've thrown her to the bed by now! Why wasn't he kissing her?

Maybe he was reconsidering this.

Take him over the finish line, Bettina!

Dazed bewilderment.

Trehan could only stare, riveted by his Bride's pert breasts and taut nipples, savoring her every stroke upon his skin. How long he'd gone without a single touch!

This creature belongs to me, he told himself again. *To me alone—*

The sorceress grasped his hands, pulling them down to her soft breasts.

The contact roused him from his enthrallment. With a strangled groan, he covered her flesh with his palms, molding it.

Why did other vampires always warn of obstacles inherent in mating with an otherlander? Trehan's mate was demanding that he stroke her breasts, the ones she'd been eager for him to see.

When he gave them a reverent squeeze, she moaned low. Her reaction made him shudder, a sensual haze clouding his mind once more.

And then she swept her hands down his torso, lower . . . lower toward that aching, engorged part of him. As she grazed her nails along his waist just above his sword belt, his throbbing shaft strained for her touch.

Finally, he found his voice. "You are so lovely."

She briefly stilled at his words, tilting her head.

His lust-addled brain determined two things: she truly didn't want him to talk; *nothing* could interrupt this blooding.

So he resolved to say no more, determined to do whatever it took to come inside her. At the thought of pinning down her writhing body to spend deep within it, need surged within him, as if a dam had been breached.

He clasped her upper arms, tracing them into her bed. She gasped as he positioned himself over her, but then she whispered, "Yes, *yes*."

Her hair spread out behind her, a backdrop of shining waves. Her scent was drugging. She arched her back, drawing all his attention back to her breasts, to those jutting nipples. Did they throb as badly as his shaft? Were those stiffened peaks driving her mad?

He rubbed his thumbs over them, gave each a light pinch as he watched her reaction.

"Oh, gods." She licked her lips, staring up at him with heavy-lidded eyes. As her irises began to glitter from her passion, she whispered, "Kiss me. Please kiss me."

Anything! He lowered his head, slanting his mouth over hers, relishing her cry. Her red lips were smooth, unimaginably giving. He slipped his tongue between them, and she met him.

As she softly lapped, Trehan's head swam. Her mouth tasted like spiced honey mead.

He kissed her with all the pent-up passion denied him over lifetimes. With each sweep of his tongue, he grazed his straightened forefingers over her nipples, until she was undulating beneath him.

When he tore his mouth away to run his lips along the slim column of her neck, she breathed, "I've needed this. Needed you." She sounded delighted—and *relieved*?

He craved relief as well. For now the pressure in his cock was turning into pain. He rose up on his knees, unbuckling his sword belt, tossing it to the floor.

"You know you can do anything to me," she murmured. "I'm yours—I always will be."

He groaned. *Want for nothing?* No more. His wanting for this female was primal, undeniable, bordering on . . . savage. He dropped his head to her chest, kissing all around one nipple, tasting her luscious skin.

"Yes!" She sank her nails into his back. "*More*. Please! P-put your mouth on it."

With a growl, he complied. When he closed his lips over one peak and it puckered to the tip of his tongue, she gasped. When he flicked it, she moaned, "That feels so *good*."

His new Bride was so responsive, he knew he could make her come just from this. Another night, he would, tormenting her until she begged him for release.

She threaded her fingers through his hair, holding him in place as he began to suck.

Her taste was bliss—her cries, the scent of her dark hair, the way she moaned with each swirl of his tongue.

What a gift he'd been given with this sorceress!

Impulses warred. He wanted to suckle her for hours, to lick her sex and taste the orgasms he'd wrung from her. He wanted her pale hands gripping his cock, her red lips sealing around it as he thrust.

To feed his length inside her . . . inch by throbbing inch.

Haze. Losing control. He snarled against her breast,

increasing his suction as he drew his head away. Then to her other nipple. *What would it be like to pierce that taut peak with a fang? Blood from the sweetest little font.*

Where had that disturbing thought come from? His kind considered biting another to be a savage taboo. Were his fangs beginning to ache? *Ignore them.*

As he sucked, he palmed her breasts with greedy hands, possessively clutching her. When her arms fell limp over her head—*letting me do as I will*—his worry faded. He drew back and gazed at his woman, pride firing inside him.

Panting breaths between plump, red lips. Hips rolling with need. Nipples wet and swollen from my tongue. His heart thundered for her. Forever for her.

She's stunning.

All she needed was his bite, emblazoned on her skin. *No, ignore these forbidden thoughts! Think only of mating her.* He could scent her desire. *She* needs *to be mated.*

With that idea in mind, he snatched off her skirt, leaving her in only her mask, her jewels, and those leather boots.

"Oh! P-please go easy." She swallowed audibly. "This is about as far as I've ever been before."

A virgin! Misgivings arose. How young *was* she?

Yet she didn't attempt to cover herself. Any lingering doubts dwindled when she gave a needy whimper, spurring him on.

Must prepare her body. A virgin would need extra care. He supposed. *Never been with one.* He couldn't remember bed play before her, seemed to have forgotten anything he'd learned in his youth.

He dipped one hand, glancing his palm up her supple thigh.

"Yes," she sighed, "oh, yes. You've made me *ache*

here." Her knees fell wide open for him, spreading her slick, blushing folds, and one thought arose: *She is* o comoara, *a treasure. My treasure.*

Soon he'd be buried to the hilt inside that lush heat. His cock pulsed in readiness. Pre-semen beaded the crown, dampening the front of his pants.

Again her fingers skimmed across his waist, back and forth before sliding lower behind the material. Just as he reached between her legs, she worked her hand into his pants.

Her soft palm gripped him; he cupped her hot sex.

He gave a curt, shocked yell, almost coming spontaneously; she moaned with abandon.

Even as he reveled in her wetness, her touch jolted him—nimble fingers clutching at his shaft, gently tugging. The foreign sensation drove his hips forward for more.

He could feel her swollen little clitoris budding beneath the heel of his palm; her dizzying scent made him *crazed* to taste her there.

Then her hand started to move on him. "It feels so . . . *amazing*," she said in a tone filled with wonder.

She'd never even touched a cock before? Amid all the turmoil he felt, tenderness arose for his sweetly innocent mate.

But then she squeezed it, murmuring, "My darling, I need this inside me ever so badly."

Too much! Seed climbed until the pressure grew agonizing. He was about to come, would never last as he sank his length inside her virgin sheath and took her maidenhead.

"Stroke me," he commanded her. He would get this out of the way, then see to her pleasure all night. Claiming her repeatedly.

She hesitated, then tentatively rubbed his shaft from hilt to tip, and again. As he petted her quivering flesh, he grew mindless, unable to stop himself from fucking her hand with short pumps of his hips.

His testicles tightened. His cockhead swelled. He knew he had only a second before he ejaculated for the first time in centuries. Two choices. Rip down his pants—or raise his wetted fingers from her sex to his lips.

The latter won. As he sucked her cream from his fingers, he groaned around them, beginning to spill into her hand.

5

Bettina had been lost in this experience, awash in every unfamiliar sensation and sound.

Cas's increasingly desperate groans. The heat of his skin as it slickened with sweat. His measured thrusts giving way to frenzy, until he was grinding against her fist.

Then something spurted over her hand. Hot. Liquid. Her eyes flashed open.

Semen?

Cas gave a deep bellow, his mighty body jerking as jet after jet of his seed erupted. How was this *possible*?

Could I have wrung this from him? Her brief flare of happiness was doused by confusion. No, he couldn't produce it, not until he'd had sex with his mate. Certainly not *outside* of her.

Had he already found his female and broken that seal, only to be untrue to his fated one? Had he lied to Bettina?

Once he'd emptied himself, once the violent shudders had subsided, he collapsed atop her with a satisfied grunt, nuzzling her neck. When she tugged her moist hand from his pants, he reached for his ripped shirt, using the tail to wipe away his come before tossing the garment away.

Which she supposed was *considerate*?

Then his fingers returned between her legs. She gasped when his thumb circled her clitoris, his other fingers teasing her opening. When she felt his erection already growing against her hip, that smoldering desire mounted even stronger than before, momentarily erasing all misgivings.

She'd gone her entire life without this kind of pleasure; why did it feel so critical to her now? Her body relaxed, her legs helplessly spreading for more of his caresses.

"Ah, my wanton little sorceress"—his heated words fanned over her ear, making her nipples pucker against his damp chest—"you are a treasure." Still lazily petting her, he began to kiss down her body, grazing his lips over her collarbone, then between her breasts. "Now let me attend to you."

Even as she trembled with delight, she wondered why Cas's voice sounded so raspy. Just from his arousal? And was he talking about licking her down there? The idea excited Bettina—but why wouldn't he claim her? "Don't you want to make love to me now?"

Finish line . . . so *close*.

"Soon. But I've had a sample of your taste, *dragă mea*, maddening me. First I feast. . . ."

That did *not* sound like Cas—

But his warm breaths over her navel felt so good, made her shake with eagerness. "C-Cas?"

The male tensed, cursing in a language she'd never heard. *"What did you say?"* He rose up above her and pinched her chin hard.

She began to sober up as panic raced through her. "You're not Caspion!" she cried, shoving at his chest.

Red flags had arisen before, but she'd been a slave to her senses, to the pleasure radiating outward from his every kiss, his every stroke. She'd assured herself that his voice was desire-roughened or that she was simply drunk.

"Caspion?" he grated. "So that is the way of it? You believed I was another when you gave yourself so freely!" He captured her wrists in one fist.

"Release me!" she ordered as she fought to get free. "Who *are* you?" She couldn't see, but she could *feel* tension rolling off him, could hear the rage in his voice. Violence would follow.

Just like before.

Confusion rocked her, that familiar terror arising. She'd learned all too well how vulnerable her body was to attack!

Why does this keep happening to me? Tears welled. She whispered, *"N-not again."* But he wasn't listening.

Between gritted teeth, he said, "I am Prince Trehan Cristian Daciano. And you are my woman." Pinning her arms above her head, he vowed, "After tonight, little Bride, you will *never* mistake me for another again. . . ."

Raw instinct burned inside Trehan, aggression overwhelming him. The need to mark his mate grew irresistible, not necessarily for blood but for *dominion*.

For possession. *She's mine.*

Biting simply wasn't done—but his control faltered. Goaded over the edge by jealousy, he knew he would answer the call.

She wants another. My female craves another male in her bed.

"Bride? *V-vampire?*" she cried, fighting his hold on her wrists. "Wait, wait!"

He spied her pulse fluttering in her neck. His fangs sharpened to tap that spot—never had they been beyond his control, never had they *throbbed* to pierce flesh. No vampire could resist this temptation.

But a Dacian would be expected to.

Compared to his hunger, that thought was too dim to be heeded. He leaned down, parting his lips to lick her neck, instinctively preparing her for his bite. Just below her collar, soft, pink skin beckoned him. "I feel your pulse against my tongue. Ah, your flesh . . . it tastes so *sweet.*"

If her skin tasted like this, her blood would be like heaven. Hot, rich, heaven sliding down his throat.

Over. His restraint gone—

"Don't bite me!" she pleaded. "Don't hurt me!"

Hurt her? "I don't want to hurt you . . . I can't stop this."

"P-please don't."

You're going to fucking bite her? Like some savage vampire? You're a godsdamned Dacian! "If you've any defenses, sorceress . . . use them . . . against me now! *Stop* me."

He heard a sob, felt moisture on her face. Tears? She was *crying?*

Her small body trembled against him as she whispered, "I-I *can't* s-stop you."

The idea of her in such distress cut through his frenzy. Somehow he forced himself to draw back, to *not* plunge his dripping fangs into her.

Behind her mask, her glinting eyes darted. Darted blindly? He waved his hand in front of her face. Nothing.

Then he remembered—Sorceri senses were nearly as diminished as a mortal's.

Reason whispered, *Your little Bride is terrified, can't see in the dark, has no idea who's in her bed.*

Instinct screamed, *Mark her! So another male can't take what's yours!*

With every ounce of willpower he possessed, he released her, surrendering his prize.

She jerked upright, scrambling across the bed from him, snatching the bedspread to her chest, eyes still darting.

She hadn't been able to see Trehan whatsoever. She truly had believed that he was Caspion.

So what will she think of me when she gazes upon me for the first time? Perhaps he oughtn't to be kneeling there, bare-chested, with his spend drying in his pants, for her initial impression. He rose, yanking on his coat and slinging his sword around his hips. His tattered shirt was ruined beyond use.

"Wh-why would you do this to me?" she whispered, her mask askew. "I don't know you." She dropped her face into her hands.

It was everything he could do not to touch her, to comfort her. *But I'm the one she fears. . . .*

He'd frightened his Bride. *Because I'm not Caspion.* Yet another reason to kill him.

How excited Trehan had been to find her, how optimistic—but it'd all been an illusion, her sensual responses meant for another.

Each of the things he'd so enjoyed with her was now tainted. When she'd stroked Trehan's shaft to come, she'd believed it was that demon's. When she'd whispered, *"You know you can do anything to me. I'm yours—I always will be. . . ."*

The thought sent his anger skyrocketing once more, his fangs sharpening again. Trehan wanted her to tell *him* those same charged words, whispering them in *his* ear.

With a vile curse, he reached for a candle.

The strike of the match made Bettina jump. As a candle alleviated the darkness, she saw that the vampire was turned from her, leaning with one hand against the wall. His head was down, his broad back heaving with breaths.

He dug his fingers into the stone as he clearly grappled for control. "You awaited *him* this night?" he bit out, launching his other fist against the wall, sending rock shards flying.

She gave a cry, briefly ducking under the cover.

At the sound, he tensed even more. "You fear me. You *shouldn't*. I will never hurt you," he grated. "Gods know if I haven't yet . . ."

"B-because I'm your Bride." She could scarcely wrap her mind around that.

"Yes."

"Are you a natural-born vampire?" Born vampires couldn't tell lies.

"What you really want to know is if I can speak untruths. I can't. I wouldn't anyway." His voice was deep, his words marked by an accent she didn't recognize. "Lying is counterproductive and illogical."

"Oh." She found her tears drying. The fear that so

often dominated her life had receded—and she didn't know why. Maybe because this vampire had somehow kept himself from biting her even though she'd blooded him—and *infuriated* him. His restraint reassured her somewhat.

Instead, other emotions arose. She was humiliated and still drunk, and her body felt like a stranger's.

Ah, gods, she'd just gotten with some foreigner vampire named Trehan Daciano. *Not* with her beloved.

This male had touched her as no one had before. "You wanted to bite me though? Isn't that what your kind does?"

"I've never bitten another."

That was difficult for her to believe. Every vampire she'd ever met—and there were many, since her demonarchy had allied with the Horde in the past—had eyes red from bloodlust.

When he turned, she caught a glimpse of his eyes before she averted her own. *Clear of blood?*

"Look at me, then. Know the male you belong to."

She cautiously returned her gaze.

He was handsome, she supposed, in an angry, brooding way. He had chiseled cheekbones and a strong chin. His wide, masculine jaw was clean shaven. His hair was thick and black, his irises like onyx from his emotions. She wondered what color they would be normally.

Individually, his features were pleasing. Together, they appeared too severe, his expression harsh.

Body-wise, he was as tall and muscle-packed as Cas. *Mistaking them now seems a touch more plausible,* she drunkenly reasoned.

But overall, he wasn't nearly so glorious as Caspion—the standard by which she judged all males.

Though the vampire had ordered her to look, he appeared uncomfortable with her frank stare. She supposed it was rude to gawk like this, but she'd never seen a shirtless vampire before. And they *had* just been intimate.

Her gaze dropped to his muscular chest. What an odd crystal he wore—

"Tell me your name, female."

Her head snapped up. "I'm Princess Bettina."

"Bettina," he said with that unusual accent. *"Bettina,"* he repeated in a huskier voice, as if he liked the way her name rolled from his tongue.

His supremely talented tongue. She almost shivered, recalling how he'd used it on her breasts—licking her nipples, wickedly flicking them. Beneath the sheet, they hardened once more.

"And of what kingdom are you princess?"

"Why should I tell you anything?" Then his earlier words sank in. *"Belong* to you? Did you actually say that? I don't even know you! Y-you took advantage of my . . . state, allowing me to believe you were another. You were silent just to keep up the ruse!"

When his expression darkened even more, anyone in their right mind would have been afraid. Yet her oh-so-familiar fear was absent. *Because he can't hurt his Bride.* Plus, tendrils of sunlight had begun creeping into the candlelit room. Surely he'd be driven away in moments.

"I don't perpetrate *ruses,* sorceress."

"Then why were you quiet?"

"I followed *your* request for silence!"

Oh. She had shushed him, hadn't she? How could the night have gone so wrong?

This vampire had found his Bride—her—and had acted on instinct. Bettina was the one involved in a ruse—seduction. "You know I said those things because I thought you were someone else."

A muscle ticked in that broad jaw of his. "And I reacted as I did because I was keen to see what pleasures you intended. Keen to know 'how right I was to come to you.' Your eyes were promising irresistible things."

She gasped.

"His loss, female; you *delivered*. It seems I savored treats meant for another."

Now she glared. "You are amazing!"

"Parts of me, at least."

Her cheeks flushed as she remembered her awed comment when she'd touched her first erection. Struggling for composure, she said, "How did you get past my barrier spell?"

"With ease."

Arrogant male! "Why are you here?" Surely he wasn't one of the competitors. "Are you the first clear-eyed Horde vampire?"

Seeming to grapple with his temper, he said, "I'm not of the Horde."

"Then what? Why are you in Abaddon . . . ?" She trailed off, her gaze fixing on his sword, on the cross-guard over the grip. The forged metal was distinctly rounded—

"A crescent moon?" she cried. "Oh, gods, you're the one Cas spoke of, the Prince of Shadow! You're the assassin from the Realm of Blood and Mist come to kill him!"

The vampire didn't deny this. "He broke the laws of my people. He must pay."

Now everything Cas had told her began to make sense. *An assassin without equal . . . the last thing I'll see is a crescent moon.* "Please don't hurt him! He didn't realize he'd done wrong."

"Understand me, Bettina, the only thing he didn't realize was that I could find him here. I will dispatch him just as I have thousands before."

He didn't say this in a boastful manner—more like he merely stated an unavoidable truth.

Though Caspion was a powerful warrior, everything about this male convinced her that Cas had been right to fear for his life. There was a chilling lethality about the vampire, a confidence in his own cold-bloodedness.

"And what is your interest in a wastrel like him?" he demanded. "Besides what you obviously intended to give to him."

"He's no wastrel! If you hurt him, I will *never* forgive you!"

Baring his fangs, he grated, "We'll sort this out back in my home."

"What gives you the right to accost me like this, to try to abduct me?"

"I told you who I am. I've told you what you are. You've blooded me. I didn't choose for this to happen with you. Fate decided this. And now we must bow to her commands."

"You *can't* trace me from Rune!" *Olden ways.* She was trapped on this plane—until she wed. Raum had used that damned summoning medallion to prevent her from leaving.

"Can't I?" The vampire reached for her, his gaze intent.

6

When Trehan yanked her naked body to his chest and tensed to trace home, two things happened: he didn't budge her; pain shot through his palm.

He released her, staring down at three deep wounds in his hand. *"What the hell is this?"* he roared while she scrambled back under the sheet. "Where is your weapon?" As he wrapped his bloody palm with the ripped sleeve of his shirt, he saw what had caused his injury. When he'd grabbed her upper arm, her gold band had ejected *spikes*.

Clutching the sheet over her chest, she breathed, "It *worked*." He detected pride in her expression before she dropped her gaze once more, fiddling with the armlet. With a flip of a hidden lever, the spikes retracted.

All at once, he understood—that was *her* book collection. Those were her drawings. Weapons, gold-smithing, design . . . "You *made* that?"

She shrugged.

Clever little sorceress. *How did she craft a pressure sensor—*

No! With a sharp shake of his head, he reminded himself that he had larger issues to deal with. Namely, how to get her back to his home. "Are you under an enchantment?" He began pacing with frustration, unable to seize the Bride who was just before him.

Blood still ran from his palm. *Should've sampled hers!*

Could this night possibly decline any further? "Why was I unable to trace you?"

She pursed her lips, her glare telling him she'd answer no questions.

As a natural-born vampire, Trehan was, in fact, physically incapable of lying. If he even attempted to, the words would make his throat burn like fire. So what could he promise to get her to cooperate with him? "Bettina, if you answer my questions, we could leave together—and perhaps I need never return for Caspion." Of course he would return.

To be marked for death by Trehan Daciano was to be as good as dead.

Her eyes went wide. "I'll tell you anything!"

Anything to save that bastard. Had Trehan actually thought her clever? She had no sense if she favored Caspion—and she was *still* slurring.

My Bride, the mistress of the legendary House of Shadow, is a drunken, senseless Sorceri. His ancestors must be tracing over in their graves right now. "How can I take you from here?"

"My godfather has a summoning medallion, one I'm tied to. He's used it to ensure I remain in this kingdom until the tournament ends."

Trehan had heard of those kinds of medallions,

knew they were an archaic means to control . . . demons. "You're part demon?" *Yes, the night can decline further.*

No, no, she had neither horns nor fangs. She looked like a fragile mortal, if anything. Scarcely a hardy demoness.

"My mother was a Sorceri, my father king of this demon realm," she said with a touch of smugness, but Trehan was in no way impressed with royalty.

My Bride is a drunken, senseless halfling. Of all the potential mixes in the Lore . . . This creature was the product of two of the most opposite immortal species.

As far from a proud, logical Dacian female as possible. He exhaled. No matter. Bettina was still *his*. "How do I procure your medallion?"

"It's being offered up as a prize," she said in a deadened tone. "For a tournament."

"You're the orphaned princess. You're the trophy?" *Declining still further.*

She shrugged. "There's an invitation on my dresser."

He glanced around, then traced to retrieve the old-fashioned parchment.

RAUM, THE GRAND DUKE OF THE DEATHLY ONES,
AND MORGANA, THE QUEEN OF ALL SORCERI,
REQUEST THE PLEASURE OF YOUR ATTENDANCE
AT A TOURNAMENT FOR THE HAND
OF THEIR GODDAUGHTER,
PRINCESS BETTINA OF ABADDON.
VENUE: THE IRON RING; RUNE, ABADDON
WHEN: THE NINE DAYS BEFORE
THE SANGUINE MOON
WHAT: FIGHTS TO THE DEATH
PRIZE: THE CROWN OF THE DEATHLY ONES AND
THE SUMMONING MEDALLION OF BETTINA

In smaller print at the bottom:

FULL-MOON MARRIAGE CEREMONY TO FOLLOW FINAL
ROUND OF TOURNAMENT. ALL ENTRANTS GUARANTEED
MYSTICAL PROTECTION OUTSIDE THE RING.

"Guardians?" Trehan nearly crumpled the parchment. "How old are you?"

"Twenty-two."

His jaw slackened. "So young?" He'd amassed centuries' worth of strength, could have seriously harmed her tonight. "An entire kingdom is up for grabs. Do you know what types of males will be entering this farce?" Trehan had spied a sample of them near the combat ring.

"I agreed to the tournament."

"Why in the gods' names would you? And why would you ever surrender your blood for a summoning medallion?" Talismans like that were common enough in the Lore. But the demon had to give up blood willingly for it to work.

She murmured, *They willed it.*" Before he could ask what she meant, she attempted a brisk demeanor. "Once the competition begins, I will be completely prepared to wed whoever may win." Yet her voice broke a bit on the end.

Completely prepared—*and terrified.*

"But you're regretting your decision now? Is that it?" Realization hit him. If Caspion had bedded her this eve, the tournament would be canceled. "That's why you were trying to seduce the demon!" His relief was profound. "So he'd save you." *And now I will save you.*

"I was trying to seduce Caspion because I love him. I always have, and I always will."

Trehan felt as if he'd had his fangs knocked down

his throat. Of all the males in the world. That death demon was notoriously popular with females of all species, had plowed through half of Dacia's maids before he'd absconded in the night.

My Bride is in love with my target.

If Trehan's mate had been another vampire, she would feel the same urgency and need for him. But when a vampire was blooded by a female of another species, that foreign Bride might feel nothing for him.

This one feels nothing. "What if I decided to simply steal the medallion—and you?"

"It's protected."

"I'll breach that spell as easily as I did your barrier magic."

"The medallion is held in a glass case that's been protected by Morgana, using the full force of her magics. It can't be taken, only won by my future husband."

Trehan knew of Morgana, knew she was one of the most powerful sorceresses ever to live—because she controlled the abilities of *all other Sorceri.* Though Trehan was a learned Dacian, he wasn't egotistical enough to believe he could easily circumvent her spells. "You must know of a way to seize it."

She shook her head. "I don't. I'd tell you if I did."

"You'd tell me, but only to save your precious Caspion." Again he grappled with his temper, with a jealousy so raw he'd never experienced the like. "And what will he do to save *you*? Is he entering the tournament?"

In answer, she glanced at the coverlet.

"No? So it's either me tonight or one among the males lining up below? I would think you'd be more receptive to me. Surely I'm a better alternative."

"At least none of them want to murder the male I love."

Barely controlling his rage, he ignored the pain in his palm and clutched his sword hilt, something he never did. "The male you *love* is in a brothel right now; I'm here with you." His words hit home, making her flinch, but he took no satisfaction from it. "You've some skill in seduction, for a virgin. You'd be wise to use it right now." He could scarcely believe he'd said that to her. In the past, he'd spoken only after careful consideration of his words.

It seemed this jealousy was eroding his reason, his impulse control. Trehan, a Dacian, had nearly *bitten* her.

She met his gaze. "I'm sorry that I'm your Bride," she began, clearly trying to sort out the exact right thing to say. A difficulty in her condition. "I'm sorry that my heart's already taken. But if you harm him, you will *break* me." Tears welled in her eyes once more. "Please . . . *don't.*"

To protect his realm, Trehan must eliminate that demon; his Bride would never forgive the murder.

He needed to think. To approach this rationally. Which was impossible when the tears in her eyes affected him physically, and when the memory of her pulse against his tongue still made him thirst for the forbidden.

"I've told you everything I know," she murmured. "I'm begging you to leave Abaddon."

Begging me to leave her.

He didn't need this! He should be grateful for the increase in power his blooding had brought him—and the release he'd stolen with Bettina—then move on with his duties.

He could enjoy other women now that she'd brought his body back to life. He could still father heirs, could repopulate his house. As far as he knew, he was the first of his cousins to be blooded, which meant he'd just become the strongest.

Old longings could still be realized. *I could have a female and offspring—and the strength to protect them all.*

Trehan would be damned if he'd compete for Bettina's affections, especially not against someone so unworthy as Caspion. As the sun began to spill into her bedroom, he said, "Farewell, Bettina of Abaddon."

"You're leaving?"

The hopefulness in her tone cemented his decision. "I am."

Yet then her face fell. "To try to steal my medallion?"

"I return to my home."

Her eyes widened. "And you'll spare Cas?"

"Not at all. I have no plans to come back for you. But I definitely will for him. It's a done thing, Bettina. Resign yourself."

"Please, no! I'll do *anything*." Her face flamed as she asked, "Don't you need to . . . to claim me?"

Yes! The temptation to sink into her virgin body— to lose himself in the silky wetness that he'd touched, he'd *tasted*—nearly had him reaching for her once more.

With a nervous swallow, she dropped the sheet to her waist. "V-vow not to hurt him, and I'll be yours."

His gaze locked on her breasts, on those taunting nipples. *She'll sleep with me to save him.* Gods, the pleasure would be unimaginable. His cock hardened, twitching within his damp pants. Yet again, his fangs sharpened.

But he refused to force himself on a female who didn't want him. "You're in an impossible situation, girl. The more you plead for the demon, the less I'm inclined to want you." The more she pleaded, the less he *wanted* to want her. "The next female I take to my bed will be there because she craves what *I* alone can give her."

When burning rays of sun spilled into the room, he took one last look at her, then disappeared.

7

After Bettina tossed on a robe and ripped off her mask, she all but dived for Salem's bell, ringing it frantically.

"What's bloody wrong with you, chit?" the nearly empty jug on her coffee table demanded.

"Have you been watching over Cas?"

"I have. I morphed wiv the ceiling directly over the bed of the strumpet he's been pile-driving for hours. He's been doing things to her that you would not believe. I'll just pop off and get back to me post—"

"Wait." Bettina ground her teeth, reminding herself that it wasn't as if she and Cas had any commitment between them.

And it isn't like I haven't been with somebody else tonight.

"Go back to the *strumpet's*," she bit out, "and tell Caspion that I met the vampire sent to assassinate him."

The air shivered around her, the only indicator of Salem's emotions. No longer was he in the jug. She sensed him occupying a curl of her hair.

Right at her ear, he yelled, *"An assassin was in your apartments? Why the bloody-ell didn't you call for me?"*

Bettina jumped. "Just go get Cas! I'll explain everything to the two of you."

"I should have been here wiv you. And what if this leech returns? I'll tell Raum—"

"No! I don't believe there's a danger now that the sun's risen. Now go!"

Three minutes later, both Salem and Cas returned to her rooms. Cas was half-dressed, reeking of perfume, his horns and mouth smeared with lipstick. His shirt was unbuttoned, revealing flawless bronzed skin and more lipstick all the way to his navel.

What faceless female had enjoyed Cas's body over the night? Gods, the jealousy stung! Sometimes Bettina was glad that she didn't still possess her Sorceri power, could only imagine what she might be tempted to do in a fit of pique.

She gazed down at her splayed fingers; even after all this time, she expected power and light to boil up from her palms. Instead, emptiness tolled inside her.

A hollowness that nothing can alleviate. . . .

"You *saw* him?" Cas demanded as he pulled on a boot. "He was here?"

"Yes. In the flesh." *And in my bed.*

"How are you still alive?" Somewhat dressed, Cas laid his roughened hands on her shoulders, much as the vampire had done. "He never leaves anyone alive! It's forbidden for him to be seen by otherlanders!"

She swallowed. "I'm . . . well, I guess I'm an exception."

Salem shimmered through the room, possessing one of Cas's hands, but the demon shuddered, flicking his fingers with disgust.

Salem alighted, settling back into her hair. "Divvy, princess."

"The thing of it is . . . I'm his Bride."

As Cas gaped, Salem said, "So the demon pissed off some vampires, and they hired an assassin who recognizes you as his mate? Oh, this just gets better and better."

"That's about right."

Cas opened his mouth to speak, closed it, then tried once more before saying, "You *blooded* him?"

"Why do you sound *that* disbelieving?" She tightened the sash on her robe with snappish motions. "Some males actually find me attractive, Caspion."

"I know, I know. But—"

"And don't make it sound like this is *my* fault! I was asleep in my bed minding my own business when he appeared in my room."

"Because he was looking for me!" Cas backed away from her, swiping the back of his hand over his lipstick-stained mouth. "I've put you in danger, put you in that bastard's sights." Then he frowned. "Why is the vampire not here, trying to steal you?"

How embarrassing. She stared at the floor when she admitted, "I think he left me . . . because I told him of my feelings for you. He was angered." But not toward the very end. Then he'd seemed detached, unaffected by what had taken place between them.

"The bloody Prince of Shadow," Cas said. "Angered. What have I done?"

"How did he get past my warding spell in the first place?" She'd been completely vulnerable. What if he'd had ill intent? Her hand went to her throat. Could the

Vrekeners get in at will? That spell had been in place since the castle had been built—was it expiring?

"The vampire turned to mist," Cas absently said. "He's got centuries of experience foiling barriers. I was certain he could get to me."

"Mist! Vampires!" Salem exclaimed. "You two are talkin' about a *Dacian*?"

"He told me his name was Daciano," Bettina said. "What exactly is a Dacian? I thought they were the Horde's boogeymen. Super-vampires of legend."

Cas muttered a harsh curse. "They are *secret*. Anyone who knows of them dies! I'll not speak of this in front of Salem."

"As if I can't find out all soon anyway," Salem said. "I'm a *phantom*. Well, a sylph. Don't you two understand that there're no secrets kept from Salem? None." He addressed Bettina. "Like when the princess noshed hallucinogens last year at a—what do the mortals call it?—*rave*."

How could he know that?

To Cas, he said, "Or what you did wiv those two Lykae sisters one full moon? Almost lost a hand that night, yeah?"

Cas swallowed uncomfortably, looking shamefaced. *What happened with the she-wolves?*

"Fine. You know things," Cas said. "But how can we be assured that you haven't been telling all this to Raum?"

"Because Raum has two gears: jolly and furious—bear hug or battle-ax to the brain. He can't hide reactions. Now, you two, decide: Salem as ally or enemy?"

She narrowed her eyes. "Why do you want to be involved in our lives if not to tell Raum all you learn?"

"Because I can't fight, eat, drink, sleep, or wank. It's difficult to get a leg over when you *don't have legs*! I want in on the intrigue! Now, demon, what did you do?"

Bettina sank down on her settee. "Oh, for gold's sake, Cas, just tell him."

With a grated sound of irritation, he said, "I *left*. Once you enter Dacia, you can't leave without special permission. It's granted very rarely for native Daci—and *never* to kingdom newcomers."

"Did no one tell you these rules?" she asked.

"I thought I could get around them, or that my sponsor would call the dogs off. At worst, I believed I'd have sanctuary here. I never told them I was from Abaddon, still don't know how their killer reached me here so quickly. He can't have ever been here before." Cas rubbed his palm over his face. "And how in the gods' names did he find you?"

"I have no idea. I just woke up and there he was."

Cas cast her a puzzled look. "How could he leave if his blooding wasn't completed?"

When Bettina studied her hands in her lap, tension rolled off him, so strong she gazed up again. Never had she seen him so furious. Even Salem had begun to blur the air with his anger.

"He forced you?" Cas grated. "I will gut him before he ever has a chance to strike at me!"

"No! It wasn't like that."

Salem snapped, "Then what *was* it like?"

Taking a deep breath, she said, "I was tipsy. I thought he was Cas." Her cheeks felt like they were on fire. "I was . . . receptive."

Cas drew his shoulders back. "You couldn't tell that it was another?" he demanded, clearly affronted.

"The room was dark! And we weren't doing much . . . talking. But no permanent damage has been done. I'm still a virgin. Just perhaps a jot more *educated*."

Cas reached forward, lifting her gold collar. "At least he didn't bite you."

She recalled how hard Daciano had fought not to. *I will never hurt you. . . .* "He stopped himself when he saw I was upset."

"A *very* lucky break for us. To be bitten by a vampire is . . . altering." He glanced away briefly before facing her once more. "I'll find a way to protect you from him. Somehow. He might be ancient and skilled with a sword, but I'll figure out a way. When he returns, I'll make my move."

She didn't share Cas's optimism. *That chilling lethality . . .* "Wait, you said ancient?"

"At least nine centuries."

How very . . . *old*. She didn't know how she felt about that. But for Caspion, this was disastrous. Age brought strength to immortals. "He said he has no plans to return for me, but he definitely will for you, Cas. Do you really think you can defeat a professional killer? A long-lived Dacian? You certainly hadn't earlier—you were convinced that he'd end you."

"That was before you were involved. Now I have to find a way."

Salem said, "That's the thing about an assassin—wiv each kill, he risks capture or death himself. A long-lived assassin means he wins *every single time*."

Cas rubbed his throat again.

Bettina pressed her advantage. "There's only one course of action. Enter the tournament. Raum and Morgana guarantee each contestant's safety out of the ring. The vampire couldn't touch you. And you know you can beat anybody who enters."

Though he wasn't as powerful as he could be—death demons garnered strength from each kill and his job had been to track, not *execute*—Cas was an excellent swordsman, and he could trace.

A flicker of hope rose in his eyes. Then he shook his head. "And if I win? What then? Say I eliminate this assassin afterward and wed you. You would deprive my fated mate of her male? I'd be making both of our lives miserable."

Her mind cried, *I might be your mate*. "You can't know it's not me. And I'm free to love whoever I want to." Unlike many Lore species, Sorceri didn't have a mystical fated mate per se. But they did wed and form lifelong bonds.

"I'm sorry, Bettina." His expression looked genuinely remorseful, his blond brows drawn. "I can't enter."

Disappointment threatened to engulf her, but she strived for a calm tone. "I see. I could ask Morgana for help against the vampire." Bettina's godmother was just like a big sister.

That one did not ever, ever, *ever* want to cross.

Yet Bettina was desperate once more. "She doesn't arrive until this eve—won't stay on this 'wretched demonic plane' any longer than necessary—but I could ask her then."

Morgana reviled all demons, still couldn't believe her best friend Eleara—Bettina's late mother—had wed one. But the sorceress might actually agree to help Cas just to thwart the vampire.

Morgana would interpret Trehan Daciano's actions with Bettina as a *trick,* and Sorceri were supposed to be the tricksters—not the trickees. The great queen might kill the vampire for that alone.

Cas took her shoulders again. "You can't tell anyone else about this! No one is supposed to know the Dacians even exist. Already too many know. I'd be betraying Mirceo even more."

Mirceo? "But Morgana can help—"

"Vow to me, Tina. You would put the Sorceri at risk, put yourself more at risk!"

When he looked at her like this, with his blue eyes glowing with feeling, she could deny him nothing. She mumbled, "I vow it."

"This is all fine and good," Salem said, "worrying about Caspion. But you have *plenty* on your plate to be worrying about. Not every female in the brothel was lucky enough to be serviced by him. I saw other competitors inside. A trio of two-headed Ajatars. Cerunnos. Even a pus demon—oh, 'scuse me, an excretorian—was there."

Ajatars had metal teeth and breathed fire. Cerunnos were snakelike humanoids. Excretorians leaked pus from every pore. She turned to Cas. "Please don't leave me to this fate. They will cancel the tournament completely if I'm not a virgin. Can't you just . . . would it be so bad . . . ?"

"Bettina," he began gravely, "there's something you should know."

8

"Show yourself," Trehan demanded of his seemingly empty apartments. He sensed danger looming. A regular occurrence for him in Dacia.

His gaze flickered over the shadowed corners of the gilded sitting area, then up to scan the vaulted ceilings. He stole a quick glance down the two adjoining corridors. One led to his bedchamber; the other opened up into a wing with unending bookshelves.

When only silence greeted him, he returned to his task: researching.

He'd assured his newfound Bride that he had no plans to return for her. *True at the time.* But now . . .

The idea of never seeing her again made him crazed.

She'd asked him, "What do you want from me?" He wanted to go back in time and answer: "Everything! Everything that is mine by right!"

But he'd done the rational thing—and left her. Never had he regretted a rational decision.

Might I now?

He'd told himself he simply didn't have enough information to conclude anything about her. He needed to contemplate this in a logical fashion, gathering facts.

So he'd turned to his books, retrieving a tome on vampire physiology, the weighty *Book of Lore,* and a recently published history of the various demonarchies. Laying the books out on one side of his large desk, he'd set the tournament invitation on the other.

In the physiology manual, Trehan confirmed the harsh realities of his situation. Unless a vampire claimed his Bride completely, he would be filled with aggression, irrational jealousy, and uncontrollable sexual urges.

Perhaps Trehan should have agreed to her offer and taken her. Aggression? Check. Irrational jealousy? When he thought of Bettina responding with such abandon to Caspion, Trehan traced to his feet, wrestling with a murderous rage. Check.

Uncontrollable sexual urges? Upon returning home to wash and change, he'd grown achingly hard just from the evidence of his release in his pants. After all, he hadn't scented or seen it for the better part of a millennium.

The book also said that a vampire must penetrate his mate with his fangs. As the demons and Lykae did. *Which we consider barbaric.*

But this book had been written about vampires—in general. Dacians were different, superior to other factions like the Horde and the Forbearers. He assured himself of this, even as he recalled how badly he'd craved biting her.

Dominion . . .

With an inward shake, he turned to the demon history book, to the Abaddonae entry.

Aptly named, the Deathly Ones derived strength from every kill they made, so historically they'd been at war more often than not. Their plane was an isolated swamp realm of no consequence, with a typical off-world time variance.

Time, like life, moved more slowly in Abaddon. . . .

Princess Bettina was the first daughter born in generations, described as "elfin" in appearance. Though a halfling, she'd inherited no outward demonic traits, yet she was reputed to possess a notable—but undisclosed—Sorceri power.

Fascinating. A delicate, little sorceress born into an archaic and violent demon world.

Her paternal ancestors had fought proudly and died in various battles, most often with other demonarchies. Just a decade earlier, her father, Mathar, had gone to the aid of one of his Pravus allies, perishing on the front line.

Apparently his sorceress queen, Eleara, had been killed by Vrekeners just after Bettina's birth. Those winged creatures were mortal enemies of the Sept of Sorceri, considering themselves a check on Sorceri evil.

Trehan could find no more history on Eleara's side, so he read in the *Book of Lore* about the Sorceri in general. Distantly related to witches, each was born with a root ability that they considered akin to a soul.

Their species was one of the weakest of all immortals—at least in matters of physical strength and healing—so they adorned their bodies with protective metals, especially gold.

They had no claws, so they wore metal ones. The masks they favored unsettled their enemies.

They were at once merry wine drinkers who worshipped gold—and fearful magicians, living in constant dread of ceding their powers to another.

What was Bettina's power? Why hadn't she used it against him when he'd been on the verge of taking her neck?

With these three books, he'd established a trio of facts.

His physical need wasn't only grueling, it was dangerous.

Though her line was partly demonic, it was proud and worthy.

The little sorceress would be under constant threat and would need him as well.

But some things couldn't be uncovered through books, and Trehan had more questions than answers regarding his Bride. He wondered what her personality was like, what her favorite color was. What were her hobbies? What made her laugh?

He considered what he *did* know about her.

She would bravely—if wrongly—sacrifice herself for the male she loved. She was sensual and curious about sex; no innately cold Bride for him. Yet again he recalled that shy grin as she'd bared her breasts. She wasn't brazen by nature, but when pleasured, she grew beautifully wanton.

Judging by her book collection, she was fixated on her craft. Trehan was as obsessed with arms as any Dacian, probably more. He surveyed all his weapons displayed in gold cases and thought, *She creates weapons; I wield them.*

He gazed down at his injured hand. *Ah, but she wielded one as well.* Was that to be their initial common ground?

The wounds were fading; he found he didn't want them to. No, he hadn't sunk his fangs into her flesh, but she'd given him her own bite. When he remembered the blood welling across his palm and her flash of pride, for some reason he grew aroused once more.

Glancing from the invitation . . . to his books . . . back to the invitation—

Cold steel pressed against Trehan's neck.

Must be Viktor. He wondered if his cousin would finally land a deathblow. They'd been trying to kill each other for hundreds of years.

"You let me take you unawares?" Viktor grated. "What occupies your thoughts so completely?"

"Not completely occupied." Trehan prodded Viktor with the blade he'd managed to slip from his sword belt, the blade now pressed against Viktor's scrotum.

Viktor laughed at Trehan's ear. "I might temporarily lose my balls, old man, but you'll lose your life."

"I've been castrated before. The regeneration was such that you might find my headless fate preferable," he said, cursing his carelessness. Tonight was a night of firsts for Trehan: allowing Viktor to take him unawares, leaving a target alive, his blooding—even his rejection by a female.

Viktor hesitated, then backed away. "It won't prove amusing to end you without a fight." He loved nothing more than fighting. Not surprising—he was the last scion of the House of War, *the wrath of the kingdom.* "Take out your sword, Cousin."

With a weary exhalation, Trehan sheathed his short blade, then drew his sword. The weapon was one of the only belongings he truly cared about. It had been given to him by his father with the instructions: *"Be an example, Son."*

Ignoring the twinge in his injured hand, Trehan traced to face Viktor. Though their temperaments were directly opposed—one cold and methodical, one warlike and rash—their looks were so similar they could have been brothers.

Viktor narrowed his green eyes at Trehan. "You're even more pensive than usual. Trouble with your target?"

You have no idea, Trehan thought as he launched the first strike.

Viktor deflected it, and the clang of steel echoed in the spacious library.

"It was that new demon, right?" Viktor asked as he charged. Trehan neatly dodged his sword. Centuries of nearly constant battles between them had made them both superlative swordsmen. "Caspion the Tracker, the one all the females favored?"

All the females. Even mine.

Viktor feinted left, making a short jab to the right; Trehan arched his back, narrowly escaping the sword tip.

"Did the great Trehan actually leave a target alive? No, no, because then you wouldn't be back here." Another thrust.

Trehan parried. "I didn't engage him," he answered, half-tempted to tell his cousin everything. If not Viktor, then whom could he confide in?

No one.

Their relationship was complicated, to say the least. As the last members of their respective houses, they'd been trying to kill each other for most of their lives, yet there was no one Trehan would rather have at his back if they fought a mutual enemy. Viktor also kept his cousin's secrets, refusing to sully himself and Trehan with court politics, preferring to settle their grievances by combat.

Trehan swung; Viktor blocked. Their swords connected, quaking in their hands.

"You're strong tonight," Viktor observed with approval. He venerated strength and relished violence.

Viktor was perpetually disappointed that their hidden kingdom afforded no chance for open conflict. As he'd once said while in his cups, "I'm the general of the world's proudest and most perfect army—one that will *never* go to battle."

Strike; swift parry. Slash; deflect.

"What is this I hear?" Viktor suddenly exclaimed. "Ah, Trehan, your heart beats! That's where this new strength hails from."

A vampire derived strength from age, Dacian blood, drinking straight from the flesh—and his blooding. "So it does." He didn't know if Viktor was blooded. His cousin utilized an old witch's spell to camouflage whether he had a heartbeat or not.

Trehan had a theory about that. . . .

"Where is your new Bride?" Viktor risked a glance past Trehan. "Why were you *reading* when I stole upon you?" A look of confusion followed. "Why are you not rutting her even now? Perhaps I'll find her sprawled across your bed with a soothing pack of ice between her legs?"

"You're crass." Another flash of his sword. "That's my Bride you speak of!"

Another parry. "Then where is she?"

"There were *challenges* inherent with her." He traced away from Viktor's charge, appearing feet away; the blade sliced the air where Trehan had just been.

"Tell all, Cousin!"

"It doesn't matter. She wouldn't be suitable for me." Bettina had her own realm to rule. She could scarcely be expected to live in this underworld with him.

She's in love with another.

"Did you claim her?" Viktor asked.

A sharp shake of his head. "And it's just as well. Once I take the throne—"

"So certain you'll be king?" *Slash.*

Dodge. "Unfortunately, yes. You know I'm the logical choice."

He was the most qualified to rule, but in fairness, each of the contenders had strengths. Trehan had cultivated an order of trained assassins. Viktor controlled the military. Their cousin Stelian governed who entered or exited Dacia. The youngest male cousin, Mirceo, was the most beloved by the people and had a loyal ally in his little sister, Kosmina.

However, Trehan was the most "Dacian" of the royals, believing in this kingdom, like a religion.

"Ah, that vaunted Dacian logic," Viktor sneered, feinting a trace to the right, then striking to the left. With a well-timed block, Trehan deflected, but Viktor's leg shot up, booting Trehan in the stomach.

If Viktor wanted to fight dirty . . .

Between breaths, Trehan grated, "Perhaps you wouldn't resent that trait in others . . . if you weren't the most *il*logical of the family?" Like a blur, he swept down, kicking Viktor's legs out from under him.

Just before Viktor's back met the floor, he traced to his feet. "King Trehan? Never while I live."

They faced off once more. "You're too hostile and rash," Trehan said. "Mirceo's too self-absorbed and hedonistic, not to mention young. And Stelian is nearly too drunken to handle his responsibilities as gatekeeper."

"And *you* are too emotionless."

I haven't been tonight. Gazing down at Bettina's eyes, watching them glitter with need, Trehan had been filled with emotion. He hadn't been emotionless when he'd come in his Bride's soft hand. . . .

Distracted once more, he barely dodged Viktor's next strike.

"The people would wither under your stifling rule, Trehan. You *are* the sword of the kingdom, a cold, unfeeling blade."

"This is a debate for another night."

"So be it. Back to your missing Bride . . ." He trailed off, his gaze landing on Trehan's desk—on the invitation. Before Trehan could reach the parchment, Viktor had snatched it up, swiftly perusing the writing. "Abaddon? I've been there! Used to go watch the fights. The mist blends with that fog so seamlessly, you know. Wait, this is her, isn't it? 'Challenges inherent'? I should say so. She's a godsdamned tourney prize!"

"Enough, Cousin."

"Not even close! Why are we wrangling over this crown when you can just go get another one?"

"I have no interest in that kingdom—solely the girl."

"The one who just happens to be under the protection of a Deathly One and the most powerful sorceress ever to live? Did you try to steal her from them this eve?"

"I did," Trehan admitted. "But she's bound to that plane."

"Wait, she's a . . . a *demoness*? Again, why are you not bedding her right now?"

"For the record, she's half sorceress. And she knows my target. They're . . . close. She will hate me forever if I kill him."

"You don't have a choice."

"And why's that?"

Viktor rolled his eyes. "Because you're a slave to your duty, to your house."

Over the last millennium, Trehan had sacrificed *everything* for the good of Dacia. For once in his life, would he have what *he* desired? "What if I . . . wasn't?"

Viktor backed away, unsure what to do with that. "Perfect, selfless Trehan Daciano entertains selfish thoughts? This I must explore. Truce for one eve?"

Trehan exhaled. "Pour the mead." Once he cautiously sheathed his sword, Viktor did as well.

"Tell me about her." Viktor traced to the sideboard, selecting a crystal decanter filled with mead-laced blood.

"She's young. Lovely." *Talented, creative, innately sensual. With the sweetest skin I've ever imagined.*

"How young?" Viktor handed him a glass topped off with crimson.

After a hesitation, Trehan said, "Kosmina's age." Mirceo and Kosmina were so much younger than the elder cousins that they called each one "uncle."

Viktor's lips parted. "You're jesting."

"Not at all." He took a drink, but found the blood tasteless. Again he wondered what Bettina's would be like.

Observant Viktor narrowed his eyes. "Did you *bite* her?"

Came so close. He recalled how his fangs had ached to pierce her—completely beyond his control. Like an ungovernable erection.

Would he be able to stop himself from tasting her blood if given a second chance? How did other Dacian males keep themselves in check?

Is something . . . wrong with me?

"You did!" Viktor raised his glass. "How very deviant of you, Trey! Did you mark her skin? Did you take her memories into you?"

"Don't be absurd." One of the reasons Dacians disavowed drinking from the flesh was because of the *cosaşad*—the ability to read memories through blood. When a *cosaş* took blood directly from the flesh, he took his prey's memories into his own consciousness, even from the merest drop on the tongue. The coldly rational Dacians believed this to be a pollution, an intrusion into their pure minds.

If I'd taken Bettina's memories, what would I have witnessed? Probably scenes of her lusting after Caspion. Trehan just stopped himself from crushing his goblet.

"Thinking about it even now?" Viktor said. "I can't believe you used your fangs on her—Trehan the Perfect is actually perverse!"

"I didn't bite her." He glanced up. "You look disappointed. So eager to see me fall?"

"But you *wanted* to."

Will fantasize about it for the rest of my life. "If I did, I'd never admit anything so shaming to you."

Viktor gazed away. "You might have once." He took a deep drink. "Back to the matter at hand. What are your options with the girl?"

"Kill Caspion. Forget her and move on." As he said the words, they burned like a lie. Forgetting her *wasn't* an option. Could he possibly move on?

There were so many questions surrounding her, so much to discover. He felt as if he'd read the first page of the most absorbing book he'd ever opened, only to have it slammed shut. "Second option: kill Caspion, find a way to steal the girl's medallion, then abduct her." Would she truly hate Trehan forever? Surely in a few decades she'd get over her displeasure.

Viktor shook his head decisively. "Morgana's magics won't be circumvented, not even by the likes of you. We have no spellcaster to aid you, much less one who could take her on. *Logically,* you know stealing the medallion isn't an option. A campaign like that would be doomed to fail." He lowered his drink, growing very serious about the topic.

This could be because Viktor had identified an enemy in Morgana, one who was thwarting the desires of a fellow Dacian. Or perhaps he was sensing imminent violence and hoping for a part of it. Maybe Viktor wanted to help because he sought to damage Trehan's chances at the throne.

Likely all three motives.

For a brief moment, Trehan considered that Viktor might be moved to help because once, long, long ago, they had been friends. Then he dismissed the idea. They had too much history between them.

Trehan said, "I'd contemplated appealing to her godparents before the tournament begins. But how exactly would I present my case? Should I say, 'I can't tell you who I am, what royal line I descend from, where I hail from, or what my properties *used* to be. But give me your ward anyway'?"

"What about stealing her after the tournament—but before the full-moon wedding?"

"Back to the summoning medallion. Whoever wins it will control her movements."

"If you entered, you'd have to leave the mist? To be seen by all?"

Trehan just stifled a shudder. "Yes. By all."

"You'd be banished—and then I wouldn't have to kill you," Viktor said smugly. "At least not pressingly."

Trehan gave him the look that comment deserved.

"Just think, you'd be king of one realm at least."

"That's actually a negative for me. Ruling a rainy, backwoods swamp plane filled with Deathly Ones? What do I know about ruling demons? Or about rain, for that matter?" He waved to indicate Dacia's stone sky. "And why would they accept a nameless vampire to govern them? Clearly, the tournament is not an option. I could never turn my back on my kingdom and abandon my house, not when the Dacians need a king."

"There's another who could rule us."

Trehan drank deeply, keen to get to the mead. "Lothaire again?" Lothaire Daciano, the Enemy of Old, was a three-thousand-year-old vampire gone red-eyed and insane from bloodlust—a prime example of why Dacians refrained from drinking others.

Lothaire was half Horde, half Dacian. *Wholly mad.*

Did he have a claim to the throne? Undoubtedly. His own house had always ruled.

What he lacked was a grasp of reality. Though the cousins had intermittently kept tabs on him, they'd never revealed themselves to him. "You'd truly accept a red-eyed king?" Horde vampires drained their prey to the quick, becoming addicted to the power and madness that act brought. Lothaire was rumored to have countless memories rattling around in his head.

In fact, it was said that he used the *cosaşad* to his advantage, drinking chosen victims *just* to get to their secrets.

"Perhaps I admire him," Viktor said. "His bargaining is masterful. He would bring his fabled book of debts to the kingdom like a dowry."

Lothaire's book was also legendary. For millennia, he'd maneuvered Loreans into life-or-death situations, offering to save them—for a price. Rumor held that his debtors had vowed to do *anything* he asked of them when he called in the debt, and that he'd recorded their bargains meticulously.

"He's probably the strongest vampire alive," Viktor continued. "We could do worse for a king. Besides, I thought you'd be all for it, eager to end all our family animosity."

"Don't you tire of it?"

"Who are you talking to, Trehan? I *live* for animosity."

And Viktor had plenty of cause for it. Trehan's own father had killed Viktor's. Of course, Viktor's mother had slain Trehan's. Throw in Stelian's parents and Mirceo's and they had all ended up dead eventually.

The blood vendettas of the Daciano houses were legion, inherited from their ancestors, with each generation adding new ones. "Then why would you even consider Lothaire?"

"Maybe I have no desire to be king either," Viktor said. "Perhaps I only fight for it because I know I'd be better at it than any of you. Give me a vampire who's actually more powerful than I am, and I'll help guide him as he rules."

From what Trehan had heard—and seen—of Lothaire, the male wouldn't prove easy to "guide."

Viktor viewed the invitation once more, this time with a look of lust on his face. *"Zeii mea." My gods.* "Fights. To the death." He actually groaned. "You could be *in* that ring. And with your clear eyes, everyone would think you're a Forbearer." One among an army of turned humans who didn't drink from the flesh. Viktor smiled evilly. "They'll believe *you* are weak, having no idea what you really are. Already an advantage."

Trehan gazed down at his drink, lost in thought. The fighting didn't factor into his decision whatsoever. If he chose to enter the tournament, he would win. Period.

Instead, his thoughts centered on another battle. *Could I possibly win Bettina's affections?* On that score, he was much less certain.

"Come, Cousin, there's more that you're not telling me."

Trehan quickly glanced up, the words falling from his lips: "She's in love with another. With . . . Caspion."

Damn it, what did she see in that demon? If those two had had some kind of relationship, then Caspion hadn't been true to her, had been in a brothel this very night.

Viktor winced. "Bloody bad luck, Trey." He sounded genuinely sorry for Trehan.

And yet tomorrow Viktor would plot to murder him all over again.

Unless I'm not here.

"He must die," Viktor said. "Even Mirceo has accepted that."

Mirceo had been Caspion's sponsor into the kingdom, using all his influence to campaign for the demon's acceptance. Mirceo had never expected Caspion to bolt, a first for the charming Dacian.

"You have other assassins under your command," Viktor pointed out. "Get someone else to kill the demon."

Trehan rubbed his brow. "By my hand or by my command won't make a difference with her."

"Is the demon entering the tournament? Then you could kill him in combat."

"I haven't relinquished Dacia yet, Cousin. If I decide to enter—"

"You'll enter."

"—then I will have spent my entire life in service to the kingdom, only to abandon it in a time of need, for a female who doesn't even want me!"

"It makes sense that she would prefer Caspion," Viktor said in a thoughtful tone. "Apparently, he is irresistible to females—and not a few males. There's a reason Cousin Mirceo petitioned for him to enter Dacia. Alas, the demon is much better-looking than you are, old man."

Trehan scowled. "I'm barely older than you are."

"You said your Bride was young. She likely doesn't know her mind yet. Her feelings for Caspion could be nothing more than a schoolgirl infatuation with a dashing demon."

Bettina *was* woefully young, and she'd obviously been overprotected. Perhaps she simply hadn't been around other males? She might have bonded with the one given most access to her.

Or was this only wishful thinking? He knew his looks didn't compare to the demon's—admittedly Caspion was . . . without flaw—but Trehan had other laudable qualities.

I'm a good killer. A talented scholar. Fuck. How could she possibly resist?

Then why has fate chosen her *for me?*

Bettina, Princess of Abaddon, was the only female

in existence—and in all times past and future—who'd proved to be his Bride. . . .

He reminded himself that she *had* responded to him. She'd inhaled deeply of his skin, moaning in reaction. She'd moistened her bloodred lips as she'd investigated him with her soft fingertips. She'd murmured in a throaty voice, "My gods, I love your body."

She'd delighted in touching me.

If he could seduce her into a similar situation, he could make her realize who'd awakened those feelings in her.

He had to believe that, given the chance, he could make her desire him again.

But that was the crux of this all: the mere *chance* would cost him dearly. His house would perish forever, his duty—and honor—with it. *Competing in that tournament will cost me* everything.

"You've obviously got it *bad,* old man," Viktor said. "The girl burned a hole in your brain, did she?"

Trehan recalled how she'd looked in the throes of passion—her shimmering eyes pleading for more of his touch—and muttered, "A fiery arrow through the fucking temple." She'd quivered against his hand, so close to coming for him. . . .

"What are you going to do?"

"What any logical male would."

Viktor raised brows. "Then *I* am at a loss. Enlighten me."

Trehan said, "I'm going to gather more information about her before rendering a decision."

9

Morgana would arrive in minutes, yet Bettina sat in her cooling bathwater in a daze, unable to muster any outrage that Salem had been watching her bathe again.

Her interaction with the vampire had left her feeling battered—not to mention Caspion's confession this morning.

When she'd all but begged him to make love to her, he'd said, "You're my best friend, and I love you like a sister. Tina, it wouldn't feel right. And after the night I've, uh, spent, I don't even know if I . . . can."

While she'd rocked on her feet as if slapped, Salem had sneered, "But pile-driving a hooker for hours felt right? Maybe the manwhore's all whored out? Maybe wittle Cas can't rise to the occasion?"

Caspion's flushed cheeks had confirmed Salem's jab.

If she'd ever needed a wake-up call . . . Cas felt no

physical attraction to her. Period. Why was she forcing this with him?

But every time she wondered when she'd become *that* girl—the one chasing after a guy who would never love her—she'd recall all their years together.

When she'd been orphaned after her father's death, she'd gone from crying herself to sleep, feeling completely alone—with not a friend in the world—to waking up each morning filled with anticipation of seeing Cas's smiling face.

He'd been a lifeline.

Whenever she berated herself for holding on to false hopes, she remembered his reaction when he'd first seen her injuries. With his eyes watering, he'd barked orders to get her help, urging, "Stay with me, Tina." When they'd started to set her bones, no demon tonic would put her under. He'd roared as she'd screamed.

Later she had heard that he'd destroyed his home, blaming himself for not protecting her, bellowing with frustration. Was that the reaction of a big brother? She hadn't thought so. Of course, she had no siblings for comparison.

For sixty nights, he'd tried to avenge her, but failed. *No one* could avenge her. . . .

Now, as the sun began setting, her nervousness ratcheted up. The vampire might return for Caspion soon; the tournament was definitely about to begin.

No more stalling. She stepped from the large pool in her bathing chamber. This room was as medieval as everything else in Abaddon, but through miraculous feats of engineering—and the work of behind-the-scene ogres—she had managed to score hot, running water all the way up in her spire.

Tossing on a robe, she asked Salem, "Got an eyeful again, didn't you?" Life with a sylph roomie—her resident peeping phanTom—had drilled out much of her modesty.

"Of course," Salem answered from the foggy mirror above her sink. "How do you always know?"

Bettina's five senses might be humanlike, but her sixth sense was strong. Well, except when she was tanked on demon brew. And besides . . . "I know, because you *always* do it."

She swiped her sleeve over the glass, then studied her reflection. No better than before the bath. She still looked hungover and exhausted. When she'd finally managed to drift off to sleep this morning, her customary nightmares had plagued her.

"I don't understand why you spy on me," she said. "It's not like you have a body." A servitude curse—for some mysterious crime—prevented him from becoming corporeal. And though he was still telekinetic, he couldn't *feel*.

"I won't be like this forever. Why, one day I'll be a real boy! And this gives me much masturbation fodder for the future."

She rolled her eyes, hoping he was kidding. When he'd arrived here three months ago, she'd made the mistake of picturing him as a harmless, genie-type sprite, much as Raum still thought him.

The first time Bettina had sensed Salem spying, she'd figured if he wanted a peep at small breasts and zero hips . . . *knock yourself out.*

Then she'd found out more about the "notorious" Salem from Morgana and her coterie, who'd known him before his curse. Apparently, Salem had been a ruthless warrior who "dripped sex appeal."

Bettina's innocent genie bath time had taken on an awkward new dynamic.

"You look like utter ass, chit," he said now, nudging a glamour trinket toward her.

Morgana had given it to her to conceal all her wounds after the incident, but there was still some magic left over. Should Bettina do a cursory camouflage, so her godmother wouldn't spy anything amiss?

Morgana was already hypercritical about Bettina's looks, finding her lacking compared to Bettina's mother, Eleara.

Bettina remembered one of her earliest visits with Morgana: "Oh, for the love of gold, you are an odd, tiny thing, aren't you?" she'd said with a frown. "Your features can't decide if they want to be impish like a demon cub's or arresting like Eleara's. Hmm. Well, little freakling, be of cheer, for it can only go up from here. . . ."

At the memory, Bettina set the glamour away. She *wanted* her godmother to know something was amiss. *No less than my entire life.*

"Still having the nightmare?" Salem asked.

"Unfortunately." This afternoon, Bettina had shot upright in bed, midway into one of her panic attacks. Ever since her beating, she'd been plagued with them. Her body had been tight with strain, her skin covered with perspiration. Her lungs had felt constricted as if by a vise.

She'd peered around her room, assuring herself, *I'm in my home. Those fiends aren't here. No Vrekener has ever come to Abaddon. . . .*

Bettina had two goals in life. One of which was to feel safe again. She could remember what it was like *not* to have fear constantly creeping up on her. She remembered life without her debilitating attacks.

She used to be able to walk the town without a care, used to be able to visit the rain forest by herself. Now she couldn't exit the castle unescorted, could scarcely navigate the interior of it alone.

Her episodes seemed to be getting worse. And last night's break-in had been a serious blow to her recovery. Despite a warding spell, the vampire had entered her room "with ease."

"You should talk to someone about it," Salem suggested. "Get it off your chest."

She rubbed her pounding temples. "Are you offering to be a sounding board for me?"

"Only if you want to hear your mirror snore. From what I've been able to piece together, I'd be bored silly."

She glared, unable to tell if he was joking. "Then why are you still here?"

"I found out a lot about our mysterious assassin. Did a little digging, calling in favors from some very old phantoms. No one knows secrets like phantoms."

"Tell me," she quickly said, beyond curious about the vampire Daciano.

"It's rumored that his people live inside the hollowed-out mountains of an entire range. No one in the Lore can prove they exist, not even the most skilled phantom spies. Caspion could very well be the only outsider at large who has seen Dacia and lived. They'll remedy that soon enough."

Bettina's hands fluttered to her throat. Why wouldn't Caspion agree to enter the tournament? He'd prefer death by assassin over her? Was he so averse to exploring even the *possibility* that she was his?

Salem continued, "Their species is proud, powerful, but they *never* engage wiv the outside. If a Dacian is seen outside of the realm by an otherlander—that's what they call us—then he's mystically forbidden to return. Except for in your case. According to my sources, the Bride of a Dacian *is* a Dacian, to their way of thinking. So he could go home. But not after he comes for you tonight, before all and sundry."

"He's not interested in me. Remember? He flat-out told me he had no plans to return for me, and he can't lie."

Naturally Bettina was delighted by the idea of his never returning—if that meant Cas was safe. Yet a tiny part of her also had to wonder why males found it so easy to pass her over. She'd never heard of a vampire ditching his Bride. Ever.

"You can't see, but I'm shrugging." In a contemplative tone, he said, "Can you picture living in Dacia? Learning all about the Realm of Blood and Mist? I'd give me right invisible arm for a chance at that."

"Living underground, inside a mountain? With no forest? Never to feel the sun on one's face?" *Nice place to visit, but . . .* "Let's just say I'm glad I don't have to worry about Daciano returning."

"I'm telling you, he'll be back. And if you ever go to Dacia, I'm tagging along," Salem assured her. "Oh, and by the way, your patroness contacted us, wants a new piece. Something 'seductively lethal.'"

Another commission? Bettina experienced a thrill. Though she'd been selling jewelry for years now, it'd never been about the compensation; her parents had left her plenty of wealth, which Raum continued to grow for her.

If Bettina's first goal in life was to feel safe, her second was to walk down a busy street and see someone wearing her creations. She'd daydreamed about it, wondering how she'd react.

After the incident, she'd changed her focus, designing adornments with a dual purpose—jewelry pieces that doubled as weapons.

She hand-fashioned old standbys—like rings with poison reservoirs—as well as body jewelry: mesh tops that could ward off a sword blow, armor-piercing brooches, collars with embedded blades.

Sorceri coveted such accessories, but high-quality pieces were often hard to come by.

Bettina liked to call her work "lethal luxe" or "blood bling." Salem laughingly deemed them "slaughter chic," avowing that "Deadly is the new black."

Whenever anxiety threatened or she was dwelling on her tragedy in the mortal realm, she adjourned to her workshop and created in a frenzy.

When Salem had first seen her like this, he'd sneered, "Look at the Keebler elf, wiv her wittle tools!" Then he'd grown intrigued with her creations, securing her first patron—for a hefty finder's fee, of course.

"Here's the downside," Salem said now. "Patroness wants it in two weeks' time."

"So quickly?" Bettina hastened into her workroom, scanning her jeweler's benches. She was as proud of her workshop as she was of the pieces produced there.

She had collected a master's set of cutters, polishers, burs, and drills. On one bench, old-fashioned swage blocks and mandrels sat beside state-of-the-art, propane-fueled solder guns and hot-air pencils.

On another bench, she had design sketches and a backboard filled with spools of gold chain. Dress dummies stood at intervals throughout the space.

To cheer her after the incident, Salem had occasionally made them dance.

"Two weeks? What am I going to do?"

Salem answered, "Give her the field-tested armlet, if you can clean the vampire funk off it. Still can't believe you got the spring mechanism to work."

Bettina had told him how it had successfully pierced Daciano's hand. "I want to keep that one." Though Patroness was a style setter—and a fearsome female—Bettina couldn't part with the armlet. It symbolized a little victory, her first since the attack.

"Your call, but if I were you, I'd almost be more afraid of disappointing your Patroness than your godmother. Speaking of which . . ."

"I sense her too."

"I'll let you and the womenfolk get yourself all tarted up." With a "Laters, dove," Salem disappeared, abandoning Bettina.

She hastened from the workshop just as the front doors to her spire whooshed open.

The only thing greater than the pull of Trehan's home was his curiosity about his Bride. Yes, he'd decided to return to Rune, but only to fact-find.

Or so he kept telling himself. *Yet I packed a bag?*

As Trehan ran his fingers down the spines of treasured books, he wondered if his mind was playing tricks on him, misremembering how good it'd been with Bettina.

Those moments of pleasure couldn't possibly have been as sublime as he thought them. Her clever weapon and drawings couldn't have been as fascinating.

However, he'd prepared for any eventuality, packing clothing and other essentials. Inside his coat, he carried an ancient silk standard of red and gray, symbolic of blood and mist—of the kingdom he loved more than anything.

Yet again he surveyed his apartments. If he chose Bettina, he'd be leaving behind a millennium's worth of accumulation—a fortune in gold, his extensive arms collection, artwork, about two hundred thousand books.

He'd be leaving behind his history, his very identity.

After a sleepless span, Trehan still wavered. Of one thing he was certain. *I'd kill for another feel of her in my arms.*

Instinct rode him hard, an uncomfortable position for a logical Dacian to be in—because instinct was rarely logical.

Yes, his father had told him to be an example. Trehan seriously doubted his father had meant an example of what *not* to do.

"Uncle Trehan?" a soft voice called.

He traced to the sound, finding his "niece" Kosmina standing by his bag, a troubled look on her face.

She and her brother Mirceo were the last of the House of Castellan, the castle guard. *The heart of the kingdom.*

Kosmina was such a contradiction. She was completely innocent in matters of love and painfully bashful. Her clothing was always demure—today she wore a traditional gown, floor-length with the collar nearly reaching her chin. Yet at the same time she was a mistress of arms—and a merciless killer.

Trehan had helped train her with weapons. He suspected that each of the cousins had secretly had a hand in raising her. *I have so much more to teach her.* Yet after today he may never see her again; whereas the male cousins traveled outside Dacia, Kosmina had never been beyond its stone borders.

"Uncle Viktor said you were leaving." She shyly glanced up at him from under blond bangs.

"Rest easy. I might be returning directly. I only go to observe, just as I often do." He frowned. "Mirceo doesn't suspect you've come here?" Dacianos didn't usually meet in private—unless a fight was imminent. The last thing he needed was Mirceo appearing, sword in hand, to defend his sister's life.

As if I'd ever hurt her. Trehan pinched the bridge of his nose. Distrust and dread marked their family, just like a curse.

If only it were so easy as that. *Curses can be broken.*

"I keep telling him that you won't harm me," Kosmina said. "Stelian's the only royal you'd truly kill."

"Is that so?" Trehan asked with a hint of amusement at her conviction.

She outlined a pattern of the rug with the toe of one boot. "You found your Bride?"

"I did."

"Will you have offspring now? I'd like to be an auntie."

He exhaled a gust of breath. *Offspring.* When he'd been younger, he'd longed for his Bride, for a family of his own. As ages whispered past, he'd lost hope.

Now he could mate another female and beget young. But children with Bettina . . .

Would never see Dacia. Would never grow the House of Shadow.

"I don't know, Kosmina. My Bride doesn't care for me at present."

She glanced up, brows drawn. "Then she doesn't *know* you."

"I appreciate your confidence." He still couldn't believe that his Bride and his niece were about the same age.

If some lecherous, centuries-old male lusted for Kosmina, Trehan would gut him so slowly.

And still *I go to Rune?*

"I'll keep your home and your collection as you left them, Uncle, just in case. But I hope you make a life out there." Her light blue eyes went dreamy. "Every day, I imagine leaving this place."

She was forbidden to leave the kingdom. In this, he agreed with his cousins; it was too dangerous.

"I imagine it will be like waking up, like rising from a coffin and coming to life."

"Coffin, Niece?" She described herself as if she were dead. "Come now, it's not so bad. Life is good here. You're safe from the plague." Afflicting only the females of their species, the sickness was deadly even to immortal vampires. *Deadly—or worse.*

"Good here?" she queried softly. She pointed to his favorite seat. "Then imagine sitting there, reading the same books. For another thousand years."

The idea made him feel vaguely nauseated, her point delivered. For one so childlike in many ways, she was uncommonly observant.

He managed an even tone as he said, "Imagine the alternative: never seeing my home again, allowing my house to perish when so many have died for it." Years wasted, waiting for something that would never be? Years spent fighting, only to abandon those vendettas?

Those vendettas defined him. His duty defined him.

Without those things . . . *I will not be who I was.*

"We're all slowly moldering down here," Kosmina said, "as good as dead, just waiting for a deathblow. At least you'll be free now."

"As good as dead?" he scoffed. She exaggerated.

"Mirceo said all of the royals—except for him— were 'in stasis.'"

Trehan pulled the invitation from his coat pocket. *Have I been "in stasis"?* If so, nothing could upend his entire existence quite like this tournament.

A marriage ceremony. Death matches in a stadium. The crown of the Abaddonae.

Me, a demon king?

When he gazed back at Kosmina, he found her eyes watering. "There now, Niece." He chucked her under the chin. "I'll probably return anon."

As if he hadn't spoken, she said, "I will miss you."

He picked up his bag, then gazed around for another look. *A last look?*

"Uncle Trehan?"

"Yes?"

"Do you want to hear something sad?" He raised his brows. "Your leaving is the most exciting thing that's ever happened in my life. . . ."

10

Morgana stood at the doorway in all her furious majesty.

"You are not yet dressed, and I am *unamused*," she snapped as she swept her gaze over Bettina, still clad in her robe. Three slaves—powerless Sorceri known as Inferi—trailed in the sorceress's wake, weighed down with cases of cosmetics and accessories. "Ah, you've been working on your trinkets, haven't you? What an . . . adorable hobby."

"They're not trinkets." Bettina's shoulders went back. "They're art; I'm an artist. And it's not a hobby— I sell more than I can make."

"Of course you do, dearest freakling." Then she frowned. "Where's your phantom? The notorious Salem? I don't sense him."

"He stepped out to let me get ready."

When her godmother made a moue of disappointment, her Inferi as well, Bettina asked, "What exactly is Salem notorious for?"

"Why don't you ask him?" Morgana's attention was already on Bettina's wardrobe. "Now, we have scant time! Raum, curse his demonic soul, will be here at sunset to escort you." She waved her hand, and several outfits flew out of Bettina's wardrobe, landing on a divan. Then she turned to Bettina. "Let's see what we have to work with." Morgana shoved her in front of a full-length mirror, stepping behind her.

The difference between the two women was striking. Voluptuous Morgana wore a gauzy scarlet skirt, an intricately wrought gold top that concealed her breasts—barely—and a connecting jeweled collar. Claw-tipped gauntlets covered her hands and forearms.

Her pale blond hair was interwoven throughout her gold headdress. The piece was substantial, fanning out behind her like a barbed sunset, so wide it had narrowly cleared Bettina's doorway.

Her mask was black with inlaid onyx, highlighting her lustrous eyes, her nearly black irises.

Morgana was resplendent; Bettina was . . . Bettina.

On almost every day of her life, she was reminded of her own ordinariness. The male she loved considered her nothing more than a plucky—sisterly—tagalong. Her godmother, a renowned beauty, considered her the awkward spawn of Bettina's late mother.

Strangely, the Dacian had gazed at Bettina as if she were the most beautiful creature in the world. Of all the females the vampire had ever met, *she* had been the only one who could bring him back to life.

And the things he'd told her! For him, Bettina's eyes hadn't been promising good things, or even seductive things, but *irresistible* ones. He hadn't merely found pleasure with her, he'd savored her "treats" because she'd "delivered." He hadn't simply enjoyed her taste; it had *maddened* him.

Just thinking about his husky tone as he'd uttered these shocking things made her face and chest flush—

"You appear overtired," Morgana said with a critical eye. "This won't do. You must look your best when you're presented this eve."

"I believe you mean *displayed*."

Morgana's three Inferi froze in their unpacking, amazed that Bettina would contradict the great queen.

Ire flashed in Morgana's fathomless gaze. "Need I remind you that you agreed to this tournament?"

"Only because I didn't understand what it would really be like. You made it sound like a noble affair filled with romance and pageantry." Bettina had pictured hot suitors from allying demonarchies battling fiercely for the right to call her wife.

"I will forgive this insolence, chalking up your behavior to nerves." Morgana's eyes glittered with warning, silvery pinpoints dotting her dark irises—the rattle before a bite.

Immediately backpedaling, Bettina said, "Nerves, yes, of course." She could *feel* Morgana's power brimming. Which made her wonder, *Why did I ever vow not to tell her about Caspion's predicament?* Her godmother could eliminate the vampire assassin with a flick of her hand.

The tiff forgotten, Morgana directed her Inferi to get to work on Bettina. "Hair, dress, makeup, jewelry, mask." *Clap clap.* "We want the princess looking *elaborate*! But not necessarily *ostentatious*. Though she could never upstage me, I don't want her to appear to be trying to."

Bettina sighed and cooperated, dutifully raising her arms, closing her eyes, puckering her lips. Resisting Morgana was impossible—and for others, *deadly*.

Raum had once asked Bettina, "How can you even tell your godmother loves you?"

"One, because Morgana keeps visiting me in a realm she hates. Two, because I keep surviving the visits. . . ."

Within minutes, Bettina had been transformed. She wore a cropped, sleeveless top of gold mesh, with slightly thicker mesh to cover her breasts. Her skirt matched, slit up the sides, to show off her jeweled garters and silky thigh-highs.

Her mask was made of bold jade-green feathers that jutted up like small wings well past her head. Her thick hair had been wrapped around her diadem, holding it in place.

"Well?" Bettina asked.

"You are pensive, and it affects your looks. You're not exactly a great beauty anyway. Mouth too wide, cheekbones too sharp. You appear to your best advantage when you smile."

Last night in the dark, her smile had made the vampire's breath hitch. *Why do I keep thinking about him? He's not returning.*

Then Morgana's words sank in. "Do I really *need* to appear to my best advantage?" Bettina dared to ask. "The competitors aren't here for me." Morgana opened her mouth to argue, so Bettina said, "Oh, there might be some that are attracted to me. But at best, I'm an . . . an *afterthought.*"

"Afterthought? Do you actually *care* what they're thinking whether before or after?" She tsked, examining her costume claws. "You should be thanking your godparents for this opportunity. You told us that you wanted to feel protected. To Raum's archaic way of thinking, that means a *protector*. In any case, this is for your own good. Or have you forgotten that night?"

"As if I ever could." *As if you'd ever let me.* The humiliation of the court, her cowardly screams echoing from this spire as they'd set her bones . . .

"Do you remember what you told me when we were tucking your ribs back into your torso like little babes under a blanket?"

Bettina nearly retched. "I-I remember." She'd promised them *anything*.

"Everyone in the kingdom heard you shrieking like a banshee," she continued. "Then *I* arrived, soothing your woes."

Morgana had scratched her with a toxin-dipped metal claw, and the world had gone blessedly black. . . .

Before an attack could seize her, Bettina hastened outside to the balcony, breathing deeply of the twilight air. She peered upward, some part of her expecting to feel the whoosh of wings at any moment. If she couldn't trust her barrier spell . . .

Just when she'd begun backing off the balcony, Morgana joined her. "Still afraid they'll come here for you?"

"Occasionally." *Always.*

"That's not rational. There's never been a Vrekener in Abaddon. Why would they chase you down?"

"Vrekeners never abandon their hunt." Yes, she'd once been a mouse beneath a hawk's talon, and she'd escaped. But she knew the hawk would never rest until it had recaptured its prey.

"How could they even reach this plane?" Morgana asked. "They can't trace or create portals. They can't simply fly *really, really hard.*"

I know this.

"There were rumors that the elders of the Vrekener clan vowed to end the killings after Eleara," Morgana said in an inscrutable tone. "Didn't you tell me that your attackers were an offshoot group, acting outside of orders?"

Bettina gazed down at her shaking hands. "I believed so." Though Vrekeners condemned spirits, the four who'd targeted her had been drunken—and their violence had seemed . . . personal. *We've been watching you, Princess.* "I-I can't be sure."

"Perhaps if Raum can actually eliminate them, you'd feel safer."

For Bettina's willing participation in the tournament, her godparents had made her promises. Raum would send a cadre of demons out to hunt down and secretly assassinate all of Bettina's winged attackers—as yet, those Vrekeners remained untouchable. Morgana would locate and return Bettina's power to her. The sorceress remained coy as to whether she'd retrieved it or not.

"I'll feel safer once I get my power back." Bettina had once been a *Queen*—not yet a royal one—but a mystical one. A Queen was someone who had better mastery over an element or force than anyone else. She'd been the Queen of Hearts—

"It didn't help you the first time."

"No. But I would learn to control it better, would practice more. Have you located it?"

Morgana quirked a mysterious blond brow. "Don't worry—you'll have it before you wed."

Bettina sighed, turning her attention to the rain forest beyond the city. Deep within those giant moonraker trees, closeted in vines, was her folly—what used to be her favorite place in Rune. But since the attack, she'd avoided any place with trees.

It was almost worse that she could always see the forest from here, forever out of reach.

She trained her gaze far below. Thousands of demons and other Loreans had flocked to the streets, tossing confetti over the procession of combatants.

Brightly colored pavilions and tents circled Abaddon's famed Iron Ring—an enormous stadium with a caged arena. A grandstand overlooked all. Bold standards hung limp in the still, humid city.

Bettina surveyed the procession, shuddering at many of the "suitors." The pus demon wore rubber boots and gloves to catch the filth bubbling from his skin. A pair of Cerunnos slithered along the cobblestone streets, leaving sidewinder trails in the confetti. A crocodilae shifter went shirtless, the better to show off his speckled, platelike skin.

"Look at the males below." *This is actually happening.* She'd wanted to feel safe; those entrants were terrifying. "They're repulsive."

"Not *all* of them. I dated a coil of Cerunnos once—they're not as bad as one would think." Morgana tapped her claw-tipped finger against her bottom lip. "Regrettably, no Sorceri are expected to enter. Even assured of my involvement, they all think this contest will be fixed. Or that it will come down to simple brute strength."

If the Lykae were the physically strongest breed of Lorean, the Sorceri were among the weakest.

Morgana frowned, then said, "Of course, I could *force* the issue—if I thought a champion of ours might actually survive."

As the Queen of the Sorceri—both royal *and* mystical—she had absolute mastery over her subjects and all their individual powers. She could order any member of their species to do anything, and they would be compelled to obey. Or she could simply steal their powers.

Morgana wasn't a beloved ruler, but she was content to be a dreaded one. "Alas, poisons are frowned upon in these matchups." The Sorceri were famed toxinians. They didn't necessarily make them, but they certainly utilized them.

"I don't suppose you've finally stolen the power of foresight and have seen a good ending for this."

"Foresight?" Morgana scoffed. "Never. Oracles go soft in the head. I'll take my blind alleys and my sanity any day."

"Surely you're going to steer the course of this thing?"

"I cannot, by thought, action, or deed, affect the outcome of this tournament. But I did negotiate with Raum so that you would have some influence over the competition," Morgana said. "There will be a lady's choice round. Consider it a safety clause. Don't ask what that entails, because I'll say nothing more on the subject."

Bettina's question died on her lips. *I hate it when she does that.* "Are there any contestants here that you would accept as *your* husband?" she asked innocently.

"For gold's sake, Bettina, you know I'll never wed." She flicked her fingers in a dismissive gesture. "I'm surprised that demonic wastrel you call friend hasn't entered. Raum's certainly for that."

Really? *Wait, why does everyone keep calling Cas a wastrel?* Did no one see past the devil-may-care skirt chaser? He'd nabbed his first bounty at fourteen and had been risking his life to collect more ever since. Cas was determined to earn respect in this kingdom, one death demon at a time.

Oh, where was he? Bettina would have thought he'd be here to see her off. She didn't spy him below either.

Maybe he'd fled Rune to escape Daciano? Would she never see Caspion again? Then she swallowed. Or had the vampire already returned?

Surely Daciano wouldn't have come back until night was full upon them.

"You told me that you would give anything to feel safe again," Morgana said. "These competitors are feared champions."

"Many of them are dangers *to me*!"

"Whoever wins is who you're supposed to have," Morgana said blithely.

Bettina glared. "The Sorceri don't believe in fate."

"I will clarify: Whoever wins will be the strongest, most cunning, most powerful competitor. Potentially all of the above. *That* is who you will have for your husband."

One problem. A Cerunno could be all those things.

Morgana sighed. "If you don't approve of your new husband—and really, Bettina, when did you get so persnickety?—make yourself a widow. Bettina the Black Widow! Then you'll rule all by yourself with no irksome male to influence you. Just as I do."

Bettina's lips parted. Part of her suspected Morgana *wanted* a monster for her ward, just so Bettina would have to kill him. Morgana wanted to toughen her up—after all, Eleara's daughter had come crying all the way home. A wedding-night execution would be just the thing!

Bettina would certainly lose her reputation as a pushover.

"And what about the Abaddonae?" Bettina asked her. "Why would they tolerate a Cerunno as king?"

"*Tolerate?*" Morgana's many braids drifted around her head as if an invisible wind blew, and the gold pieces on her body thrummed—her anger manifested. "You're about to be their queen. They'll *tolerate* whatever you choose to give them. Always remember that." Smoothing her hair, inhaling for calm, she said, "Besides, you know these demons worship strength— might maketh right, and all that. They'll accept whoever wins."

A knock sounded on the door. Bettina stepped back inside her sitting room.

"Oh. How surprising," Morgana sneered, following her in. "Raum is right on time."

Her godfather strode in, clad in his ceremonial armor, his dark horns polished. His breastplate bowed out to cover his barrel chest. His black beard hung nearly to his breastbone and was neatly braided.

Whereas Morgana had scarcely cleared the doorway's width with her headdress, Raum barely cleared its seven-foot height. Even the vampire hadn't been quite so tall.

Stop thinking about him!

"How's m'girl?" Raum gave her a wink. "I know what you're thinking. Raum is handsome as the devil, eh?"

Bettina smiled fondly at him. Though her father had been kind, some part of him had always seemed . . . distant. Raum had doted on her, making up the lack. But he wasn't perfect; he'd been raised in a feudal age, and he treated Bettina like a damsel—who was continually in distress. He saw her as a fragile doll among the demons, a rare hothouse flower.

Still, he'd been flexible in some regards—right up until she'd been attacked.

After directing an expected scowl at Morgana, Raum extended his arm to Bettina. "You look lovely. Are you ready to descend?" With obvious reluctance, he offered his other arm to Morgana. "Shall I trace the two of you?"

"Only if you want me to make merry with your intestines," Morgana replied sweetly. She never allowed herself to be traced, always traveling via a portal spell.

Bettina didn't particularly care for it either. Unfortunately, her demon half hadn't enabled her to teleport on her own, so she always felt like a failure whenever someone so easily did it.

Could nothing *about me be demonic?*

"But you may escort us." Morgana took Raum's arm, "accidentally" smacking him with her sharp headdress.

Dual-purpose pieces at work . . .

The three rode the elevator—manned by ogres—down to the ground floor, then started toward the Iron Ring at the outer edge of the town, near the great marsh.

With each step, the tension between her guardians grew and her own mood deteriorated even more.

I feel like a sacrifice—one shove away from a volcano opening. And still she felt more dread for Cas than for herself. *Think of other things. . . .*

All the fanfare distracted her to a degree. The tournament was a formal occasion, with Abaddonae donning their best clothing. Many male demons had pierced their horns with gold loops, while females rouged their much smaller horns.

Older demons clacked around in antique armor,

the pieces squeaking from disuse, but the details and designs were more ornate than on modern armor. Bettina studied the engravings and raised filigrees with interest.

Finally they reached the ring. Roughly an acre in size, the arena was surrounded by stadium seats and completely caged in by iron bars. Jagged spikes protruded inward at every crossbar. Fog curled around the macabre structure, held at bay by the blue and orange flames dancing above enormous torches.

At opposite ends of the ring were a grandstand and the entrance to the warriors' sanctum, a series of catacomb-like tunnels. Running deep beneath the ring, the sanctum was like an underground bullpen for competitors to await their matches.

The grandstand was a large covered stage, swathed with precious silks. Bettina's Sorceri sensibilities couldn't help but thrill at the bold riot of colors. Sometimes Rune could be . . . bland.

Two long banquet tables stretched along either side. One table was filled with demon lords and ladies who bowed and scraped for Raum. *Not so much for me.*

They were all aware that she'd been attacked and physically defeated. Yet she was also the great Mathar's only offspring. Her subjects didn't quite know what to do with her.

Fitting. *Folks, I don't quite know what to do with me either.*

The other table was peopled with masked Sorceri dignitaries who simpered before Morgana.

Again, not so much for me. They all knew she'd had her power taken. When Morgana wasn't looking, they treated Bettina like an Inferi.

Not a real demon, not a real sorceress. Imposter . . .

In the center was another dais and a table for Bettina, Morgana, and Raum. Directly below them was the sign-in station, with weighty scrolls stacked like logs. Those contracts were thicker than one of Raum's burly arms, enumerating what must be thousands of rules.

As each contestant—with his entourage of squires and delegates—finished his processional, he would file into this station to sign a scroll, entering into an unbreakable pact.

Beside the scrolls was a quill and a dagger, because the contestants signed these pacts in blood. Bettina was privy to few rules, but she knew that the only way out of the tournament was to win—or die.

It was all so wretchedly . . . medieval. Most of the Lore's demonarchies were.

She picked up a schedule of events from her place setting. The first night's contest was to be announced. The next several nights would involve individual bouts within the Iron Ring. Night seven was indeed lady's choice—a *mystery* round. *Even to the lady* . . .

The semifinals would be held on night eight, with the final round and wedding occurring on night nine.

Bettina peered over the crowd, searching in vain for Cas, wanting him here with her. Instead she was flanked by Morgana on her right and Raum on her left, like bulwarks.

As the lengthy procession drew closer, her anxiety escalated. She turned to Raum. "Why are so many creatures entering? Abaddon's rich, but not wildly so. Our climate is hard to get used to."

He briefly buried his face in an oversize tankard of brew, then said, "Because your loveliness is legendary—"

"Raum. Please."

He made a gruff sound, then said, "Some are glory hounds, but mostly it's the Accession. War has routed many Loreans from their homes. Others are champions for an entire species, who hope to win the throne and give their peoples a place to live. Some are emissaries of a sort, looking for an alliance for their realms. Still others are pawns, controlled by powerful masters, who'll merely cede the crown if they win."

"You'd let a pawn win me?"

"We can't exactly prove who's a pawn until after the tournament."

Bettina narrowed her eyes. "There's more you aren't telling me."

"There's a last class of competitor. . . ." He patted her hand, a consoling gesture. "The condemned."

"Excuse me?"

"They were sentenced to die for various crimes in their home planes. Their only option is to compete in this, win, then turn over the crown to the ruling power."

Bettina was aghast.

"All that matters naught!" Raum assured her with the gentlest tap on her shoulder (when he would've whaled someone else on the back). "I still have hope that Caspion will enter and defeat them all."

Hope? He and Morgana both seemed to have pinned all their hopes on, well, *hope*. Bettina wanted something more concrete, thank you very much. Besides, Caspion had no intention of entering.

"I've seen the way you look at him," Raum said. "That lad's the one you want, isn't he?"

He doesn't want me back.

Under his breath, he said, "Morgana fought me on him, said she saw you with someone 'more exotic.' But if Caspion enters, she can't say anything." Raum gazed around. "Where is he anyway?"

"I haven't seen him all day."

"There are still a couple of hours left until the entry deadline."

Morgana jabbed her with an elbow. "Here comes the first contestant. Now remember, don't bow your head too deeply. Even if your subjects are mere demons, you still have royal blood. . . ."

One by one, squires and delegates introduced their champions. Morgana provided continual—and scathing—commentary, as regular as a laugh track.

Most were representatives from the various demonarchies, which pleased Raum. Several storm, ice, stone, rage, and fire demons were in attendance. Even a winged Volar demon entered. Not to mention the excretorian, who left a trail of pus on the sign-in desk.

A few contestants stood out. A snarling Lykae, with his ripped shirt and wild eyes, was surely a pawn. His three cloaked "squires" manhandled him to the sign-in station, then collared him away.

"Those three are warlocks," Morgana murmured. "An ancient order called Those Best Forgotten." She and Raum shared a look. "A-list," she said in a *yesss!* tone.

Raum, however, appeared uneasy, like a teenager whose illicit party had outgrown his sire's den.

Morgana added happily, "And right before the Accession!" That brutal immortal war—when all factions were forced to battle for supremacy. With each day, the warring Pravus and Vertas alliances strengthened. . . .

Next, two handsome centaurs approached, their sharpened hooves ringing on the walkway. With their bows strapped across their bare chests, the pair gave Bettina a flattering show of attention.

After them, a Horde vampire lord bowed courteously, but his bloodred gaze was restless—so different from Daciano's. Once the lord signed in, he hissed at the Lykae, his natural-born enemy.

The sole troll in the procession was enormous, its shoulders nearly as wide as it was tall. Bristly hairs dotted its body, covering its lengthy tail. In one grubby hand, the creature carried a spiked club bigger than Bettina's body.

She muttered to Morgana, "Now we're just being ridiculous."

Morgana shrugged. "The tournament is open to all."

There were the fire peoples: a Chimaero with skin that turned to flames and three Ajatars, dual-headed dragon shifters. Then came the snakelike competitors: two Cerunnos—princes of the Serpent Lands—and Meduso, son of Medusa.

"That one has a poisonous tongue," Morgana supplied in a delighted tone. "Haven't you heard? Once you go snake, you never go back."

Bettina sighed. *I feel like I'm on the Island of Misfit Toys.*

During a lull in the procession—the next demon appeared to be falling-down drunk—Bettina rubbed her hand over her nape, sensing something amiss. *More than what's* obviously *amiss?*

Naturally, most in attendance were watching her, but for some reason, her sixth sense was clamoring with awareness. . . .

11

Hidden in mist, Trehan had traced to Rune, back to the drawbridge he'd crossed such a short time ago. He'd stowed his belongings beneath it, then moved toward the Iron Ring.

Though the deadline to enter was imminent, Trehan still hadn't made a decision. Probably because he hadn't yet laid eyes on his Bride.

Instead, he'd glided along the periphery of the crowd, studying the large arena and the massive stadium-style seats overflowing with spectators.

He'd tried to imagine what it would be like to kill in front of them. For so long he'd hidden his skill—now to possibly display it in front of thousands?

Soon the grandstand would be in sight. *She* would be in sight.

Ever cold, ever logical, Trehan didn't make impulse decisions. Whenever someone tried to create a sense of urgency to move him to action, he dug his heels in, preferring absolute *in*action.

But he feared that once he saw her, the need he'd felt last night would redouble, his control faltering.

Over and over, he thought, *Your Bride or your house? Your female or your kingdom?*

No more stalling. He raised his gaze to the stage . . .

There she was.

Under the bright arena flames, his dark-eyed halfling looked like his most fevered dream in her jewels and revealing silks. Her dark hair was plaited into shining braids all around her face. Her jade-green mask highlighted her brilliant eyes.

First thought: *Fuck the kingdom.*

A sharp shake of his head. *Steady, Trehan. Be rational, investigate.*

Beside her were a male demon and a sorceress— must be the demon duke and the Queen of Sorceri.

Though Bettina seemed oblivious to all the gawking eyes on her, he did *not* like that most of her body was displayed to a multitude of covetous male gazes.

That's my *Bride they lust after.*

Despite her penchant for baring her body, her face was again concealed by a mask. *I haven't fully seen her face, and still I consider this.* But even as the thought arose, he realized that didn't matter. The physical was only part of what attracted him.

Still hidden, Trehan traced to a line of demonic contestants, listening to their conversations.

One young animus demon admitted to another, "I don't have a choice. Either I enter or my father will kill me."

A pathos demon said, "Of course I want the crown. Doesn't mean I won't breed on her for three litters a year."

A rage demon said, "The halfling's part sensual sorceress, part lusty demoness. I'd fight for a single night with a creature like that, much less an eternity. She's as good as beneath me."

The last two comments made Trehan's vision blur with rage, his fangs sharpening uncontrollably. *No, be reasonable. This isn't you*—

Reasonable? When all he wanted to do was rip out their arteries with his teeth?

Could Bettina hear any of these exchanges? She held herself very still, very regally—a detached beauty. So different from the shy seductress of the evening before.

But then, for just an instant, he saw a glimpse of fear in her eyes. His predator's gaze detected that wildly fluttering pulse in her neck.

Trehan might have resisted his mounting need to claim her, might have resisted the call of her blood. Yet her fear was intolerable to him.

He examined her more closely. Now that he knew what to look for, he could see her trembling. And why not? This wasn't a tournament for her hand—this was a virgin sacrifice, a spectacle.

The instinctive need to crush whatever threatened her hammered at him. The need to make her foes die bloody . . .

When the last of a line of roughly two hundred and thirty suitors had been presented to Bettina, she sank back, rubbing her forehead. Morgana reached over and pinched her chin, turning her face left to right. With a scowl, she shooed her ward away. A brief reprieve?

Trehan traced behind Bettina, secretly following her as she retreated to an alcove deep within a garden.

Gods, he liked the way she walked, liked the way the ends of her hair swayed back and forth just above her taut ass. With each step, a pale, gartered thigh flashed out from underneath her slinky skirt.

His swift erection didn't even surprise him. Nor did his lustful thoughts. *Gods, female, the things I would do to you. . . . I'd rip those garters away with my fangs, your panties too. Then I'd spread your long, svelte legs wide and bury my tongue between them.*

To claim the kiss he'd hungered for last night . . .

Everything about this woman aroused Trehan literally beyond reason. A fiery arrow through the temple? *Will I ever recover from the shot?*

After taking a seat on a bench, she turned to talk to a . . . *plant?* "Any sign of him?"

"No. I've looked for the last two hours, checked every whorehouse twice."

She glared at the plant, then murmured, "Did you see the way those entrants looked at me? I'm surprised they didn't want to check my teeth."

The plant replied, "Actually, one of them plans to remove all your teeth, so that you can handle his 'penile girth.' His words, not mine."

Who the hell had made that remark? *Someone soon to die.* Entering the tournament would afford Trehan the opportunity.

"Enough!" She started visibly shaking, her big eyes full of woe.

Trehan wanted to end that mouthy plant. *Then I'd enfold her in my arms and tell her that all will be well.* He found himself easing closer to her.

"I know what they plan for me," she said. "Oh, why won't Cas come?"

Always she thinks of that fucking demon.

Just before Trehan reached Bettina, Caspion appeared beside her, steps away from tracing directly into Trehan!

"Tina," the demon murmured, reaching for her.

She rose, her face crumpling as she launched herself at Caspion.

It isn't his right to embrace her. She is mine! Only centuries of honed self-discipline kept Trehan from ripping them apart. *Investigate, Trehan. Delve. You know so little about her. . . .*

Caspion whispered something in her ear, something Trehan couldn't hear. She gave him a wobbly smile, gazing up at the demon with open adoration. Hearing of her affection for Caspion was one thing, seeing it another.

Kill him. Trehan's hand fell to his sword, but before he could act, Caspion traced away with Bettina in tow.

Where had that bastard taken her? Trehan's gaze darted. When the two appeared on the grandstand, he exhaled with relief.

Only to tense once more—Caspion was striding toward the *sign-in table*? When the demon lifted the quill and dagger, the crowd cheered.

That son of a bitch! Trehan recalled the invitation. All competitors were mystically protected. With a swipe of the blade and a scratch of the quill, Caspion had entered the lists—removing himself from Trehan's reach.

At least until the tournament ended.

I can wait till then to kill him. Caspion might not even make it past the first round. Another might do Trehan's work for him.

Or I could enter. Two birds with one stone. He'd have no choice but to kill Caspion.

And Bettina would have to forgive me. . . .

Raum, the apparent master of ceremonies, motioned for the crowds to quiet down. "Tidings to the Abaddonae, fiercest of all the demonarchies!" More cheers. "And also to those from offplane who've journeyed here for our—humble—little tournament." Laughs sounded. "Together with my cohost, the all-powerful Morgana, we welcome you."

When he indicated her with a jerk of his chin, she rose. Without a wave or gesture of any sort, she swept her gaze over the crowd as if staring down every single attendee.

Only when the crowd had grown utterly silent did she sit again. She whispered something to Bettina, something that made the girl nod warily.

"Now, the stakes of this contest are high. Each round is to the death, yet one will have no fighting at all. Perhaps a game of wits? Ah, but never a game of chance! You have to *earn* Princess Bettina's hand, proving yourself worthy of her line."

Raum held up a gold case—the one that housed Bettina's summoning medallion? "Yes, the stakes are high, but the rewards are commensurate. The victor will win dominion over the fair princess herself!"

Dominion. Trehan nearly growled.

Bettina's face heated, her fists balling. She was clearly unhappy about her circumstances; so why had she allowed herself to be offered up? Last night, she'd said, *"They willed it."*

Then Raum held up a crown. "And the right to rule the Deathly Ones."

An armored storm demon—from a demonarchy infamous for its harems—shouted, "I'm already a royal. I'm only here to plow the princess!"

Guffaws sounded. Bettina flinched as if struck. Just as Trehan tensed to attack the male, Morgana stood once more, with her braids coiling like whips. In a clear, ringing voice, she snapped, "Respect—is—not—*optional.*" Swirls of sorcery radiated from her.

Raum gave Morgana a quelling look, then asked the crowd, "Now, have all the competitors been accounted for? The deadline nears."

Your female or your kingdom? Trehan stared hard at his Bride, compelled to be near her, to be touching her this very instant.

Just then, she glanced down at her twining fingers. When she looked up again, her eyes were watering, her little mask askew.

Should I protect her, even if she doesn't want my protection?

"We have two hundred and twenty-seven?" Raum said.

At the demon's words, Trehan's thoughts began to race. *Entry about to be closed. Ready to feel thousands of gazes upon your back, Trehan? Think! Enter, and you will not be who you were.* Which might be good. *I only leave the coffin to kill.*

Have I been moldering? Have *I been as good as dead?*

He was a loner by nature, with a sacred duty to murder, taught by experience to trust no one. Added to that, he lived in a closed, hidden society that worshipped reason and believed in the absolute control over one's emotions.

Surrounded now by all these new scents, sights, sounds—by all this *life*—he realized the answer.

Trehan *had* been a shade. But like the dead, he was the last one to know it. *No wonder killing comes so easily to me. I'm halfway to the grave myself.*

Yes, he'd been buried in the earth like some dormant thing—an unfeeling machine. What would await him should he decide to rise?

Remaining dormant was comfortable. No sharp emotions, no uncontrollable urges.

No regret for all his many years already wasted in that static state.

Think, Trehan! To pursue Bettina would mean forsaking everything he'd ever loved and embracing everything that had ever challenged him.

Your kingdom? Or the one who first awakened you . . . ?

12

Raum gazed around at the crowd. "Then the lists will be considered full—"

"*Hold demon,*" a male called from the back. "You've one final competitor."

Bettina would have recognized that deep, accented voice anywhere.

She squeezed her eyes shut. The vampire was *here,* somewhere in the crowd. And he planned to compete?

Just when she'd thought the night couldn't possibly get worse.

Earlier when Cas had told her he would enter, with his shoulders back like some sigh-worthy hero of old, her heart had leapt. Then at the sign-in desk, he'd qualified his actions: "There, Tina. If I'm marked for death anyway, I might as well try to save my best friend from a nightmare marriage."

And now this?

"Is that another vampire?" Morgana murmured in an intrigued tone.

Bettina opened her eyes and drew a shocked breath.

There Daciano was, striding toward her, his face grim with determination. The light of the grand torches sheened off his black hair.

Tonight his clothing was more regal, the fine lines and cloth looking like they'd cost a pretty karat. He also wore a full-length trench coat of black leather that fitted flawlessly over his broad shoulders and narrow hips.

The fog seemed to part for him; the crowd certainly did. Even among the strapping Abaddonae males, his towering body stood out. He could have traced, but he chose to walk, heightening her suspense.

Last night, she'd asked herself, *What foreign assassin would dare target a Deathly One in his home plane of Abaddon?*

This one. Trehan Daciano. A professional killer.

This isn't happening. Why, gods, would he return? And why *enter*? Why not wait to finish his mission until *after* the tournament?

Her gaze slid to Caspion, standing slack jawed outside the ring.

Then she remembered: once seen like this, Daciano could *never* return to his home.

No wonder Cas was stunned!

The vampire hadn't spared him a glance, his attention solely on Bettina. Initially the Dacian's eyes had been a deep green. Yet when his gaze locked on her, they flooded with black.

As they'd been last night.

With his every step closer, awareness pricked her senses—the heat of the flames, the scent of her goblet of wine, the way the damp night air clung to her bare arms.

All she could think over and over: *That vampire was in my bed, touching me as no other had before.*

As he closed the distance, she felt increasingly weak and breathless, as if a flash-fever had taken hold.

How could merely looking at someone make her react *physically*? One word arose in her consciousness. *Dalit.* In Demonish, it meant *lightning*—in addition to another quaint, old-timey meaning.

"Who is that *gorgeous* male?" Morgana asked.

Bettina had never heard her sound so interested in a stranger.

The vampire wasn't gorgeous to Bettina, but he was . . . striking.

"Oh, my gold, is he a Forbearer?" Morgana asked.

With his clear eyes, Daciano looked like one. No one would ever guess he was from the fabled Realm of Blood and Mist.

Once he neared the lower grandstand, Bettina subtly shook her head, warning him away, but he didn't break his stride.

Earlier when Caspion had approached the sign-in table, the crowd had cheered for one of their own. As the vampire approached, everyone grew silent.

Crickets. A dog barked in the distance. A demon cub gave a cry.

"Your name?" Raum asked in puzzlement.

"I'm called the Prince of Shadow," Daciano answered in that resonating voice.

"Where do you hail from? What is your standard?"

"I hail from nowhere you know." The vampire retrieved a beautiful antique-looking banner of red and gray from his coat, handing it to Raum. "This is my standard. I enter for the hand of Bettina."

He can't lie? Then he's not here just to kill Cas? He wants to marry me? She just stopped herself from fanning her face.

Why can't I catch my breath?

Her godfather cast him a studying glance. Raum couldn't bar the vampire entrance, but surely he would demand more information.

Instead Raum examined the standard, returned it, then offered Daciano the blade and quill. "Well then, Prince of Nowhere. Sign your name."

Still holding her gaze, the vampire dragged the blade across his palm, blood welling. Without hesitation, he signed, never looking down at the contract, never taking his penetrating eyes off her.

Bettina could tell Morgana was glancing from the vampire to her and back, but didn't acknowledge her godmother's curiosity.

Once Daciano's entry was complete, Raum announced, "The lists are filled! The tournament has officially begun."

Cheering sounded from the spectators before Raum quieted them once more. "Now, on the first night of the tournament, we will have a melee. All competitors will go in unarmed, race to reach strategically placed weapons, then kill at will."

"Oh, I've always enjoyed a spirited melee!" Morgana said, as if she were talking about a potato-sack race. Then she gazed past Bettina, her eyes gleaming with approval—no doubt ogling the vampire.

When Bettina refused to look at him, Morgana tapped her chin with a metal claw. "You don't appear to be an *afterthought* with that one, dearest freakling. You appear to be the *only* thought."

I've done it then. Trehan had stood up in front of thousands of gaping Loreans, pledging himself to winning Bettina. He'd stepped from his comfortable shadows directly into the spotlight, under the crushing weight of the crowd's scrutiny.

No longer was he the enforcer of Dacian laws. No longer did he live among books, merely *reading* about social interactions. He wasn't just an observer; he was present and involved, with an unshakable purpose: *I will possess her.*

He'd left behind all he loved, but he'd also shucked off his deadening existence. And at this moment, excitement over the future outweighed his regret of the past.

This close to Bettina, he could scent her light perfume and sweet skin, could hear her shallow breaths as she studiously ignored him.

Yes, I will possess her—and I'd do far worse than this for the privilege.

He almost looked forward to battling for her favor. Killing was what he did, was all he knew. And Caspion? He was a mere obstacle to be dealt with when the time came.

Somehow Trehan would devise a way to seduce her once more. *I'm betting everything that she'll respond again.* Perhaps he should do as the madman Lothaire did, and bargain with her?

Before the tournament began tomorrow night, Trehan would ready himself, gorging on blood and perhaps finally sleeping for an hour or two. Many of the demon lords would imbibe this eve, were already drunken. Tomorrow, they'd be compromised. Trehan would have another advantage. *Not that I'll need it—*

"But there's a twist," Raum announced. "Night one . . . begins in five minutes."

Gasps sounded. Those drunken lords sputtered their protests.

"Two hundred and twenty-eight will enter the Iron Ring before the gate slams shut," Raum said, his voice booming with finality. "You'll kill until the great horn blows. Though many of our contestants will never get to hear it. . . ."

13

As the competitors filed off to the ring, Bettina chewed on a fingernail, the fingers of her other hand drumming.

Just moments ago after Raum's announcement, Caspion had traced to her side, smoothed a braid behind her ear, then bravely set off to the warriors' sanctum.

Daciano had strode off as well, yet he lingered outside the ring. Awaiting something from her?

"So, Raum, who do you think will be the bettors' favorite?" Morgana asked.

Raum dragged his face from his tankard. "No Abaddonae would bet against their own."

Cas, my demon, who's about to be locked in that cage! Bettina started on another nail.

Morgana slapped her hand down. "I believe I'll put karats on the clear-eyed vampire."

Bettina's gaze darted to Daciano. His overall demeanor was *bored*. But she could see his cunning gaze taking in his enemies. She suspected she was about to witness the lethality she'd only sensed before.

Would he target Cas immediately?

Turning to Bettina, Morgana said, "I believe the Prince of Shadow is particularly motivated. He looks like his heart is in this. His *beating* heart."

Bettina stifled a gasp. Of course Morgana had figured out who Daciano's Bride was. But Bettina couldn't think about that now.

"The leech is blooded then?" Raum asked, taking another gulp from his mug. "Wonder what his Bride has to say about this?"

She's pissed! And terrified for Caspion. "If Cas can trace, he'll be safe in there, right?"

Morgana snorted. Raum uneasily pulled at the collar of his breastplate.

"Couldn't he just continually teleport around the ring if he wanted to?" Bettina asked. "Or if he got injured?"

"If he wasn't caught fast by a stronger opponent, then yes," Raum said. "But tracing is not without its perils. To strike an accurate blow you have to materialize fully for a split second. And whenever you disappear, you risk losing sight of your opponent, something no warrior is keen to do."

Morgana added, "Plus you run the chance that someone will predict where you will reappear and be waiting with, say, a raised mystical sword. I killed my last demon that way." She made her voice like an innocent girl's as she said, "Oh, no, please stop with your tracing! It's confusing my feeble female mind!" She abruptly made a chopping motion against the table. "Then SLASH."

Raum looked unimpressed with her theatrics. "It's also physically draining, especially for the injured. The ability is a great advantage, but it also brings great risk."

Talking around another fingernail, Bettina asked, "If a competitor gets into trouble, what's to stop him from teleporting back home or something?"

"The blood pact they signed."

So Cas was well and truly trapped? If he . . . died, she didn't know how she'd recover.

The highlights of her history with him flashed through her mind—all the things he'd done to win her heart. Cas taking her to her first baseball game and patiently explaining the rules. Teaching her to drive a mortal car. Escorting her to fashion shows and art exhibits, even when he was so bored he could barely stay awake.

He was young, and sometimes he could do stupid things, but he was bighearted. She'd recently found out that he'd been secretly giving food and clothing to other foundlings, using some of his newfound influence to set up apprenticeships for older orphans.

Everyone was always so dazzled by his looks that they never realized he had substance—and *loyalty*. She knew he would give his life to protect hers. . . .

Bettina's reverie was interrupted when one of Morgana's Inferi hastened over to the queen with a written message. The sorceress snapped, "What fresh hell is this?" then tore open the black seal.

In a completely *un*smooth attempt to be smooth, Bettina stretched her arms, leaning back for a look at the page. She caught a few words—"portents," "Gilded One," "rising," and "Accession"—before Morgana wadded up the paper so hard her metal claws dug into her palm.

The Gilded One was La Dorada, the Queen of Evil—and Morgana's nemesis, thought to be dead.

With a curse, Morgana rose, shoving her chair back with a wave of her hand.

Bettina dared to ask, "La Dorada is rising?"

In a distracted tone, Morgana answered, "Do excuse me. Someone needs to die." Over her shoulder, she told Raum, "In my absence, keep this tournament . . . interesting."

"Absence?" he sputtered. "You can't leave! You're the cohost!" He leapt up and followed her, arguing with her as she and her train of Inferi hastened toward her travel portal.

As soon as Bettina was alone, the vampire traced beside her and grasped her hand.

Aware of the spectators watching her, she tried to appear calm as she hissed, "Release me!" between gritted teeth.

He didn't. His hand was hot, swallowing hers.

She inhaled his crisp scent, and memories of the night before overwhelmed her—which infuriated her. "You told me you wouldn't come back for me!"

"I said I didn't *plan* on returning for you. I've since changed my mind." His eyes were now green, his gaze narrowed with intent. "Listen to me, female. Your Caspion will live or die this eve based on my actions."

She raised her chin. "So certain you'll defeat him? I'm not convinced. And if you did strike him down, I'd hate you forever."

"Then convince yourself of this—I will influence the others, telling them that Caspion the Tracker is a kingdomwide favorite who must be eliminated early. Unless . . ."

"Unless what?"

"You vow to grant me a boon, one to be determined later." He spoke over her sputtering: "And I will not only spare him, I'll dispatch any competitor you choose."

"You're blackmailing me?"

"Consider it . . . bargaining."

"Why should I trust you?"

"You know I don't lie." Leaning down, he murmured at her ear, "Tell me a target, or tell Caspion good-bye."

She quickly said, "How am I to choose? I want them all gone!"

"Then promise me even more favors. Accept me as your champion, and I'll rid the entire ring of life."

After this night's humiliating procession, she was tempted—with the exception of Cas, of course. But until she determined what type of "favor" Daciano might demand, she'd limit the exposure.

To *one*. Bettina found the serpentine entrants the worst. The mere thought of mating with one of them made her gag. Not to mention the idea of delivering *eggs*. "Fine. I vow to the Lore to grant you a boon, if you spare Cas and dispatch the larger Cerunno."

Daciano gave her a formal bow. "As you wish." Then he shrugged out of his coat and handed it to her. "Hold this, Bride." Such a trivial request, but it made it appear that they were already together. "Naturally, if I have an opportunity in the ring, I could expand our arrangement . . . ?"

"For more of these boons? Forget it."

"Know that I'll kill the Horde vampire for free." At her frown, he explained, "I will require his tent for the duration." And then he was gone.

Trehan stood within the Iron Ring, surrounded by stands of gawking Loreans, but he focused his mind on what was at stake.

Her. Bettina.

Now, like so many times in the past, he had a sanctioned kill to make. He marked his prey—the Cerunno his Bride must fear above all the others.

Trehan gave a cursory glance over the weapons available: lances and varieties of spears, war axes, maces, swords, and two different types of whips. One was coiled razor wire, the other coated with a viscous layer of oil—a whip of fire. He was a master with all these.

He noted that many of the competitors were studying the placement of the weapons, deciding which would suit their own strengths best. But few were studying their opponents. Fools. Weapon choice depended upon the opponent.

Try felling a Cerunno with a spear and see where that leaves you. . . .

Besides, within moments there would be far more weapons than those alive to wield them.

Trehan made quick calculations. The males most likely to give him any competition whatsoever: the incredibly fast Cerunnos, the other vampire, the three Ajatars, the rabid—and therefore unpredictable— Lykae. The two massive stone demons as well. They could make their muscles so rigid that blows would bounce off them, as if off stone.

The Horde vampire stared hard at Trehan, no doubt trying to assess his strengths. He would believe Trehan was a weaker Forbearer, a turned human.

Ah, but that ravening Lykae was barely able to refrain from attacking the red-eyed vampire even now. Could he be counted on to keep that Horde lord occupied?

And the Cerunnos? Trehan had stalked them in the past, had observed them in battle. He knew how they distracted your attention with their sword work, while their tails slithered up behind you. . . .

When Raum returned, apparently from arguing with Morgana, he signaled for demon guards to close the enormous iron gate. The other entrants' muscles were tensed. Trehan's were relaxed.

I've prepared my entire life for this tournament, even if I hadn't known it—

He felt a vibration beneath his feet. Then another. Footsteps. Something was coming, something with *mass*. A last competitor?

Just before the gate closed fully, a being emerged from the fog, heading for the ring.

Trehan raised his brows as he craned his neck up. And up . . .

The things I do for my Bride.

14

"What—is—that?" Bettina murmured as a giant demonlike creature entered the ring.

He stood well over ten feet tall, with pebbly green skin like a toad's. He sported not one, not two, but *three* pairs of horns. Rising straight up from his forehead were two slimy yellow ones that matched the color of his slitted eyes; two more capped his muscular shoulders; a third pair jutted from the backs of his elbows.

Fangs protruded up from his bottom row of teeth. A line of mottled tusks jutted down from its chin, like a bony, spotted beard. Lengths of chain crisscrossed his otherwise bare chest, holding up a leather half-tunic like suspenders from hell.

At each step, the packed-clay earth quaked beneath his boots.

Raum bit out a curse. "Goürlav."

Mutters sounded in the crowd.

—"That's the Father of Terrors."—

—"He's a pre-demon, a *primordial*."—

—"If a drop of his blood hits the ground, a monster will spring up."—

Looking furious, Raum said, "For once, the rumors have it right."

"I don't understand? What will happen?"

"If anyone so much as nicks one of his veins, he'll spawn hideous new creatures bent on annihilating anyone who thinks to harm their 'father.'"

Cas was about to be caged in—with that nightmarish being? "Can't we kick the primordial out? Why wasn't he in the procession?"

"The procession was just a formality. Someone signed a proxy contract to enter him. There's no way to expel him, no barring entry to any Lorean."

Raum's craggy brow furrowed, sending a chill of unease through Bettina. This was the first look of regret he'd evinced over the tournament.

He'd been so positive that this was the right course—good for commerce, "good to show other Loreans that we're a free and open kingdom." He'd waved away all her concerns, and the concerns of the people; Bettina had overheard him assuring his cronies that a demon of some kind would have to prevail.

They'd surely never expected a demon of the primordial variety.

As the gate clanged shut behind Goürlav, Bettina's stomach lurched. There was so much danger to Cas. Over all their years together, he'd been a lifeline, a mentor, a guide, and a protector. Now Bettina wanted to protect *him*.

But couldn't. No amber light boiled up from her palms, no destructive sorcery.

She reminded herself how skilled Cas was, how quick. *He's safe from Daciano. . . .*

"Might as well get this over with," Raum muttered. He gave the signal.

At once, the great horn sounded. The crowd's roar grew deafening.

Many competitors charged for weapons, and within seconds the clang of steel rang out.

Then came . . . *chaos.*

Blood sprayed as if from moving fountains; bone cracked. Yells of agony carried over the drum of the crowd.

The Volar demon flew above, then dove to strike a fire demon, its razor-sharp talons slicing through flesh. *So reminiscent of the Vrekeners . . .* She flinched and gazed away.

The smaller Cerunno had used its meaty tail to spring up to the top of the cage, coiling around the bars to suspend its body upside down. Swinging like a grotesque pendulum, it snatched an unsuspecting foe up to his death.

Caspion had seized a razor whip, using it to lasso a centaur's neck. Though the creature kicked and reared, Cas used all his considerable strength to tighten that noose.

"Come on, Cas!" Bettina yelled.

Tighter, tighter . . .

Suddenly the centaur's head popped off, neck spurting arterial blood. Abaddonae yelled with delight.

And with that one kill, Cas had just become more powerful, a death demon collecting strength.

The Lykae slashed and mauled, biting the throat of its opponent until head and body no longer connected. The pyromasters hurled balls of flame; competitors screamed as their skin sizzled.

The scent of roasting flesh increased Bettina's nausea. Any lingering fog in the area evaporated away in the heat.

The other vampire seemed to have Daciano in his sights, but the Lykae began stalking the red-eyed lord, keeping him on the run.

Goürlav? He squatted near one side of the cage, running a knife under his claws, casually cleaning them. Everyone gave him a wide berth.

With cold, precise moves, Daciano methodically cut his way toward the larger Cerunno, which had a crocodilae shifter coiled in its serpentine tail. Though the shifter heaved its body in a death roll, it couldn't get free.

The Cerunno widened its jaws and struck. Fangs the size of blades sank into the shifter's thick hide over and over, puncturing its neck until the Cerunno simply pulled the creature's head free, like a joint of tender meat.

It gave a short victory hiss up to the sky. Mistake. Daciano used that brief second to trace behind it.

The vampire's sword flashed out so quickly, Bettina didn't actually see the blade slicing through the air.

The creature whirled around to attack Daciano.

But the movement made its head slide from its sheared neck, tumbling to the blood-soaked ground. Daciano's sword cut was as clean as a laser incision.

Raum patted her shoulder, startling her. "There, m'girl, that should make you feel better! A Cerunno down. See, I told you this would work out. And look at Caspion." Cas was easily winning a hand-to-hand skirmish with another demon, and actually looked to be . . . enjoying himself?

Her gaze slid to Daciano again. Sheathing his sword, the vampire traced once more, dodging a spear jab to the back, then attacked one of the storm demons, the one who'd called out those vile things earlier.

With what looked to be a practiced maneuver, Daciano seized its horns; the armored male bellowed and thrashed.

To capture such a warrior in his hold . . . Her lips parted. The vampire's strength was unimaginable.

Then Daciano cast her a steady, questioning glance, as if to ask, *A boon to be rid of this one too?*

Her temper got the better of her as she recalled the demon's disgusting words. *I'm only here to plow the princess!* Feeling not an ounce of regret, she gave a nod.

Arm muscles bulging beneath his shirt, Daciano shifted his grip. Without so much as a sound—or even a change of expression—he twisted the demon's head on its neck. One rotation. A second. Then he ripped it free *with his bare hands*.

Before the demon's head had bounced beside its fallen body, the vampire had already seized a second demon competitor. Another questioning glance at her.

So that was what he meant about expanding their arrangement!

Bettina bit her lip, peering around. How bad could these boons be? Daciano wouldn't hurt her; he'd proved that last night. She was his Bride, so he'd want only what was best for her, right?

And he might die in tomorrow's bouts, or even momentarily! How many boons could he collect on before he got killed?

Or maybe she was simply drunk on this power?

Another nod; one instant later, the male was dead.

As she watched Daciano fight—no, *fight* wasn't the right word; as she watched him ruthlessly execute his opponents, she fully comprehended why Caspion had been certain he would die.

Trehan Daciano's trade was killing. And he was a master of his trade.

Yet as long as he was doing her bidding, he was like an extension of her—a weapon to be utilized. Oh, yes, the power!

Daciano grabbed the repulsive pus demon—who'd actually made a kill—and flashed her an expression that said, *Well?*

She got greedy. Another nod to the vampire . . . then another.

Before she'd realized how deep in she was, she'd agreed to five boons. *I won't agree to any more. That's it!*

But then she saw Caspion besieged by enemies, teaming up to take him out. Assuming he was a kingdomwide favorite? Daciano hadn't needed to point that out after all.

One Ajatar had lashed Caspion's leg with a whip, preventing him from tracing. A second raised a handful of fire, readying to bomb Cas with it.

She turned to her godfather, begging under her breath, "Raum, the horn!"

"Caspion will pull out of this. He must! If I end it now, everyone will know why. He will lose the respect he's earned."

"Please! He could *die*."

Raum couldn't be moved. "Might maketh right, Bettina."

Only one thing could save Cas now. *Help him, Daciano!* she inwardly cried. Gods, she would do anything, would agree to any number of boons to save Cas.

As if he'd heard her, Daciano glanced up with a scowl, then to Cas and back. He held up five fingers.

She nodded instantly, not even pausing to consider what this would mean in the future.

At once, Daciano traced in front of Caspion, his sword slashing out with breathtaking speed. With one swing, he cleaved through the waists of the Ajatars—and the whip holding Cas. Another swing, and Daciano's bloody sword took the pair's four heads.

Cas staggered back in confusion, no doubt wondering why Daciano hadn't slain him as well. Only then did Raum give the signal to end the melee.

Just as the great horn began to sound, Daciano vanished, reappearing once more before the Horde vampire.

Slash.

The red-eyed vampire's head toppled as the horn's blast faded. . . .

At least three dozen others had fallen—although the melee had lasted *not ten minutes.* Even the blood-thirsty crowd had quieted, gaping at the carnage.

Gradually the remaining contestants dropped their weapons, backing away from each other. Most began limping toward the sanctum entrance. Their eyes burned with emotion—rage, fear, even excitement—from the hell they'd just endured.

But not Daciano. His eyes were a steady, compelling green—and locked on her.

Raum counted the fallen then announced, "So concludes the first night! Congratulations to the one hundred and ninety-two survivors. Tomorrow will commence the one-on-one, randomly drawn bouts. Each contestant may bring one cold weapon into the ring—a sword, a lance, a club, a mace, and so on. The bouts begin at sunset. Good eve!"

A group of jubilant young Abaddonae had already surrounded Cas, but Daciano remained amidst the bodies, blood splattered over his clothing, rivulets of it running down his grim face as he gazed up at her.

He'd killed so ruthlessly, yet so . . . calmly. Bettina had never seen anything like him.

And she owed that dangerous male her *favors*.

He'd taken out five competitors just for her and had saved Cas. But not for long. *If Cas faces Daciano, he* is *as good as dead.* A small sob escaped her lips.

Daciano simply stared at her, as if there were nothing else on earth worth beholding.

15

Trehan was up to his ankles in blood, viscera, and writhing corpses.

Freshly slain bodies of all species would often twitch, but immortal corpses and body parts clung tenaciously to life. Severed hands still clenched and unclenched. Mouths opened on soundless screams. The faces on severed heads changed expressions before freezing into grimaces of pain.

He supposed it was fitting that Bettina see him like this, without shadows to conceal him, his true nature exposed. *This is what I bring to you.*

If you need a protector, this *is what I offer.*

Her lips were parted, her eyes wide behind her mask. He inclined his head to her, acknowledging for whom he'd fought.

Tonight he'd been Bettina Abaddon's champion. And *zeii mea,* it'd felt good to kill for her!

When he started for her, she gasped, turning to Raum, who was now waylaid by outraged delegates, each demanding his champion's release from the blood contract.

—"I never would have entered my son if I'd known Goürlav would be in the lists."—

—"Not to mention the remaining vampire! Who the hell is he? What is his line?"—

—"The word *contest* indicates a *fighting chance,* demon!"—

Apparently those idiots hadn't realized that Raum was not to be ordered about. The grand duke's chest was bowed even more, his horns straightening with hostility.

Bettina wisely turned from that group without a word. She glanced at Caspion, who was surrounded by a throng of admiring demonesses, which clearly irritated her.

That wastrel had a female like *Bettina* wanting him. But he was too stupid to see what was just before him.

His loss. *If it's the last thing I do, I'll make sure of it.*

The vampire was coming for her. So naturally, Bettina had chosen to flee.

Of course the one time she'd hoped for Morgana's intrusiveness in her life—if anyone could devise a way out of a bargain it would be the wily sorceress—her guardian had left. Raum was busy, Salem nowhere to be found.

Cas was . . . occupied.

Bettina glanced over her shoulder. *Vampire still*

nearing. She peered around for *anyone* to talk to, but suspected Daciano wouldn't be stopped anyway.

When he traced in front of her, she drew up short. *Snared.*

"We've ten favors between us," he grated, taking back the coat she'd forgotten she still held. "Are you prepared to pay what you owe?"

She parted her lips to answer, only to fall silent as she peered up at him. "Your eyes were green the entire time."

"Why is this noteworthy?"

"All that killing and blood, all those screams and flames, and you're unaffected." In a way, he reminded her of . . . of *gold*—a noble metal that didn't react to most other elements.

"I'm accustomed to death and all its faces. But when I think about last night, I'm *utterly* affected." At once, his eyes flooded black.

In turn, she grew breathless, flushed, that awareness redoubling. The more she tried *not* to think about last night, the more images arose in her mind . . . his big hand between her legs, his hot mouth on her nipples.

Voice gone husky, he murmured, "Your irises grow lighter, female. I'm not the only one who enjoyed what happened between us."

She swallowed. "Because I thought you were another." She glanced over at Cas. A horde of females cooed over his slight injuries, jockeying to fondle his muscles. Bettina wondered if she had any place at all in his thoughts.

Daciano gripped her upper arm, drawing her attention back. "I ask you again, will you pay what you owe?"

She raised her chin. "Up to a point."

"To a point? That wasn't one of the terms of the deal."

"I'm still a lady—a princess! I expect to be treated as such. And I'm still embroiled in this tournament. As soon as this farce began, I knew I'd be held to certain . . . standards." By ancient law, Bettina could be stoned to death for breaking the terms of the contract. "I won't jeopardize my life by sleeping with you."

"Meet me in my tent at midnight, and I promise you," he said, his voice dropping even lower, "that I will treat you *like a lady*." Such innocuous words, but the way he said them . . .

"What if I can't sneak away tonight? I won't be alone." Salem would surely tell Raum if he learned of this. And her godfather would shift to second gear—battle-ax to the brain.

Which would probably only get Raum killed by the menacing vampire.

"Then I'll come to you."

"That's not possible," she snapped. "I'll figure something out." She thought she could get the guards outside her doors to take the night off, but would Salem balk? "This will count as . . . *five* boons."

"One."

"Three," she countered. When he inclined his head in agreement, she asked, "Which tent is yours?"

"The quarters of the slain vampire. Look for my standard."

Then he disappeared.

She sagged, yearning for the privacy of her rooms. Now that her royal responsibilities were over, nothing was stopping her from returning. Nothing except for herself.

The winding, foggy lane to the castle was a short stroll filled with beings, but to her, it rolled on . . . and on . . . and on. . . .

She could call guards to escort her, but her kingdom was a safe place. It would send the wrong message. Plus, she didn't want others to know of her fear. In the Lore, fear equaled weakness. Weakness eventually equaled death, even for an immortal.

There are crowds all around, she told herself, *nothing can get me.* But then, she had been within earshot of crowds when the four had attacked her.

Bettina remembered getting dressed with friends before going out that night. She'd thought, *A rave out in a poppy field—what could possibly go wrong . . . ?*

Though her bones had healed seamlessly, at times like this she could swear she still felt the fractures aching.

Rubbing her arms, she took a few tentative steps, breaths shallowing, anxiety constricting her chest. Anxiety and *anger*—at the Vrekeners who'd twisted her. At herself for becoming a shell of the old Bettina.

She'd once been bold(ish) and quick to laugh, generally happy. She had never imagined she'd end up like this—a timorous, incapacitated mess.

Sheer will netted her a few more steps. But when she made it to a well-lit storefront, she froze, glued to its safety as if soldered there.

Someone would soon come along to walk with her. *Surely. For now, think of other things.*

As she feigned interest in a shelf of figurines on sale, her thoughts returned to Daciano. He'd entered for her hand—not because he was a glory hound or because he'd been condemned on his home plane.

No, apparently he'd surrendered his home forever.

And once the tournament had begun, that vampire had been the only one who'd acknowledged her, acknowledged that he'd fought for her. No one else had even looked at her. Not even Caspion.

Cas had been helpless not to respond to those battle groupies surrounding him, especially the voluptuous demonesses. *My hips will never be that round, my breasts that plump.* The one bad thing about freezing into immortality? If unhappy with your appearance, you were eternally screwed.

Yet even the slim demonesses got a swoon-inducing grin from Cas. In fact, it seemed there was only one female he didn't respond to.

Me.

Five minutes passed. Ten. She'd begun meandering through the store, picking up a figurine here, a vase there. But soon, the shopkeeper started insisting that Bettina take them all as gifts, refusing any offers to pay.

"No, please. I'm just resting a bit inside your lovely store. I couldn't accept more." And there went another vase into a bag.

Bettina was unable to leave, and equally unable to decline the merchandise without insulting the kindly shopkeeper.

I don't even like *knickknacks!* Morgana would never have this problem. Bettina's deadly patroness wouldn't. Those two Sorceri females *always* got what they wanted. *Why can't I?*

When the shopkeeper began looking for a larger bag, Bettina inwardly groaned.

Ultimately, she accepted all the offerings with a strained smile, then forced herself to turn toward the exit.

Outside, the buildings loomed taller, the alleys twisting narrower and darker. As she cautiously peered upward, that familiar seed of anxiety started to seethe in her chest—the one that wouldn't stop growing until she was covered with sweat, shaking with fear, gasping for breath.

She was trapped, standing at the threshold like an idiot, clutching her sack like a life preserver.

I hate this! When did I become that *girl—the push-over afraid of her own shadow?*

She knew her fear was irrational. There'd never been a Vrekener in Abaddon. If one managed to enter this plane, the Abaddonae milling around would never let it hurt their princess.

The demons would trace into the air and attack, asking questions later. She *knew* this.

So why wouldn't her body listen to her mind?

"Bettina!" Caspion? He'd left his admirers for her? "I've been looking for you!" He jogged up to her, still spattered with dried blood from the fight. He glanced around, lowering his voice. "You're alone here? Aren't you afraid?"

Salem and Cas were the only ones who knew about her phobia. "It isn't so bad tonight." Not a lie—she hadn't had a full-blown attack yet.

He didn't look like he believed her. "I'll walk you back." He took her bag with a frown—he knew she wasn't a knickknack type of person—then offered her his arm. As they started toward the castle, relief breezed through her. The shapes of the buildings morphed to normal, the alleys opening up like mortal freeways.

"You fought really well tonight, Cas. I was so proud."

"Did you see what Daciano did?" Before she could answer, he said, "Bastard muscled into my skirmish just for the chance to kill me himself! I was about to get free of that whip even without his interference."

Not true—and Bettina was almost glad it wasn't. *Otherwise I bet five boons for nothing.*

"The vampire returned for you."

She gave a slight nod. "I could scarcely believe it."

"I was only in Dacia for a short time. But from what I heard, Trehan is like *Mr. Dacia.* He loves his kingdom more than any of them. You two must've had, uh, some night." He seemed to be looking at her with a new regard, which flustered her.

"What are you doing here, Cas? I thought you'd take another female"—or two, or three—"home with you. Aren't males usually keen to after a battle?"

His shoulders went back. In a steady tone, he said, "No others for me, Tina."

With a tremulous smile, she murmured, "Really?"

"People would talk. I would never insult you like that."

Her smile faded. "I appreciate your consideration." People already talked. She was the subject of pity, the weird halfling hopelessly in love with a strapping demon.

"Now that I've entered, everything has changed."

"How so?"

"I will figure out a way to defeat Daciano. Some-how. And I will win you. We'll rule together, and we'll be good at it. I will endeavor to always be true to you. I consider us betrothed; I have since I signed my name to enter."

"Endeavor?" she said softly. "Will it be so difficult?"

"It's not exactly my nature. And you're not my mate." He raked blond locks off his forehead. "I *did* warn you, Tina. You have to be patient with me."

She sighed. He *was* trying. "I know. And I appreciate all you're doing. But why are you so certain you'll defeat the vampire? Daciano seemed formidable"—*unstoppable*—"in the ring."

"I'll study him, discover his weaknesses."

If only it were so simple. "And what about Goürlav?"

"I'll figure it all out. Don't fret over me."

Of *course* she would fret over him. She'd been doing it for nearly a decade.

Cas escorted her to her secreted castle entrance, but didn't follow her in.

"You're not coming up?" she asked, though she wanted to work anyway.

"We can't do that anymore. People will talk if I go to your spire."

She raised her brows. "Most of the combatants will be in a brothel tonight, but I'm expected to go to my lonely bed?"

"That's the way of this world, I'm afraid." His expression darkened. "I'm concerned about the Dacian returning to your apartments. He *cannot* have access to you, Bettina."

"I thought a vampire could never hurt his Bride."

"I'm not worried about him hurting you. I'm worried about him pressing his claim, trying to bed you fully."

"Salem will boot out any unwanted visitors."

After a moment, Cas nodded. "Tomorrow at sunset, I'll escort you from here and bring you back after my fight. Consider it a date," he said with an affectionate smile.

Surely he knew what effect that look had on her. "A date."

"You've been proud to call me friend, Tina. I'll make you proud to call me husband. I vow this."

And there went her heart.

"If you want to leave this spire, you must contact me first."

"You know I'm too scared to go about alone." *Will I be tonight?*

"True." He gave her a brief peck on her forehead, then traced away.

As she rode up the elevator, she considered what Cas had said about discovering the vampire's weaknesses. He couldn't get close enough to Daciano to learn anything meaningful.

But I can.

Inside her suites, she removed her cloak and mask, calling out, "I'm back."

In a distracted tone, Salem answered, "So you are. Big night, then? Lots of developments."

Floating closer to her, he said, "I told you the vampire would return. What was he talking to you about on the stage?"

"Nothing important."

"Your little chin-wag wiv him was the subject of *much* discussion. He was all proprietary with you, like you'd known him a while."

"I never saw him before last night. You know that."

"You held his things for him while he fought," Salem pointed out.

"Because he foisted his coat on me!"

"Perception is reality, chit. The wily leech wants others to think you're his."

Chit? She was a princess! Why did everyone forget that?

Because you let them. . . . She remembered Morgana

had once told her, "With your actions, you train others how to treat you."

"I don't want to talk about the vampire," she said. "I've got work to do." She turned toward her workshop, planting herself at her drafting table.

Again and again she attempted to sketch a new piece, but she was stumped. She needed a unique design, something Patroness had never seen.

She tapped her pencil against her bottom lip, her thoughts turning to tonight. Even if she decided to go, how was she supposed to get from point A to point B alone, without an episode?

To go undetected, she'd have to choose the most deserted route. A recipe for disaster.

Which would be stronger? A panic attack—or her vow to give the vampire what he asked for?

Bettina rose, stretched in a futile effort to relieve the tension in her shoulders, then began to wander aimlessly, still debating what to do.

She found Salem in the sitting room, unusually quiet, using telekinesis to thumb through her celebrity magazines—luxuries imported from the mortal realm.

She paced up and back; he turned a page. Repeat.

They continued like this as her grandfather clock ticked on. . . .

Toward midnight, she knew she had to get rid of him soon. But how?

"Princess." Salem suddenly occupied the door. "Going out for a spot."

"Pardon?" Yes, she wanted to get rid of him, but what if she'd actually wanted protection? "You're leaving me? What if I'm afraid the vampire might return?"

"Tonight I'm on a mission."

"What kind of *mission*?"

"The kind that takes precedence over protecting you from a vampire *who will never hurt you*."

"Tell me what you're talking about."

"I'm going to spy on Goürlav, try to puzzle out a way to kill him—without bringing ruin on the kingdom. Otherwise you just got engaged to him tonight."

She shivered at the thought. Before she could ask more, he said, "Laters."

Alone. One less obstacle to prevent her midnight meeting.

Bettina poured a glass of wine with a shaking hand. Dread over the short walk to the field of tents mingled with a different kind of anxiety. What favors would Daciano want from her? What might he demand? Maybe he'd ask for a repeat of what had happened last night.

More kissing, more touching.

She was so *curious* about him, about his reactions to her—about males in general.

If only she could remember her first sexual experience more clearly. Though much was foggy, three things had been etched into her mind: the pleasure of his mouth on her breasts, the new and wondrous feel of his shaft, and the scalding heat of his seed.

Face flushing, she drank deeply. She thought about sex as much as the next twenty-something halfling, and Daciano had given Bettina her first taste of real passion.

In turn, she'd blooded him, giving him his first release since his heart had stopped beating; had it been all he'd hoped?

How could it have been? She was hardly an experienced sexpot. Add "sexually untutored" to her list of deficits.

Damn it, how could she be insecure about this—she hadn't asked for him to steal into her bed!

Okay, say I go . . . Yes, she'd promised to give him boons. But she hadn't vowed to perform them blindly. She needed to set parameters tonight. Then she'd proceed to learn everything she could about him to help Cas.

Salem will figure out Goürlav; I'll handle the vamp.

This worry might be all for naught. Most likely she'd freeze at the castle entrance, unable to venture forth. Or would her vow compel her to skulk down darkened lanes—alone, powerless—exactly the sort of place where enemies were wont to hide?

She inhaled deeply, struggling to block her mind off from those memories. To no avail.

We've been watching you, Princess. Those fiends still lived, could very well be watching her right now.

A mouse might escape from a hawk, but never for long.

She flung her glass against the wall, hating her fear. Hating herself.

16

Trehan often awaited his targets. He had crouched upon roofs in the night, leaning against chimneys. He had hovered above them as light as mist. Always, he studied them before he struck.

Now he stood in the foggy drizzle upon a rooftop outside Castle Rune, awaiting Bettina—to *watch over* her. After the way those drunken entrants had spoken about her, he would never allow her to walk through the encampment alone.

Earlier, he'd collected his bag of clothing and weapons from beneath the bridge—he supposed some part of him had always known he'd enter the tournament—then traced to the fallen vampire's tent.

Inside, he'd found an ornate desk and chair, a divan, golden goblets, carafes of blood, and a bed of furs on the ground, as was the vampire way. Amenities and luxury for the taking. The Horde had always been wealthy.

So he'd unpacked his few belongings. In his haste, he'd been forced to leave behind so much. But he had the two items he truly treasured: his father's sword and the scry crystal. The former was sentimental; the latter was priceless.

After hanging his standard outside the tent, he'd made himself at home—because that was the closest thing he had to one now.

A short *conversation* with the dead contestant's vampire squire had gained Trehan a new servant as well.

Now in the streets below him, the mad scramble of delegates and contestants spying on each other had begun. Soon he'd have to undertake a fact-finding mission of his own. But for now, his focus was on Bettina.

Through the fog, he spied movement at the base of the castle. A concealed door was opening, revealing her at the threshold. She wore a cloak that covered her hair and most of her body, as well as a mask. But he could still see she was panting, her gloved fingers digging into the doorjamb.

She looked as if she were a vampire about to check the time—with a sundial.

Eyes darting behind her mask, she took one halting step out, then another. By the time she reached the closest building, she had to stop and lean her slender frame against a wall for balance as she nearly hyperventilated.

She dreads meeting me this much?

And why wouldn't she? He'd forced an overprotected, virginal—and very young—female to sneak to his tent for an assignation. In her mind, he was almost a stranger, and she would have no idea what he might demand.

No doubt she imagined the worst, and now her nerves were frayed. Guilt scored him.

But then a scavenging kobold, a sort of reptilian gnome, knocked over a basket near her, scuttling away. She jerked away from the clatter with a cry and flattened herself against the wall. Chanting something between breaths, she pressed one hand to her forehead as she swayed.

Surely this was more than nerves, more than virginal misgivings. She was utterly terrified.

Her trembling brought to mind the moments from last night when he'd been struggling not to bite her. Though he'd been nigh mindless in the grip of his blooding, he now recalled two words she'd whispered, *"Not again."*

She'd thought he was about to hurt her; clearly someone already had. Another vampire? Trehan didn't think so—she'd shown no more reaction to that Horde vampire at the tournament than to any other contestant. Then who?

She *was* like the most absorbing book he'd ever encountered. *How to turn the page?*

Suddenly that strange and inexplicable frustration from months before returned, the dread that had woken him. He rubbed his chest. What had called to him so sharply then? It must have been related to her.

Protect.

Trehan traced behind her, secretly wrapping her within the mist. As his blood female, she was of his kind—even if she didn't accept that yet—and the mist was a part of them all.

She soon calmed, not completely, but enough to steady her breaths and continue on to the tent.

He had to uncover what his little Bride feared. So he could destroy it.

Of course, he was the last person she'd confide in. But there were other ways to learn about her. His gaze fell to her neck, to her wildly beating pulse.

Using one of Lothaire's tactics had brought about this meeting. Perhaps if this bargaining with Bettina proved successful, Trehan would employ another of the Enemy of Old's tricks. . . .

I made it! Somehow Bettina had walked—alone at night—all the way to the vampire's tent.

She glanced around the empty space. So where was he?

"Bettina," he intoned from behind her.

She whirled around with a cry. "Y-you startled me."

The vampire was studying her with a quizzical glance. Right now, his eyes were a steady, dark green. They were handsome.

He was handsome?

He wore black leather pants, the cut more old-fashioned, but they looked good on his muscular legs. His tailored white shirt was made from a light material that did nothing to disguise the latent strength of his chest, those corded biceps and broad shoulders.

The sight made her frown. She'd had the run of his body last night—but she'd *wasted* her chance to satisfy her curiosity. Great. She dragged her gaze up to his.

When not wearing a scowl, his face was . . . pleasing. He'd certainly cleaned up well after the melee.

She felt safer with him than out on the street, even found the tension leaving her shoulders, her temples and jaw. In its place, that heated awareness returned, bringing with it irritation. Was she actually attracted to this vampire?

Every time he was near her, those molten feelings returned—she seethed inside, not with anger, but with *something*.

"Please sit," he said, ushering her to a divan. "Shall I take your cloak?"

Parameters, Bettina. "Look, Daciano, I came here to pay off boons, but I didn't agree to open-ended *favors*. I want to set a time limit for this meeting. I suggest twenty min—"

"You'll stay till dawn." His tone brooked no argument. "Your cloak?" he asked again, as if she hadn't spoken.

There went that plan. With an aggrieved air, she removed it, handing it to him. Or *trying* to.

For a long laden moment, he just stood there staring at her body, his eyes smoldering.

She'd deliberately worn a more modest outfit, one her godmother would consider "frumpy." Bettina's top of braided gold strands barely molded to her breasts; her jade silk sarong was split high, but only on one thigh. Accessories: a jet black mask, small diadem, and black full-length fingerless gloves. No flirty garters or thigh-highs.

All in all, this was demure by Sorceri standards. She'd seen Morgana attend a state dinner in nothing more than a micromini and glorified pasties.

She delicately cleared her throat; he exhaled a gust of breath, finally meeting her gaze and reaching out to take her cloak.

"Arresting, Bettina," he said in a roughened voice. "Quite literally."

Bettina was a design geek, a virgin who'd failed to seduce the male she was closest to. Now this vampire was looking at her as if she were a femme fatale. And for a crazy moment, he'd kind of made her *feel* like one.

"Would you like a drink?"

"I guess." *Desperately.* "Sweet wine if you have it."

"No demon brew?"

"Never again. The one time I tried it, a vampire appeared in my bed."

With raised brows, he traced to pour her a glass. She thought she heard another exhalation. Had she rattled the centuries-old vamp?

Taking a seat, she surveyed his appropriated tent. A fire burned in a copper pit, the smoke venting out through a shielded opening in the canvas. Though a light rain had started outside, the interior was snug and warm.

The floor was a platform of wood, covered by luxurious rugs. A desk and chair occupied one side of the tent, that log-like scroll of rules on the floor beside it.

A deep bathtub stood in one corner, while a sprawling pallet of furs lay directly atop the platform in another. No raised bed for him—because vampires slept as close to the ground as possible.

As he poured himself a goblet of blood from a warmed carafe, she said, "I can see why you wanted this tent. It screams vampire."

A slight frown. "You and I are not so different, Bettina."

"We are *wildly* different."

"Not so much that we can't find common ground."

"Oh? Is that why I'm here?" she asked, adding dryly, "To look for 'common ground'?"

He simply said, "Yes." Offering her the wine, he asked, "Were you worried about someone seeing you on the way here?"

She accepted it. "I wanted to avoid that, yes."

"You seemed . . . on edge walking here alone."

"You *spied* on me?"

"I watched over you," he corrected, sitting beside her. "I would never let you walk alone this late at night."

Bettina supposed that should irritate her, that she should rail at him for being a stalker and hate him even more.

Instead, the realization that she'd had a deadly guard watching over her the entire way was . . . reassuring. "That was your mist. You surrounded me." She'd perceived the cool, comforting embrace of it, but hadn't known what it was. It had blunted her panic attack.

Not all by myself, then. "So you truly can turn into vapor?"

He inclined his head. "All Dacians can. A talent born from a time before we came upon our mountain realm, when the light was too great and the shadows too few."

Before she could ask him more about this, he said, "Were you that nervous about meeting me? Or was it more?"

More, so much more! "I have no idea what you'll demand." And yet she wasn't *frightened* of what he might do. Again, she felt no trepidation where he was concerned.

He gazed away, looking troubled. "I told you I'd never hurt you. If given leave, I'd do nothing but protect you."

He'd seen her reaction outside; she didn't want him to think he was responsible for that. *Not* out of concern for him. She simply didn't want the vampire to think he'd intimidated her. "Look, I just don't like to walk alone at night. I might have . . . issues—ones that I don't want to speak of."

Naturally, Trehan wouldn't rest until he was fully versed in these *issues*. "Your kingdom is secure. Most beings cower before your guardians. Not to mention that you're a sorceress. What issues could you possibly have?"

Her eyes narrowed with irritation. "We're not friends, Daciano. We're not confidantes. Why should I tell you anything about myself? *You* are a threat to me. You blackmailed me today."

"Unfortunate but necessary." He leaned forward on the edge of the divan, resting his elbows on his knees. "Now back to the subject at hand. You whispered 'Not again' when you thought I was about to hurt you last night."

She glanced away, clearly trying to remember what she'd said.

"Has another vampire touched you?"

"No!"

"A sorcerer then?" he quickly asked, setting away his goblet. "I read that Sorceri constantly battle for powers. Was yours stolen from you?"

"Another subject I don't want to talk about!"

Trehan sensed he was close to the truth, so he pressed on mercilessly. "I also read that your kind consider a root ability akin to one's soul?"

She peered hard into her cup. It shook in her hand. Her expression was a mix of sadness, frustration, and . . . shame.

This fragile creature had been violated like that? Someone had dared steal her power.

He was awash with pure rage—an unfamiliar emotion for him. *Give me names, the scantest direction!* Yet he leveled his tone when he asked, "What was your root power?"

In a voice just above a whisper, she said, "I was a . . . queen. The Queen of Hearts."

"What could you do?"

"I could make a being's heart stop. For all time. I could make an enemy's chest explode."

"Did you wield it to defend yourself?"

Staring past Trehan, she murmured, "I didn't have time. They dropped from . . . I-I never saw them."

"Them?" More than one? Barely managing to rein in his fury, he bit out, "Direct me to these thieves, and I will slaughter them."

She glanced up at him, clearly startled by his tone. "No one steals from us, *dragă mea*."

17

Bettina felt raw. Trehan Daciano now knew a secret only a handful of others shared. How had he gotten under her skin like that? And why was he so adamant about avenging her? "There is no *us*, vampire. Again, I'm here under duress."

"Tell me who hurt you."

"You've known me for twenty-four hours. Yet you're willing to wade into danger, risking your life to avenge me?"

"Yes."

"I'm not a vampire. I can't wrap my mind around this spontaneous protectiveness."

"That part is not much different from a demon's mate."

Apparently, I don't get that either.

"Twenty-two years ago, my Bride was born. For two decades she's been without my protection. From what I can glean, that span of years has been treacherous for her. Simply put: someone hurt her—I need to make that being *suffer* in unspeakable ways."

Daciano's strength and will were nearly palpable, a heady combination. She finally understood why some women were hopelessly attracted to dangerous men. Not that *she* was. But she could see it.

"Can your power be returned to you?" he asked.

"Morgana has promised to do just that before I wed."

"A condition of this tournament? But isn't she worried about who the victor might be?"

"She doesn't see the horrific ones as . . . horrific. I just know that this tournament is very important to her." Bettina had begun to suspect that there was more to this entire event than she could fathom. Was this a Lore power play, a twist in the great Accession?

Were they all cogs in a wheel? And if so, who was turning the crank?

"Does your godmother possess your power now?"

I'm losing faith that she'll find it. Bettina shrugged.

"So she doesn't. What if *I* returned it to you?" he asked, his eyes flickering green to onyx once more. Apparently, he was keen on this idea. "And then I could punish those foolish enough to harm you. Give me direction, and they will die bloody."

Die bloody. How *tempting.* She imagined each of those four Vrekeners squirming on the ground in his own blood, voice hoarse from screams. Would they beg for mercy as she had?

But she had no names, no direction to give Daciano. Besides, she'd never tell the vampire what had happened to her. It wasn't his business—and it was humiliating. "I can't talk . . . I *won't* talk about it."

"Just tell me—was it a sorcerer who struck against you?"

"I'm under *Morgana*'s protection; no Sorceri would dare. And if a sorcerer had stolen my power, then I'd be an *Inferi*, a slave." Because of Bettina's halfling lineage, it was possible for her to be both a demon royal—and a Sorceri slave.

"Vrekeners hunt your kind."

"They do. Have forever . . ." she murmured, her thoughts shuttling back to that night.

Early in the attack, the leader had used that scythe of black flames to siphon away her power. She recalled thinking, *At least they aren't planning to kill me, wouldn't go to this trouble.*

Then she'd remembered: they would steal her sorcery just to prevent it from being reincarnated into a newborn Sorceri upon Bettina's death.

Once the leader had finished stripping her of her power, he'd roared, "Your kind killed my father, crippled my brother forever!" as he'd launched his boot into her face.

She shuddered now, and Daciano noticed.

"You might as well tell me, Bettina. Eventually I will find out."

Refusing to have more of her past laid bare, she inhaled for calm, then attempted to steer the conversation back to the tournament. "You assume you'll be alive that long? You could meet up with Goürlav tomorrow. I heard his blood spawns monsters."

The vampire gave her an indulgent look. "I'll deal with Goürlav when the time comes."

"How can you be so confident? You're not invincible," she said, hoping she sounded natural. If she had to tolerate Daciano's interrogation, she might as well help Cas. "You're not without weaknesses."

"No, I'm not. Nor am I inclined to discuss any with you so you can relay them directly to Caspion."

She flushed guiltily.

"Bettina, you don't have to reveal details, just tell me where to hunt."

A place hidden in the heavens that no demon—or vampire—has ever reached! A place protected from all sorcery! Bettina stood. *Enough of this.* She set her glass on his desk, then headed toward the door.

"Wait, woman." He traced in front of her, blocking the exit.

"Already I don't want to be here. I don't want to be with you. And you just keep digging."

"At least tell me if you're still in danger."

"That's more digging!"

He inhaled deeply. "I find myself in a position I've never been in before. I'm besieged by . . . instinct. And you are the focus of it."

"What does that mean?"

"It means I *need* to kill. For unending years, I was naught but death, with no judgment, only duty. But now . . ."

"*But now* we're done talking about my past, or I'm leaving."

He parted his lips to say something, thought better of it, then said, "Very well." He ushered her back to the divan, handing her drink to her and reclaiming his own. "What would you like to speak of? I'll accommodate you."

"You know more about me than I'd supposed. I know very little about you and your kind."

Another slight frown. "I'm not used to explaining

what I am. Unless it's to someone I'm about to kill. And what I have been for over nine hundred years has changed drastically in the last twenty-four hours."

Cas had said that Daciano was at least eight centuries old. But to hear it from the vampire's own lips . . . "You're over *forty* times my age?"

Had a flush colored his chiseled cheekbones? "Give or take."

"You were—give or take—eight hundred and eighty years old when I was born!"

Voice gone low, he said, "So now you know how very long I've waited for you to come into this world."

Now she felt *her* cheeks flush. "You said you were a prince. Is your father king of the Dacians?"

"My father's long dead. I'm one of several contenders for the throne." He glanced down at his goblet. "Or I was."

"You really can't return?"

"No."

She almost felt guilt about his loss. Then she remembered she'd never asked him to give up his realm. "But now you intend to be the king of the Abaddonae?"

"I have absolutely no aspirations toward that. Though I understand that co-ruling this plane is expected of me, if I intend to live my life with you."

The vampire made it sound like the crown—which every suitor coveted—was a necessary evil he'd put up with to be with her. Even Cas must desire the throne, if just a little.

Flustered, she fiddled with her mask—her nervous tell. His gaze fixed on her hand. "What weapons have you tonight?" he asked, pointing to the four rings on her right hand. "There must be more to those than meets the eye."

Was it any wonder that her jewelry designs had become so . . . dark? Sometimes she thought she might have gone mad without that creative outlet.

And for some reason, this vampire was intrigued by it.

Her guardians considered her craft demeaning. Caspion scratched his head, unable to understand her compulsion to create.

She remembered the day she'd called a meeting with Raum and Morgana to discuss her education. "I want to learn more about design. And mortals are surprisingly good at it. They use computers and tools I can only dream of here."

"What would you do with this knowledge?" Raum had asked. "Continue with your hobby?"

"It's no hobby. I've been commissioning my pieces here and there to acquaintances. But I'm thinking bigger. I want to sell them . . . I want to sell them on the open market!"

They'd looked at her as if she'd grown two heads.

"Become a tradesman?" Morgana had hissed.

Bettina had corrected her: "A trades*person*. . . ."

Now, in a coaxing tone, the vampire said, "Come, Bett, show me what weapon I'll encounter tonight if I displease you." Was there a hint of a smile on those grim lips of his?

"Fine." She demonstrated how the rings interlocked to form brass knuckles.

He gently grasped her fingertips, holding her hand to examine the rings thoroughly. At the contact, some kind of electric charge passed through her, like a bolt of . . . *anticipation*.

He must have felt something too. His voice was huskier when he asked, "You devised this yourself?"

"Yes." She stiffened, drawing her hand away. "All by my little self." Why were others always so surprised by this?

"It's clever."

Chin raised, she said, "I can see a problem and visualize a solution."

"What design are you working on now?"

"A commissioned piece."

"You sell your work?"

She bristled. "What of it?"

"I have a niece who is obsessed with weapons. She would love to have something like this."

"You want to *commission* a piece?"

"Absolutely. And then I'd insist on watching you work."

Bettina blinked at him. "You really are interested?"

"I'm a weapons master. You create weapons. I think it's fascinating."

"You don't have a problem with your Bride being in trade? It's not exactly decorous. I thought an old-fashioned vampire like you would want me to quit."

"Though I'll be loath to let you out of our bed for any reason, I'd never try to restrict something you enjoy."

Another fitful adjustment of her mask. *Let me out of bed?*

"And as for the trade stigma, I've lived my life obeying the rules, *enforcing* the rules. I cast off that rigid existence to be with you. Perhaps the beauty of being a queen is that you get to do whatever you like."

"I'm not naïve." *I might be naïve.* "I know that's not how the world works."

"Then change the world."

The world? She could barely change the subject.

"For now, let's discuss this commission," he said.

"How would you even get the gift to your niece?"

"Not easily. She never leaves the kingdom, so I'd have to send it through another one of my family. I'm not shunned by them all. Well, not exactly. Let's just say that I suspect I haven't seen the last of the Dacianos." There seemed to be a wealth of emotion in that statement, but she couldn't decipher it. Relief? Grief? "When will you finish the piece you're working on now?"

She mumbled, "Probably sometime after I actually start it. Which should occur after I figure out what to create."

That hint of a grin teased his lips once more.

"My patroness is very exacting, and I've sent her weapon after weapon. She wants something new."

"The piece you wear now is only a few modifications from being a *bagh nakh*." Brass knuckles with claws jutting out.

Now *she* had to grin. Not many threw that term around. "I already made her one."

"With the spikes curling inward along the palm or jutting out over the knuckles?"

"Out." Then she admitted, "I've never seen any curling in." That would be a great twist. A lady's indignant slap would never be the same.

"Have you ever heard of a *bichawa bagh nakh*?" When she shook her head, he said, "I wish I could show you. I had a collection such as you wouldn't believe." His dark brows knit. These reminders of what he'd given up must be sharp.

His look bothered her, and she couldn't understand why. *You made your bed, vampire.*

And still she found herself saying, "Maybe you

could draw one?" She crossed to the desk, rooting through drawers until she found paper and a pen.

With a nod, he traced to the seat, collecting the paper. He began to sketch the baseplate and curved claws of the basic weapon, his outline surprisingly competent. Was there anything he couldn't do?

Outside the storm picked up, but the lazy fire gave off just enough heat. She found herself relaxing, sipping her wine as she watched the drawing take shape.

Yet she kept getting distracted by him. Her eyes flickered over his hair. It was thick and straight, reflecting firelight. Had she run her fingers through it last night?

She noted the expanse of his shoulders beneath that tailored shirt and his great height—sitting down, he was nearly as tall as she was standing up. Then her gaze lingered on his face. His masculine features formed an expression of thoughtful concentration.

His eyes really were a mesmerizing shade of green. She'd seen that color before. In the deepest forests of Abaddon.

Perhaps Morgana had been right in her assessment.

Looking at Daciano's lips brought to mind his heated kisses last night. Whenever she'd imagined kissing Cas, she'd envisioned accompanying sighs, handholding, and laughter.

But now, with this vampire, her thoughts weren't quite so innocent. Surely that was because she'd actually kissed Daciano. Of course her *imaginings* would be different; *reality* was intruding!

Breaking her stare, he said, "The basic model would be fine to use against a human. But for an immortal you need more tissue disruption."

Tissue disruption. Gods, he was talking Weapon to her.

She was actually enjoying herself. She hopped up on the desk, tilting her head down to watch him work.

He paused, his gaze sliding to the slit of her skirt. She crossed her legs; he snapped the pen.

How . . . thrilling. She'd never had such an effect on males before. She could almost feel like a sorceress again, enthralling a vampire warrior.

That didn't mean she needed to play with fire. She handed him another pen. "The drawing, Daciano."

His broad jaw clenched, he gave a subtle nod, then continued. His fingers were dexterous. She remembered more vividly how he'd secured her breasts in his possessive grip as he'd suckled her. She remembered how those clever fingers had trailed down her torso before petting her between her legs.

Slowly, tenderly, hotly.

He'd certainly been dexterous then, with an art all his own.

She didn't need to be thinking about this right now! If she grew aroused, he would know, could probably hear her heart speeding up right now—

At that moment, one of his pen strokes went erratic. He paused, seeming to catch his breath before the pen moved once more.

When she glanced down next, he'd drawn a blade jutting from one end of the baseplate. "That's a static blade?" she asked. "It's always extended?"

In a hoarse voice, he said, "Yes, but if you can figure out how to eject spikes from an armlet, you can surely create a switchblade to eject from the baseplate."

"So it'd look like it was shooting from the bottom of my fist?"

"Precisely."

So that was the modification. Patroness would *adore* it. Maybe Bettina and Daciano *did* have some common ground.

Eyes anywhere but on her, the vampire slid the page over.

If Trehan's female could guess even half of his thoughts at this moment, she'd run screaming from the tent.

With her so accessible on the desk, he could sweep her over in front of his chair and grip her knees, easing her thighs open.

He'd compared Bettina to a book before; now he dreamed of spreading her wide and devouring her, sampling her as he'd dreamed of all day. His shaft swelled painfully as the fantasy played out in his mind.

He wouldn't let her go until she'd come half a dozen times for him. Against his tongue, her drenched sex would quiver, hungry for his shaft to fill it—

Control yourself, Trehan!

Easier said . . . When she'd hopped up on the desk, her bared thigh just inches from his hand, he'd wondered if she was a tease—or if she truly had no idea how much she affected him.

He suspected the latter. He also suspected she was catching on, and *enjoying* her newfound feminine wiles.

Gods help me.

Already her mannerisms had bewitched him: the way she absently licked wine from her red lips. The way she adjusted her mask when she was discomfited. The way she gazed up at him from under her thick lashes, taking his measure with those exquisite eyes.

When she'd tilted her head to analyze his drawing, her thick mane of hair had swept over her bare shoulder, sending him awash in her scent.

And, *zeii*, her smile. Earlier, when she'd realized she was enjoying herself, her lips had curled, the smile coming easily. Immediately, his mind had turned to ways he could coax another from her.

Everything about her made him want to either crush her in an embrace—or pin her hips as he pounded between her legs.

Worse? He was certain she was getting aroused as well.

But he'd governed his urges. He knew how important this interlude was. It was their beginning. An eternity of pleasure lay before them if his campaign with her proved successful.

He was building trust, demonstrating their commonalities. His actions followed a formula, but the method seemed to be working.

Next, he would deploy the second stage of his plan, using her desires to his advantage. He stood and moved before her, greatly looking forward to it.

She gazed up at him with those entrancing eyes. Success would find her in his arms, her moans in his ear.

Failure? Would find her with her hands all wet . . .

18

Looking for all the world like he was about to kiss her, the vampire eased closer until she could perceive the heat coming off his body.

Lips parted, brows drawn, he reached down to gently cup her face, tugging her to him—

She shoved against his chest. "Stop! This is not why I'm here."

He eventually released her, his gaze narrowed.

Analyzing me. She knew vampires were an inherently logical species, but she'd never met any who exhibited that trait. Their minds had been tainted by bloodlust, their irises—and even the whites of their eyes—gone red from it.

She'd never met a clear-eyed vampire before, and now she was the object of this one's study.

"One boon, then—for a kiss."

She gave him a disappointed look. "You want my favors to be, well, sexual? Is that why you've maneuvered me into this bargaining? You're hardly playing fair."

Curling his finger under her chin, he said, "Do you really think I'll play fair when the prize is so dear?" With his other hand, he reached for her mask, gently unlacing it to remove the silk. Seeming captivated by her face, he bit out, "*Zeii mea,* beauty, you speak to me of playing fair? You've vanquished me with one move."

Her cheeks heated furiously. Why did she feel such a thrill at each of his compliments? Because others' compliments were so rare?

She reminded herself that he was a stone-cold killer, clearly a manipulator. He was so much older, with lifetimes more experience than she had. "You told me you wouldn't return for me. You seemed perfectly okay with the idea of never seeing me again. Now this? I want to know what changed."

"*Me.* For centuries, I lived a life of service, never desiring anything for myself. And now I do desire." He eased closer to her. "Bettina, I desire beyond reason."

His scent and heat permeated her senses. Did all vampires smell this mouthwatering? Maybe as a predatory tool to lure quarry like her? It was *working.*

Again she felt weak and breathless, the flash-fever returned. It seemed like her body was so busy struggling to regain equilibrium that her thought processes suffered. "I-I have a hard time believing you'd leave your home, a home you treasure."

At her ear, he rasped, "To treasure you."

He could be smooth, she'd give him that. But then she remembered that he planned to kill Caspion.

She drew her head back. "Why? You know nothing about me. Your blooding makes you attracted to me. Your *desire* is actually just a quirk of fate."

"Does the blooding affect me? Yes. I *need* to protect you, to claim you, to"—he stopped himself—"to . . . possess you in every way."

What exactly did that mean? What had he been *about* to say?

"But you also fascinate me. Your creations intrigue me."

"You're a flatterer."

"Never. A teller of truths."

"You can tell me all the truths you like, vampire, but I'm still not going to kiss you. Not tonight. Not ever."

"I see. Very well, Bettina."

Funny. She'd thought he would put up more of a fight—

Suddenly his arm wrapped around her, mist filling her vision. One of his fingers pressed over her lips.

A split second later, another vampire traced into the tent, a younger squire who looked nervous, twitchy—and fearful of Daciano.

Ah, gods, she was seen!

But the squire quickly set about his duties, paying no attention to her.

She squeezed her eyes shut as if that would hide her from his gaze.

After a few moments, he asked, "Anything else . . . my lord?" His voice broke midsentence.

She peeked open her eyes. The young vampire hadn't even glanced at her. Was she *hidden* in Daciano's mist? Was that even possible?

"That will be all," Daciano said. "Do not return until gloaming tomorrow."

When the squire disappeared, Bettina said, "He couldn't see me?"

"You're my Bride. I can hide you."

"That was too close!" She shoved against Daciano's chest, but he didn't release her. "This is such a bad idea—wait a second. Why did that squire *ready your bath*?"

"You told me earlier tonight that you expected to be treated like a lady."

"Yes, so?"

His eyes bored into hers. "A lady tends to her lord's bath."

"What are you talking . . ." She trailed off. "You're not my lord!" She gave another shove that he didn't even seem to register.

"A boon says I am tonight."

"This was a—a carefully orchestrated trap! You planned all this, manipulating me!"

"Yes."

When he simply admitted to things like that, it seriously undermined her outrage. "You're insane."

"Perhaps all these unredeemed favors have gone to my head."

"You're not even in need of a bath."

"A bath can have other purposes. Here are your choices: you tend to my bath—or I'll tend to yours."

The look in his eyes told her that he was leaning toward the latter.

To have this male running soap all over her naked body . . . ? What would that be like?

Gaze dropping to her neck, he said, "I could demand far worse than this."

Such as a drink? Was that what he'd meant when he'd said, "possess you in every way"?

"Bettina, you didn't have to agree to our bargain."

"Of course I did. I would have done anything to save Caspion."

Some dark, primal emotion flashed over his face, and his arms tightened around her. "Have care, sorceress. You tread upon perilous ground."

She swallowed with fear. Strangely, not for herself, only for Caspion. "You still want him dead. So why save him earlier? It only increases the likelihood that *you* will have to kill him."

"If we're pitted against each other, I won't have a choice but to defeat him, so you'll be more likely to forgive me. If I hadn't saved him today, that would have been a choice you might *not* have forgiven. Besides, these favors will help me win your affections of my own accord—not simply because my competitor no longer exists."

"So that's what motivates you? Competition with Cas?"

He gave a humorless laugh. "Soon you'll find there is no competition with that demon. What motivates me is the lovely prize I'll possess." He set her away to begin unbuttoning his shirt. "And you'll stall no more." His gaze raked along her body as he began to bare his. Again, she fought the need to fan herself.

When Daciano removed his shirt, she turned away, but not before she got a look at his muscular chest in the firelight.

His skin was smooth—and completely unmarked from the melee. In the ring, he'd been saturated with blood. But only from others?

She also glimpsed that crystal around his neck. His clothing style was simple and unembellished; she wondered why he wore that lead.

Is he removing his boots?

Keeping her back to him as he undressed was more difficult than she would have supposed. What woman wouldn't crave seeing the vampire's body, especially after touching it in the dark the night before?

But for Bettina, it was even worse. She had an artist's eye, and right now that sensibility was clamoring to see this male naked. *As a subject. Nothing more.*

His pants landed over a chair to her right. She swallowed. *He's naked in this tent with me.*

When he descended into the water, she snapped, "I'm not doing this," even as she mused, *I should have peeked.*

"Then prepare for worse."

Her thoughts ran riot. Scrubbing his back *was* preferable to a thousand other things he could have demanded. "But I've never bathed anyone before."

"I'm confident you'll stumble your way through this."

She scowled up at the ceiling. Oh, how bad could a bath be? She would refuse to wash any part of him below the waist. *I won't get caught up like I did last night.*

Because this time she'd know he wasn't Cas.

"It counts as five boons," she said. Then she'd have only two left after this, and her greedy gaze could be appeased to an extent. His back was *plenty* to start out with.

"Three," he countered.

"Four."

"Agreed," he said.

Okay, only three *left.* With straightened shoulders, she turned toward the tub. *I can do this.* As she approached, she realized the water was sudsy and steaming, concealing his body from just below those developed pecs down.

Which was a good thing. It *was*.

She knelt behind him, beginning to remove one glove.

He turned sharply, twisting to watch her, as if he didn't want to miss even this small unveiling.

Flustered again. When she began to roll it down her arm, she *did* feel like she was stripping—for him. By the second glove, his eyes were flickering.

Once her arms were bared, he handed her a cloth and soap, and their fingers touched. Another current seemed to leap between them. He glanced up quickly, as if to gauge if she'd felt it too.

Whatever he saw appeared to satisfy him. At length he gave her his back.

In the steam, a few locks of his hair grew tousled about his neck. Black, black hair that gleamed like jet. His leather tie caught her attention. "You don't want to remove your crystal?"

"Never," was all he said.

She wondered where he'd gotten it. Had a former lover given it to him? "Fine." She assumed a business-like demeanor, unwilling for him to know how much this prospect alternately excited and dismayed her. Soaping up the cloth, she rubbed it across smooth, taut skin from one of his shoulders to the other.

Repeat. He wasn't the only one who could be methodical. One shoulder to the other. Repeat.

Had that movement been a bit more leisurely? Perhaps; his muscles flexed in response.

He'd killed with those muscles. He'd killed *for her*.

Inward shake. Another sweep of the cloth. "Do you always have unwilling females bathe you?"

"You're a first in many regards." Without warning, he snagged the cloth from her. "Continue without it."

"Why?" Was that *her* voice sounding so breathless?

"You enjoyed touching me last night." He stretched his long arms along the sides of the tub. "It's my hope that you will again."

"This was your plan? You think to seduce me like this?"

"Yes."

How could one word hold so much confidence? She swallowed, but did continue running her palms over his shoulders and neck.

Yes, she'd always had an artist's eye. She looked at things in terms of relief and shadow, color and contrast. Because of the nature of her work, she paid attention to form and function.

And now she could see the shapes she'd only felt. She could take her time registering the utter might of his body.

The raised muscles around his shoulders. The indentation above each of his bulging biceps. The strong fingers now clutching the side of the tub.

She couldn't decide which of her senses Daciano appealed to most. Tactile, visual? Not to mention his vampire scent. She wasn't even surprised to find her slick palms slipping lower down his back, exploring him.

Outside, the rain began to pour, the wind to howl. Inside was all sultry warmth and glowing firelight. Her eyelids drooped to half-mast, then slid shut as she lost herself in sensation—the texture of his skin beneath her sensitive fingertips, the unyielding form of his sculpted back, the heat rising from the water, from his very body.

For her work, she honed and tweaked, iteration after iteration, until she found her creation faultless.

I wouldn't change an inch of his body. Not one single inch.

As she wondered if she could grow addicted to this . . . this *exploration,* she kneaded his neck. He exhaled a relaxed breath, sinking back into her hands.

She went up on her knees to reach farther forward—and possibly to steal a peek. But the water still concealed him. All she could make out was a shadowy shape at his groin, that enticingly *large* shape she'd stroked. Had it pulsed in the water?

How *titillating.* She would give karats to see it.

Too late, she realized she'd dipped her palms over his shoulders, down past his collarbone. She was officially tending to his "front."

Relaxed no more, he grew tense as a spring trap, even as his knees fell wide.

Instead of alarm, excitement coursed through her. Her hands slipped lower.

His knuckles went white as he gripped the side of the tub. The metal began to bend under the pressure. . . .

19

Don't drag her into the water . . . don't force her hands down.

Last night Trehan had restrained himself—barely—and had been rewarded with her desire this eve. Tonight he must do the same.

Bettina wasn't immune to him, and he was one step closer to seducing her. Which meant he needed to deny instinct once more, and use his *mind* to win her. *Remember the plan!*

Again, easier said . . .

Even now her dainty hands glided over his collarbone, her graceful arms lightly draping over his shoulders.

Even now her breaths fanned over his damp ear. Each exhalation made his cock jerk hungrily beneath the water.

His Bride was teaching him much about himself this eve, awakening him even more. He'd never known how sensitive his ears were. Or his shoulders. Or the back of his neck. . . .

When she'd begun kneading his muscles, he realized his plan had worked all too well. She was lost to sensation.

A sensual little sorceress. His Bride was *o comoara*. A treasure.

Comoara mea. My *treasure*.

Was she leaning forward to get a look at his shaft? She'd felt it; now she must want to see it. Though he wasn't often the subject of scrutiny, he was about to be.

Zeii, I want to show it to her. The idea aroused him unbearably; his hips began to rock. *Would his be the first one she'd seen hard?* Definitely the last one.

Should he take himself in hand and present it . . . ? The notion faded when she rubbed her palms lower than before.

This had been *his* plan. *His* seduction. Now he could barely think. *Was my chest always this sensitive—*

She grazed his nipples; he hissed, bowing his back for more, clenching his fists on the sides of the tub.

When his fingers dug furrows into the groaning iron, she went still.

He'd frightened her, ruining this—

She grazed them again.

"Bettina!" he roared, bucking his hips uncontrollably. For a brief second, cool air met his upthrust cock.

She gasped at his ear, making him shudder. She'd seen a glimpse. How would she react? What would she do next?

She leaned in closer, until the side of her face was touching his. *Her lovely unmasked face.* Skin to skin. Panting, she eased forward even more. When the corners of their lips were flush, his parted in surprise.

Though it was torture, he went motionless. *What will she do next?*

He held his breath. His cock pained him as never before. His body began to quake—

Then came one sly dart of her little tongue . . . the lightest dab at the edge of his mouth, just inside his parted lips.

Thought fled.

With a roar, he traced to his feet to seize his prize.

The vampire's hands shot out for her.

"*Wait!*" Bettina cried as she tumbled from her knees to one hip.

He froze. Gradually, he straightened. Between ragged breaths, he said, "I'd never hurt you, Bett. *Never.*"

She frowned up at him. That thought hadn't crossed her mind. If she'd feared him, then she wouldn't have been trying to tease him to distraction—so he'd thrust his hips and show her his erection again.

Her one fleeting glimpse as it'd breached the surface of the water left her beset with curiosity. *With desire.*

In lieu of thrusting, his standing completely naked in front of her worked too.

Oh, my gold, how this works.

He must've realized she had no fear of him because he put his shoulders back, must've realized that she'd craved this view because he lifted his chin.

"You want to see your male?" he grated, masculine pride suffusing his tone.

"My male?" *A male. This male . . .*

I'm staring up at a naked, fully aroused vampire. Blooded and in his prime.

She felt giddy, as drunk as she'd been during their first encounter. The sight of him like this not only aroused her, it *delighted* her.

The fire was to his right, illuminating his glistening skin, shadows and light at play. Under her gaze, every sinew of muscle contracted, rippling. Water streams licked over every mighty rise, over every rigid fall.

Drops sluiced down his chest to his navel, meeting at that dusky trail of hair leading down, *down*.

When her gaze followed, he said in a gravelly voice, "This is what you do to me, Bett." His accent was thicker than she'd ever heard it.

She was transfixed by his erection—again, *giddy*. Her peek had been just the tip of the iceberg. *So to speak*. At the thought, a laugh escaped her.

Which made him scowl and cross his arms.

Had she actually tried to convince herself that she would view him as a subject of study?

Uh-huh. For my art.

She couldn't even *think* that with a straight face.

"*Strange little sorceress*," he suddenly murmured in a wondering tone. "You're . . . happy."

She gave an absent nod and began lovingly taking in every detail of his manhood.

Crisp black hair circled the base. Just below it, his heavy sac tightened before her eyes. The shaft was veined, the skin so taut. The engorged head strained toward her, as if toward her parted lips.

What would it be like to feel that firm crown at her mouth, like a plum warmed in the sun? She grazed her fingertips over her lips as she imagined it. Would the vampire shudder and groan if she pressed her tongue against him there?

"Ah, Bettina, your eyes go light," he rasped. "Have you looked your fill?" Were his legs quaking?

My fill? No. Not at all.

Planes, textures, colors? Proportion! His body taken all together was a tableau of perfection—a masterpiece she needed to appreciate more fully.

One that was making her wetter than she'd ever been in her entire life.

He inhaled deeply, and his body shot even tighter with tension. Could he tell how he affected her? Of course, he would scent her.

What would he do next? She wished she had more experience with these things.

"The way you look at me, woman . . . I could come under your glittering gaze. I wager my merry sorceress would like to see that."

She'd only felt it in her hand before. Form and function. She thrilled to watch her creations work, to perform as intended. She wanted to *see* this part of him . . . release. "Now that you mention—"

He scooped her up. In an instant, she was weightless, traced to his bed.

"Oh! What are you going to do?"

His words like a growl, he answered, "Pleasure you." He covered her with his big wet body, wrapping his brawny arms around her as his lips descended to hers.

And it felt *wondrous.*

This time she didn't break away, didn't deny him. When he touched his tongue to the seam of her lips, she parted them, letting him taste her.

She knew there was a reason she shouldn't be in bed, kissing a naked vampire, but her thoughts were still scrambled from the sight of him.

Against her lips, he said, "*Zeii,* I've craved your kiss, all this long day. Craved more of what I found in your bed."

"Was last night really the first time you . . . ?"

"*Came?*" he groaned the word. "First time in centuries."

"Did it . . . did it feel good?" *Was I too clumsy? Too inexperienced?*

"Ah, gods, female, it felt very *good.*" He licked at her lips. "Your soft little palm wrung me dry. I can't even look at your hands without getting hard." With that, he took her mouth totally, those firm lips claiming hers. Sensuous flicks of his tongue coaxed hers to meet him.

She did eagerly, but he kept their kiss slow, fierce— devastating. How could he be so good at this after so long without?

Each stroke of his wicked tongue drew her ardor to the fore, making her wild for him. She wriggled her body closer to his, to his warmth and palpable strength.

Were his hands busy at her waist? Ah, her sarong. *Oh, gone!*

His kisses stifled any halfhearted protests she could have managed. Had he just wedged his hips between her thighs?

Yes! That glorious shaft pressed over her panties, its length like a brand from her mons past her navel.

More kisses, more movement. Her arms were over her head. Wrists briefly in his fist? A whisper of sensation on her breasts?

He'd removed her top? Yes, cool air tickled her

nipples—until the hot, slick skin of his chest shoved against her naked breasts. She moaned into the kiss.

When he hooked a finger around the side of her thong, she comprehended that it was the only barrier left between them. She jerked her head back. In a strangled voice, she said, "Vampire, my panties!"

"Off! *Yes, dragă* . . ."

"No, they stay!"

With a rumbling sound of disappointment, he flexed his hips. His erection rode over the silk, over her mons, leaving utter pleasure in its wake.

"Doesn't matter. I'm still going to make you come, female." He gave another thrust that rubbed right over her clitoris. As she cried out, he said, "And when you do, I want you to moan *my* name."

His deep-toned voice and commanding words were like a stroke over every part of her. The hot pressure of his shaft was heavy on her clitoris. She rocked against it for more heat, more friction.

More *anything*. Desperate, she undulated her hips—just as he drew his back. His penis slipped down to prod right at her entrance, *stayed only by the silk*.

His head snapped up, his gaze meeting her widened eyes.

"Wait!" She squirmed to the side, until the head of his penis wasn't tucked into her cleft. "T-too fast! You know I can't have sex!"

Forehead against hers, he rasped, "I want inside you, Bett. More than I've ever wanted anything in my entire existence." Gripping her waist, he dragged her right back under him. "But I know we must wait."

"I'm trusting you, and I don't give my trust easily."

"At the end of this tournament, I'll rip away your

silk and bury my length so deep in you. For now, no sex. Just pleasure. It's my woman's turn. . . ."

He cupped her ass with splayed fingers, angling his hips, positioning the base of his erection directly against her clitoris. Then he tightened his arms around her, squeezing her until every inch of them seemed to be touching.

The weight of him atop her was rapturous, the heat of him seeping into her. His fingers bit into the curves of her ass, holding her still for him, holding his hardness exactly where she craved it. She couldn't rock against him, didn't need to.

She was pressed so tightly against him that she could feel his shaft throb, could feel his heart thundering against her tingly breasts.

So tightly against him that when he moved, they moved as one.

He brought his lips down on hers once more. This time the kiss was more forceful, deeper, as if he wanted to mark her with his lips.

As she moaned into his mouth, their tongues danced and their breaths meshed. They were nearly molded together and she wanted his body closer still. Why wasn't he closer?

More moans, his hoarse groans. His penis felt like it had swelled even more. The friction grew, until she was so close. Her first orgasm with another . . .

He broke their kiss. "Gods, woman! I'm already at the edge. My fangs grow sharp."

"Um, okay." Surely he wasn't hinting that they should end this. *So close.*

In a ragged voice, he said, "You know what this might mean, Bett."

It means he's so aroused, he's losing control. Like her. "Just as long as we don't have sex."

"Ah, dragă . . ." He took her mouth with another hard press of his lips, more bold strokes of his tongue. She met him every one.

She was shivering, her body tensing, readying for her orgasm. On the brink of wet bliss—

Then came the tang of . . . blood.

20

Shocks jolted up and down Trehan's body from his head to his toes, before convening in his shaft.

He'd nicked her tongue. *Zeii mea,* her blood straight from the flesh. If her kiss had brought to mind mead, her blood was a glimpse of heaven.

An injection of perfect pleasure seared his veins.

He shuddered, growling against her lips. The tip of his hungry tongue licked hers for more, hunting for that tiny nick.

Dimly, he remembered how taboo this was, even as he sought more. *A perversion?*

No, connection! Sharing her essence felt . . . pure. *"Dulcea!"* he groaned between kisses. "So *sweet.*" How could this possibly be wrong? The sense of union was almost like intercourse.

But she broke away. "Y-you tasted my blood?"

A drop of crimson stained her bottom lip, taunting him. His eyes locked on it, his cock hardening even more.

"Look at me, Daciano! You took my blood?"

He forced himself to meet her gaze. The way she stared at his eyes, he knew they must be stark black with thirst. "Yes."

In a panicked tone, she said, "Can't you see a person's memories?"

Her anxiety seemed to prick at him, paining him. "I've never taken another's blood."

"Answer the question!"

"I believe I possess that ability."

"Let me go!" She thrashed against him until he released her.

Again, I surrender my prize.

Scrambling to a sitting position, she draped an arm over her breasts, shoving her braids out of her face with her free hand. "You'll see mine!" She was looking at him with disgust.

Deserved disgust. Any of his acquaintance would do the same. Trehan supposed he wasn't much different from a vile Horde vampire. Or from Lothaire, the furthest fallen of the Dacians.

And yet Trehan knew he wouldn't rest until he'd tasted her again.

From this night on, I'm a true vampire.

That raw, familiar feeling of violation rose inside Bettina. Her palms itched to unleash her power on him; she felt unwhole without it.

He could witness that night! At the thought, she nearly swayed. The humiliation of another seeing her like that . . . broken and naked on the floor of Castle

Rune's court. Coated with blood and liquor. Their laughter still ringing in her bleeding ears.

She darted for her sarong, hastily tying it in place. The vampire's gaze followed her every movement, locked on her as she worked her top over her head. But when she scurried for her cloak, he traced to his clothes, stabbing his legs into his pants.

"This would have happened eventually, Bettina. I can't control my fangs any more than I can stop myself from hardening every time I'm near you."

In a dry tone, she sneered, "Because I'm *such* a tempting siren."

Brows drawn, he rasped, *"Yes."*

Seriously undercutting my argument! "Why did I trust you? I want you out of my sight!"

"You can't leave."

"Watch me!" She dragged her cloak on, marching for the exit. But just outside his tent, her feet froze. The rain had eased somewhat, but now the fog was thick as soup, visibility nil. At least for her.

She would have to brave that murky gauntlet to reach home. Right before her eyes, shadowy buildings moved, narrowing the alleys. The street grew darker, the air thick with foreboding.

That seed of anxiety burned. Vertigo threatened. Her heart began to pound in her ears, her eyes to water. Fear was a great steel fist wringing her chest free of air.

Her bones ached, actual pain arising where her ribs had ruptured her flesh.

All too clearly, she remembered how the skin of her torso had tented over her displaced ribs—like cloth over a dull needle. *Only a matter of time.* A kick to her side had sent the needle up and through her skin. . . .

The back of her hand found her lips. *I want those four dead! Why won't they die . . . ?*

"Bettina?" The vampire was right beside her, studying her with eyes that were now steady and green.

He'd betrayed her and she couldn't even manage to leave his company, couldn't slam the tent flap in his face as she stormed off.

I hate this, I hate this, I HATE this!

"What is it, little Bride?"

Swallowing back bile, she said, "I don't . . . I don't like walking in the rain."

"Of course," he said, his expression unreadable.

He knows, he knows! Just as she'd started to shake, she found herself outside the concealed door to her castle. "Y-you traced me?"

"Bett, you never have to walk alone again."

And with just those words, her anxiety ebbed. Which infuriated her! How could he affect her so easily?

How could he have taken her blood?

Daciano could now witness scenes of her life, could see her at her lowest. He would learn of her cowardly, irrational fears.

Then she berated herself. Why should she care what he saw? Her entire court had seen her as a victim, an object of pity.

Bettina feared her *vanity* had something to do with her anger. She didn't want this handsome, devious vampire—who already seemed obsessed with her—to see her fall. Because he *liked* her, was attracted to her, seeming charmed by everything she did.

His response to her had been such a balm after Cas had admitted to feeling no attraction to her, that he'd entered the tournament because he was marked for death anyway.

Once a warrior like Daciano saw what she'd really been like—sobbing, begging for mercy—he'd disdain her as well. His lacking Bride.

And then I'll never experience him like this again. Where had *that* thought come from?

"*Dragă*," he grated, "tell me who hurt you."

When he grazed his knuckles over her cheekbone, she turned her face away.

"Very well. But I'll have one more boon from you. . . ."

Trehan waited until a light glowed from her bedroom before returning to his tent. For a loner, he found parting from her surprisingly . . . *paining*.

Inside, he picked up one of her silk gloves, left in her haste. So slim, so small. His fragile female—who'd been attacked by more than one fiend. Who still suffered.

She'd frozen outside, with her heart racing so fast he'd thought she would pass out.

Again and again, he'd reflected over the day in Dacia when he'd awakened with that unusual restlessness, that dread. He'd suspected that he'd somehow sensed her pain and terror, even when buried deep in his kingdom.

Now he was sure of it.

Instead of saving her, he'd been closed up in that coffin of a mountain, frozen in that city, that godsdamned *library*, never seeing her—never *seeking* her.

I left her to fate. Unforgivable. Her broken plea echoed in his mind. *Not again. . . .*

Tonight he'd learned much about his Bride, about her fear—and her desire.

Her desire taught him that her body—and her affections—could be won. Her fear taught him that she needed help to heal.

Trehan's plan had now transitioned and expanded. *Win the tournament, find and slaughter her enemies, capitalize on her passion.*

He'd taken her blood, the first step in locating her foes. Even though he'd never harvested memories, he assumed that he, like other Dacians before him, was a *cosaș.* Once he slept, he would dream scenes from her past, reliving them from her point of view.

I know exactly which memory of hers I need.

He traced outside once more, peering up at her room. Her light was still like a beacon, calling him.

Trehan suspected he knew who'd attacked her—if he could dream her memories of them, then it was possible that he could use the crystal to find them. No plane was safe from Trehan, no hiding place too remote.

Wrong an assassin's woman, and he will make you pay.

"Bettina of Abaddon"—he gazed upward, higher even than her spire—"your enemies' days are numbered."

"Well, well, well. The princess was out catting around," Salem said when he returned to her suites, just minutes after she had.

Shit. She hadn't yet had time to recover from the events of the night. Her lips were probably still kiss swollen, her hair even more of a mess than usual.

"Careful, else you'll get a rep." He chuckled. "Soon you'll be as notorious as me."

"And what precisely were you notorious for?"

He gave another laugh. "For how fine I looked. And for how fine I fuc—"

"Okay, then! All clear," Bettina said in a rush. *Bath time just got weirder.*

"I'm giving you an aloof yet mysterious shrug, dovey."

She rolled her eyes. "I thought you were going to be out spying all night."

"Oh, I was. For instance, I saw you in the vampire's tent, squirming against his naked body like an eel in heat."

"An *eel*?" What a fetching visual. *Yep, sexually untutored.* But the vampire hadn't had any complaints. No, he'd been full of praise. "Are you *trying* to insult me?"

"I don't make the news, I just report it."

"Reported it to Raum, no doubt?"

"I haven't yet. Any reason not to?"

She began to pace. "I thought we were *allies.*" Had she left her mask and gloves in the vampire's tent? Shit! "And it didn't *mean* anything with Daciano."

"No? Tell that to the fuck knots in your hair."

"Salem! I made a deal with the vampire that I would go see him if he spared Caspion in the melee."

"Grinding wiv a vamp to save poor ole Cas? Wow, you *are* noble. If you'd come any closer to closing that *deal,* you'd of fucked up beyond remedy. Remember, you're supposed to be a virgin? And from what I saw, Daciano was in the glide path."

How close he'd been. . . . "I have to know—are you going to tell Raum?"

"No harm, no foul. So far. I'll keep my invisible mouth shut, *if* you don't meet the leech again."

"Not—a—problem." She still couldn't believe Daciano had taken her blood.

Worse? She couldn't believe that her main problem with it was probably vanity.

Maybe he wouldn't see her memories of that night. Maybe he wouldn't see anything—because he'd die in the ring tomorrow. "Wait. Why do you care if I see him or not?"

"I'm not one to pull my telekinetic punches, Princess, so I'll tell it to you straight. After my night of spying, I'm convinced Goürlav's about to be your new gent. Which means your cherry best be unplucked."

At the thought of marrying the primordial, chills danced up her spine. The Bettina-the-Black-Widow option would fly out the window. Even if her power was returned, it wouldn't likely be enough to take Goürlav out. Not when newly restored and unpracticed. "Nobody can defeat him?"

"I found zero weaknesses. Zilch, fuck-all. None of my contacts in the network know anything either," he said. "You saw the heads rolling tonight. Think of the amount of blood someone would have to spill to take his. Barrels. It'd spawn a legion of Child Terrors."

"I'll prevail upon Morgana. There's got to be some kind of sorcery we can use."

"You do that. In the meantime . . . you were really into that leech."

Into him? Like when she'd been a split second away from orgasming against his insistent shaft?

Like when she'd tasted her own blood in their kiss and for a moment had considered just going with it? "I was there only for Caspion."

"Yeah, you looked like you were completely swamped with thoughts of Cas. By the way, that demon of yours rose a notch in my estimation."

"Oh, was his pile-driving even more vigorous than last night?"

"No. He went home. Alone."

21

*N*ight two. Well past midnight. Drunk again.

Bettina slouched over the banquet table, head propped in her hand, a glass of wine tilted precariously in her other hand. Her eyes were glazed over from watching fights for umpteen hours.

Die already, she inwardly cried for the hundredth time.

She gazed around, noting that she wasn't the only one drunk; all of Rune was in rare form.

They'd been imbibing since sundown and the demon brew was beginning to hit them, sweeping over the crowds like an apocalypse of drunk.

Initially, the ring had been divided into several different cages so the matches between less well-known contenders could occur simultaneously. Still, they'd taken ages to complete. At midnight, guards had removed the inner cages to prepare for the heavy-weight contenders like Goürlav, Daciano—and Caspion.

Pretty much all of the kingdom's females had rallied around "Abaddon's fair-haired son." Even the males were coming around.

He was slated to fight the remaining Cerunno last, and she'd been on edge all night. Goürlav's match was up next, with Daciano's bout against the giant troll to follow.

Like all the competitors, they'd been required to wait in the sanctum for hours.

Morgana had long since returned to her castle, located in her own private Sorceri plane. Early on she'd endured two matches, yawning widely, even at the gruesome ends. Assured that Bettina had dressed scantily enough to be worthy of the Sorceri name, she and her Inferi had portal-ed away.

During the ring changeover, Bettina had spied Raum escorting two pretty nymphs backstage.

Which left her all alone at the table. Winners could have come and visited her after their bouts, but they always left, never joining her at banquet. Each one intended to marry her in mere days; none of them made an effort to get to know her better.

Well, except for one. A vampire with the most sublime body she'd ever imagined—who'd provided her with the most erotic vision she'd ever witnessed.

When Cas had shown up today at sundown, she'd barely been able to look him in the eye.

He'd gone home alone the night before, trying to make it work between them, while she'd been moaning into Daciano's mouth.

But she wouldn't be seduced again. *Tonight,* she and Cas had started over. . . .

She waved for a refill, glancing over her shoulder at the other banqueters. Again the grandstand was divided between armored demons and gold-clad Sorceri.

On the demon side, the table was laden with platters of suckling pig, rack of lamb, wild boar, venison. Tankards of demon brew abounded.

Most Sorceri, however, were strict vegetarians. On their side, fruits and vegetables were arranged in elaborate platters and towers, and sweet wine flowed from crystal decanters.

Bettina definitely preferred their table. When she was young, she'd tried to eat like a demon, to have one thing in common with her subjects. She'd been as successful in that as she'd been in growing horns, getting strong, or learning to trace.

Hey, at least I can be summoned!

Different as the two groups were, both sides were sauced. The demons openly pawed the serving girls. The Sorceri flirted with their coy looks that could say a thousand things.

Most of the latter had remained to enjoy the wine, but also to watch their new favorite—the Prince of Shadow.

He was responsible for a good part of Bettina's exhaustion, for her fitful sleep over the course of the day. When she'd first drifted off, she'd suffered her usual nightmare; yet then the subject—and the nature—of her dreams had changed.

In reverie, her mind had replayed the night with him. She'd relived endless kisses and slippery hot flesh. She'd eagerly revisited that image of him standing before her clad only in firelight.

Over and over, she'd awakened on the verge of orgasm.

A day of sensual torture. Yet she'd been unable to do anything about it, because of the last shocking favor Daciano had asked of her.

Don't touch yourself.

She'd been flabbergasted. "Pardon?"

"Over the day, if you feel need, don't act on it. That's the favor I want from you. Then you'll owe me only two boons."

"Why would you want this?"

"So you will crave me as I do you."

"More plots, more plans?"

"When the prize is so dear . . ."

Sensual. Torture.

He'd kissed her, aroused her to the brink of release, then forbidden any relief. She didn't know how she was going to face him tonight.

Maybe I should pull for the troll.

Trehan wanted to begin his match—so he could end it. At last it neared, next after Goürlav's.

He was keen to see his Bride once more, to determine whether she'd kept her end of their final bargain last night.

He'd caught only a glimpse of her as the tournament had begun. She'd narrowed her eyes at him, seeming particularly irritable—not the demeanor of a sexually satisfied female.

Yet Trehan hadn't been able to talk to her, compelled by his contract to join the other competitors in these dank catacombs.

Water seeped from slimy stones. Kobolds hissed and scurried in the distance. Crude benches had been carved into the walls. Male voices echoed throughout this labyrinth, voices tinged with fear or bravado.

Trehan said nothing to his opponents, instead re-living the day he'd spent—a day of need and denial.

He hadn't accessed her memories yet, because he hadn't slept. Uneasy away from her, he'd returned to her room, just for a glimpse of her sleeping to tide him over until sunset. He'd found her in a fitful sleep, her brows drawn as a nightmare tormented her.

Wrapping her in mist, he'd secretly lain beside her in the darkness of her curtained bed. Her silken locks had haloed out over silken sheets, her lips parted so temptingly.

As he'd stared at her face, he'd been overwhelmed with feeling, as if centuries of yearning had risen in a single moment:

I want her draped in mist, under my protection. I want her in my bed, gazing up at me with those glittering eyes as I enter her. I want her pleasured cries in my ear and her blood upon my tongue. . . .

Yet then her dreams had grown sensual. She'd raised her slim arms over her head, spreading her legs, her hips rocking, rocking . . . until she'd awakened in the dark with a gasp, on the verge, having no idea he was less than a foot away.

His fangs had shot as hard as his shaft, just as un-controllable. He'd wanted both buried inside her.

In the past, he'd observed Horde vampires blood-taking in deranged attacks. Needless to say, the victims hadn't enjoyed it. But what if Trehan took Bettina's lei-surely, painstakingly?

There were females rumored to find pleasure from a male's bite. He'd wondered, *Could* my *female?* It would be a perfect exchange. *She'd give me blood, and I'd make her come. . . .*

At that thought, it'd taken every ounce of his control not to reach for her. But she was already angered with him. Finding him in her bed would only add to her pique. So he'd clenched his fists and suffered with her, telling himself she would be sorely in need this eve, and he could use that to his advantage.

When she'd drifted back to sleep, the same thing had happened again and again.

He couldn't plant dreams—he was no dream demon—but apparently the mist had brought him to mind.

Trehan *hoped*. If he even supposed that those hungry little moans had been for Caspion . . .

Once she'd awakened for good, he'd forced himself to leave, wondering if she could possibly refrain from caressing her trembling body. From masturbating her sex during her bath.

Delicate pale fingers against rosy flesh.

When he began to grow hard—even in this foul place—he shook his head. *Focus, Trehan! Concentrate on the task at hand. Study your opponents.*

He peered across the dingy corridor, gaze landing on the troll. Armed with a massive club, the creature was large but lumbering, with foot-long bristles dotting his body. Not exactly threatening. Yet Trehan had noticed in the melee that weapons had *shattered* against those bristles. They must be as strong as titanium—and dozens of them sprouted from its throat.

Trehan thought he spied a sliver of space between them. Basically he'd have to slice his sword perfectly—through an opening the width of his flat blade.

If he missed and his sword broke, he didn't know how he could relieve the troll's body of its head.

One shot.

With a mental shrug, Trehan turned his attention to Goürlav, hoping to spy some weakness. Yet the demon merely leaned back against a wall, eyes closed, breathing deep and even.

Trehan could glean little, other than the fact that the pre-demon's body had been made for war. A rippled plate of bone covered its heart; those tusks hung down from its chin, protecting its neck like a shield. Three pairs of horns only added more protection. Even its green eyelids were thick, doubled over with many scaly folds. All vulnerabilities defended.

How to deliver an immortal death blow—without spilling a single drop of blood?

There had to be a solution. Every conundrum had one. *What I wouldn't give to research this in my library.* He rubbed his palm over his nape, feeling another's gaze.

Ah, Caspion studies me. Though incredibly young—not much older than Bettina—the demon wasn't without skill. Trehan suspected he would advance far in the tournament.

Trying to uncover my weaknesses, whelp?

In times past, Trehan had few. If the sun threatened to burn his skin, he'd always been able to turn to mist. Now he had to keep that talent hidden. Fortunately, he also possessed the ability to half-trace: manifesting himself just enough to be visible—and poised to attack—yet still insubstantial enough for the sun's rays to pass through him.

No, Trehan's greatest weakness was one brand-new to him: any threat to his Bride.

Caspion chose that moment to trace in front of him. "You often take advantage of innocent young females, old man? Stealing into their bedrooms?"

"Not one in an eternity." Trehan viewed him as he might an annoying insect. "You feel misplaced anger toward me. I've done nothing to you. Yet."

"You sneaked into the room of my best friend and future wife, compromising her."

"Future wife?" *Control your anger, Trehan, lest it control you.* "And how would your fated demon mate feel about your marriage to another?"

"You're a prick, Daciano. No wonder Bettina hates you."

Hates me? "So you *know* she's not yours. She indicated to me that you hadn't planned to enter—did you change your mind to avoid my sword for mere days?"

"I entered *for her*. And we won't know if she's mine until I bed her for the first time."

The idea of them together enraged Trehan. His fangs went sharp as he imagined her saying those words to Caspion: *You can do anything to me.*

Calm! Control! "You and I both know you won't get out of this tournament alive, boy. I had to save your forsaken life in the first godsdamned round. I could have ended you then."

"I had that under control!" His horns straightened with aggression. "And the only reason you helped me is because you want to kill me yourself."

Trehan had helped solely for an advantage with Bettina. *Considering last night, I'd do it again.* "Right now I very much wish to kill you myself."

"If you do that, you'll devastate Bettina."

"Which is regrettable. Luckily, as you pointed out, she's young. I'll make sure she recovers." *Why am I baiting him?*

"She loves *me*. She always will. She might be your Bride, but she'll never be your wife."

Trehan clutched his sword hilt, fury burning inside him. *Control your anger. Control your instinct.*

His rational mind knew Caspion had no fated claim on Bettina. After this conversation, Trehan also knew that the demon didn't feel love for her—at least, not romantic love.

But his heated instincts still demanded satisfaction, a swift death as punishment. Since encountering Bettina, Trehan had been inundated with a ferocity unlike any he'd ever known.

Control . . . control. Inhale. Exhale.

The horn blared then. Ignoring Caspion, Trehan turned his attention to Goürlav, due to fight the young animus demon this round.

Goürlav eased his massive body to his feet. Had he been slow to move initially? Had his primordial joints creaked?

Or was he feigning weakness?

Instead of tracing, Goürlav stomped from the sanctum to the ring, his horns scraping the top of the twelve-foot-high entryway, gouging the rock. His horns were unmarked.

The animus demon followed with leaden feet. Sweat covered the male's pallid face. When the iron gate closed behind them, he lost control of his bladder.

Trehan traced to the gate to watch the bout. Caspion made a frustrated sound and followed.

Just outside the ring, a cadre of Rune's soldiers had gathered, readying to fight Child Terrors, should any arise from Goürlav's blood. They needn't have bothered.

As the match began, so would it end—abruptly.

With one blow, Goürlav sliced his opponent from

balls to scalp. Another sword strike took both halves of his victim's head.

Goürlav gave a monstrous roar to the sky then disappeared, likely returning to whatever hell dimension he ruled.

Trehan glanced at Caspion, finding the young male's eyes narrowed, his expression determined. Trehan imagined them both sharing a singular thought: *I will do anything to keep that creature from Bettina.*

22

The vampire's match was next.

Once Rune's guards had cleaned up the remains of Goürlav's opponent—who'd been halved like ripe fruit—Daciano and the troll entered the ring.

The vampire was dressed all in black, again in tailored pieces of obvious expense. Bettina alone knew what he concealed beneath those garments.

His unique sword was at his side. His one *cold* weapon.

The troll was at least a dozen feet tall, wearing what looked like the largest—and rattiest—toga Bettina had ever seen. It thumped its spiked tail aggressively, but Daciano ignored his opponent, instead gazing up at her, alone at her table.

His lips were thinned with intent; she now knew how sensual they could be.

Bettina wasn't even surprised when that electric thrill coursed through her body. So she pointedly ignored him, hiding her face behind the rim of her over-size goblet.

As soon as the gate clanged shut, the troll raised his club in the vampire's direction, spitting the words: "I'm going to gut you and feed on your entrails! I'll take your head and suck on it like a sweet!"

The horn sounded. At once, the troll swung; Daciano feinted left and dodged the blow.

"And then I'll slurp from your gullet!"

Daciano moved right and struck so fast, she couldn't see the flash of his sword.

Blood began to seep around the troll's bristly neck like a crimson scarf. The creature's expression was one of shock as its body and its head crashed to the ground with all the grace of a demolished building.

The crowd went silent. She saw others around her blinking, as if they hadn't seen the fight correctly. Daciano had dispatched his opponent with one blow, and not a drop of blood on his immaculate clothing.

After a stunned moment, the Sorceri cheered.

Again, the vampire gave Bettina a formal bow, acknowledging the prize.

She scowled. She didn't like the effect he had on her, didn't like how out-of-control her body felt, while he appeared completely self-possessed.

He wiped his sword on the troll's toga, sheathed it, then traced to Bettina. When he took the seat beside her, Sorceri on the grandstand cheered again. It seemed to take him a moment to realize their fanfare was for him.

The muscles in his neck tensed, his unease noticeable.

The secret assassin who'd been *naught but death* was quickly becoming a celebrity. How odd that must be for him. Over his shoulder, Bettina spied other Sorceri females gazing at him with blatant attraction.

Which irritated her. *For no reason!*

He took her hand, pressing a gentle kiss to the palm, making her gasp. At her ear, he murmured, "You worked off a boon over the day. Good girl."

Was it that obvious? She felt her cheeks go hot. Delicately clearing her throat, she asked, "A vampire taking a seat at a banquet? What exactly do you intend to eat?"

His smoldering gaze landed on her neck. Had he just run his tongue over one fang?

She almost shivered. "Don't even think about taking my blood again. I'm still pissed at you."

In truth, she couldn't muster much anger over that. He *had* tried to warn her, and it wasn't like he'd pierced her neck.

Since last night, her outrage over his taking had cooled to . . . curiosity? Maybe even titillation? Whenever she recalled his reaction to her taste, she experienced a forbidden thrill. *"Dulcea!"* he'd groaned. Sweet.

If he did harvest her memories, then the damage was already done. She told herself yet again, *Don't cry over spilled blood.*

Or maybe she was just drunk.

"I apologize, Bettina. I have little control with you."

Me, Bettina the Freakling, making a centuries-old vampire lose control. She sighed. *Delicious.*

"As for this banquet, I *can* eat," he said. "And drink wine." He took *her* glass and drank a healthy swallow before handing it back. Proprietary. *Perception is reality.* "I'll do both if it makes you feel more comfortable."

Daciano was all charm again this eve, looking handsome and noble. She was immune. She *was*. Damn it, she was starting fresh with Cas. From *this* minute on.

She would not let this vampire plant any more doubt. Because today, when she'd tried to picture *Caspion* straight out of the bath, she'd seen nothing but deep green eyes, black hair, and a chiseled body wracked with vampiric lust.

Daciano could make her doubt her own heart, if she let him! "Comfortable, vampire? Trying to close the gap on all our many differences?"

"Yes."

Flustered, she glanced at the program for the night. The next fight was between two fire demons. She didn't care either way who won that meet. In fact, the only rounds she cared about were Cas's, the vampire's, Goürlav's, and, weirdly—the Lykae's.

She didn't understand why the wolf couldn't restrain the beast inside him. All the Lykae males she'd met before had been brimming with sensual charm, hot Scotsmen with wicked grins and a repertoire of clever innuendo.

But this creature was brimming with pain and confusion. Earlier when it'd won its match against a rage demon, it had begun to feed on the demon's corpse. Cloaked warlocks had drugged the Lykae and hauled it away. Its handlers. Disgusting.

And there was nothing she could do about it. The powerless queen. In more than one regard.

When she waved for a refill, Daciano frowned. "Do you always drink so much?"

"No, but if it bothers you, I'll drink much more often." She thanked the attendant.

"I can use it to my advantage."

At the rim of her goblet, she said, "Oh, and how's that?"

"You're soon to see. Now, tell me, what creation have you this eve?" he asked, lifting her hand, examining the sizable ring on her forefinger.

Normally she took every opportunity to talk about her lethal luxe, even as people's eyes glazed over, but her tone was put out as she explained, "Standard-issue toxin delivery." She'd created a flip-top reservoir on the bottom of the band.

Most Sorceri owned at least one poison ring. Her kind were talented toxinians—who didn't hesitate to practice their craft. She demonstrated the function for Daciano, turning her palm up and flipping the lid on the full powder well.

"So you would dump that in someone's drink?"

"Yes, or I could blow the poison into someone's eyes, like I was blowing a kiss." Exactly the reason why mimicking a blown kiss was a heinous insult to Sorceri.

"The craftsmanship's flawless." He appeared proud. Yet then his expression grew lustful, as if his pride had only stimulated his desire. "Planning to poison someone?"

"One leech is making the short list."

"My clever sorceress has a tart tongue this eve." Leaning closer, he rasped at her ear, "When last night it was so exquisitely sweet."

Not going to fan myself. Wine! *Gulp.*

"Come back to my tent."

"Why would I do that?"

"For a time, you enjoyed yourself there."

Enjoyed? Understatement. For a time, she'd been crazed with lust. Just remembering his hard, damp chest against her breasts made her nipples tighten under her bandeau top.

Apparently he noticed, because he had to clear his throat before saying, "And it's still your turn, Bett."

Turn? What did he— *Oh!* She flushed, wishing she'd worn a full face covering instead of a narrow bandit-style mask. Her pink cheeks were on display for all to see. "You like embarrassing me."

"I'm a vampire—naturally I'm going to love it when blood heats your cheeks." Before she could pull back, he'd grazed the backs of his fingers below her mask. "It's beautiful. *You* are beautiful."

He can't lie. Wait, speaking of mask . . . "I left things in your tent. I need them back."

"Impossible."

"Your squire could find them!"

"They remain secure in my possession."

What could he possibly want with them—

"Did you dream of me when you slept?" he asked.

She raised a startled glance to him. "What? N-no!"

His lips curled. "Liar."

"And what about you?" she demanded. "Did you dream my memories?"

"I didn't sleep. I haven't since I met you."

"That's not good for your tournament."

"You saw me fight. Did you see any ill effects?"

"You're arrogant."

"I'm Dacian. You can't have one without the other."

She wondered what he'd done today instead of sleeping. Had he found another to relieve him of that erection? Judging by Caspion's past example, she assumed males had sex every night without fail. "And how did you occupy yourself during the daylight hours?" Had her tone been arch? She raised her glass.

"I spent the day with my Bride."

She nearly choked on her wine. "You wouldn't dare come to my room while I slept!"

He merely raised his brows.

"Does my barrier spell do nothing?" Great, to live without protection, high in the sky where the Vrekeners ruled!

"It's imperfect. But for others it would be sufficient."

"And what exactly did you do with me today?" She could only imagine. Had he seen how her dreams had affected her?

"I lay beside you and shared your suffering. You're desirous, *dragă*," he rasped, his accented words making her melt. "Come with me, and I'll pleasure you till you scream."

When her mind started to blank again, she gave her head a sharp shake. "Caspion is about to fight in the next heat. I'd never abandon him with no support."

A bitter laugh. "Won't his throng of female admirers *support* him?"

"He's escorting *me* home afterward. We have a date."

"A date?" Daciano bit out. "You have no bond with him. Though I can scarcely comprehend it, he doesn't want you in the way I do."

Again, was it so obvious? "Why would you say that?" Could everyone see it?

"He was in a brothel two nights ago. In Dacia, he had a new maid every night."

"Caspion and I are starting anew. We discussed it today. He considers us betrothed from now on. Therefore I *will* be waiting here for him."

"And I will be damned before he enjoys a passion I stoked."

"I'm not leaving this table, vampire." *No matter how seductive you are.* "If you try to trace me back to your tent, I'll introduce you to the weapons I *didn't* show you." A dagger strapped to her ankle, for one.

"Then you leave me no choice."

"What does that mean—" She jerked upright when she felt the vampire's callused palm at her knee. She tried to pry it away, but he was far too strong. She had to settle for clamping her legs together.

"It seems I'll have to pleasure you here."

"Stop this!" she hissed when he began making lazy circles high on her thigh.

"You have the softest skin, sorceress. Are all the females of your kind so soft as this?"

"Go find out. Your . . . Bride gives you a pass. Just leave me alone."

She didn't want his touch; apparently her body disagreed. Her nipples hardened even more, her breaths shallowing. She squirmed in her seat, dismayed to find her panties were growing moist. Her clamped legs seemed to weaken, the muscles lax.

How could he affect her so quickly? Yes, she'd had dreams of him, and yes, he'd taken her to the very verge two nights in a row—but they were surrounded by people! "I-I draw the line, vampire." The indignant tone she'd attempted fell flat.

He gave her that indulgent look. "You'll learn that there is no line between a vampire and his Bride." As his hand trailed higher, he murmured, "I can feel you tremble. It won't take much to bring you over the edge. I'll ease this ache and have you relaxed and sated in my arms."

He wanted to make her come—right here? "You're mad." Then she bit her lip. *To be fair, I do ache.*

No! "Someone will see."

"My hand isn't the only one busy under a table, I promise you." All around them, couples were furtively touching. "No one is paying attention to us."

"Y-you care nothing about my reputation!" she cried. "This isn't fair."

"As I said before, the prize is too dear for me to fight fair. Doesn't it feel good, *dulcea mea*?"

My sweet. In a hazy part of her brain, she wondered if he called her that as an endearment or if he was referring to her taste again. "You know it feels good, but someone will notice."

"So my touching you isn't the issue. It's just that you don't want others to see."

"You're twisting my—I never said that." She was already panting, her breasts swelling. The peaks jutted lewdly beneath her top. She clutched the tablecloth in her fists.

He worked his hand between her legs, but didn't force them open. "Spread your thighs and let me give you pleasure," he rasped. "Come, Bett, I won't stop until you're writhing from it."

"Daciano, please, you can't do this here."

"Shh, shh." His soothing murmurs only heightened her arousal. "I left you unsatisfied, and I vow to you that I never will again."

She squeezed her eyes shut. This male wanted to give her hot, wet, bliss—and gods help her, she craved it.

"Open your eyes, *dragă*. Now no one can see us."

Mist had filled the grandstand. She couldn't see anyone but him. They might as well be alone, cocooned in the sensual heat surrounding them. It dotted her skin, glittering like dew in the morning.

"You are part of it, Bettina." Again he sounded proud.

Something was affecting her. One second she felt like she was floating, the next like she was tethered hard to the male beside her.

He dragged her across his legs, settling her sideways over his lap. With his arms wrapped around her, she felt almost a sense of relief, as if she'd yearned to be even closer to him.

Yes, tethered even more tightly to this vampire. . . .

"Open for me." Her legs eased a touch wider; he growled low with approval.

Then his hand glided higher, rucking her skirt to the side. She held her breath as his fingers began delving into her panties. Strange—she thought he was holding his breath too.

When his fingers slipped to her sex, he groaned at her ear, *"Wet, so fucking wet."*

Struggling not to whimper, she bit her lip again.

"Woman, you madden me"—he ripped her panties free with one forceful yank—"at every turn."

"Vampire! Don't . . ." She trailed off—because he'd begun to stroke her.

With infinite tenderness, he rubbed his thumb up and down her clitoris, the rest of his fingers teasing her opening.

Nothing could possibly feel this good. She needed more. *How to get more?*

"I love how sensual you are, Bride. Even now you're rocking to my fingers, as if I'd petted you like this a thousand times."

Am I? She gazed down, shamelessly watching him fondle her bared sex. With his thumb making slick circles, he crooked his forefinger, breaching her only with his knuckle. And it was—

Rapture.

"Ah, gods," she whispered. Sure enough, she was slowly undulating to his touch, wanting it deeper, the pressure greater.

"You'll do that when you're beneath me," he promised her. "Look how hard your little nipples strain against your top." She felt a ghosting sweep of fingertips across them, making her shiver. "Did you like when I sucked them?"

His words and his sinful voice worked together, stoking her desire like a forge. "Vampire, you really want me to . . . to . . . *here*?"

"Yes. Tell me you'll let me do anything to you."

Her brows drew together. "You know I can't say that, can't allow that."

"One day you will."

Why were those words so important to him?

"For now, you'll come for me." The wicked things he was doing to her . . . pressure right at her core, then a tickling sensation, then more pressure.

When her head lolled, he cradled the back of it with his free hand. Holding her so gently, he brought his forehead to hers, pinning her gaze with his own— as if he wouldn't *let* her look away.

The intensity of his eyes, the need in them . . . she found herself tunneling her fingers into his thick hair, clutching him close.

"Open for your male, Bett," he said, his voice hoarse. Below, his fingers continued their play.

She surrendered completely, mindlessly spreading her thighs for the vampire.

The pleasure was so great she feared its end. Eyes pleading, she whispered, "You won't stop?"

"Never, *dragă*."

"But what if I cry out?"

"I can make your release softer, less intense. Would you like that?"

In a miserable tone, she said, *"Nooo."*

He gave a strained chuckle. "I didn't think so."

She was panting—half panicked, half *out of her mind* with lust. "Daciano, it's so strong. . . . Oh, gods, I *am* going to scream. I-I won't be able to stop."

"Press your mouth against my neck."

She laid her hands on his chest, leaning her face closer. . . . Against her lips, she perceived the smoothness of his skin. His vampire scent was just as drugging as it'd been last night, making her moan.

When she buried her face in the crook where his neck met his shoulder and inhaled deeply, a sound rumbled from deep in his chest. She felt it beneath her clutching palms.

With each of his strokes, she moaned against his neck harder and harder. She parted her lips, licking his delicious skin.

The *taste* of him sent her right to the edge, hovering. . . .

23

Trehan was in an agony of bliss. He was about to bring his Bride to come for the first time in their lives. His cock felt like it'd explode. And she'd just started *licking his skin.*

His head fell back as his fingers stroked her. The heel of his palm rested on her tiny thatch of hair, her folds plump and slick in his hold. *My gods, her tongue is* flicking *against me.*

Teeth clenched, he gazed upward, fantasies tangling in his mind. He imagined her hot little tongue, pictured her tracing it over the very tip of one aching fang. Or tucking it against his sac as she masturbated him with her soft hand. Or dragging it along the length of his shaft as her eyes gazed up and held his.

"Vampire," she whispered with a wet swirl that had his hips bucking, grinding against her lush bottom. "Need . . . to . . . *scream.* . . ."

"I'll take care of you, Bett. Just let it come." Right before her cry burst from her, he splayed the fingers of his free hand over one side of her face, cupping her head closer, pressing her mouth harder against him to muffle the sound.

Her body stiffened. Her lithe muscles tightened so beautifully. Her fingernails bit into his chest. Then . . .

Release.

She bucked to his fingers, screaming against his neck.

When he felt the entrance to her sheath clamp around his knuckle, his cock surged in his pants, desperate to claim that virgin flesh.

As she writhed, his fangs went sharp as blades. *What would it hurt to graze them over the pale curve of her shoulder, the swell of her sweet breast . . . ?*

At the idea of piercing one little mound, he nearly lost his seed, but he refused to repeat his shame from their first night together.

When she could come no more, she pushed at his hand. After a few last fleeting strokes, he finally relented, removing it from her drenched sex.

The impulse to lick his fingers again was undeniable.

Her taste! *"Mieroase rai,"* he groaned against his fingertips. Honeyed heaven.

Inhale. Exhale. Control. This was for her. *Only for her.* Control.

As they both sat catching their breath, she leaned her head against him—allowing him to hold her. He didn't ponder his fortune, just rested his cheek against her forehead. He was surprised by how satisfied he felt—when his shaft throbbed just beneath her.

Yes, satisfied. And proud. *I've waited lifetimes to do that.* With each of her shivery aftershocks, his shoulders went back farther.

"No one saw?"

He pressed a tender kiss to her hair. "No one, love. They'll believe a fog bank rolled in. In a moment, I'll make it fade."

"But I . . . there were sounds—"

"That carry differently. Anyone nearby was too busy taking advantage of the cover of mist, I assure you."

"Okay." To his astonishment, she nestled closer to him. Just as he'd promised, she was relaxed and sated in his arms.

In moments, she'd be angry, the spell broken. For now, he squeezed her body close, savoring every second.

He found himself musing, *Why not this place? Why not me?* She could be his queen, and they could share this realm. He hadn't given the crown of the Deathly Ones much consideration, but now he had to wonder.

Perhaps I could still be the sword of a kingdom, another *kingdom.* All this could be theirs. *Not such a bad fate at all.* No more constantly watching his back, no more looming battles.

Bettina finally drew back, her heavy-lidded eyes sparkling and her red lips curling, as if she'd forgotten where she was—and whom she was with.

She looked adorably drowsy and tipsy, her mask atilt; he wasn't even surprised when his heart thudded like a stack of books dropped from a height.

"Look how smug you are, vampire."

"Am I then? Know that you can be smug for the rest of the night, while I'm still limping from this agonizing erection." He rocked it against her.

"Oh!" Her face flamed. "It's nothing less than you deserve. I hope it stays that way." She scowled. "Or something else, *worse*—"

The great horn sounded, signaling the end of the fire demons' match.

"Cas!" At once, she shoved against Trehan, trying to shimmy away from him.

With a vile Dacian curse, he let her, giving her a few seconds to straighten her clothing before he waved his hand, gradually clearing the air.

Spell broken. Now he needed to concentrate on another aspect of his plan. *Will I be able to stay away from her long enough to prepare . . . ?*

After soldiers removed the charred, headless corpse of the loser, Caspion marched into the ring. The crowd cheered even louder than they had last night.

Trehan had noticed that the demon's standard—one curved horn wrapped in some kind of vine—now adorned many of the shopkeepers' windows.

A clearly inebriated Raum returned to the grandstand, tankard attached to his meaty hand, clothing in disarray. He frowned at Bettina and Trehan sitting together. She shrugged helplessly.

After a hard look at Trehan, Raum quaffed his drink, then announced, "And next we have our own Caspion the Tracker, beloved son of Abaddon!"

At that, so many demonesses tossed their garters at the ring that it soon had a ceiling of lace. Bettina looked like she could barely control her jealousy.

Something else we've in common.

Caspion hammed it up for the audience, raising his sword. They went wild.

And what would this crowd sound like if Trehan was the one who slew him? Sentiment so strong could be turned around, but only by a far more charismatic leader than Trehan.

And what if I can't turn her *sentiment from the demon?* He had many advantages over Caspion: age, strength, wisdom. Bettina valued none of these things.

Caspion's words played in his mind. *She might be your Bride, but she'll never be your wife.* And perhaps, deep down, a small part of Trehan feared the demon might be right.

Yet there's one thing I can do for her. One thing to win her. . . .

When Caspion's challenger, the remaining Cerunno, slithered into the ring, Bettina's nervousness redoubled.

Trehan could hear her heart racing for that demon. *And I envy him every beat.*

As Raum announced Cas's competitor, Bettina turned up her glass. Now she was drunk *and* disgusted with herself.

She was supposed to be here supporting Cas. Instead, she'd been letting a vampire give her a mind-scrambling orgasm.

And just as memorable as the experience? How Daciano had looked afterward. His shoulders had been back, his lips curving. His tousled black hair had tumbled over his forehead.

His onyx eyes had been *devilish*.

If she'd thought that vision of him stepping from the tub had been sexy, that look . . . those eyes . . .

Oh, how had this night gotten so out of hand? In close proximity were the male she hoped to marry and the first male to give her an orgasm. If only they were one and the same!

She motioned for another refill.

"You feel guilt?" the vampire asked under his breath.

"Of course I feel disloyal to Caspion now."

He didn't like that answer at all. Between clenched teeth, he said, "Remember that if it weren't for his selfishness and shortsightedness, you wouldn't be in this position. *He* brought me to your kingdom." Then, seeming to rein in his temper, he added, "You don't have to watch this. Come away with me."

"You can't expect me to leave?"

"Yes. I can. You are mine, Bettina. We are fated. We've shared blood between us, *pleasure* between us. You've come against my palm and I in yours."

She grew flustered yet again. She couldn't deny the truth of his words, but that didn't matter right now. "If you think I could be anywhere but here at this moment, then you don't know me at all."

Raum swerved back to the table, then gave the signal.

The horn sounded. Caspion and the Cerunno faced off.

Caspion's horns had straightened with hostility, his sigh-worthy countenance now fierce.

But the Cerunno was so powerful, its muscles rippling beneath its scales.

"You worry for naught," Daciano told her. "Unfortunately, your demon will win this match. Even more unfortunate, he'll advance far in this tournament."

"How can you be so certain?"

"He's strong for his age and will get stronger with each kill. He's not without technical skill."

Never taking her eyes off the ring, she said, "But not on par with yours."

"No. Not with mine."

"And you'll use all that skill to kill him."

"If pitted against him."

When Cas narrowly dodged the Cerunno's first sword strike, she gasped. She could *feel* the vampire's eyes on her, but this was Cas! *Of course* she would react.

A second swing by the snake. Another close miss. Cas's tracing helped, but the Cerunno was lightning fast.

Bettina began wringing her hands in her lap. She chanced a quick glance at Daciano, found his face suddenly inscrutable—but, oh, his eyes were black as night.

"If you don't want to witness my worry, then leave," she murmured, her attention back on the fight.

He didn't reply.

Why wasn't Cas trying to strike the Cerunno? She knew he was better than this! She turned to Raum, assessing his expression. His craggy brow was furrowed. *Not good.*

The Cerunno charged again; finally Cas defended. Their swords clanged in the night, once and again. Sparks leapt when metal kissed metal. As the two males circled each other, the great torches illuminated Cas's sweating face and the Cerunno's shimmering scales. Neither could gain the advantage.

Then she noticed the snake's tail was elongating, creeping up behind Cas while he concentrated on deflecting sword strikes.

Just when she was about to yell, "Look out!" other spectators beat her to it. Cas tried to trace too late. The serpentine tail had already wrapped around his legs and hips, holding him in place. He fought to hack his way free, but the snake's sword warded off each blow.

All the while its tail coiled higher and higher around Cas's torso, constricting, weakening him.

Bettina watched in disbelief as the Cerunno clamped its own arms around Cas's, crushing his body until Cas's beautiful face flushed with blood, veins bulging in his temples.

"Ah, gods, no. Raum, do something!"

Cas slumped, his arms going limp. His sword clattered to the ground.

"No. No. *No!* Raum!"

"I'm so sorry, Tina." He laid his hand over Bettina's. "Look away, m'girl."

Powerless, she could do nothing but watch as Caspion was crushed in that hideous creature's grip. "No. This can't be happening!" *What I wouldn't give for my power!*

To Raum, Daciano grated, "You give him too little credit, demon."

Bettina clung to the vampire's words. He was the expert, he would know if Cas was doomed—

Like a shot, Cas twisted his head, raking one sharpened horn across the Cerunno's throat. Blood spurted from its severed jugular.

Forced to stanch the flow, the Cerunno eased its grip enough for Cas to trace to his sword. With a roar, Cas swung.

The Cerunno's head hurtled high across the ring. The shocked crowd erupted into cheers.

Bettina sagged, her eyes watering.

Raum gave a bellow of relief and joined the cheering, not even attempting to appear unbiased.

As Cas caught his breath, he managed a grin, eventually recovering enough to raise his mottled arms over his head and egg the spectators on. He was loving the attention so much that she couldn't prevent her lips from curling.

Her glorious Cas. She was so proud of his victory, happy that he was happy.

Daciano broke the spell. "Bettina, there is a limit."

Without looking at him, she asked, "What does that mean?"

He took her hand, smoothly returning her panties. "One day you'll convince me that you'll always want him." Just before he traced away, he murmured in her ear, "Take care, lest you lose a male who'll desire only you—and gain a male who'll desire only others."

24

Discovering more about Bettina was critical—because Trehan was failing to coax her attentions away from that fucking demon.

He traced back to his tent, his mind focused on the task ahead: access her memories.

Which meant sleep. He was running out of time to complete all the things left for him to do. If he'd turned his back on his kingdom only to lose his Bride as well . . . ? To have neither in his life?

He would have no identity. No future. *I will not be who I was.*

Nor who I want to be.

Must sleep. Removing his sword, he lay back on his bed, struggling to dictate the direction of his thoughts. *Do* not *replay how she looked coming in your hand, Trehan. For gods sakes, do* not *revisit the slick heat you just reveled in.*

But her scent lingered on the furs, tantalizing him. Last night, her hair had fanned out over his bed as he'd rocked his shaft against her sex.

When only the hot, soaked silk of her panties had barred him entrance to her core . . .

Too much! He groaned, his shaft straining against the confines of his pants. Once he unfastened them and his length sprang free, he grunted in relief.

He took one of Bettina's gloves and wrapped the cool silk around his aching length, pretending it was her palm gripping him. *Should've kept her panties.*

As he began to stroke, he fantasized that she told him, *"You know you can do anything to me, Trehan. I'm yours—I always will be."*

Only to him would she make those promises. . . .

His fangs sharpened, dripping in his mouth for her. He dragged his tongue over them, sucking on his blood, pretending it was hers.

Like a true vampire.

Trehan had begun remembering more from his youth; as a lad, he'd stroked himself to fantasies of sinking his fangs into a trembling female while coming inside her. He recalled that particular fantasy could make him ejaculate until his back bowed.

Now he imagined piercing Bettina's slim neck. *Drawing her scorching essence into me as she writhed from her orgasm. Her sex would squeeze my cock with greedy tugs. As she gave her blood, her body would demand my seed—*

When he began to spend, he yelled her name; his back bowed violently.

When he wiped himself clean and redressed, he shuddered, grieved to be parted from her.

When he drifted to sleep, he knew he'd dream of her.

My memories? Or hers?

He woke not even an hour later, straight from reverie. Though he hadn't experienced the memory he'd sought, he'd seen something he could scarcely describe.

The world through Bettina's eyes.

Her memories were . . . sublime. She noted details he would have missed, searching out beauty in everything from a spider's web to a weathered basket. When he compared her way of seeing to his, he felt as if he had a layer of film over his eyes.

He *was* awakening. After living so long as staid, boring Trehan, he craved more.

He'd also learned much about her personality, confirming all the facets he'd already admired. Indeed, she was remarkably intelligent, she was sensitive, and *zeii,* she was lusty.

That night in his tent, she'd viewed *him* with an artist's eye. And she'd liked what she saw. Just as he'd observed, she'd been *happy.*

She'd marveled at his erection, musing what it would be like to part her lips for it and touch the tip with her tongue. She'd wondered if he would shudder and groan.

Yes, Bettina. Yes, I would.

He groaned now, just from the thought of it.

During that day he'd spent with her, as she'd slept, she *had* dreamed of Trehan. She was intrigued by him, reluctantly attracted to him. She'd absently thought of his eyes, *I've seen that color green before. In the deepest forests of Abaddon.*

If only Caspion didn't stand between them.

Trehan also had some of her memories of that demon. Caspion had saved her from a lonely and friendless childhood, accepting her as others in her kingdom hadn't. He and Bettina had traveled all over the mortal realm, exploring together.

Jealousy clawed at Trehan. *I should be the one to show her the world.*

As he sifted through his dreams, other memories arose. He'd learned that she resided with a phantom warrior. One who spied on her bathing? The fuck that would continue!

And Trehan had seen the dynamics of her relationship with her godparents. She'd once thought, "Why do I topple over whenever they push? Because I've never found my footing?"

He'd even experienced her using her power. A little over a year ago, two ghouls had gotten loose in Rune, cornering her in an alley. Instead of being frightened, she'd blasted them with her power, stopping their hearts. Starved of blood, their organs had shut down. The creatures had thrashed on the ground, howling with agony.

The memory had been so intense that Trehan now splayed his fingers, feeling his palms tingle as if he himself had wielded her power.

That innate sorcery *had* been like her soul. It'd been so intrinsic that magic would emanate from her body whenever she'd experienced strong emotions. Heated whirls of light had marked her happiness, her excitement.

Now . . . nothing.

Trehan had to get it back for her. *Or,* he thought darkly, *help her steal another Sorceri's.* What *wouldn't* Trehan do for her?

A fiery arrow to the temple? There was no recovery from it.

But he still lacked the memory of her attack. *I must see what happened to my Bride.*

To find her foes and make them pay—

He sensed another's presence inside the tent. Eyes flashing open, hand shooting for his weapon, he traced to his feet. "You won't catch me unawares, Viktor. Cease trying."

His cousin materialized in front of him. "That's not my intention. Remember, I'm in no rush to kill you now."

Trehan didn't even argue the impossibility of Viktor managing to do that. "We still have a blood vendetta between us." *An inherited one, but all the same.*

"That's the thing about vendettas. There's literally no expiration date." He tsked at Trehan's appearance. "You look like hell, old man."

Understandable. He'd had little sleep and less blood. When he'd tried to drink a meal earlier, he'd spat out the contents of his goblet. He feared all blood would be tasteless after Bettina's. "Are you here for a reason?"

"Truce for the eve. I'm here because I need your assistance."

Trehan glanced at him with surprise. Viktor simply didn't ask for help. *This ought to be good.*

Another male voice sounded: "We *all* need your assistance." Mirceo? He'd just appeared inside the tent, along with Stelian.

All the royal male cousins in one place. At least, all the sane ones.

"Truce?" Trehan raised his sword. "I'm supposed to believe that the four of us are in one tent—and we're all getting out alive?" Each of them was dark haired and tall, each bearing the Daciano stamp upon their faces. Yet they were no family. "I haven't any patience for your jesting. Draw your weapons."

Viktor shrugged. "I vow to the Lore that we hold no ill intent toward you."

"Tonight, at least," Stelian added.

A vow to the Lore couldn't be broken. "I don't know why you've come, and I don't care. I've my own concerns now. A *life* of my own."

"It appears your suit goes well," Viktor said.

"What do you know of it?" Trehan demanded, but he feared he knew. The Dacians were observers. . . .

Viktor smiled widely. "Your Bride is lovely in mist."

"You *watched* us?" This shouldn't surprise him, but, gods, it *enraged* him.

"I was mainly watching the fights. And we turned Mirceo's head away," Viktor said. "Eventually."

Trehan didn't know whom to attack first. Their gazes had been on his Bride's trembling body; they'd seen her skin kissed with Trehan's mist. His fangs went sharp.

"Such aggression," Stelian said disapprovingly. "You're as bad as Viktor usually is. Your blooding has turned you savage."

"The better to bite your throat out with, Stelian."

"You'd attack when my sword remains sheathed?"

Damn them! None had drawn.

"Look at those fangs, Trey!" Viktor exclaimed. "Still maintaining that you haven't bitten your Bride?"

Never bitten her. But he'd taken her blood. *And I'll do it again.*

Stelian turned up his flask. "You *can* learn to control your fangs, Cousin."

Can I? Trehan shook his head hard. "Fight me, or leave! My break from you was clean."

"And it was your leaving that opened up a dialogue among the three of us," Mirceo said.

"What are you talking about?"

Though Mirceo was normally a male who took little seriously—a notorious hedonist—his gray eyes were grave. "We've realized that we've all been fighting for something we don't want to win. You gave up your right to the throne. But here's the thing, Uncle. None of us want it either."

"I don't understand."

"I'll reach my immortality soon, might not even have a year left." Mirceo was nearing the time when he would freeze forever, the time when he'd stop breathing and his heart would cease beating. When he could no longer have sex. "The last thing I want is to be mired in this feud."

Though Trehan had vague memories of intercourse as an enjoyable pastime, Mirceo's entire life revolved around bedding—females, males, anyone who'd have him.

"Why should I rule others when I can't even govern myself?"

Good point.

Stelian took a nip from his flask of blood and mead. "And I am the gatekeeper—"

"A task that already cuts into your drinking?" Trehan interrupted. Whereas he had once been friends with Viktor and a fond "uncle" to Mirceo, he'd never tolerated Stelian well.

Stelian's parents had been the most devious of all. Just two decades ago, his widowed father had murdered

Mirceo and Kosmina's parents, then disappeared. Tre-han had hunted him down and slain him. *To this day, they all must suspect me of it. . . .*

Stelian scowled at Trehan's statement, but he didn't deny his love of drink. "We all know that in a secret realm, a gatekeeper possesses far more power than a king. I can be one or the other, but not both. I choose my current position." *As the guardian of the kingdom.*

Trehan could scarcely believe what he was hearing. The two of them had battled nearly to the death as many times as Trehan and Viktor had. "And your rea-soning, Viktor?"

He shrugged. "I'm the last of the House of War, and frankly, that's all I want to do. I'm given to under-stand this is a bad trait for a king to possess."

There had to be more to it than that, but Trehan wouldn't push for details in front of the others. "So what do you three plan?"

"We install Cousin Lothaire as monarch," Mirceo said. "And then the discord will end. Just as predicted."

At the hour of her death, Lothaire's mother, Ivana, the rightful heiress to the throne, was said to have cursed Dacia with unrelenting strife.

Until Lothaire was made king.

I wonder if Lothaire the Enemy of Old knows exactly how accurate his trailing name is. . . .

Mirceo had seen enough strife in his short lifetime to believe in the curse. Trehan, however, had been alive long enough to know that the wily Ivana had likely just predicted more of the same underhanded maneu-vering already in play. Dacia's finite amount of politi-cal power and territory made for a situation rife with conflict.

"How much damage can Lothaire do?" Viktor said.

"We don't aggress other kingdoms, we don't have civil unrest—other than what we royals get up to—and we're bloody hidden! He'll be a figurehead. And by rights, the throne *is* his."

Trehan shook his head. "The last time I saw him, he was half out of his mind, searching for Dacia in the dead of winter—naked." The vampire's white-blond hair had been saturated with blood, his pale skin covered with it, his eyes glowing red like coals. "Oh, and he was also bellowing in Russian for someone to 'fucking fight' him."

Like the rest of them, Lothaire pursued a vendetta, and he coveted the crown of the Dacians to a blistering degree. Too bad he couldn't find his own kingdom. "He murders for sport, he feeds without restraint, and he sleep-traces uncontrollably." Like sleep walking— only he could awaken *in a different world*. "The Enemy of Old is a madman."

Mirceo said, "We've been watching him, Uncle. This idea is not as implausible as you'd think. He's found his Bride."

This was a new development.

Viktor added, "I understand your hesitation, Trey. But I've seen him with his female. Even in the grips of blood lust, he doesn't ravage her. And he's been setting off purposely, as if for some kind of mission. Which indicates at least a degree of sanity."

Trehan narrowed his gaze. "And you want to find out what this mission is."

"Exactly. We've found his lair in a mortal city called York—"

"It's *New* York," Stelian said with a roll of his eyes, as if he'd explained this before. Then to Trehan he added, "He's going farther afield, to locations we can't predict. We can't follow his movements—not without your crystal."

Trehan gave a laugh. "Which will *never* leave my sight."

"We figured as much," Viktor said. "You must lead the way, then!"

Trehan had only to imagine Lothaire's face, and it would direct him to the Enemy of Old. Then he could trace his cousins to the vampire's location.

Trehan turned to Stelian. "You're actually in agreement with this?" His hulking cousin revered Dacia and loathed change.

"It's rational to explore the possibility, to determine if Lothaire's truly improving." Stelian took another drink. "We require little of your time. Your days are free."

No, they really weren't. Damn it. *And still my duty to Dacia calls me.*

Though Trehan's memories of Lothaire gave him pause, the idea of restoring a rightful king to his throne appealed to his sense of order. Trehan might be breaking other rules now, but the rules of succession for the Dacian crown should be inviolable.

Yes, he was warming to this idea.

Viktor said, "You should know, however, that there might be a catch with his Bride."

"Isn't there always?" Trehan said. "Can't wait to hear it—but first, I've a catch of my own. . . ."

25

For the last several days, Bettina had been particularly *un*motivated to work.

The first couple of nights after her close encounter with Daciano on the grandstand, she'd wandered her rooms after the evening's battles, aimlessly pacing, her appetite gone. For endless hours, she'd fretted over Cas in the ring—and replayed her three interludes with Daciano.

But then, fearing Patroness's displeasure, the deadline looming, she'd powered through and now had much to show for her efforts.

She'd sketched diagrams of every moving part and cut each individual mold, getting closer to the fabrication stage. *So what materials will I use?*

She thought of her great and powerful Patroness, with all her fiery red hair. Rose gold. Of course.

Picking up a diamond file, she began to smooth the edges of the last mold. With a project this intricate and complex, the parts had to be exact, with machinelike precision.

She could have requested an extension on this deadline, but it helped to keep her mind occupied as the tournament dragged on.

Night after night, she'd flinched with each hit Cas took and sagged with each bout he won; she'd fretted as Goürlav handily advanced, without so much as a single injury.

Night after night, she'd wondered why the vampire had made no move to speak to her since he'd pleasured her in the mist.

He had appeared, killed quietly and efficiently, then vanished.

In his bout against the remaining Ajatar, he'd walked through flames, his outline illuminated—no panic, just pure will as he'd made his kill, collecting one head, then the other.

Against the Volar demon, he'd demonstrated just as little emotion. With his face expressionless and his eyes that impassive green, Daciano had winged the creature, then taken its head effortlessly.

Many of the Abaddonae were speculating that he was a turned human, a Forbearer. Some of them believed he must be the oldest Forbearer ever turned, considering his strength and his control with tracing.

Most had deemed him chillingly cold.

If she had a gold piece for every time Cas had muttered, "Bastard's got ice in his veins" . . .

But Bettina thrilled to watch him fight. As someone interested in mechanical precision, she could appreciate his daring but methodical style.

A killing machine.

Yet she'd also seen him as no one else had—his grim face alight with pride, his eyes dancing. . . .

Even if she could deny that she'd missed him, she couldn't deny that her body hungered for more of what he'd given her.

Her only exchanges with him? After each of his matches, he'd given her a bow in acknowledgment, then he'd leveled that penetrating gaze on her.

Recalling how his irises changed as he beheld her—forest green flooding black—made her shiver even now.

She could imagine his look said: *I'm fighting for you. Soon you'll be mine.*

It made her feel like the most desirable woman in the world.

Others had started to remark on the way he looked at her, nicknaming him the Prince of Obsessions. Bettina Abaddon—an object of obsession?

She couldn't quite buy it either.

Besides, if he was so obsessed, then why had he made no move to contact her? Salem had mentioned that he was never in his tent during the day. Where would the vampire go if barred from Dacia?

She'd noticed that his clothing was often in disarray, as if he'd traced into the ring directly from another fight. He would have mud splashed across his pants or a ripped shirttail. Once he'd had snow on his boots and a spray of crimson on his sleeve.

What? Did he have a part-time job or something?

Maybe he'd simply tired of the chase. She replayed his parting words continually. *Lest you lose a male who'll desire only you . . .*

The idea of losing him brought on a wave of sadness. Which made no sense; if she loved one male, how could she feel things for another?

Admittedly, things were strained between her and Cas. The more he tried to be on his best boyfriendly behavior, the more distance seemed to yawn between them.

Whenever he remained at an endless banquet with her—instead of running off with his rowdy friends—he could be the picture of attentiveness. Until he inevitably slipped up with a longing gaze at the exit, or a buxom serving wench distracted his attention.

Then he'd look guilty, like he was inwardly berating himself. Which made *her* feel guilty for dragging him into this. Would he forever gaze at other females, wondering if *that* one might be *the* one? Would he forever imagine attempting other demonesses to find his fated mate?

She wasn't eaten alive with jealousy like before—not after all the things she'd done with Daciano. No, she was more contemplative about Cas's insistence that another female would be his. What if he'd been right?

What if I've been . . . wrong? Maybe it hadn't been a matter of their different stations or his insecurity over his birth. Maybe it hadn't been a matter of his sown oats.

She and Cas had never been ill at ease with each other before. At times she feared they were trying to wedge their relationship into a mold that would never fit.

Speaking of which . . . She glanced down at the mold she'd been filing, gawking at the pile of shavings. *Ruined.* She chucked it into the wastebasket, then squeezed her forehead with frustration.

Everything was changing, her life altered by this

tournament in unforeseeable ways. And possibly for nothing.

Raum had visited today with some startling news—

"Honey, I'm home!" Salem called out, returning from his daily duties: spying. Entering the workroom, he occupied a length of chain on the backboard. "Damn, chit, maybe you want to file the shavings down too?"

She glared. "I'm preoccupied, *okay*?"

"And I'm holding me palms up in surrender—but it's fake. 'Cause I never surrender. So how much longer till you finish?"

"I'll complete fabrication before the round tonight, attaching the palm grip to the four top rings. Basically everything but the spring mechanism and the sneak blade. When I get back, I'll do that and then etch the rings. You can send word that she'll have it tomorrow."

Which was an important step. Bettina straightened her arms, clutching the edge of the workbench. *Because if Goürlav wins, I'll be seeking asylum in Patroness's kingdom.*

Of course, without her medallion, Bettina couldn't exactly escape her new husband's clutches.

They still had no idea how to defeat the primordial, and there were only three rounds left—including tonight's lady's choice round. She'd secretly been hoping that this round would afford her the opportunity to take out the primordial herself.

"What's going on out in Rune?" she asked Salem.

"Commerce," Salem said in an impressed tone. "Lots and lots of commerce. Your backwater kingdom is now a hot tourist destination."

As the final battles neared, fans of all stripes— sometimes literally—had arrived on the plane, filling inns and eateries. Young Loreans were camped out around the Iron Ring, playing music and building bonfires.

"And whatever Morgana's got going on down in the ring is drawing folks by the droves."

The sorceress had commandeered the arena for the entire day and night, hosting opening acts before tonight's round. "Any scoop on the competitors?" Their number had been cut down to just six. Most possessed the ability to trace. Four of them were demons—including the primordial. "Maybe you have news about Goürlav?" she added hopefully.

"He's here less and less during the day," Salem answered. "I got nothing. Even the spies I'm spying on who are spying on other spies got nothing."

Salem had reported that intrigues, subterfuge, and cheating were rampant.

"Do you have any idea what tonight's round will entail?" All Bettina knew was that the remaining six would dwindle to three.

"I just shook me head. Wiv Morgana, expect the unexpected, yeah?"

"Maybe I'm supposed to decide which competitors will fight each other."

"Or maybe you just snap your fingers and take out three." Salem made a snapping sound. "Including Goürlav."

"I'd been hoping the same. What about the rest of the competitors?"

"I spent the morning as the ceiling in the warlocks' tent. Found out that the hobbies of Those Best Forgotten include long walks on the beach and sacrificing nymphs on altars. I mean, who'd want to hurt a nymph? That's like kicking a rainbow in the nuts. And they're doing things to that wolf . . . well, let's just say they're shy of humane."

Salem had already told her how those *handlers* baited the poor creature before his rounds, bringing his ferocity to the fore.

"Why can't he rein in his beast?" She knew his kind spent years learning to control the wolf within, always fearing that it'd take over.

"It's not a rollicking good time of a story." When she waved him on, Salem said, "The male was . . . human. The warlocks turned him to serve them. Apparently, they do that kind of thing a lot."

A turned Lykae would have *no* chance of mastering the new beast inside him, not for years—if ever. Until then, you'd have a brutal killer on your hands, which was why so few were ever transformed. "So the warlocks just wind him up and let him go?"

She could imagine Salem nodding.

An added bonus? Besides being the strongest Lore species, the Lykae also happened to have unfailing fighting instincts. "Does the wolf have any idea what happened to him?"

"Dunno. Depends on how long ago he was turned. He might have flashes of lucidity. We better hope for one of those flashes if he goes up against Goürlav. Those Lykae claws would spill some serious Child Terrors. Can you imagine—"

"I don't *want* to imagine! This is happening under my watch. Most outsiders believe *I* rule. But I'd never condone the slavery of that wolf. I'd never condone anything that might bring Child Terrors to Rune!" With snappish movements, she began cleaning up the slivers.

"No argument here," Salem said in a consoling tone. "By the way, I happened to stop by the leech's again. Actually found him inside."

She briefly stilled. "And?" she asked as if she couldn't care less.

"You don't sound interested. It's nothing. Shouldn't have bothered you wiv—"

"Fine! Just tell me about him."

"I found him sitting in his darkened tent, mindlessly sharpening his sword as he stared at a crystal on his desk. His fangs were sharp, eyes black as pitch. The furs on his pallet were shredded. Not exactly the behavior of a cold and rational sort. He looked like he was about to—oh, how do I put this?—go out and *fuck shit up*. Take me word for it, still waters run deep wiv that one. And when the cold ones go, they go big."

Daciano had neared the limits of his control with her, but he'd always pulled back. So what had affected him so much?

Salem said, "Did you know there are Abaddonae who have started backing that leech?"

"Over one of their own? Or another breed of demon?"

"Hell, I can almost see it myself. Almost. He's kept it in his pants, thereby keeping you safe from a stoning. Hat tip to the vamp on that one—'cause you sure as hell weren't barring the gates to your lady garden." Over her outraged sounds, he continued, "He fights like no other, and you fancied him."

"I did not!"

"Fuck knots don't lie, chit."

"But I love Cas."

"Know that I'm rolling my eyes right now." At her

glower, he said, "*Of course* you love him! In a certain way. You were two orphans that hit it off and bonded. He was your only friend in this entire kingdom. Pair that uncommon tie wiv his uncommon good looks, and *any* female's judgment would get cloudy. Trust me on this—I used to leave chits addlepated whenever I walked by."

"You were uncommonly good-looking?"

"Hotter 'n Beckham wiv a better body."

That got her to raise a brow.

"In any case, you're young—*too* young to know what love is."

Exactly what Daciano had said. "How old are you, then?"

He gave a dramatic sigh. "Old as air. And probably still too young to know what love is. Though there was this one. Almost thought she was me kindred."

A phantom's mate.

"It ended bad though—"

The outer exit to her spire whooshed open. Bettina frowned in Salem's direction, imagined them sharing a questioning look.

Morgana called, "Freakling!"

Bettina and Salem hurried to the sitting room. "What is it?"

"We need to talk about Raum at once."

This was weird. Earlier Raum had visited—to talk about Morgana.

"Hello, hot-and-bothered," Salem said to Morgana. *Al-low, hot-n-bovvered.*

The sorceress's gaze found Salem's vicinity. "Phantom, is that you?" Her imperious stance softened as she *fluffed her hair.* Bettina had never seen her godmother like this.

"Here in the flesh. So to speak," he added. "What's doin', trix?"

"Oh, with *me*?" She examined her costume claws. "Just been supervising today's Morganapalooza. I put together some opening acts down in the ring. They're quite popular." Her demeanor was boastful, her words laced with an I'm-kind-of-a-big-deal undertone.

"Opening acts? Like what?"

"Kobold tossing, ghoul cage fights. And the Morganza of them all: a nymph floor show."

What's a floor show?

Salem seemed to know—the air blurred around him, signaling his eagerness. He hastily said, "I should go do a patrol, you know, down 'round the ring-al area. For security purposes. For the good of the kingdom. I'll let you two talk." And then he was gone.

Morgana gazed after him and sighed. Then she turned to Bettina with a hard look. "Pour the wine."

They took their glasses out onto the balcony. Feeling safe with the sorceress, Bettina only gazed upward once. "Okay, tell me. What's a floor show?"

"Did you never see *Rocky Horror Picture Show*?"

At Bettina's blank look, Morgana's lips parted. "*R.H.P.S.?* I've been remiss with you. I can see that now." To the sky, she murmured, "Eleara, forgive me." To Bettina, she said, "Floor show: noun, nightclub acts that include singing and dancing. For my purposes, they are sexy acts. Or sex acts. I can't remember which package I ordered."

"I see." No wonder Salem blazed.

"Now, I must depart soon to change for my referee duties, but this couldn't wait. I don't want to mince words"—as if she ever did—"but I don't believe your godfather has located the fiends who attacked you. With the end of the tournament nearly upon us, I don't think he can uphold his end of the bargain."

"What makes you say that?"

"Those Vrekeners are likely deep into the air territories. Exactly how are death demons going to trace to a location like Skye Hall? It *moves*. And they can only teleport to places they've previously been. Say they actually bag a Vrekener and force their hostage to take them aloft to the Hall—is Abaddon to wage war? Because that's what Raum courts."

Bettina squeezed her goblet, surprised to find it bending in her grip. "They declared war on us when they nearly assassinated me, the future queen of this realm! And what about Eleara? They *succeeded* with her. What's to stop them from wiping the Sorceri out completely?" *From wiping* me *out?* "Why can't we do anything?"

"Though it's difficult for our kind to wage a war— when we can't *find* our enemies and their stronghold is *impervious* to sorcery—we're not without victories. Why only six hundred years ago, Sabine decapitated the Vrekener leader, while her sister Melanthe maimed his son! All in one night! It's said the son can't fly without grueling pain to this day. A Vrekener who hates to fly? That must count for something."

Sabine and Melanthe were both legendary for their deeds. As the Queen of Illusions, Sabine could make her victims see their worst nightmares. She'd used that power to seize the leader's own mystical scythe—and behead him with it.

"In any case, don't you think I have non-Vrekener concerns in my own queendom?" Morgana continued. "Portents bode ill; a nemesis rises."

"La Dorada." When Morgana didn't deny it, Bettina said, "Is she alive?" La Dorada was the Queen of Evil, which meant that she could control evil beings. Including Morgana.

A sorceress who could master Morgana—as easily as Morgana could master her. Which one would get to the other first?

"I don't yet know if she lives," Morgana said. "Considering her arrival may harken the apocalypse, I've made this a *bit* of a priority. Besides, *Raum* was tasked with Vrekener disposal. Yet whenever I ask him about his progress, he's very evasive."

"He said the same thing about you concerning my power."

"What?" And there went Morgana's braids. "How dare he cast aspersions!"

"Do you have my ability or not?"

"And now you doubt me. I'm wounded. Terribly. If I weren't wearing a face glamour of indifference, you'd see my eyes glinting exquisitely."

"Just answer me."

"Do I? Don't I? You'll have to wait and see if your godmother has kept her word to her most beloved goddaughter."

Bettina didn't know what to think. Frustration welled inside her. "I'm upholding *my* end of the deal, and if you two aren't—"

Morgana dipped her claw in her wine, then flicked it at Bettina.

She glared, wiping the wine from her cheek with a swipe of her shoulder. When Bettina flicked wine back, Morgana retaliated with a wave of her hand; suddenly a bank of snow tumbled over Bettina.

Bettina gritted her teeth, brushing off her shoulders.

"That's how you say 'The subject is closed' in Yeti." Expression darkening, Morgana added, "Shall Abaddon have its first blizzard?"

And just like that, the matter was closed. *I hate it when she does that.*

Morgana's pique disappeared as swiftly as it'd arrived. "Look at the crowds. I can *hear* your tax coffers growing fatter by the second. Raum is wily in that, at least."

"Why do you disapprove of him so much?"

"I don't disapprove of him. I *hate* him. He's demonic and coarse. He fought me fang and claw over the lady's choice round. Tonight he'll see how right I was to include it."

"Still don't care to tell me anything about it? Such as if I'll have a chance to take Goürlav out?"

"A chance? Hmm. There is a chance. And that's all I'll—"

"Say on the matter," Bettina finished for her. She set her dented glass aside, resting her elbows on the railing, peering below. Something caught Bettina's eye. A raven-haired female was sauntering through the crowds—though others were steering clear of her.

It had to be the odd spectator who'd been showing up every night. She had pointed ears and wore T-shirts emblazoned with PRINCE OF SHADOW #1! The strange fey creature brought buckets of theater popcorn that she never ate. She tried to start waves and chants, cheering Daciano on.

"Morgana, do you know anything about that weird female who shows up for each night's fight, the one who wears trashy T-shirts?" Was she a former lover of his?

Bettina sniffed to herself. *If so, that bitch ooooolllld.*

"Hmm? Don't concern yourself with her."

"You didn't answer my question. How is she connected to the Prince of Shadow? Tell me." The female looked like a Valkyrie. Considered "good guys" in the Lore, the Valkyries were major Vertas players.

We don't get many of her ilk here. In times past, the Deathly Ones had sided with the more nefarious factions of the Lore. For this Accession, Raum had already made gestures to ally with the Horde and other demonarchies aligned with the Pravus.

"Your eyes go bright, freakling. Are you jealous of the female? After all, *you* are the Shadow Prince's Bride."

"Of course I'm not jealous." *I might be jealous.*

"He looks at you as if you're a virgin vein. There's much to be said for obsessive hunger." Morgana patted her hand knowingly. "Solid partnerships have been built on less. Did I mention that I spoke with him the other night while he awaited his bout?"

"You did *what*?" Questions about the raven-haired spectator disappeared.

"I told him, 'You must be a Forbearer.' He merely said, 'Must I?' then turned away. That dripping disdain—so sexy!"

Morgana had *no idea* how sexy that vampire was. *I do. Because he was mine for three brief encounters.*

"I decided I wanted his tongue on me; I couldn't decide if I wanted it still attached to his mouth or not. So I held off. Now I'm glad I did, since you're so possessive of him."

"I'm *not* possessive." Morgana together with Daciano? The idea made her want to screech.

"And there go your eyes once more. Raum has shown favoritism at every turn, gunning for a demon king. It would serve him right if you wed a vampire." With a chuckle, she turned to leave.

But at the doorway, she gazed back with a thoughtful look on her face, offering Bettina cryptic wisdom: "Remember, freakling, the greatest thing about having power is the mere *having of power*. Use the latter well, and you'll never have to use the former."

26

Just hours ago, Trehan had been in his tent, sharpening his gleaming sword, grappling with a fury so strong it scalded him inside.

Now he sat at his desk, cleaning his well-bloodied sword, face spattered with gore—and still struggling to rein in his overwhelming rage.

I'm backsliding.

But didn't the term *backsliding* indicate that he'd reached this level of fury before? He'd never known it as he had on this day.

After wading through Bettina's memories, he'd finally seen things he couldn't unsee. *I did things I'd* never *undo.*

He peered at the burlap bag at his feet and the plain black staff beside it. *Think of something else,* he told himself. The tournament began in minutes. *Change the direction of your musings.*

What else was there to think of besides Bettina? What else . . . ?

Ah, Dacia. *My former home.*

Would the Realm of Blood and Mist soon have a new king?

After days of tracking Lothaire all over the world and spying on the vampire's luxurious *York* penthouse, the cousins had learned much about their potential ruler—and his Bride.

Indeed, there's a catch. Lothaire's female was Elizabeth Peirce, a human "mountain girl" peasant. She was pretty for a mortal, with long dark hair and an intelligent gaze.

But humans perished so easily.

Unfortunately, transforming her into a vampire would be nigh impossible. Females rarely survived the transition, and never with Horde blood, polluted and dark as it was.

Lothaire was indeed on some kind of mission; Trehan would bet his soul that the Enemy of Old sought some way to make his Bride undying.

Lothaire's mission—combined with his madness—had made for some precarious episodes. To ensure his and Elizabeth's safety, the cousins had been forced to secretly intercede—up until the time when secrecy had no longer been possible.

The Enemy of Old now knew they were tracking him. . . .

But with each day, the vampire was healing under his female's influence. At times, he'd proved as calculating as any Dacian.

Pros: Lothaire was more powerful than any other vampire and would make a mighty regent. Cons: He remained bloodthirsty—in all senses of the term.

Still, Mirceo had already voted to install Lothaire. "A red-eyed king who bites others with impunity? My ballot reads: *yes*," Mirceo had said with a wink, shocking the older three cousins.

Trehan had scowled at him. "Biting isn't . . . Dacians simply don't bite others," he'd said, sounding prudish and old, even to himself. "Keeping our blood untainted is what separates us from the Horde."

"Really, Uncle? You know mated Dacians must taste each other's blood. Even if no one speaks of it. Perhaps with such a king as Lothaire, bloodtaking will be taboo no more?"

"Exchanging blood could happen accidentally," Stelian had pointed out, "but a bite is consciously done. We're above such needs."

Apparently not me. Maybe Trehan had Horde blood in his ancestry . . . ?

Viktor was on the fence about installing Lothaire, saying, "He's much worse than I'd thought. The only way I'd agree is if he figures out how to bond with his female and make her immortal. Oh, and if we withhold as much pertinent information from him as possible." Why? "So he has reason to keep us alive."

Stelian had grown dead set against Lothaire.

And Trehan? *I am . . . ready.* New ruler or not, the kingdom was no longer Trehan's mistress. Now he was free to serve another completely, a wide-eyed halfling he would kill to possess.

To protect. *Zeii mea, I want to protect her forever.*

Today, at last, he had begun.

"Welcome, all, to the Morgana show!" her godmother announced to the crowd.

Bettina sighed. *This is going to be a long night.* She

gazed around the grandstand, noting all the changes Morgana's minions had wrought over the day.

Sorceri banners of crimson and purple now swathed the area, like slashes of paint on a gray Abaddon canvas. Crystal domes levitated above the great torches, the glass casting brilliant prisms over everything.

Was it just her, or had the Sorceri banquet table lengthened—while the demon table had shortened? And no meat graced the demons' feast, which Bettina thought was unnecessarily cruel.

Raum sat beside Bettina on the dais with his goblet all but attached to his face. He was cruising toward battle-ax mode, casting Morgana black looks.

There had to be a story between those two, something more than Bettina knew.

Morgana was in rare form tonight, dressed in her most impressive pieces. Her gold bustier was encrusted with diamonds—she called the piece her "Valkyrie slayer"—and her full-length skirt was *sequined* with more diamonds, hundreds of them.

Across her face, she had sapphires affixed in the shape of a mask. Her eyes glowed with her amusement, lighting the gems. But her headdress was the most awing sight to behold, a fan of gold, studded with mismatched jewels—choice heirlooms from all the Loreans she'd slain over her long life.

Bettina couldn't lift the piece by herself. Three Inferi had to heft it atop Morgana's shoulders. Yet the sorceress carried it with aplomb.

Now Morgana cupped her hand to her ear. "I said, *'Welcome to the Morgana show!'* "

Sorceri cheered—frantically, as if their lives depended on it. *Wise.*

Apparently dissatisfied with the level of applause,

she announced, "*I* am the one who sponsored the preceding spectacles, including the *floor show*—"

The crowd erupted into cheers and foot stomping.

Guess my subjects are big on floor shows. Good to know.

"Silence!" Morgana commanded. At once, everyone went quiet. "Tonight's round is the lady's choice. It will have much, *much* more tension and emotional poignancy than the other mundane rounds." Sly look at Raum. "This is a contest of wits—the only muscle used will be *the brain*."

At last Bettina would find out what this was all about.

Morgana waved to the guards at the sanctum gate. "Bring forth the competitors." The six remaining males filed out to stand in a line below the grandstand— Goürlav, the Lykae, the remaining fire demon, the last stone demon, Caspion, and Daciano.

Just looking at the vampire brought on a pang of feeling. Which meant . . .

I have more than just Cas to worry about tonight.

For once Daciano wasn't gazing at her but staring out into the misty night, clearly preoccupied. What had happened to him today? What turmoil had Salem witnessed?

"Six of you will enter. Three will die," Morgana told them. "Now, the rules of this round are simple. You have ten minutes to return here with an offering for Princess Bettina. She will rate them from favorite to least. The trio whose gifts rank lowest will lose their heads."

Bettina's jaw slackened. It was one thing to see males battling it out to the death—having to decide exactly who would perish was another thing altogether. She bit out to Raum, "You knew about this?"

He patted her hand, looking anywhere but at her face. "Over before you know it, m'girl."

Tonight Morgana had made her the judge and jury. For *three* beings. Bettina would all but execute them herself.

As Bettina bristled beside Raum, Morgana continued, "Whoever *wins* tonight will go directly to the final round, awaiting the victor of tomorrow night's semifinal match."

Cas caught Bettina's eye, mouthing, *Just made the finals.* Of course he was jovial; he knew he was safe. He could bring her dirt, and she'd adore it.

"The runner-up," Morgana said, "will receive a tour of Rune tonight, guided by Princess Bettina herself."

Tour? Tour!!!

"You will bring your offerings to the sanctum, then return here," Morgana said.

Daciano's face was as impassive as ever, but his eyes were black. Bettina sensed that this challenge had taken him off guard.

"Beginning *now*." The great horn punctuated Morgana's words.

Once the contestants had hastened, traced, or were wrangled away, Morgana turned to Bettina. "Let's see how well your 'suitors' know you. It takes so little to make a sorceress happy. All we need is gold, wine, gold, bold color, merriment, gold, power—"

"I'll pick Goürlav's as last," Bettina informed her godmother, "and be done with him."

"Alas, you must answer honestly." Morgana sipped from her goblet. "Just as the terms of the contract will compel those entrants to return—despite their prospects—you'll be compelled to tell the truth."

Their prospects? They were returning to a fifty-fifty chance of death. Dread suffused her.

Though Cas was completely safe, what if Daciano offered her something she detested?

"And besides," Morgana said, "you won't be privy to which contestant offered which gift."

"What?"

27

Trehan's options were few.

He'd already procured his "gift" for Bettina, but it was the type that should be given with explanation and tact. Otherwise, she might react badly to it.

Screams, fainting, retching—all possible.

He knew his Bride could be . . . skittish at times. However, his offering *was* something she'd dreamed of, and her guardians would be pleased.

All beings in the Lore would be put on notice.

If Trehan wanted to signal to Raum and Morgana that he was a male who should possess their ward, this was a solid move.

But thinking of her fears made him doubt. Ever cold, ever logical Trehan was unable to make a decision.

Is this a rational play?

Or do I merely want to demonstrate what I alone can give to her? Demonstrate it to the entire realm?

Was it ego—or daring?

Two minutes left. He might have the opportunity to prepare her; he'd have to chance that.

Exhaling a breath, he traced back to the sanctum, the burlap bag slung over his shoulder. Unable to spy out what the others' gifts were, he grudgingly handed his bag to attendants, then returned to the ring.

Each contestant looked pleased about his gift, except for the dirt-coated Lykae; he just appeared rabid and half-drugged.

Morgana raised her hands over the six, commanding, "Kneel."

None of them did. Trehan even shared a look with Goürlav: *the fuck?* Trehan Daciano knelt before no one—

Suddenly an inconceivable pressure hit him, as if anvil blows had landed atop both his shoulders. His knees slammed against the ground, his legs nearly buckling under the force. All of the contestants had been shoved down, the fire demon suffering a dislocated shoulder. The ground shook when Goürlav was put to his knees.

The gold decorating Morgana's body vibrated, heated air diffusing around her. Trehan perceived her power surrounding them. Swift, fierce . . . *dark*. "Perhaps next time you'll obey promptly when a Queen orders you. *Obedience—is—not—optional*."

Each of the contestants had his arms jerked behind his back, his wrists fettered by her sorcery. Like a shot, six swords appeared, floating through the air to position themselves before the six males.

One sword directly against each competitor's throat.

If Trehan so much as swallowed, he'd slice himself. Out of the corner of his eye, he spied a cadre of warriors standing at the ready to fight any Child Terrors, should Goürlav's blood spill.

Everything became clear.

Instantly upon Bettina's decision, three heads would topple.

By the time the six had returned, Bettina had been close to hyperventilating. It hadn't helped that Daciano looked troubled about this round, his brows drawn.

In the past, he'd been so confident. Now he seemed to be trying to communicate something to her.

Goürlav was enraged, his yellow eyes slitted, spittle dribbling from a rotted fang down to his fossilized beard. Caspion looked cocky. The poor Lykae squirmed against Morgana's hold, chuffing with confusion.

Had his warlock handlers chosen well, or would the former human die for their mistake?

The fire and stone demons appeared stoic, but their horns were twisting with their panic.

This entire situation was killing her. Six swords at six throats? No muss, no fuss, no disputing the verdict.

This *would* all be over before she knew it.

Cas chanced a wink at her. Whatever he'd given her would likely be recognizable as *his* offering.

Thank gods for that.

But what if Daciano had stumbled with his choice? What if *her* choice made that sword slice through his neck—the neck she'd licked and nuzzled her face against as he'd pleasured her?

Never again to see his devilish eyes go black with emotion . . . ?

Her own eyes started to water behind her mask. Why had this decision fallen to her?

Morgana called, "And now, the gifts!"

More guards conveyed the procession of tributes toward the grandstand. One held a single envelope, one a velvety-smooth jewelry case, and another led in two stallions of a rare silver color, an exquisitely matched pair. Next came a bulging wagon full of gold. So much of it that even she raised her brows. Behind that was a rare phoenix, its feathers so brilliant she nearly had to shield her eyes.

Last: a bulky burlap sack?

Murmurs sounded, demons craning their heads to get a better look at the bag.

Already Bettina had made a decision about one of the gifts, a deadly decision. Dear gods, what if it was the vampire's? Trehan Daciano might be about to die.

And it took this realization for her to admit that there *was* something compelling between them. Maybe it *was* fate or his blooding or just unparalleled chemistry. Whatever it was, she wanted to explore it.

Would they never get the chance?

Morgana opened the envelope, announcing in a ringing voice, *"For those of you in the audience, the envelope contains two tickets to deadmau5. Dead mau five?"*

"Deadmouse," Bettina corrected in a whisper. A techno act she'd been wanting to see in the mortal realm. Clearly Cas's gift. No harm would come to him tonight.

Yet her sense of relief for Cas couldn't override her worry for Daciano.

Next, Morgana opened the jewelry case and announced, *"The royal jewels of the long-fallen Peace Demonarchy."* As she laid them on the dais table for

Bettina to examine, she said, "Look at the pretties, Bettina!" She was gleeful, as if these gifts were being offered to her. "Is this not the *best*? You love jewelry."

True, but Bettina didn't like to be given it. The quality was always inferior to what she could create. Bettina would just wind up melting this gift down.

She shrugged; Morgana rolled her eyes, then called, *"Next!"* A soldier led over the horses. *"Behold—the fey king's prized stallions, stolen from the legendary realm of Draiksulia."* Over her shoulder, she said, "Look at the ponies!"

Sadly, Bettina wasn't fond of horses, and she was fairly positive that they hated her. She'd been thrown when little and had never climbed back in the saddle.

"Prancing, prancing ponies for Bettina?" Morgana queried. "No? Seriously?"

When Bettina gave another slight shrug, Morgana's expression turned woebegone. "But how they *prance*."

Bettina was seeing all new facets to the great sorceress. Before, Morgana had simply been her moderately evil godmother. Now Bettina was beginning to understand that she was a woman with her own concerns—such as the apocalypse—and her own wants and desires—such as prancing ponies and Vrekener extinction.

"Next! Ah, and here we have a phoenix, the sole male from what is thought to be the last flock."

What was Bettina supposed to do—put the bird out to stud? Advertise online? Though she adored the phoenix's vivid colors, she considered it cruel to take it away from its flock.

Not so for Morgana. "Think of the masks we could make from those feathers! No? Oh, come on! Really?" She gazed heavenward with frustration.

When the wagon of gold rolled out, its wheels groaning under the weight of all those riches, Morgana called, *"This one needs no description! Behold a sorceress's fortune in gold!"*

She winked at Bettina. "Looks like *somebody* wants to live. What's that smell? Ah, yes, it's *desperation*. . . ."

Then came the last gift. She and Morgana shared a look.

"What could be in that bag, Bettina?"

When she held up her palms, the sorceress waved a hand toward the sack, using her power to open the fastenings.

In a rush, the contents spilled out and bounced across the stage.

28

Bettina frowned when Trehan's offering lay strewn before her, as if she didn't comprehend what she was seeing.

And Trehan realized he'd erred this eve.

Despite all the wise choices he'd made over the centuries, despite all his sage counsel that had helped others . . . when it had truly counted, his logic had failed him. He'd made a colossal mistake.

One that might cost him his life—and, worse, cost him Bettina.

He didn't fear death; he'd lived long enough. No, Trehan feared never seeing her again. He dreaded what would happen to her in the coming days. *Likely wed to Goürlav, if the demon advances—and if my cousins fail to protect her.*

"I'll assist you with Lothaire," he'd told the three of them, "if you vow always to safeguard Bettina. . . ."

Now regret hammered at Trehan. He'd thought he could personally present the bag to her, gentling her reaction; he hadn't expected to be at sword point while Vrekener heads bounced before her eyes.

With no warning.

Realization was dawning on Bettina's pale face, and there was nothing Trehan could do to remedy this, forced to watch helplessly.

"Heads, Bettina!" Morgana cried, clasping her hands to her breast and batting her eyes. "A bag full of them! Just like you've always wanted!" Trehan could hear the sorceress adding under her breath, "Not the most original of gifts, true. But these do appear to be *fresh*."

Bettina looked like she was about to vomit.

Fuck.

Zeii mea, I've . . . failed. After the momentous day he'd experienced?

Before dawn, he'd shot awake, fresh from a dream. For days he'd failed to access the memory he'd sought from Bettina's drops of blood.

Finally, he'd succeeded; he'd relived her attack.

Her *beating.* Trehan had felt everything, every last second of the horror as a tender young girl was savaged by winged fiends in the name of "good."

My Bride *savaged. Her limbs broken at angles, her skull and pelvis cracked. Two ribs rupturing her skin. Blood painting her body.*

Long after she'd accepted death, when she'd ceased screaming and her pleas had fallen silent, they'd still brutalized her.

Only Raum's summoning had saved her from slowly burning to death.

Trehan had awakened to his own howl of rage,

covered in shredded fur. His fangs had been sharp as razors.

Hungering to punish, he'd envisioned flesh rending beneath his fangs, arteries plucked with his claws. Dear gods, yes, to *punish*.

Breaths heaving, he'd collected his sword, gripping his talisman. Trehan had hoped that with her memory of those attackers, he could use their identities and the crystal to trace directly to them. Sword in hand, he'd pictured the first one's face, then begun to trace, having no idea if this would work. . . .

It had been night in the air territories, the shadows plentiful. He'd smiled, baring his fangs, knowing he was a chilling sight.

One by one he'd meted out retribution for his Bride; one by one he'd gathered their heads.

Trehan and Bettina were indeed connected. Her attack *had* happened the day he'd had that ominous sense. Had his Bride been calling out through the ether, calling for her male?

I answered today.

He'd returned to Rune still filled with rage, but knowing he had to win this round tonight.

Yes, an eventful day to die. Momentous.

Disastrous.

Strange—he'd never truly failed before. Figured his first time would result in his death.

Can't stop shaking. With unsteady steps, Bettina sank down in her seat.

The contents of that bag had shocked her, then dredged up horrors she'd desperately tried to bury.

She knew it was Daciano's offering to her. He was the only one who could've accomplished this feat.

Just as Bettina had feared, he'd read her memories. He'd seen her most private moments like a voyeur in her mind.

Morgana turned to her with a slow grin spreading across her face. "Are they who I think they are?"

Bettina started to speak, had to cough before she could utter: "Vrekeners."

Somehow the vampire had traveled to the air territories and wrought vengeance.

Their grimaces of pain in the torchlight were so very reminiscent of their masks of rage, lit by a pale yellow moon. The scent of crushed poppies . . .

She furtively pressed the back of her hand to her mouth, fearing she'd throw up. Judging from the disfiguring marks across their faces, they'd *died bloody*. Just as Daciano had promised.

She gazed over at him. His mien was as stoic as ever, but deep down he had to fear he'd made a mistake.

With sheer glee, Morgana announced to all, *"And lastly, we have the most wanted foes of Abaddon, executed and delivered."*

Surprised murmurs sounded throughout the stands, so few understanding the meaning of those trophies.

Raum hoisted his tankard above his head, not bothering to disguise his delight. The pressure to find her attackers had just been lifted.

Bettina glanced at Cas. He looked infuriated that Daciano had done what he'd been unable to.

Back to the vampire. Finally she discerned a hint of emotion on his face, his eyes flickering.

She thought that he was . . . *sorry*—not about the ultimate outcome of this round, but that he'd upset her. *Why present them like this, vampire?* Yes, she'd wanted them dead. *But why like this?*

"Time for the results!" Morgana said.

Bettina dutifully rose, pressing her hands against the table to steady herself.

"Which three gifts do you like least? *Princess?*" Morgana prompted more forcefully.

In a deadened tone, she answered, "The horses."

The fire demon directly beside Daciano cried, "Wait—"

But Morgana had already waved her hand to wield the mystical sword. His head bounced to the ground. "And next?" she asked in a breezy tone.

Bettina grew even more nauseated.

When the Lykae saw the first head topple, he began grappling against Morgana's hold with all the brutal force in his body, his ice-blue eyes wide. Whimpers broke from his chest.

"Princess?"

Did the Lykae believe they were all being summarily executed? Did he understand anything that was happening?

Does he believe he's . . . next?

"Princess! Which gift?" Morgana's expression turned sinister. Under her breath, she said, "Each second you dally, the wolf's ungodly strength tests my powers. Take care that I don't accidentally swing for Caspion's head."

Bettina gave a wary nod. Just as she murmured, "The jewels," she spied a flicker of clarity in the Lykae's eyes. The ice-blue color faded as his gaze darted around him with . . . *comprehension.*

The former human had surfaced from the wolf's grip—to find himself bound in an iron cage, surrounded by blood-thirsty demons. A frantic bellow erupted from his chest.

Have I just killed him? Were the jewels from the Warlocks? Bettina twisted toward the sorceress. "Please, Morgana—"

Morgana had already waved her hand; the Lykae yelled one word: *"Brother!"*

His call still echoed, even after his head rested next to his limp body.

Bettina swayed, her jaw slackening. But Morgana simply tossed a temporary glamour over her, erasing any expression.

Inside, she was sick—about this tournament, about her existence, about her very world. *How long can I be powerless like this?*

How long till she became as hard-bitten as Morgana hoped—or as weak as Raum expected?

Trehan swallowed, feeling cold steel against his throat, yet unable to trace away, unable to fight.

Such a gamble. Such a fool. You gave her fucking heads, Trehan?

"Lastly, Princess?"

The crowd was silent as a grave.

Bettina gazed at Trehan, as if to gather strength for her last pronouncement.

He stared back, taking her face into memory—

"The . . . phoenix."

The stone demon roared, "No, you can't!"

With a shrug, Morgana waved her hand once more. His muscles bulged, hardening like stone, but the sorceress's power was too great. Another demon down.

Trehan just kept himself from sagging against the sword in relief. He, Caspion, and Goürlav would survive the night.

"And now for the winner! Which gift do you like best?"

Wagon of gold, concert tickets—or a seemingly impossible revenge?

Yet again, he and Caspion would be in competition. Now that Trehan hadn't been decapitated, his confidence over his offering rose. *She'll choose mine.* Anyone could give her tickets or riches. But not vengeance.

"I like . . . the tickets best."

"Caspion the Tracker advances to the final round!" Morgana called with fanfare, but no real excitement.

Well-played, demon. The crowd roared, feet stomping the stands. Raum whistled shrilly, whaling his massive hands in applause.

Had Trehan actually thought Bettina would prefer any gift over Caspion's? Two fucking passes to some kind of mortal entertainment.

And now I face Goürlav tomorrow.

"Which gift is your runner-up, Princess?" Morgana asked.

Bettina sounded sick as she said, "The . . . heads."

Face Goürlav, have Bettina take me on a tour?

Any night of the week.

Trehan might die in the ring. He'd be damned if his Bride didn't send him off with a smile on his face.

Bettina's gaze kept straying to the Vrekener heads. Just looking at them provoked so many emotions inside her—fear, revulsion, yet there was also relief.

She'd reasoned, *I would pay Goürlav's wagon of gold for those heads. Which means Daciano should earn the runner-up spot.*

Points deducted for presentation, though. Their glassy eyes seemed to be staring at her accusingly.

She shuddered, her stomach churning even worse. *Need to get off this stage.* Before she humiliated herself in front of everyone. . . .

"Excellent!" Morgana called. "Goürlav the Father of Terrors will meet the Prince of Shadow in the semi-finals. The winner will face Caspion the Tracker of Abaddon on the night of the full moon. This eve's festivities have ended. You may leave. *Now.*"

At that, spectators scrambled away.

When Morgana's floating swords disappeared, the three surviving competitors stood.

Cas traced to her, laying his hand on her shoulder. She quaked beneath his grip.

Too much to process. Aside from the shocking development of the Vrekeners' deaths, Bettina was rocked by the outcome of this round. Because of her choices, three entrants were dead, the fates of three others altered irretrievably.

Some part of her truly must have thought she could take out Goürlav with her lady's choice. He remained, and he was seemingly unbeatable in the ring. Which meant . . .

The vampire will die tomorrow.

Cas will die the next night.

I will wed a monster.

Too much—

"What is this runner-up *tour,* Morgana?" Raum demanded, hurtling toward battle-ax mode.

Matching his tone, she said, "It's a done thing, demon. Challenge me not."

"Sending m'girl off with that strange leech. I won't have it!"

Daciano traced to the grandstand at that moment. The vampire stood silently, gazing at Bettina with concern, a question in his eyes.

All sweetness and light, Morgana said, "Ah, the gentleman vampire comes calling. Why don't you meet her in an hour or so, Prince? Give her time to decompress. In the meantime," she casually continued, "we must go sort out a petty family squabble. Never fear, I have every hope that at least two of us will survive it."

To let her go now? Trehan had to clench his fists to keep from reaching for her. Standing this close to his Bride after remaining away so long was punishing.

He wanted to hold her, to demand to know her thoughts.

As if Morgana could read his own, she cast him a foreboding look. "One hour, Prince."

Trehan decided he'd heed Morgana's warning, but only because he had work to do in the interim. Tonight he intended to show Bettina other benefits of a blood connection—namely that he could provide anything that she needed or desired, without her even having to ask.

Again Trehan's plan had transitioned. *Capitalize on her passion; eliminate her fear.*

"Back to my quarters, Caspion"—Raum reached for Bettina, then an indignant Morgana—"we're away."

"Get your paws off me, you oaf—"

The sorceress's words were left hanging as Raum traced them. Caspion scowled at Trehan, then followed them. *He* was considered part of the family?

She's my *fucking Bride. Decreed by fate!* I *am her family, with a tie greater than any of those three.* This would be the slowest sixty minutes of eternity.

An hour of wondering what they were telling Bettina. Probably browbeating her as he'd seen in dreams.

An hour of wondering how she felt about his gift.

She didn't like his offering best. But she hadn't liked it least either. Not a success, nor a failure. Gods, that female confused him!

Confusion? Another feeling he was unaccustomed to.

Coupled with that, he still battled rage over his dream of her attack. *Backsliding.*

Focus, Trehan. You've so little time.

He'd scarcely thought of his own fate tomorrow night. He was scheduled to fight an adversary stronger and faster than any he'd ever faced. One he dared not injure.

And if he lost, he'd have to depend on his cousins to get Bettina away from the primordial.

Best not lose.

Trehan traced to his tent, collecting another item he'd taken from Skye Hall today, the plain black staff. He needed assistance with it. Luckily, Trehan knew of a blind mystic of great power.

Without delay, he traced from Abaddon to a windy, lightning-lit realm, appearing in the mystic's modest shop.

Trusting another with this piece would be a risk.

With no other choice, Trehan held out the staff for the mystic to feel.

The male glided his fingertips over the wood, raising his brows in shock.

"I need this to do what it's meant to, Honorius," Trehan told him. "Multiplied by a thousand. And I need it before sunset tomorrow."

29

*G*entleman caller?" Raum shouted to Morgana as soon as the three of them had landed in his receiving room. Historically, Bettina had visited this place only to discuss the most serious of matters.

—*Bettina, your father . . . he's fallen on the battlefield.*

—*This is your summoning medallion, Tina. We only need a bit of your blood.*

—*You must be wed, m'girl. Without a protector, you risk another attack. What if something happens to me this Accession? Who will protect you?*

"Curse you, Raum!" Morgana yanked her arm away. "Never trace me again, or your horns will decorate the grille of my new mortal car!" She flounced over to one of the rustic divans, draping herself over it with a great flourish.

Bettina perched on the divan opposite Morgana, gazing around warily. Raum's spire was like an extension of him—a mix of violence and unexpected thoughtfulness.

Crossed battle-axes hung above a rough-hewn hearth. Centuries' worth of armor lined the walls. Above them were the mounted heads of monsters he'd hunted: vicious Gotohs, ghouls, and Wendigos.

But he also possessed a collection of rare scales from myriad basilisk nests. Demons held those dragons sacred. In the room's firelight, the scales gave off a mesmerizing shimmer, waves of iridescent pearl, jade, and crimson.

Caspion traced into the room, heading straight to the sideboard.

"I don't like this," Raum snapped. "Don't like the way that vampire looks at Bettina, as if he's wedded and bedded her already. As if he *knows* her."

Bettina peered at her bitten nails, watching them begin to grow back.

"And as glad as I am about the Vrekeners, I demand to know how he found them!" Raum's eyes widened, and he pointed a claw at Morgana. "You must have helped the leech! Predicted where Skye Hall would be!" Raum joined Cas at the sideboard. "When you wouldn't assist us?" He sloshed demon brew from a pitcher into a mug, then thought better of it and palmed the pitcher in his big hand.

"How? I'm no soothsayer, as evidenced by my sanity." Morgana spread her arms over the back of the divan with an insouciant grace. "And you know I tried to read Bettina's mind to give you a description of the four. But she couldn't even bring herself to picture them."

Daciano had probably been able to see deeper into her subconscious than Bettina herself could.

"Your hand is in this, sorceress!" Raum insisted, adjourning with the pitcher to his oversize desk.

"One more time, Raum—the Hall is impervious to Sorceri. We can't find it, reach it, attack it—"

"And I'm to take your word on that?" Raum all but yelled, "I don't trust you as far as I can throw you!"

Morgana snapped, "The feeling is mutual, I assure you!"

Cas slid Bettina a glance that said: "This is so messed up." She flashed one back: "I know, right!"

She felt as if they were two siblings watching their dam and sire fight.

Wait. *Siblings?* Were her feelings turning . . . *sisterly* toward him?

Morgana said, "Ah, Raum, you're just angry that the vampire did something supposedly impossible! When *you* couldn't." With a pointed look at Caspion, Morgana added, "When even the vaunted 'tracker' couldn't track them."

Cas glowered. "Because Raum ordered me off their trail! Eventually I would have found them somehow!" To Raum, he said, "I always did before. Yet you commanded me to stop searching. You as good as handed this revenge to the vampire!"

Raum slammed his fist against the desktop, rattling writing utensils and skull paperweights. "I gave that order because you were exhausted. You'd barely finished transitioning to immortal, hadn't even harvested a death yet! And I didn't want you to repeat what Mathar did!"

Everyone fell silent. "What? What did my father do?" Bettina finally asked.

Raum scowled, knowing he'd said too much.

"Raum?"

At length, he muttered, "He hunted your mother's killers until it nearly drove him mad. He monitored Skye Hall's movements for years, trying to come up with a pattern, to predict where it would appear next. No use." Raum scrubbed his hand over his craggy face. "Mathar existed, like a ghost, as long as he could, holding out for you. Then he sought the front line of the bloodiest battle he could find, knowing it would end him."

He'd *wanted* to die? In a soft voice, Bettina said, "He couldn't live without her?"

Raum shook his head sadly. "Had no interest in that prospect."

Mathar's love for Eleara astounded Bettina. *His love for me. He'd existed—in misery—for me.*

No wonder he'd seemed distant. He'd been tormented. "So devoted," she murmured to herself.

Morgana sniffed. "Eleara was just as much so. Though *I* could never see it."

Bettina's gaze landed on Cas. Would she ever know such devotion from a male? And return it just as fiercely?

With the vampire. The thought arose without warning, startling her because it felt like . . . *truth.*

Cas met her eyes then, but again he didn't seem to *see* her. *What if I've been* horribly *wrong about us?*

"There's no finding the air territories," Raum continued. "I didn't want to doom Caspion to failure. I still don't know how the vampire located them."

Cas frowned at Bettina. "Did you tell the vampire about the Vrekeners?"

"No!"

"Outside of this room, no one knew about those four. So there's no way, unless . . ." Cas trailed off.

All eyes fell on her neck.

Raum sputtered. "You didn't . . . y-you wouldn't!"

Morgana grinned. "Did you gift the vampire with your blood?"

Bettina blurted the words: "It was an accident! He never bit me. We—we kissed and his fangs went sharp."

Cas, Morgana, and Raum groaned in disbelief.

"Oh, for gold's sake, you're really that naïve, freakling? First *R.H.P.S.,* and now this. Clearly, I'm derelict in my duties."

"This is why I still have her medallion!" Raum pointed out in a vindicated tone. "She's *too* naïve."

Cas said, "Vampires like him don't have 'accidents.'"

"He tried to warn me!"

"But you were beyond caring?" Morgana said. "It's called *seduction*. And what it shows us is that your prince is a very cunning player indeed." Her blond brows drew together. "Strange, though—an immortal male will usually become an unthinking, primal brute when fighting for his female."

Daciano a brute? Bettina couldn't see it. "Morgana, it was only the tiniest drop."

"Then maybe he harvested only your most recent memories." Her godmother examined the end of a braid, the Sorceri equivalent of navel gazing. "Haven't I changed in front of you within the last few months?" With a shrug, she said, "If he sees that memory, I'll expect a call from him directly."

Raum's eyes went wide. "Then he knows our kingdom's defenses."

Cas's disappointed look sliced through her. "The secrets I've trusted you with, Tina."

"And now Morgana's arranged for them to be together for this—this *tour*?" Raum blustered. "What if the vampire bites Bettina? You know that could prove ruinous to her."

Daciano's kisses and caresses had proved so—Bettina could think of little else—so why had no one told her to be wary of those? Then she frowned. "Why is a bite *ruinous*?"

"Because they're excruciating," Raum said. "Right, Morgana?"

Excrutiating?

In a grudging tone, the sorceress said, "Bite play *can* go badly. If the vampire's exceedingly thirsty or inexperienced. And the prince *did* look peckish. Hmm, what say *you*, Caspion?"

Had Cas's cheeks flushed? "It's like nothing you've ever felt." He sounded almost as if he were speaking from firsthand knowledge. Hadn't he described a bite as *altering*? Had some Dacian female taken his blood?

Did it . . . hurt?

Daciano *was* inexperienced, had never bitten another. Would he tear her skin?

Raum traced before her. "Promise me you'll keep your blood from him."

She craned her head up. "I promise! Believe me." Bettina had suffered enough excruciating pain to last an eternal lifetime.

To Morgana, he said, "You intend to send her off without a chaperone, to spend the night with a 'very cunning player' who's practiced in seduction?"

"You did not just say the word *chaperone* to me."

"I won't have it, sorceress. We will come to blows!"

"Oh, let's!" Morgana leapt to her feet, her eyes beginning to spark in warning, like a viper's rattle.

"Damn you, what if the vampire sullies her?"

That was the absolute wrong thing to say to the sorceress. Morgana looked as furious as Bettina had ever seen her, braids flying. "What if *she* sullies *him*? Why is it *always* the female who gets sullied? Archaic demon! You think like the primordial!"

Raum yelled the vilest of Demonish curses, basically telling Morgana to suck on his horns until they were raw. Bettina gasped. In turn, Morgana blew him a kiss, essentially telling him she'd poison him at the earliest opportunity.

"You Sorceri harlot!"

"You demonic fossil!"

Cas joined in, and the three started up once more.

Bettina stood unsteadily, putting her hands over her ears. Did none of them understand how close she was to losing it? Inside, she was at once blistered and numb, torn between alternating urges.

Cry.

Scream.

The latter won out. "Shut up, all of you!"

They were shocked into silence. She'd never raised her voice to any of them.

Turning to Raum, Bettina said, "If Mathar couldn't find the Vrekeners and you knew a tracker like Cas never would, then you never truly expected to uphold your end of our bargain!"

Pulling at the collar of his breastplate, Raum said, "I had inside information from a very reliable source."

Morgana sneered, "How. Convenient."

"And what about you?" Bettina turned on her godmother. "Vow to the Lore that you have my power! Now, Morgana."

"Freakling, I *dispatch* the orders." *Rattle rattle RATTLE.* "I do not *receive* them."

Bettina sank down on the divan once more. "So you don't. Both of you tricked me."

"I, too, have inside information," Morgana said so smoothly.

"Bullshite, harlot!"

I'll never get my power back. But she would still be queen in two nights.

Seeing Raum and Morgana and even Cas like this made her realize she had depended on them far too much. They were fallible, just as she was.

Even without her power, Bettina had better start *thinking* like a queen. Before they could start up again, she said, "What will happen now? Will the Vrekeners retaliate?"

"We'll be lucky if they don't descend upon us for this," Raum said. "I'd ordered my demons to do this quietly. If they were ever to reach Skye Hall, they were supposed to make the four *disappear*—not spill Vrekener heads in front of all and sundry of the Lore!"

"The vampire acted alone," Morgana pointed out, sitting once more. "No one can prove otherwise."

"Let them descend upon us!" Cas snapped. "Then maybe I'll get the chance to actually bloody my sword with one of their ilk. We're Deathly Ones, and we've been too long without war. We are fierce, and we can trace. They should fear us."

Raum gazed away. "They're like locusts, Caspion, a plague from the heavens. If word of this gets back to them . . . It was badly done, is all I'm saying."

"It was *perfectly* done," Morgana said. "How better to signal to the Vrekeners that we know how to reach their lair? They are not invulnerable. Perhaps now they'll think twice about ravaging an Abaddonae royal! Or hunting my subjects like dogs!" Inhaling through her nose, she said, "This conversation is finished, Raum. Your 'girl' is about to be *queen*. There will be no chaperone. Nothing more need be said. Now, go get ready, freakling."

Raum turned to Bettina, his expression weightier than she'd ever seen it. "Understand me, Tina, the blood contract of the tournament will compel me to give you and your medallion to the winner. If the vampire seduces you, Goürlav will kill you—and there won't be anything I can do to stop him."

"So certain *I* won't win the tournament, Raum?" Cas shook his head in disgust. "You each know where I stand with all this. I leave now."

"Cas, wait!" Bettina caught him before he traced. "Walk me back to my spire?"

Morgana called from the divan, "Have fun tonight, freakling. Try not to sully the vampire too hard."

Once Bettina and Cas were alone, he said, "I still can't believe Daciano found them! I spent sixty gods-damned nights combing plane after plane."

She frowned at his surly tone. *And you're so young. Just like me.* Seeing Cas like this made her abundantly aware of her own young age.

Maybe she *had* confused having someone in her heart with giving her heart to another. "Aren't you happy that they're dead? That I won't have to fear at least those four?"

Caspion held up his hand to stop her. "Just don't."

When they neared her door, she said, "Please don't be angry with me."

He stopped, turning to her with a frown. "Did Daciano get your blood that first night? Or were you with him again? When you knew it wasn't me?"

She whispered, "I was with him again."

"I promised to be faithful!" He cast her a wild-eyed look. "But you didn't return that promise, did you? Do you know how difficult it is for a male demon to go without sex? Have you never wondered why there are eleven restaurants in Rune and *twenty-three* brothels?"

"I'm sorry! I never intended to do anything with him. I got caught up, and the next thing I knew, we were kissing."

"Just like Morgana said, it's called *seduction*. I'm well versed in it." His fists clenched, his forearms bulging. "Did he come to your rooms again?"

"I-I went to his tent."

"Why in the hell would you do that?"

"Cas, please . . ."

He laid his hands on her shoulders. "Tell me!" His horns had straightened ominously.

She'd never seen him so angry. She grasped for a lie, but she'd always wanted to be truthful with him. "The vampire told me . . . he would spare you in the melee."

"So that's why he aided me? My gods, Bettina, he forced you to do things by threatening my life? You whored yourself for my safety?"

"No! Yes? When you say it like that, it sounds so much worse than it was."

Cas wasn't listening. "He's earned a slow death." He looked over his shoulder in the direction of the vampire's tent, his grip on her tightening. "I'll make it last—for days."

Would he go attack Daciano this second? Neither could kill the other outside the ring.

"Cas, it wasn't quite that way."

He turned back. "Then what way *was* it?"

She remembered Daciano's damp skin in the firelight, the sultry warmth of that tent. *His eyes like onyx.* She took a breath and admitted, "I didn't do anything I didn't want to do at the time."

Cas released her at once, backing up with his hands in front of him. "Do you want *him* now? Is that it? I can't stop this tournament, Bettina. I can't come back from this."

"I-I don't know. I'm just so confused by everything—"

"Look at you!" Cas exclaimed. "You crave that vampire even now!"

"I do not!" *Do I?* Now that her entire existence had been upended yet again, she couldn't stop replaying how it had felt to be enveloped in the vampire's mist. Tethered to him.

Connected.

After she'd lost her power, that feeling of emptiness had tolled inside her. But the connection she'd shared with Daciano had made that ache ebb, even if just a little.

As if her growing bond with him didn't leave any room for emptiness.

"Then, by all means, have fun on your tour." Cas pointed his finger at her face. "If the vampire beds you tonight, you better pray I can defeat Goürlav."

"Please don't be mad at me!" She reached out to touch his shoulder, but he recoiled, tracing away.

She stared after him for long moments. They'd never fought before, had always gotten along with such ease. Yet just now he'd looked as if he couldn't stand the sight of her.

Turning toward her rooms, she passed the guards posted at her door, ducking her head so they couldn't see her watering eyes.

Their mewling, halfling soon-to-be queen. Who had *no* idea what she was doing.

Don't cry, don't cry....

As soon as the door closed behind her, she removed her mask and swiped her forearm over her face. How could she not cry?

She'd fought with all her loved ones, and the guilt was heavy. They were all that she had in the world. Unless she counted the vampire. *You are mine . . . we are fated.*

On top of tonight's developments, she was still trapped in this process—helpless to do anything but watch as Daciano and Cas likely went to their deaths.

Tears don't help anything. What to do? *Go outside and take in the night.* But her feet wouldn't quite shuffle her outside.

Alone on the balcony, up so high—*in the dark?* With an "imperfect" barrier spell?

Did it even matter that those Vrekeners were dead? Would more come? She suspected she'd always be crippled by fear. She couldn't just turn it off....

What to do? Work! Yes, she'd lose herself in creation.

She hurried into her workroom, inhaling deeply as she entered. The familiar scents helped to center her. When all the world seemed to be dismantling around her, creation was her one constant.

In the next half hour, she could finish fabricating the piece for Patroness. All she had left to do was attach the two moving parts of the weapon—the all-important spring mechanism and the blade. Then etching, then completion. So close.

And once she'd finished with work? How to handle this eve with Daciano?

As she gathered the needed tools, she imagined what she'd say to him. First she'd rail at him for taking her blood.

Before, she hadn't known for certain whether he'd harvested her memories. Now she did. She was sick of everyone walking all over her.

After she railed, she would demand answers! *Did you take my memories on purpose? Why gift me with those heads in such a manner?*

Are you . . . are you afraid of dying tomorrow?

Salem shimmered into the room. "What's wrong wiv you, chit? You look like you're about to cry. And in your workroom, no less? This is the seat of nirvana for you."

"Why are you even asking? I know you heard my conversation with Cas."

"That's fair."

"I broke my promise to him. He's denying his instinct, making sacrifices to be with me. But I betrayed him."

"He wants *credit* for not diddlin' a whore?" Salem occupied her earring. "Bully for him that he hasn't been dippin' his wick in all the hookers in Rune—*for a few chuffin' days out of his immortal life.* Really? He wants a biscuit for keepin' it in his pants? Try not havin' sex for eighteen years!"

Salem's Cockney accent was so thick tonight; at any second, she expected him to say, *"P-please, sir, I want some more."*

She shook her head. "You won't turn this around, sylph. *I* am at fault."

He slithered around her neck to her other earring. "Does Cas compliment you? Does he hold your hand?

Does he ask about your interests? Have you two had a chin-wag about what your future'll be like?"

When she opened her mouth to answer yes, Salem added: "In detail?"

She closed her mouth.

"After each bout, he hams it up for his adoring tarts and longs for his randy ways. He's not *tryin'* to fall for you."

Bettina glared. "Cas never wanted any of this to begin with! He never wanted *me*. I dragged him into this."

"And so far, you've saved his life! Though I do think Goürlav'll wipe the floor wiv 'im."

She flinched as if struck. But her voice was toneless when she pointed out: "Goürlav will only face Cas if he wins. You assume Daciano will lose?"

Silence. She knew she was getting a *duh* look. "And that's a shame," Salem said, "because the vampire's in it to win it wiv you."

"In it to win it?"

"Besides giving up his home, he's interested in your interests, and he's willing to compromise. I saw him chokin' down wine for you. He thinks you're the mutt's nuts. You could've done worse."

"I've only known him for so little time. I can't just turn off my feelings for Cas like a spigot. And if I went from utter love of Cas to utter love of Daciano, what does that say about me? At best, that I'm fickle. At worst, that I'm as young and stupid as everyone seems to believe."

"No one expects you to turn off your feelings— they'll always be there—just start seeing 'em for what they really are."

Had she begun to? Whenever she imagined marriage, she'd begun to think only of . . . Daciano. Whenever she thought of Cas, she kept replaying all the milestones of their friendship.

"The demon's your best mate, as in *friend*. Some other female out there is his other kind of mate. She ain't you."

Bettina was starting to believe this. If she and Cas had been fated, then why was there so much strain between them—especially when they tried to act like a couple?

Oh, what did it matter how she felt? So long as Goürlav still lived, Bettina's two choices of men were about to become . . . none.

She snatched up her soldering torch and adjusted the flame. Work! The fire blazed in front of her watering eyes.

"You know those raves you used to attend?" Salem said in a cautious tone. "You look like you're havin' a bad trip. Just slow your roll, chit."

"I'm *fine*." Flame to metal. Spring mechanism. Seamless adhesion.

"Look behind you, Princess! The dummies are dancing."

She heard them moving, but didn't glance up.

"Oi! Those soddin' dummies are *boffin*'."

She set the flame aside, slammed her palm against her workbench. "Please, Salem!"

The dummies stilled as if affronted. "Fine, then. Should I go spy?"

"Yes. Absolutely. *Go*."

"Maybe some of me sources'll give up details about Goürlav—now that their delegates are dead and all."

"Sounds like a plan," she said absently, lifting the torch once more. Soon she was lost in the process, working in a frenzy.

"I'm going, Princess."

Still here? She blew on the last heated section of metal, examining the assembled piece. Pride welled in her chest as she doused her torch. It was just like Daciano's sketch.

Yet when Salem finally left, a presence remained.

30

"You're early," Bettina murmured to Trehan.

She'd sensed I'm here? He appeared fully. "And you're extraordinary," he bit out, marveling at her.

She'd been utilizing a soldering flame, her movements precise—and so quick that a mortal wouldn't have been able to discern her hands.

Her gaze had been one of total focus as her nimble fingers wrought such a formidable weapon. Her eyes were still glowing, her irises sparkling.

A thing of beauty to watch.

When he'd first arrived, his lingering rage over her attack and his marked confusion had felt like two animals clashing inside him. That turmoil had faded as he'd watched her.

She was here, healthy and safe, with him now. The Vrekeners were dead. And she was so fucking beautiful.

His lessening fury had been replaced with *lust*. The

more he'd watched, the more aroused he'd grown, re-calling how those delicate fingers had smoothed over his body just as eagerly.

Had he ever been so hard?

She set the new weapon in a special cradle, then turned to him. "We have a lot to talk about."

He cleared his throat before saying, "Don't let me stop you from completing it."

She seemed at a loss. "I've never worked with any-one but the sylph in here."

"That impudent being who just left?"

She gave him a look that said *You have no idea.*

That sylph was the one who watched her bathe? *A discussion for a later time, Trehan.* "Come, Bett, you look like you're almost finished." He traced beside her, examining the piece. "Not a single rivet?"

With an aggrieved air, she said, "I'm not a cobbler, Daciano."

"No, you're not." His lips curled. "No vampire has a more talented Bride than I."

She reached up to straighten her mask, only to real-ize she wasn't wearing one. "What about your tour?"

"This workshop is the one place in Rune I longed to see. It's impressive. Tell me what I'm looking at."

In a begrudging tone, she said, "That bench is for fabrication, this bench is for assembly. Over there"—she pointed out a third one, topped with a wooden set of antique pocket drawers—"I do detail work: engrav-ing, etching, poison loading."

He reached for one of the drawers. "Your poison collection?"

She shrugged. "I wouldn't touch that without a glove."

"Ah," he said, dropping his hand. "You must be at the detail stage."

"My patroness likes elaborate flourishes. After you leave, I'll etch designs along the top rings."

"I know you want to finish the piece now."

She nibbled her bottom lip. "You could come back in an hour."

He crossed his arms over his chest. "Not a chance."

She gazed from him to her project. "There are a lot of things unsaid between us. I have . . . questions."

"I'll answer anything you ask me. But indulge me with this."

Another sideways glance at the weapon.

"So close to completion," he said in a coaxing tone. "It will be all you think of tonight. I'll bet this final etching is your favorite part of the process."

She glanced up in surprise. "Fine. If you'd like to be bored, I'll continue."

Allowing him to see a new facet of her? This concession had to mean something. Maybe she was accepting him more.

She moved the weapon to the third bench, fastening it in a cushioned vise, then opened a small chest.

"Those are?"

"Precision hand tools." The files and chisels were works of art in themselves, each with a polished ivory handle. She confidently plucked out the smallest chisel, one with a tip not much larger than a pen point.

"Do you know what you'll engrave?"

"Scenes from her home realm," she answered absently, clearly ready to get to her task. "Um, you're blocking my light."

"Just so." He traced back, leaning against the nearest wall.

With one hand, she began wielding the chisel, sure cuts across shining gold. With the other, she smoothed away slivers, brushing her thumb over each groove.

She had total focus on her work—he doubted she registered his presence any longer. When she pulled her glossy hair over her shoulder, narrowing her sparkling gaze, he wasn't even surprised that his heart beat wildly.

Her movements grew faster and faster. Before his eyes, patterns began to emerge over the rings, scenes in relief. On one, she etched a dragon; on another, what looked like a well. She depicted a castle on the third. Before she started the last one, she closed her eyes and ran her fingertips over each image.

Exactly as she'd imagined exploring his shaft. He swallowed hard, and furtively adjusted it now.

Along the fourth ring, she engraved a wild, spray-tossed seashore. When she puckered her lips to blow away any trace shavings, he just stifled a groan.

One day soon, he'd take her on this bench, with her eyes alight. Yet another reason to survive tomorrow.

She tilted her head, surveying her work, a stray tweak here, a deepened groove there. "I'm done," she said, returning the chisel to its box.

As she exhaled, rolling her head on her shoulders, he gazed from the work to her, and back to the work. So much talent! How long had it been since he'd looked at something with awe?

The better part of a millennium. "Try it on," he said, his voice gone husky.

With a shrug, she donned it. The raised etchings seemed to come alive with each movement of her hand. One press of her thumb and a vicious-looking sneak blade shot from the bottom. Another press, and the blade slipped back inside.

When she removed the piece, placing it in its cradle, more pride shone from her eyes. She turned to him. "So, we have a lot to talk about—"

He'd already traced to her, cupping her face. "I'll die if I don't kiss you right now."

Bettina gasped when his mouth met hers, her hands shooting to his chest to push him away. But his lips were so deliciously firm, and his immediate groan made her shiver.

With excitement?

How could she be excited when she still felt raw inside? Why was that empty feeling fading as he deepened his kiss?

Enjoy this, her mind whispered. *Tonight's your last chance.* Yes, to enjoy those smoldering looks, those strong arms around her, holding her secure against him. That connection . . .

When he lifted her to the bench and wedged his hips between her legs, she grasped his shoulders, delighted by the way they flexed under her palms.

His hands closed over her waist, his thumbs stroking just beneath her breasts. Her thoughts seemed to be scattering, leaving room only to register feeling.

Sensation, pleasure. *Yes, let him seduce you again.*

Seduce. She'd been warned of this. Just like everyone else, he was taking advantage of her. Again.

I am *so naïve.* Even as he kissed her, tears welled in her eyes.

When they spilled over, he froze, then drew his head back. His voice grew rough. "What is this, *dragă?*" As his gaze searched her expression, he grazed his knuckles across a line of tears.

"They told me you'd try to seduce me."

He straightened. "I'm *not* trying to seduce you."

She blinked. "Don't you want to . . . you aren't . . . oh, never mind."

"Want to?" He gently cradled her face, brushing his thumbs over her cheeks, over her tears. "I think about taking you to bed *constantly,* Bett. But I will never claim you completely, not until I defeat Goürlav. I wouldn't risk even the slightest chance that you'd be vulnerable to the primordial. Once I leave you this eve, you'll be a virgin still." When two more tears tracked down her now heated cheeks, he rasped, "Why are you crying?"

"Why not?" She dashed the back of her hand over her eyes. "Everything in my life is wrong. I've quarreled with my guardians. I've quarreled with Caspion for the first time—"

"Always that demon!" His hands dropped to his sides.

"And apparently, I'm quarreling with *you* now! I should be railing at you, not kissing you. You took my memories, you've seen inside my head. And you *knew* what would happen if we kissed that night. You got me to a point where I didn't care if your fangs were sharp. It was a calculated move on your part."

"Yes," he admitted.

"I hate it when you do that!"

"I did want your blood—so that I could find your foes. But it was also true that I had very little control over my fangs. I've worked on my control ever since that night."

"And what about your actions in this round of the tournament? The Vrekeners might consider your move an act of war. I won't have been queen for a day before they descend upon us, bringing strife to my people."

The vampire's eyes flickered. "They declared war on your realm when they attacked the sole heir to its throne!"

Her lips parted. Exactly what she'd said to Morgana earlier today.

"They stole the root power of a great sorceress." In a softer tone, he said, "Bett, they executed your mother."

And indirectly killed my father as well. She pinched her forehead. "I understand *why* you killed them. I thank you for that! But you shouldn't have revealed them in public."

"Of course I should have. It signals to the Vrekeners that they aren't beyond our reach. They *can* be found, and there will be swift consequences to their actions."

"You sound like Morgana." *With your actions, you train others how to treat you.*

"In this, she is right. I come from a closed realm, one hidden like Skye Hall. If anyone were to find his way to us in Dacia, the kingdom would be rocked. The Vrekeners will be as well. Failing to retaliate would tell them that they can do whatever they please to you and your kind. Eventually they would attack you again. They would not stop."

She knew this. The hawk would find the escaped mouse. "How did you find the Hall?"

"I didn't, not precisely." He pulled out the leather lead he always wore, showing her the attached crystal. "This is a scry talisman."

"You own an *authentic* scry crystal?" Did he never run out of surprises?

"It's been passed down from my ancestors for generations. I've only to imagine a being's face, and it will lead me to him."

"You told me my enemies would . . . die bloody."

His fangs sharpened, but then he seemed to make an effort to control them. "Unimaginably so."

"It looked like you tortured them?" Had he given them as much pain as they had her?

In general, she was a compassionate person. But like most Loreans, she savored when her foes suffered.

"I did."

"I think I'd like"—she swallowed—"to know more about that."

He studied her face. "I wanted to uncover where your power is being held. They were resistant at first, but ultimately I learned of a vault."

She nodded. "That's where they store our powers."

"Only the leader knows where it is, and he was out of the territories. I couldn't reach him with my crystal, because I've never seen him. But understand me, Bettina—we'll get your power back. I won't rest until we do. Clearly no one steals from my Bride and lives. I've only just begun this endeavor."

For some reason, she started to believe him.

Then she remembered tomorrow's match. "Did you . . . enjoy hurting them?"

"Every second of it," he hissed. "Before I took each one's head, I forced him to say your name."

"Why would you do that?" They'd died with her name upon their lips?

"I wanted each to acknowledge why death had come for him, to whom he was paying the ultimate debt."

"And they complied? When they knew you were going to kill them anyway?"

"By that point, they did as I commanded—so that I *would* kill them."

I'd once known pain that great. . . .

"Protecting you is my purpose in life, Bettina. I was born to defend you. To be your shield." He eased even closer, staring down at her. "After a single dream, I also became your sword, your vengeance."

She averted her eyes. "In that dream, did you see my cowardice?"

He gently pinched her chin, raising her face to him. "There were four of them. Males in their prime—"

"I begged." Shame scalded her.

"I experienced your pain. It was some of the worst I've ever felt. And I've lived so long, Bettina."

"What else did you see of my life?" She knew he would point out her weakness, her dependency on her guardians, her useless panting after Caspion.

"You view the world differently than I do."

"Of course I do. You're a brave warrior. I'm . . . not."

"You're an *artist*. You see beauty in so much, noting details I never would have seen. You have a sensibility I could only imagine before." He parted his lips, then paused for a moment, as if he wanted to get his next words exactly right. "I've spent my entire life killing. I destroy. You create. You've opened my eyes to a new world. I crave more of it. More of *you*."

After he'd experienced her memories, he wanted her *more*? She hadn't seen *that* coming.

But then his words sank in. He wouldn't *get* more, even if she decided to give it to him.

"You're talking of things to come?" *You're going to die in less than twenty-four hours!* "Your future likely ends tomorrow night. And mine? I'll be given over to Goürlav with war brewing. That creature will possess my summoning medallion, and whoever controls it, controls me. It's a bond I can't break, one I can't outrun. I will never be free."

"Your medallion will never make it from Raum's hand to Goürlav's."

"How can you say that?" she cried.

"I've instructed my cousins to do whatever it takes to save you should I fall. Three Dacians have vowed to protect you eternally. And, Bride, there's little three Dacians can't do if they actually unite in a cause."

His precautions stunned her, but her flare of hope quickly died. She didn't see how they could circumvent the blood contract of the tournament. "Raum will be compelled to hand over my medallion."

"And he will—in a bank of mist where *anything* can get lost. Should my kinsmen fail to seize your freedom, they'll trace Goürlav to a hell plane and slaughter him. They'd do it now if he wasn't protected."

Not to be wed to a monster? Could she actually remove one worry from the mountain of them?

Great. Now all she had to do was figure out a way to save her childhood love—as well as this vampire who'd invaded her thoughts, her very life.

Who'd given her this gift.

She must've looked stunned, because he grated, "When I said I'd protect you, female, I *meant* it. I'll do it from the godsdamned grave if I have to."

Such . . . *devotion*. Yet she couldn't understand how he could feel so strongly for her in such a short period of time. "You've only known me for a week."

"Time enough to know we're connected."

"Because I'm your fated, mystical Bride."

"Yes, you brought me *back to life*," he said wryly, "an event that shouldn't be discounted so easily. But we're connected by more than that. I *felt* you, long before I first saw you."

"What are you talking about?"

"At the very time you were attacked, I was roused from sleep. My chest ached with the need to protect . . . something." He raked his fingers through his hair. "It was an unformed, chaotic urge, but, gods, it was strong. I thought I'd go mad from it. Had I been out in the world, I could have sensed you better, could have found you sooner. It was my fault you were vulnerable to those four. That's why I was so determined to discover who they were—to right the wrong I did to you."

"It wasn't your fault—it was solely mine," she insisted. "I went to the mortal plane without guards. I told myself if I didn't use sorcery, I'd be hidden from their kind. But I used it unconsciously. They tracked me by it."

"*I* should have been there to watch your back!" he insisted. "After a millennium awaiting you in Dacia, I should have known my Bride would be out in the world. *Zeii mea,* I felt something that day."

"Do Dacians have a sense like that?"

"We've abilities unknown to most. But I believe that you called for your male, your protector. That night, you called for *me.*"

My male. Why did that sound so totally right to her? Had she somehow reached out to this vampire? If Daciano was in fact *hers.* . . .

Then she remembered their present circumstances. "Even if we do share some bond, it won't matter!" *The vampire's in it to win it.* But that was just it: he *couldn't* win. No matter what, they could never be together. "Tomorrow, you're probably going to . . . *die.*"

"How would that make you feel, Bettina?"

Another tear slid down her face.

He pulled her into his arms. "You would mourn me?"

"Yes!" she said in exasperation. "But just because I don't want you to die doesn't mean I'm not confused about everything. Tonight was a shock, and I don't know how to react."

"I see. You need a break from all this, a night to recharge." *I wish!* "Here. I have a surprise for you."

"I don't like surprises." She raised her chin. "Such as when heads tumble out in front of me."

In a gruff tone, he admitted, "I thought I'd have time to prepare you for the sight. I didn't want to frighten you."

"I happen to frighten very easily."

"Forgive me. For now, I've little else to give you."

She softly said, "Because you abandoned your kingdom for me."

"A worthwhile sacrifice. Now, can you trust me that this will be a pleasant surprise?"

"I don't . . . oh, very well."

"Close your eyes." When she reluctantly did, he traced her . . .

To her favorite place in all of Abaddon—her folly in the great rain forest.

She was about to ask how he knew about it, but remembered that he probably knew everything about her now.

And he still wants me.

She sighed, gazing around. Located near the marsh's

edge, the structure consisted of a marble base with ten columns, each carved to look like a different type of basilisk.

Above, over a net of gold filament, a dome of vines grew in a tightly knit riot of green. More vines stretched between the columns to fashion walls. Oversize blossoms fanned out intermittently, bold circles of vivid yellow.

My folly. Compared to Rune, the rain forest was ablaze with color. How she'd missed this place!

The vampire had slain her enemies, had taken pains to protect her from Goürlav, and now had given her this.

Then she noticed that he'd already been here, bringing furs from his tent as well as wine and food for her.

"A picnic?" She raised her brows at him. "You expect me to believe you don't plan to seduce me? You've gone and set up all those precautions to protect me from Goürlav, and yet you're not confident enough to have sex with me?"

In a husky voice he said, "Do you desire me to do so this night?"

"No!" *If circumstances were different . . . maybe?* "You just keep telling me you don't intend to have sex with me."

"Not by choice—I fantasize about it without cease!" He leaned down to rasp at her ear, "How I'll prepare your sweet little body to receive me, how I'll ease you into lovemaking so you crave me as much as I do you." As she shivered from his words, he pulled back with a sexy curl of his lips. "In any event, I said I wouldn't seduce you *fully.* Though *up to a point* is still in play."

Flustered, she reached for a mask that wasn't there, then backed away from him to stroll the perimeter. She surveyed all the pie blossoms, named so because each bloom was as big as a pie, its scent as sweet. As she ran her fingertips along damp marble, registering the sensation, the vampire said nothing. But his gaze followed her every move.

A guy who likes you wants to watch you all the time. Daciano stared at her—as if there was nothing else to behold.

"If you do win this tournament, vampire, you'll be king of this plane," she said. "Don't you care to see any of it? This is probably the prettiest place in Abaddon." And there was a natural phenomenon that took place on nights like this. *Before the rain comes the clear.* Soon a break would open in the fog bank, revealing a breathtaking scene above.

He joined her. "I want you to show it to me."

She waved a hand around. "Look on."

"I see a swamp. The flora is visually appealing, the air muggy, the trees gigantic. But I now know there's so much more. I want to see it as you do."

She nibbled her bottom lip. "I see . . . function. Nothing is static. I see the growth patterns in a line of vine: bursts of it each rainy season. Those broad leaves toward the ground are much fuller to catch the snippets of sunlight that filter through." He looked so interested, she found herself saying, "In a few minutes, if you go to the glade just there and look up, you'll see a unique sight. It's beautiful."

"You will show it to me."

Her? Walking into that clearing? In the center of all those towering moonraker trees? She nearly snorted. *Not going to happen, vampire.* Even with Daciano here, she couldn't tolerate that risk.

But wasn't this folly also flanked with those trees?

Where Vrekeners were wont to perch.

She looked at the closest tree, a massive wooden tower looming beside her. Next to it, she felt as tiny as an ant. As powerless as one.

Her breaths began to shallow as her gaze followed the trunk up and up—until it disappeared into the ghostly fog above. That oh-so-familiar seed of anxiety grew.

There could be a colony of Vrekeners up there, and she'd never see them.

But they could see her. . . .

31

Trehan saw the exact moment panic quickened inside her. Her body shot still even as her heart began to race.

"Easy, love." He was at her side in an instant, hands covering her shoulders.

Her eyes were wide and locked on a nearby tree, her breaths hitching.

"Look at me, Bett. Look at me!" He cupped her paling cheeks, making her face him. "Breathe. Inhale, exhale."

She squeezed her eyes shut, gripping his shoulders, digging her nails into the muscle. "I'm supposed to take breathing advice . . . from someone who didn't use his lungs . . . for centuries?"

"Nothing can ever touch you when you're with me," he said in a comforting tone, placing his palms over her back. She seemed so frail as she gasped for air, her shoulder blades so fragile beneath his callused palms. *My delicate little Bride.* His hands felt too large and rough against her, but when he rubbed her back, it seemed to soothe her.

"I-I want to return to my spire." Finally she opened her eyes.

He gazed down at her, studying her expression. *She's trying to get control.* He could wrap her in mist, but he didn't believe she needed it. She appeared to be tamping down the worst of her panic. "I don't think that's what you want me to do."

"Why on earth not?" Her voice was shrill, even as her breaths were steadying.

"You're reining this back in. You're beating it."

"I can beat it—back in my rooms!"

"Those Vrekeners stole more than your ability, they stole your enjoyment of this place. You can reclaim it tonight."

Her heart sped up again. "This is some kind of test? Some kind of catharsis? You'll help me past my fear? No, thanks! I don't have to do this now. One day I'll get my power back, and then I'll be cured."

"You're more than just power."

"So says the male that has so much of it!" She fretted her bottom lip. "Look, I appreciate what you're trying to do. I-I don't want to be like this—cowards don't *want* to be cowards. But I also never wanted to be the type of female who needs a male to be strong."

"Fitting. Because I never wanted to be the type of vampire who can think of nothing but his Bride. In any case, you don't need me to be strong. You simply need me here for this first step—which is that way." He pointed to the three stairs leading out of the folly into the glade.

"What can possibly make you think I'm capable of this? Why do you have so much faith in me?"

"I'd ask you why you have so little," he said. "Bett, you're teaching me how to see the world; the least I can do is help you see yourself. I've delved far into your mind. Deep down you know you're remarkably intelligent; you've considered that your talents are un-equaled; you suspect that I find you the most exquisite creature ever fashioned. You are; they are; I do."

Before she could reply, Trehan said simply, "Great-ness resides in you. Power or not, you can *become* empowered."

The vampire's words were like a bell pinging in her brain, reminding her of Morgana's cryptic comment: "The greatest thing about having power is the mere *having of power*. Use the latter well, and you'll never have to use the former."

Bettina had figured that her godmother was advis-ing, "Fake it till you make it." Or "Perception is real-ity."

All at once, the real meaning clicked. *Power is where you find it, where you* seize *it, how you wield it.*

Bettina finally understood. As Daciano pointed out, the Vrekeners had robbed her of this folly; she could steal it back from them.

She might not be able to get her ability back, but she could still be *empowered.*

It's where you seize *it!*

This was a fantastic revelation. . . . *But I'm still not going out into that glade.*

She backed away from Daciano, away from his big, warm hands. "Greatness? Are you joking? I can't do this. Vrekeners could be teeming in the trees, and I would never see them." Until it was too late.

"They could very well be."

"Wh-what was that?" Chills raced over her.

With a confident nod, he said, "There could be twenty or thirty of them. Perhaps more."

"*What?*"

"It's possible that a dozen more have landed since we've been discussing this."

"Why are you telling me this?" she cried.

"Because you're still going to walk out there."

"The hell I am!"

"If I told you none were here, would you believe me?"

How to explain this? "I *would* believe you. But my mind wouldn't . . . it wouldn't *register* it."

"Then accept that they *are* here. Now, what do you think would happen if our foes lie in wait?"

"They'll attack!"

"And then?" His voice went lower, silky with menace. "Come, Bettina, you know what comes next."

"You'd fight them?"

"I would do to them—what I did to the four." He leaned his shoulder against a carved basilisk column; at that moment he looked far more terrifying than any dragon. "You'll have a ring of bodies around you, more heads than you could ever fit in a sack. I'll let you pick which Vrekener to spare—for torture."

That shouldn't sound so utterly appealing.

"You're in a prime position, *dragă*."

"I . . . *am?*"

"If there are no Vrekeners, then you'll walk out there and reclaim this place from your enemies. If they *are* here—which I'm hoping for—you'll get to witness firsthand what happens to those who think to harm my female. Win-win; either way makes for a memorable picnic," he said dryly, his lips curling.

She stunned herself when she almost smiled in return. Maybe the connection that continued to grow between her and Daciano didn't leave any room for emptiness—or for fear.

She gazed out at the murky glade and back. *Before the rain comes the clear.* "Vampire, we could go together."

A sharp shake of his head. "You go alone."

She shoved a braid out of her face. "Oh, come on!" This mouse simply wasn't prepared to scurry into a clearing surrounded by trees, beneath a concealing fog.

And when that fog broke? What sight would greet her as she peered up at the sky? She called to mind the horrific image of a plummeting Vrekener. She imagined the rush of air from angry wings.

Win-win? She would look up and be met with either terror—or beauty.

Even with the vampire here, this would be a trial by fire.

Daciano eased closer to her, again muddling her mind with his mouthwatering scent. At her ear, he murmured, "Bett, I've dealt death in forests all over the Lore. Whenever I'm about to strike, animals, and even insects, go quiet. Listen."

She heard a cacophony of familiar sounds. Unperturbed owls, happily squeaking bats, the steady buzz of insects.

"You see so much," he said. "Now *listen* to these creatures and be assured: no predators await."

Everything out here was going on with business as

usual. Everything but silly Bettina, standing frozen, too afraid to walk twenty-five feet while the impassive world marched on.

Screw—this.

As if he'd sensed her capitulation, Daciano wrapped his hand around hers and escorted her to the folly stairs. "I'll meet you out there."

Am I really *going to do this? Sober?*

He seemed to think so. Apparently, so did some part of her she scarcely recognized.

With Daciano holding her hand, she descended the first stair.

And the second.

After a deep breath, she conquered the final one— but she curled her fingers to keep hold of his until the last moment. . . .

Just as her boot met the spongy ground, she lost that contact with the vampire and faltered, gazing back over her shoulder.

But pride lit Daciano's masculine face, his green eyes aglow with it, his chest bowed.

Great. Now I have to do this thing, if only for more of that addictive look.

The glade lay ahead. She swallowed. How had she not noticed that the trunks and roots of those trees were so monstrous, that the fog was so creepy?

But the sounds were still raucous. *Seize it!*

The twenty-five feet were the longest of her life. Her thoughts raced, keeping pace with her frantic heart-beat: *Before the rain comes the clear. Terror or beauty? Daciano is nearby. He'll annihilate any Vrekeners. Nice picnic, nice picnic. Vrekener torture.*

And then . . . she was in the glade, shoulders hunched—but still there.

"I-I made it," she tentatively called, half disbelieving. "Out to the middle."

"And so you did, love," he called back. He couldn't *possibly* sound prouder.

Within seconds, a break opened in the fog bank, just as she'd known it would. A downdraft of warm air dissipated the mist, as if in the eye of a hurricane. She was in the middle of a tunnel of clear.

She swallowed. *Terror or beauty?* With all the courage she could muster, she lifted her face.

Bettina didn't find attackers; she saw . . . a scene from dreams.

"Vampire, you're going to want to see—"

He was already at her side.

Above them, the nearly full moon was a silvery coin. Fireflies as big as Bettina's hand hovered in the sky, glowing gold, leaving tracers of light. Fluorescent crimson petals spun in the gentle vortex, twinkling red lights. Glossy leaves swirled down leisurely, moonlight striking their surface. . . .

I made it here, and I was rewarded. What other rewards had she missed out on?

She felt something shifting inside her chest.

Was she ready to traipse around town by herself? Not quite. Was she healed from her fear? Uh-uh. But right now, she felt none.

And she knew she'd turned the corner toward recovering.

Daciano didn't say anything for long moments, just seemed to marvel at the sight above them. Never looking down, he reached for her hand again, clasping it in his. "You're lifting a film from my eyes, Bett. I never want to go back to the way I was before."

She stopped looking at the sky, turning her attention to something just as remarkable—the vampire's face tipped up to the moon.

So handsome she nearly lost her breath.

His eyes were heavy-lidded as he admired the scene, as if he was experiencing bliss.

Dear gods, that's how he looks at me.

Sensing her gaze on him, he turned to stare down at her—and sure enough, his expression didn't change.

Dalit. Again that word entered her consciousness. *Lightning.* In quaint old Demonish, it also meant the bolt of desire one felt—before falling in love.

Could she leave behind her feelings for Caspion and allow new ones to grow for this gorgeous, patient, brave vampire?

Words tumbled from her lips: "What would you do if I died? If I was . . . murdered?"

His brows drew together. "I don't want to speak of that."

"You said you'd answer any question."

His hand squeezed hers. "Avenge you." He pinned her gaze with his own. "*Follow* you."

Her lips parted in amazement just as sultry rain began to fall.

32

Trehan didn't understand her sudden question, only knew that his answer had surprised her.

When she peered up at him, blinking against the drizzling rain, he sensed they were at the precipice of something and didn't dare trace her away. Droplets shimmered over her braids like a sparkling veil, her eyes so luminous.

Her expression looked . . . *lost,* as if he'd done far more than admit a simple truth.

"Bettina? Why ask that—"

Two soft hands cupped his face, tugging him down. His lips met hers. *Now* I *am lost. . . .*

He looped an arm around her waist, drawing her body against his, groaning at the feel of her. Her skin was so warm, so slick beneath his hands. Their breaths mingled, the kiss deepening, rain now pouring; the night mirrored the intensity of what burned between them.

When he lifted her up against him, her slim arms closed around his neck, her long legs wrapping around his waist. He traced her to the furs, laying her down.

Between kisses, she said, "Are we about to go *up to a point?*"

"Almighty gods, we are!"

"Will you make me forget tomorrow?"

He drew back on his haunches. "I intend to. As long as we're here in this place, tomorrow doesn't factor. Just you, me, this storm."

When he only gazed at her, she frowned. "What do you want me to do?"

"Bare yourself. Show me your pretty breasts as you did that first night." *This time, to me. Only to me.*

She bit her bottom lip. "You think about that night a lot."

"You don't?"

With a blush, she reached behind her, untying the lace of her top. When she peered up at him for courage, he rasped, "For me?"

She removed the material, revealing perfect pale swells tipped with rosy peaks. He'd seen them before, he'd kissed them before; a groan still burst from his chest.

The corners of her red lips curled. "You . . . like them."

"Like?" He covered one with his palm, giving a gentle squeeze. "Already I'm obsessed with them. I imagine an eternity tending to them and every inch of your ravishing little body." He leaned in to kiss her, promising her, *"Soon, Bett,"* just before his lips met hers. He drank in her sweet gasp.

She met his seeking tongue, lightly swirling the tip of hers against his. He loved the way she kissed—with shy laps of her tongue, welcoming lips, and now a needy moan.

One of his shaking hands cupped the back of her head; his other eased down to unravel the ties of her skirt, pulling it free.

He broke away, but only to admire the gift he was unwrapping. "Loveliness itself," he declared when he saw her in only a scrap of black lace.

Slowly, so as not to frighten her, he tugged her panties down her legs, leaving them around one slim ankle.

The sight of her body stole his breath. Waist so small, skin so sleek. Water drops trailed over taut limbs, delectable curves, and those pert breasts. The tiny thatch of dark curls on her mound beckoned. . . .

No, he was not a mere observer. As he raised his face to hers, he realized he couldn't be more present, more engaged. Scents washed over him. Warm rain lingered over their heated skin. The beat of their hearts sounded in his ears.

The two of them were a part of this storm, a part of this wild shelter.

And his female was awaiting his next move, studying him with wide, shimmering eyes.

"Do you know what I plan to do to you, Bett?"

She swallowed. "K-kiss my breasts?"

"Would you like me to?" She nodded eagerly. "Then lie back."

When she reclined across the furs, he moved over her, leaning down to lick moisture from her delicate collarbone down to the curves of her breasts. Two pouting nipples taunted him. Which to suckle first?

He groaned as he closed his lips over one, rubbing his thumb back and forth over the other. With his tongue, he flicked fast and hard. With his thumb, he rubbed so slowly.

She arched her back for more. "Ah, Daciano, what are you doing to me?"

Anything I can—up to a point. Hard and fast. Lazily back and forth. Then he switched mouth and hand.

When her head began to thrash, he left two throbbing nipples in his wake and started kissing down her flat belly.

By the time he reached her navel, she was shaking with need. But she raised herself up on her elbows. "Daciano? Wait."

"Do not stop me, Bett." His voice was a growl. "You know what I want."

"But your fangs?"

"I can control them."

"Are you sure? I-I don't want you to bite me."

"I won't take your blood again. Not until it's given." He stroked his palms up from her knees. "Do you trust me?" he asked her with a wet lick just above her curls.

"I do. I really do."

"Then part your thighs, *dragă*."

At length, she lay back, gripping the furs in her fists.

Am I to have this prize?

Though a furious blush suffused her skin, she slowly began spreading her knees. His heart twisted in his chest at this show of trust from his Bride.

Gods, yes, he would survive tomorrow!

He would live to know the full power of her desire. He'd live to claim his stunning female, to master her body with his own, to win her eternally—

She bared her succulent sex; his body reacted with an animalistic frenzy, his lusts raging.

His mouth watered for her pink, glistening folds, for the shadowy little dip of her opening. He wanted to fall upon her, devour her. His fangs ached to prick her; he'd suck on her welling flesh. His cock surged, desperate to sink into her virgin core.

When he took her luscious scent into him, he felt the beginning tremors in the base of his shaft, seed rising against his will.

About to spill? Before I'm even to kiss?

He somehow restrained himself. In an unrecognizable voice, he repeated what he'd told her the first night he'd found her: "I've had a sample of your taste, *dragă mea.* Now I *feast.* . . ."

She peeked her head up, worrying her lip. "Daciano?"

But he'd already lowered his head. When he opened his mouth and pressed it to her sex, she gasped. With his first hungry lick of her heat, he groaned, *"A mea! Dulcea mea."* Mine! My sweet.

She collapsed back with a moan of delight. "Yes, vampire, yes. . . ."

Her taste was indescribable; her essence was like a current ripping through him—tightening every muscle in his body, enlivening every dancing nerve.

Even as he tongued her with abandon, he somehow kept his fangs in check. Even when he opened his mouth wide to cover her, he didn't graze her tender flesh.

So long I've waited for this. He gazed up to see her reaction. Arms stretched over her head, she arched her back. Her breasts moved sensuously, her puckered nipples jutting toward the folly roof.

She's in love with this kiss between us, as much as I am.

Still on his knees, he rubbed his hands up her torso, possessively fondling her damp breasts, pinning them under his palms. He licked her even harder, dipping his tongue to her opening to gather wetness, then laving her clitoris with it.

My Bride, my prize, my feast.

She threaded her fingers through his hair and rocked to his tongue. "Harder, vampire," she breathed, gone wanton with need. *"Deeper."*

"Bett!" He couldn't give her what she needed, couldn't penetrate her body in any way. Not with his fingers, his fangs, his cock. Frustration seized him—*I want to be so deep in you, fucking you so hard!* His hips instinctively thrust, but his shaft found no softness to sink into.

"Trehan," she moaned. *"Please, I-I need . . ."*

With a growl, he surrendered his grip on her breasts and clutched the backs of her thighs, trapping her knees wide to get deeper with his tongue.

"Oh, my gods, *yes!*" Her broken cries sounded awed: *"Never felt . . . it's so strong . . . you make me feel . . ."*

Her trembling thighs pressed against the sides of his face as her flesh began to quiver. On the very edge, she gripped the back of his head, undulating her hips up—as she tugged him down.

Even in the throes, Bettina knew that this secreted place on her body—a place no other male had ever touched—was now *his*.

He'd claimed it with his tongue, with his lips, with his harsh growls. And she'd surrendered it fully.

Was the vampire rasping words to her between each lick? "Tell me you'll let me . . . do anything to you!"

His fingers tightened on her thighs, urging her to answer.

"I . . . I . . ." She couldn't think. Why wouldn't she let him do anything—if it felt like *this*? Did he mean sex? *Can't think.*

Why were those words so important to him?

All she knew for certain was that she needed to dig her nails into his muscular back, to lick his skin, to grind into his kiss—

Ah, gods, his wicked tongue was *everywhere*. "Oh, vampire, don't stop. . . ."

As she neared her peak, pleasure dancing within reach, her mind could generate no other thought: *"Coming!"*

An instant later, ecstasy overwhelmed her. Scorching and boundless, it coursed through every inch of her. Back arching, she flung her arms wide—and screamed.

A fierce groan broke from his chest as he bore down on her with his mouth. Though her orgasm ebbed, he licked her even more greedily. Sounding frenzied, he delved right at the entrance to her sex, where her sheath was still spasming. Could he taste her?

Too much! Writhing beneath the iron grip of his hands on her thighs, wriggling from the lashes of his tongue, she pleaded, "Oh, stop!"

He didn't; he took her clitoris between his lips. And gently sucked.

"Ah!" Lost again.

Rippling waves inundated her. Helplessly, she surrendered to them . . . just let them come and come. . . .

Once her second release subsided, he finally began kissing up her body, rasping something in Dacian, something that sounded like a promise—or a threat. She didn't recognize the words, but she recognized the *So help me . . .* tone.

"*Soon*, Bett." She thought he grated, "*As deep and hard as you need me.*"

Panting, she lay with her legs spread and—for blissful moments—not a care in the world. Again she felt like she was floating, yet tethered.

Gradually she came to her senses, keen to please him as well. He'd drawn back on his haunches, staring at her sex with such a fierce hunger that she almost became fearful.

With each second, he looked even more agonized. His body radiated waves of tension. "Ah, female"—he swallowed hard, his Adam's apple bobbing—"I can see where I would kill to be."

His comment made her want to snap her knees shut, but something told her she didn't dare.

More harsh words in Dacian followed. He repeated, "*A mea.*"

Mine?

"Vampire?" Her gaze trailed lower. His engorged shaft pulsed against his pants, the material straining.

"If you knew . . . the thoughts running through my mind right now."

Gathering her courage, she eased up on her knees and laid one palm against his face. Such a slight touch, but he quaked from it. "Daciano, I want to reciprocate."

He choked out, "Then we're . . . in accord."

Maybe it truly wouldn't matter that she was sexually untutored. Maybe he could still enjoy her clumsy kisses. She reached for his shirt; he tore it away.

"You know I've never done this," she said distract-edly, her attention fixed on the glorious muscles of his chest. *I really need to sketch him.*

"*Dragă,* you don't have to . . ." He trailed off when she reached for his pants.

"But I figure I'll make up for my lack of experience with enthusiasm."

Another groan. "If you're *enthusiastic* about this, I won't last long to enjoy it."

Enthusiasm *did* matter. She grinned up at him.

He gazed at her lips, exhaling a gust of breath. "Do you know how many times I've come while imagining those lips of yours around my shaft?"

Her brows drew together. "But you've only been blooded for a few days."

"Then you must have blooded the living hell out of me because I'm hard for you constantly. Releasing the pressure has been the only thing keeping me in check with you."

"Really?" This powerful warrior pleasured himself to fantasies of her? Bettina, the femme fatale? The idea melted away any hesitation.

She had nothing to fear from this vampire, and it might be his last night on earth. She wouldn't hold anything back. "I've imagined it too."

"I know. You wondered if I would shudder and groan if you put your mouth on me." With his vam-pire speed, he discarded his pants in a blur, then re-turned to kneel in front of her.

Between hoarse breaths, he grated, "Allow me . . . to appease your curiosity."

33

When Trehan knelt before her again, Bettina didn't immediately gaze at his rampant shaft as he'd expected.

She rose up on her knees in front of him, tilting her head as she took in his face, his chest, his twitching stomach muscles, then finally his cock—as if she wanted to savor her perusal.

Her interest in his body was palpable—and so fucking erotic. At first, she'd surveyed him with an analytical eye. But now her lids went heavy, her breaths shallowing. Those sparkling pinpoints glimmered from her eyes.

A soft moan escaped her, and her hands shot out to his chest as if magnetized. When she feathered her fingertips over his muscles, he hissed in a breath. "You touch me like you do your golds. I watched you in your workshop and wanted you to handle me with such attention."

"You're so much harder than gold," she said, voice gone throaty from her unbridled cries. "You're as hard as these marble columns." She squeezed his tensed muscles, then rubbed her palms down his torso. "That night in your tent, I only got to feel you for so brief a time, when I wanted to explore you like this for days."

You will. Somehow I'll make it so you get that chance—

She took him in hand; his hips bucked, his knees jerking wider.

"It really is unlike anything I've ever felt."

"It aches for you." He curled his finger under her chin, catching her gaze. "Forever *only for you*. Do you understand me? There will be no other."

When her lips parted, both emotion and arousal surged inside him. Half of him wanted to take her in his arms and crush her against him; half of him wanted to fit his shaft between those carnal lips.

Her halting touches grew bolder, a silky stroke here, an inquisitive heft there. "Is this like you imagined?"

He bit out, "Better than. Impossibly better."

She rubbed her thumb across the crown. When pre-semen welled to her touch, she unconsciously wetted her lips. His eyes locked on her mouth. *She's ready. . . .*

"Vampire, maybe you should lie"—

He traced from her grip, reclining on his back.

—"down," she finished with a gasp.

He tugged her hand back to his shaft, coaxing her to kneel between his legs. She did, eagerly.

"How should I begin?"

He reached out, grasping her nape, drawing her closer. "Kiss anything you want."

She tilted her head again, as if debating where to start. Leaning in, she pressed her lips to his neck, then his chest, grazing them over one nipple. She licked the other one.

Never knew I was so sensitive. His hips began to move of their own accord.

As she dipped a kiss lower on his torso, her wild braids trailed over his skin like teasing fingertips. *Don't press her head down . . . don't press her head . . .*

When she nuzzled the hair near his navel, his cock surged for her mouth. *So close to those sweet lips of hers.*

She grasped the base of his shaft. She aimed it at her mouth. He waited . . . didn't breathe. . . .

With a tentative lick, she daubed her tongue at the crown. She must have liked his taste; a purring sound of approval fanned from her lips, warm breath tickling across the head.

Enthusiasm? He was doomed.

Then she . . . lapped at the slit for more.

"Ah, Bett!"

A swirling lick around the tip followed, rendering him dizzy with lust. *Doomed.*

"How am I doing?"

His cock was under her thrall. She had more control over it than he did. With shaking hands, he piled her braids on top of her head, grating, "If only you were this good with gold." Had his accent ever been so thick?

She gazed up at him with a hint of a grin. "There's a different dimension to this, so to speak," she said, just before she closed her lips over him—and sucked.

"Zeii mea!"

That tight seal of her lips slid down his length; his eyes rolled back in his head.

With her fingers splayed around the base of his shaft, she worked her mouth up and down. Taking him deeper each time, she experimented with her clever tongue.

Any lingering inhibition burned away as she got caught up in the act, growing aroused once more.

Her intoxicating scent frenzied him. "Bett, straddle my leg!"

She didn't ask why, only complied—but her eyes went wide when he moved his leg between her own.

His hand snaked down her back to cup her generous bottom. Palming it, he pressed her against his thigh in a rocking motion.

"Oh!"

He shared her surprise. She was even wetter than before, her flesh dampening his skin. "Does that feel good, *dulcea*?" Another rock.

"*Yes,*" she moaned. As she resumed her kiss, she squeezed her thighs together and rocked all on her own, her ass moving like a dream beneath his shaking palm.

Only moments remained for him. He struggled to draw them out, withholding his seed from her. But her scent, her mouth, and her tongue were soon to defeat him.

Her moans around his shaft grew louder; she was on the edge as well.

She pulled away to cry, "*Again, vampire?*"

He bit out, "Yes, my sweet. *Again.*" When he flexed his thigh between hers, she continued her wicked kiss. Even as she moaned, she bathed his cockhead with her tongue, wrenching a groan from his chest. Then she took him between her lips once more.

She sucked; he rocked her. Sucking . . . rocking . . .

As seed climbed up his length, she ground against his leg, beginning to come . . . her throaty cries muffled by his shaft.

His throbbing cock. In his Bride's mouth. As she orgasmed.

Over.

He knew he was about to explode, knew the pressure would pump his spend up to his chin. Her first time—and she didn't like surprises. He had to stop her. Somehow he had to make her draw away.

With a will he hadn't known he possessed, he grasped her face and tugged, surrendering the wet heaven of her mouth.

"Wait! I liked that." The vampire had made her climax three times, and now he was stopping her before his own release?

"About to . . . *come*." He seemed out of his head. His skin gleamed with sweat. Whipcord tendons stood out on his torso.

"I kind of figured that out."

"Watch me this time, little Bride." Even though his expression was anguished, his eyes seemed . . . loving. "So you know what to expect the next."

She stroked his slick length, making him buck in her grip. "Are you sure?"

Between gnashed teeth, he said, "*See* what you've done to me."

"Well, I *had* wanted to see this." Another groan from the vampire.

When she started rubbing his erection, he wrapped his hand around hers. Their gazes met, and together they worked his flesh.

Beneath her palm, she could feel his shaft pulsating, still growing though they squeezed it so hard.

Just when she perceived it beginning to pump, he bit out, *"Watch me."*

Eyes gone wide, she did.

The crown erupted with pearly seed, spurting, arcing over his torso. He threw back his head and bellowed, his body wracked with pleasure, muscles straining from it.

Beauty, form . . . *function*. The vampire yelled in his language, thrashing in their grip. She was awed, speechless as they wrung his semen free.

"It's for you," he groaned as his back bowed and his spend lashed up his chest. *"Always for you."*

34

After wiping his shirt over his torso, Trehan drew Bettina to him, tucking her body against his side. He pressed a kiss against her hair, satisfaction filling him.

Warm, sated Bride. Rain. Peace. Yes, he felt at peace when he held her.

Again, he asked himself, *Why not this place?* This could be his, she could be his. Together, he and Bettina would start a new house.

"I think you like it here," she said, reading his thoughts.

"Yours is a swamp plane with frequent precipitation. I come from a cold realm with zero rain. Still, I could be so content with you here."

"Truly?"

He lazily stroked her hair. "That's not saying much, I'm afraid. I could be content on a hell plane with you by my side."

He felt her smile against his chest. From his dreams of her, he knew that she'd once been quick to smile, a happy female who liked to laugh. But this tournament had disheartened her more than anyone could have guessed.

"Vampire, what else have you seen from my memories?"

He skimmed his thumb and forefinger along a glossy braid. "I saw that you fear taking the crown of this realm."

"Shouldn't I? I'm so different from everyone here—with no horns, no fangs, no strength. Sometimes I feel like an imposter."

"You are precisely what Abaddon needs. Your subjects are warlike and raucous. A levelheaded, compassionate queen is the only thing that will keep your realm out of constant conflict. Especially during an Accession."

"I never thought of it like that." Then her tone turned contemplative. "I'm not really compassionate. I think bad things should happen to evil people."

"If anyone is *evil* to you again, I guarantee they'll meet a bad end. And that's if you don't get to them first. I experienced what it was like when you use your power."

"You did? Which time?"

"When you took down two escaped ghouls. I can only imagine the pain you can inflict. Once you're the Queen of Hearts again, I'll pity your enemies."

"My ability didn't help me with the Vrekeners last time. Channeling it took a lot of concentration—which took time. My range was limited too."

Trehan remembered that she'd had to aim her hands directly at the ghouls to affect them.

"Bett, when I first held a sword, I was too young even to swing it. You grow into a skill—you practice with it. It will become second nature."

"And if I never get it back?"

"You *will*. Until then, I plan to help you steal another's."

She seemed startled by this.

"Did Morgana not propose the same to you?"

"Well, yes. But I could never make another Sorceri feel this way."

"In any case, my offer stands."

She seemed to muse over his words, then said, "You know so much about me. Won't you tell me something about your life?"

"What do you want to know?"

"What's Dacia like?"

"Strategically and mystically hidden. Very well defended."

"Um, can you describe what it *looks like* for me?"

Her question made his lips curl. *My artist halfling needs details.* "Before you, I noted sights only for tactical advantages. But again, I will try," he said, casting his mind back to the view from his balcony. "There's a constant mist. It wisps along the cobblestone streets. Vast caverns soar above all. Fountains run with blood. The buildings are ancient, carved from the very mountain. Our black stone castle lies empty in the center of Dacia, like a bloodless heart." A constant reminder of their failure to install a regent. Though not for much longer.

"Caverns? Does it smell like a cave?"

"No, it smells of cold and blood, which is pleasing to one like me."

"It must be dark."

"In the highest peak, there's an opening capped with a gigantic crystal. It allows in filtered sunlight."

"I can hardly imagine that."

"I wish I could have shown you." Talking of his kingdom only brought to mind how much he missed it. The frothing fountains, the mist, the majestic black keep.

How would Bettina have viewed Dacia? How many details would she have seen that had escaped his notice? They'd never know.

"What was your house like?"

"I lived in the royal library, among all the books."

"You resided in a . . . library?"

"There *were* suites inside and great balconies that overlooked the city, but yes. I was most content among those shelves, so one night, I simply never left." What would she think his dwelling choice said about him?

She seemed to be giving the matter serious consideration. Then she asked, "Do you have family there?"

"No siblings or parents. But many cousins."

"Are you close to them?"

How to answer that?

"It's not a difficult question."

"I haven't talked about myself in centuries. Every detail about me has been private—or already known among kinsmen. I'm not what you'd call a . . . a . . ." What was the modern term?

"A sharer?"

"Precisely. But I will try for you."

She muttered, *"To win it."*

"What was that?" When she shrugged, he said, "Very well," and began describing his family. He recounted the blood vendettas and discord. The constant assassination attempts and battles.

He told her about siblings Kosmina and Mirceo, about hotheaded Viktor always spoiling for a fight. He briefly mentioned the hulking drunkard who was his cousin Stelian. He told her of Lothaire, their unbalanced potential king, and his human Bride—an impoverished mountain girl.

And of the other royal cousin so few knew about? That tale was better left for another night.

"It sounds like you hate your cousins."

"I don't, not really," Trehan said with a weary sigh. "We've actually become cordial to a point. I'm just sworn to kill them, as they are me."

"That's really sad. Do you have no one you can trust?"

"I can trust one of them, and maybe another—but only in certain matters. My house wars with theirs constantly. I know nothing else."

"What do you mean by *house*?"

"There are several arms of the Daciano family, each with its own house. Viktor is all that remains of The House of War, Stelian of the House of Paladin. Kosmina and Mirceo are the last of the House of Castellan."

"And you, Prince of Shadow, must have represented the House of Shadow."

"Exactly." *Except it's no more.* "Each house serves a purpose. Viktor is general of the army, the wrath of the kingdom. Stelian is the gatekeeper, deciding who enters our land. He's the guardian of the kingdom. Kosmina and Mirceo guard the castle. They're called the heart of the kingdom."

"What were you called?"

"I was the sword of the kingdom."

"The sword, but never the king? You said you were a contender?"

"Eventually duty would have compelled me to take the throne, but I never aspired to rule. I didn't believe I was particularly suited for it."

"And now?"

"Now I believe I could be a good king—if I have a clever queen by my side." He pulled her tighter against him.

"Do you think this Lothaire will do well by Dacia?"

Trehan hiked his shoulders. "The throne is his. His house ruled since the beginning of the Dacians. The head of the kingdom." Ironically, they'd been known for their dispassionate wisdom.

Lothaire—the red-eyed madman, raised among the fanatical Horde—*wise*?

"Vampire, you didn't answer the question."

"There are some admirable traits about him. If he and his Bride could ever settle down . . . if he can make Elizabeth immortal . . ." Trehan and his cousins had watched Lothaire calling in favors from his legendary debtors' book, traveling all over the world. "He searches relentlessly for the means to transform her into a vampire."

"A female?" Bettina asked. "I've never seen one."

"In Dacia we have as many females as males. The plague that wiped out their number among the Horde has never entered our kingdom."

"*How* can he turn her?"

"We believe he searches for a talisman. A mystical ring that could grant his greatest wish."

She rose on her elbow to study his expression. "Did you ever see yourself with a vampire for a Bride?"

He eased over onto his side to face her. "Before my father died, he told me not to count on having a Bride—though if it was meant to be, I'd receive a daughter of Dacia to be mistress of my house."

"Oh." Her eyes glittered. With . . . jealousy? "But now you can never go back."

"Do you think I would? Even if I could?" He brushed a lock from her forehead, unable to stop touching her. "I left for you—and I would make the same choice a thousand times over."

She seemed to weigh this over in her head. *What I wouldn't give to know your thoughts right now.*

"You sound tired," she finally said. "Maybe you should return to your tent and rest."

Even after this night's victory with her, exhaustion weighed on him. He hadn't slept a day through in weeks, and he hadn't been drinking enough to sustain himself.

"I can sleep once this tournament—and your affections—are won. I feel I'm close on both scores."

She stiffened. "*Close to winning* means *close to killing Cas.* Your speaking of your family only reminds me how close I am with him. He was there for me when my father died. He took care of me after the attack."

"That eats at me."

"Why?"

"It should have been *me*! You're confusing loyalty with romantic attachment—and friendship for love. You haven't experienced love to know the difference."

"I know I love Cas."

"Then you're confusing two types of love. Over the centuries, I've witnessed it in all its incarnations."

"Is one more important than the other?"

"They're different."

"Answer me, vampire," she persisted. "Is one more important than the other?"

"In our case, yes."

"Then say I could fall in love with you. And say I do only love Caspion as a friend. What happens to him? If you survive against Goürlav, you're going to kill Cas."

"I'm trapped in the tournament as much as you are, Bettina."

"Who's your most treasured friend? What if I had no choice but to murder him? How could we come back from that?"

"We'd find a way—because I'd know you had no choice. In time, you *will* forgive my actions."

"Maybe I could forgive you, but I'd always be thinking about it," she said. "It was because of me that Cas went to Dacia."

"What do you mean?"

"When Raum ordered him to stop searching for the Vrekeners, Cas disappeared. He couldn't take the frustration any longer, was about to go crazy. He must have met a Dacian who invited him to your realm."

Frustration wasn't the only reason Caspion had ventured into Dacia. Mirceo could be quite seductive, promising pleasures of the flesh that would boggle the mind of a randy young demon.

"I'm confused about so many things," Bettina said. "But one thing I know: I could never get past the fact that you'd killed Cas."

Trehan had believed she could eventually, that she'd see he had no choice. Now he doubted.

"The fact remains that I might not win," he said.

"And if this is my last night on earth, I don't want to discuss the future till dawn. Let's not think of it."

In a quieter tone, she asked, "What do you want to do?"

As the rain softly fell, he drew her back down against his side, heartened when she stretched her arm over his chest. "Nothing more than this, Bett."

35

Trehan returned Bettina to her spire just before the sun rose, laying her in bed, pulling the cover over her.

They'd talked the rest of the night about their pasts, their hopes, and their fears, until reality intruded with the growing light.

"You look tired." Her expression had grown pensive. "I wish I could do something to stop tonight's fight."

"We are all bound by the language in our contracts."

"What are you going to do with Goürlav?"

"*Win,* I hope."

"I'm serious. How do you kill a creature who mustn't be harmed? What can I do to protect my people if you injure him?"

"I don't plan to."

"Pardon?"

"The tales of the primordials are true. When they're wounded, their blood is catastrophic."

"Tell me."

"Legend holds that serpents, scorpions, and arachnids first spawned from other primordials, from drops of their blood—except that the original blood-born Child Terrors are as large as dragons," he said. "The only strike I can make against Goürlav is a kill strike."

She bit her lip, her face pale with worry. "Will you stay with me until the match?"

To join her in that bed and spend a lazy day talking, touching . . . ? But he couldn't. "I have much to do." He would deny himself in the coming hours, then reap the rewards later. An eternity of lazy days. *If I live.* "Should I fail tonight, it won't be from lack of preparation."

"You won't try to sleep?"

"My Bride cares for my well-being?"

She quietly said, "You know I do."

A victory! His plan *was* working. Optimism filled him. "No male could be more motivated to live." He cupped her nape. "If you're within reach, I won't go down easily, if at all. Know that, Bettina." With a final lingering kiss, Trehan forced himself to trace away.

Back in his tent, he replayed all he'd learned over the night. One thing stood out—her insistence that she couldn't move past Caspion's death.

Survive Goürlav; kill Caspion; lose Bettina? There had to be some way out of this bind.

Suddenly, the tents flaps flew open and Morgana sauntered inside.

"What do you want?"

"Yes, yes, you're welcome for my assistance with my

winsome goddaughter. By the way, the 'tour' was all *my* doing." She sat on his desk, much as Bettina had. Now it irritated him. "I've come because I want to know how you reached the air territories."

"I have ways. What concern is it of yours?"

"Great concern. One of my Sorceri subjects is likely being held against her will in Skye Hall. She was rumored to have been taken there directly after she escaped from a group of humans who imprison and experiment upon Loreans. Needless to say, she's *having a bad run of it*. So I'll ask you once more. How did you get to the air territories?"

He decided to take another page from Lothaire's playbook. "I expect I'll need more *assistance* with Bettina in the future. Perhaps we'll bargain in the days to come."

Behind her mask, she looked intrigued. "And if you die tonight?"

He didn't think this sorceress could affect the outcome of the match, but he might as well motivate her, just in case. "If I die, my secret dies with me."

Light danced in her palms, sorcery at the ready. But she didn't strike out against him. "You're very fortunate that I need something from you, Prince of Shadow." She turned to leave. At the exit, she said over her shoulder, "Should you live, we'll speak soon."

Alone once more, he reviewed what he needed for his match. But he was as prepared as possible—or he would be if Honorius came through.

Trehan considered trying to sleep; yet no matter how fatigued he was, his mind wouldn't rest. Would his problems only begin if he defeated Goürlav?

Some way out of this bind . . .

His gaze landed on the contract scroll, the one with all the rules. The one that was at least a foot in diameter. He already knew it'd been written in old Demonish.

It would take a normal scholar weeks to read through, much less translate. *Luckily, I'm no normal scholar.* With a weary exhalation, he set to his task.

The things I do for my Bride.

"What are the odds?" Bettina asked Salem, gnawing a nail.

It was late in the afternoon. Morgana and her Inferi had long since come and gone, leaving Bettina cosmeticized, masked, and formally dressed.

She'd been unable to sleep today, lightly dozing and then shooting awake with nerves. Though the vampire had made no mention of returning before the fight, she'd thought he might drop by or send a message.

Nothing.

"Bookies are laying three-fifty to one."

"Three *hundred* and fifty?" She pinched her forehead.

"Yeah, you'd basically have to have inside info to take on those odds," Salem said. "If someone—not me or you, of course, but *someone*—had spent the night wiv one of the competitors and gleaned intel, then someone—of course not me or you—could clean up."

"The only thing I know is that the vampire is highly motivated." And that he'd been exhausted. What if he still hadn't slept? What if it did finally affect his fighting? "Did you uncover any of Goürlav's weaknesses?"

"None. Just heard horror stories about Child Terrors. I don't suppose Abaddon's defenses include anything atomic?"

She shook her head. "Will you come with me to watch the fight?"

"A domestic at the grand table?" Salem sounded amused.

"Come on, it's not like anyone will see you."

Silence.

Bettina realized that she'd offended him, and she hadn't meant to. How could he not be sensitive about his circumstances? During this tournament, he'd become much more to her than a servant, and now she'd hurt him. "Salem, I'm sorry."

"Princess, I might be invisible now, but I used to be a sight to behold, a regular vision, wiv a swagger you had to *see* to believe. This corporeally challenged domestic is declining your invite."

When he shimmered away, she attacked her regrown nail. She'd fix this with him in the future. Right now, all she could think about was her vampire.

My vampire.

Maybe his blooding was doing a number on her own sense of possessiveness. Maybe after last night, she was helpless not to picture herself with him.

But even as worry for him besieged her, she recognized that she wasn't yet ready to surrender completely to him.

And he did want her to surrender. *Tell me you'll let me do anything to you. Tell me you're mine—*

Finally she remembered why those words were so important to him! She'd said them the first night she'd been with Daciano, when she'd been so drunk.

When she'd believed he was Caspion.

The vampire wanted her to say such things and mean *him*.

How maddening it must be for him to know how she had felt about Cas.

Wait, *had* felt . . . ? *I'm so confused.*

And in the midst of her confusion, she wanted to be with one person, to talk to *one* person—Daciano.

She would *never* get to speak to him again if he lost. *Three-hundred-and-fifty-to-one odds say he's about to.*

Unacceptable. He was most likely already in the sanctum. *I'll go to him there.*

Salem had left, Cas was mad at her, and Raum's guards would balk at escorting her down into the bowels of the ring. Could she manage to get there by herself?

Last night, the idea of walking those twenty-five feet had struck her as ridiculous. Then . . . possible.

Then . . . *achieved.*

Drawing on her cloak, she wended through the castle. At the exit, she hesitated to cross the threshold.

Never to hear Daciano's steely voice again? Never to feel his strong arms around her? She peered up at the sky, stunned by her thoughts.

The mouse would rather risk the hawk.

36

Trehan scented Bettina's light perfume an instant before he heard her racing heart. He spied her hastening down the darkened catacomb toward him, looking far too fragile and bright to be in this foul, dank place. As she neared, rats and kobolds scurried.

"Bett? What are you doing down here?" He put his hands on her shoulders, felt her shaking beneath his palms. "Where's your escort?"

Would she be too preoccupied to notice he had no sword belt around his waist? That his unusual weapon lay across a nearby bench?

"Don't have an escort. Needed to see you," she said in a rush. "To tell you not to die tonight."

"You came by yourself?"

"Yes."

"My brave girl!" He took her in his arms and spun her around, before setting her on her feet. "My chest swells with pride, *dragă mea*."

But she didn't share his happiness. She clasped his face and drew him down for a kiss. His mouth met hers.

Her lips were trembling—her kiss . . . fierce.

He'd always considered kisses a prelude to sex. This was different. She was telling him how she felt, and he wanted to respond in kind. He cradled the back of her head as he took her mouth with all the feeling inside him, holding nothing back.

She met him stroke for stroke, softening against him, sagging . . . until she finally drew back with a cry. "Vampire?"

"*Bettina,*" he rasped, straightening her little mask, "that was a gallows kiss."

Her eyes went wide. "I . . . I'm sorry. You need to be concentrating. I should never have come here." She glanced away, frowning at the long sheath lying on a bench.

He pinched her chin, drawing her attention back to him. "You admitted to me that you care about my well being. Is that the extent of your feelings?"

"I-I . . ."

"You believe I'll die in minutes. Come, Bett. Take pity on me and lie."

"You're manipulating me again!"

"Yes."

She groaned. "How can I stay mad at you when you agree with me like that?" She smoothed her palms over his chest. "Very well. I've grown to . . . well, it's like this—"

Goürlav stirred deeper in the bowels of the sanctum, roaring his readiness.

Damn it! "You need to go at once." Trehan traced her to the exit. "I can't take you from here, but you have to leave."

"I'll be fine." Her voice was sad, yet she seemed to force herself to smile. "I . . . I'll see you soon?"

Trehan wanted to tell her that she would, to reassure her—but even that unfounded optimism burned in his throat like a lie. So he said nothing, just stood trapped in the sanctum, watching her walk away from him.

While everything inside him screamed for him to follow.

Moments after she'd left Daciano, Bettina saw Cas, hanging out with his rowdy group of demons. Was he still angry with her after last night? He spotted her then. Would he even acknowledge her?

At once, he traced to her side, leaving his cohorts behind. "You're by yourself, Tina? Strolling around?"

"I, uh, had something to do."

"Then you're getting better. I knew you just needed to see those Vrekeners dead." Regret tinged his expression. "I wish I could have given that to you."

And Daciano wishes he could have been there for me after the attack. Bettina had needed both of them in different ways.

"Can I walk you to the ring?" he asked. "Or do you want to remain alone?"

"I've managed enough for one day. Go with me?"

They fell into step together, meandering through the town, like they had as children. But so much had changed since then. Instead of companionable silence, tension stretched between them. What was he thinking?

At length, Cas said, "Tina, I wanted to tell you I'm

sorry about yesterday. About the things I said. I don't want to fight with you."

"Me neither, Cas!"

"It just felt wrong. Can we be friends once more?"

"Friends." In the past, that word would have made her ache for more. Now she found that she longed to call him friend. "Of course. You're my truest friend. The one who's always there for me. Even when we quarrel, you're still in my heart."

In a quiet tone, Cas said, "And so is *he*?"

"Yes. I care about the vampire."

"I should never have said anything about Daciano and seduction. I can't blame you for getting caught up in your first affair—especially not with one of the Daci. They can be . . . irresistible."

Had some Dacian female tempted Cas to her bed? The thought didn't sting as it would have in the past. "Cas, I didn't mean for it to happen, but there it is. I will worry for him, just as I will worry for you tomorrow. And I can't predict how I'm going to react tonight."

"I understand."

As they neared the ring, she recognized that she'd never been more nervous in her life.

This was really happening. Daciano's fight. And everyone present was certain he was about to die.

Frustration welled inside her yet again. She was a soon-to-be queen with zero control over what happened in her own realm.

Once Cas had traced her onto the grandstand, Raum greeted her with a questioning look.

"I'm okay," she assured him. *I feel like I'll scream!* "Nothing happened last night." *I may have begun to fall for that gorgeous, patient, brave vampire who wants me to be his wife.*

Who's about to risk his life for me.

"Good. This old demon worries, Tina." Raum patted her shoulder with a rough paw, then turned to Cas. "A word, son." The two males retreated to a back corner of the stage.

Morgana wasted no time cozying up to Bettina, handing her a goblet of wine. "I told Raum you would come away unscathed from your meeting, but that the vampire might not have been so lucky. So, did my little freakling sully the Prince of Shadow? I want details."

"We didn't make love, if that's what you're asking."

"Hmm. You look exhausted."

"I know, I know. And I'm not a great beauty anyway," she said, even as she inwardly smirked. *But one vampire can't get enough of me.*

"No, I wasn't going to say that. *Attitude* makes a sorceress beautiful. And it seems you're demonstrating a touch of it—at last."

"Maybe so. But I'm still anxious about tonight. And the pressures of this tournament are weighing me down. Which you must have predicted would happen."

"Because of this tournament, your enemies are dead, your pathetic crush on the wastrel"—she jerked her chin at Cas—"is dwindling, and you're even richer than before."

But Bettina still didn't have her ability, and she was still trapped at this table, about to watch Daciano fight for his life. *Can I watch him die?* She attacked another nail. "Morgana, can't you do *anything* to help him?"

"We are bound by those cursed rules. As I told you, I cannot, by thought, action, or deed, influence the outcome of this tournament. Though I can capitalize on the results," she added cryptically.

"What does that mean?"

"I'll say no more about it."

Bettina gritted her teeth. "There's got to be something," she insisted, setting her goblet away so she could think.

Morgana suddenly gasped. "This isn't just infatuation. You're in love with the vampire!"

Bettina couldn't deal with this anxiety and fend off her godmother's inquiry too. "How could I be?" she said. "I hardly know him."

"Because you're a sorceress, who can sense her male."

"*My* male?" In the folly, Daciano had said Bettina had called for him—because he was hers. "But we don't have mates."

"Perhaps not mystical ones. Yet what if we have a single perfect affinity in all our lives?"

"I don't know who you are or what you've done to Morgana—"

"I'm quite serious. Sorceri wed for life; we choose our mates with free will. But what if something helps us along? Otherwise, how could we bond so completely? Bettina, we Sorceri *cleave* . . ." Morgana trailed off when one of her Inferi gestured urgently for her attention, then handed her a message.

Bettina studied her godmother's placid glamour, so at odds with her flying braids. "Well, what is it?"

"More reports that La Dorada's risen. But no one can confirm."

"Do you have to leave?"

"No. Tonight, it's imperative that I stay here."

"Why?"

"I'll say no more about it. This time because I *know* no more."

Whatever that meant. Bettina surveyed the gathered spectators. She wasn't the only one who feared the Child Terrors. The crowd had thinned for this fight, at least in the stands. Hundreds of demons crowded the surrounding rooftops, jostling for the best views. Those in attendance who couldn't trace had crowded to the upper tiers of the stands.

Except for that odd black-haired female. She sat alone in the front row and stared at Bettina with uncanny golden eyes. Then suddenly she waved directly at her, a cheery salute.

Out of the corner of her mouth, Bettina said, "Morgana, who *is* that black-haired lady?"

The woman had twined her fingers together and was making heart palpitation gestures over her own chest.

"I don't know her," Bettina added, "but it seems she definitely knows me."

Morgana replied, "*That* is the reason I will never have foresight. She's Nïx, a Valkyrie soothsayer. Has high hopes that the Sorceri will join with the Vertas side for this Accession." Morgana snorted at that.

The impending Accession would pit all immortals against each other, and battle lines were already being drawn. Pravus against Vertas. . . .

Raum and Cas returned then, both looking irritated.

"It's time," Raum muttered. Pausing only for a deep draft from his tankard, he raised his hands for everyone's attention. "Tonight is the battle you've all been waiting for! The semifinals, the death match without equal, an event to go down in history!"

Sporadic cheers sounded.

"First we have Goürlav, the Father of Terrors, king of hell planes untold!"

Goürlav emerged from the sanctum, stomping into the ring. Fearful whispers carried throughout the crowd. More than one family eased even farther up the stands.

The primordial had sharpened all six of his oversize horns for this event. Pointed tips jutted from his head, shoulders, and the backs of his elbows. Again, chains crisscrossed his chest, bulky metal strapped over his roughened toadlike skin. His yellow eyes were devoid of all feeling. His chin tusks looked like a dirty, fossilized beard.

This is what Morgana and Raum expect me to marry?

Raum continued, "Next we have the Prince of Shadow, hailing from lands unknown!"

Daciano stalked into the ring, his strides long and sure. His bearing was ice-cold, no hint of nerves or emotion.

A killing machine.

Cas muttered, "Never thought I would be pulling for the vampire."

Morgana murmured, "I'd sully him so hard. . . ."

As ever, Daciano was simply dressed. Black leather pants encased powerful legs. His black long-sleeved shirt molded close over his brawny chest.

The combatants had each been allowed one weapon. Goürlav grasped a sword that looked about seven feet long, and Daciano held—

A staff?

"Where's his sword?" Bettina's voice scaled an octave higher as she asked, "Is that a . . . that isn't a *walking staff*?"

Under his breath, Raum said, "What's the vampire thinking?"

Cas sounded stunned. "Bringing a stick to a sword fight?"

For some reason, Morgana gave a delighted laugh. "The weapon." In an *ah-ha!* tone, she cried, *"The Ever-Knowing One!"*

Again, whatever that meant. Daciano had said he wouldn't strike—except for the kill strike. How exactly did he intend to kill with a staff?

Dear gods, my vampire is *going to die.*

The gate clanged shut behind the competitors. With an uneasy glance at the squadron of soldiers posted outside the ring, Raum signaled for the horn.

And there wasn't a damn thing Bettina could do to help Trehan Daciano.

37

The horn was still sounding when Goürlav made his first strike against Trehan, tracing with unfathomable speed.

The primordial sliced his long sword through the air even before his body had fully materialized.

Trehan leapt back, twisting his torso to avoid the sword tip by inches. *Can't block it.* He had to remember not to wield the staff as he would a sword. Had to remember *to ignore* all his training.

Before he'd had time even to regain his fighting position, that sword whistled through the air once more. Pain seared his chest. Blood dripped from a shallow gash.

Fuck, this creature is fast. Goürlav *had* been sandbagging in other rounds. The pre-demon's body might be old, but it was deadly honed.

And Trehan couldn't fight back. *I only get one shot at this, one shot with this weapon.* He began half-tracing, making himself like air; at once, Goürlav ceased his advances, conserving all energy.

We'll be weeks like this. Trehan needed to make the demon complacent. *Which means I'll be taking a beating.* He clenched his jaw and materialized fully.

Goürlav charged once more, his sword nearly catching the staff before Trehan yanked it behind him. Goürlav's yellow eyes flickered with interest. Sensing that Trehan was protecting the staff?

Another charge.

Gods damn it! Now the demon was targeting it. *Have to defend myself—while defending it. Or I'll never leave this ring alive.*

Goürlav feinted with his sword. Trehan dodged—just as the demon launched his anvil fist right at Trehan's chest, connecting. His sternum fractured as his body hurtled through the air.

Trace! Too disoriented. Up? No, down! Plummeting. Never had he taken such a hit.

His back crashed into the side of the cage; a line of iron spikes gored holes into the back of his neck and torso before his body recoiled from the impact. Launched into the air once more, he poured blood from a pierced lung.

The second landing was like a punch from the earth. All breath left his good lung. Black dots swarmed in his vision. *Rouse yourself!*

Wait. *Hands empty?* Where was the staff?

The demon seized his body with two hands, sinking its claws into Trehan's skin. Trehan thrashed but couldn't get free; the primordial's grip made it impossible to trace. In one practiced movement, Goürlav dropped to a knee, raised the other, and lifted Trehan over his head.

To crack my spine. Trehan gritted his teeth just as the demon hurled his body, back first, down across that raised knee.

Broken? Not yet. *Can't get free; can't trace.*

Staff . . . where's the fucking—

Goürlav hefted him up and heaved him down again. Snap. Trehan perceived something giving way inside his body. *Not my spine?* He remained conscious and able to move. *Fight on!* Pummeling his fists into Goürlav's bony flanks, he searched for the staff.

Have to get free! How? How? The primordial had no weakness to exploit. *Made for war. No handholds, doesn't feel my punches—*

Goürlav raked his elbow horn across Trehan's torso, ravaging the skin and muscle beneath it. *Now he's playing with me.*

With his head forced back like this, Trehan was utterly vulnerable. But he spied something from this angle he'd never seen before. *Can it be . . . ?* He squinted to clear the dots clouding his sight.

There. A pulse point in Goürlav's neck.

Normally it was concealed by his bony beard. A visible pulse meant weakness.

Using all the strength he could muster, Trehan clenched his fist—and launched it directly at the area; with a wet bellow, Goürlav clamped his neck and reared back.

Freed of Goürlav's hold, Trehan scrambled away, lumbering to his feet. He scanned the arena. *The staff . . . must get to it!*

Everything happened so fast. He jerked his head around, spied Bettina's wan face and frantic eyes, just before he saw a line of stark black against the red clay ground.

There, just in front of the grandstand!

But the primordial followed his gaze. Goürlav slitted those yellow eyes at Trehan, then tensed to trace for the staff. . . .

"I can't watch any more of this!" Bettina cried. The vampire had been injured in several different places, scarcely able to stand.

"Brace yourself." Morgana pinched her arm, hard. "It isn't over."

When Daciano had taken a blow that sent him careening across the ring, Bettina had nearly lost the contents of her stomach. Tears had welled when Goürlav had severed the skin on Daciano's chest.

The vampire's shirt had been torn away, revealing that gaping wound, a length of bloody lacerations just beneath his pec muscles. The more blood he lost, the less control he would have with teleporting. For some reason, he looked hell-bent on getting back to his staff, the one that she'd watched tumble end over end, bouncing ever farther away from him.

Goürlav traced for it. Somehow the vampire beat him there. In a stunning show of strength, Daciano shoved his fists straight out, connecting with Goürlav's plated chest.

Now the *primordial* went flying!

Everyone gaped at the power left in Daciano's battered body, at the coldness with which he still fought.

But Goürlav was back on his feet too soon. The vampire charged toward his opponent, gaining speed. With a roar, Goürlav accepted the challenge and began tearing across the ring, quaking the ground with each footfall.

Two locomotives on the same track.

Daciano barreled into the primordial, shoulder first, as if he were busting down a door. The bone-rattling impact sent Goürlav sprawling to his back, the momentum grinding the being's body across the ground in a wake of spraying clay.

Gasps sounded all around the ring. Had the primordial's thick skin been pierced? All waited with bated breath for Child Terrors. Waiting . . .

None spawned.

Freed of his opponent, Daciano turned toward the staff. Lips thinned, he traced to it, gushing blood anew when he bent to seize it from the ground. As he straightened, he met Bettina's gaze.

Behind him, Goürlav scrambled up and ran at Daciano once more, rattling the entire ring with his steps.

"Turn around, vampire!" Why keep his back to his foe?

Whatever Daciano saw in her expression eased the grim chill in his own; his shoulders went back.

"Turn—around!" she cried even more frantically. Goürlav was nearly upon him!

Still the vampire stared at her. She whispered, "Face him. Ah, gods, *please*."

Mere feet away.

At the last moment, Daciano traced out of Goürlav's way. The primordial went lurching forward. Behind him, a blaze erupted, like . . . like *dawn*.

As Goürlav whirled around, shielding his eyes against the sudden burst of light, Bettina's jaw slackened.

The vampire was wielding the scythe of the Vrekeners, the one with a mystical blade made of flames.

The one that had been poised over Bettina three months ago.

Only now the black fire was replaced by flames that burned hotter and brighter than she could ever have imagined, like the surface of the sun.

"My gods," Morgana murmured. "Do you know what that is?"

One of the most legendary weapons in the Lore, one of only four rumored to exist.

Bettina hadn't recognized the plain black staff—the sole time she'd beheld that scythe, her eyes had been fixed on the glowing black blade.

Daciano traced into a lunge, launching himself at Goürlav, that scythe flaming above the vampire's head in a mind-boggling tableau.

Goürlav seemed blinded, confused. Too late, he tried to teleport. Daciano had already swung.

The scythe sliced through one protective shoulder horn, then the primordial's meaty neck, then another horn. Cutting like a laser.

The creature's head bounced, its mouth still moving. Its body crashed to the ground like a felled moonraker tree. Spectators froze, dread sweeping over them.

Cas clutched her arm, readying to trace her to safety. At once, Raum teleported to join the squadron of demon guards. Unsheathing his sword, he ordered them to ready their own.

Waiting . . . waiting . . .

The primordial ceded death so slowly. The decapitated body twitched and writhed. Its arms flailed as if to search for its head.

Yet not a drop of blood spilled. The unnatural flame had seared Goürlav's pebbly skin.

Cauterized? No blood? Then Daciano would . . . live?

He'll live! This was finished! The audience must've realized this just as Bettina did; they went wild. Streamers coasted down from the stands. The soldiers sagged with relief, then got to work securing the body; Raum bear-hugged anyone unlucky enough to be close by.

And the victor?

Daciano stood covered in his own blood, holding that unfathomable weapon. It cascaded light down over him, painting him like an anointed warrior. His bared chest heaved with bravely earned wounds. He seemed to have forgotten them. His sweat-slickened skin gleamed, corded muscles rippling.

Not only had he taken the Vrekeners' heads, he'd taken one of their sources of power.

And he'd used it to defeat a monster.

Morgana breathed, "I want one of him all for myself!"

Trehan Daciano was . . . magnificent.

The crowd of mighty Deathly Ones started chanting, *"Prince of Shadow."* And for a few wonderful moments, she was high from the victory, from pride in her vampire, from the roars of her people.

She narrowed her eyes to the sky. *I* dare *the Vrekeners to attack.*

Cas released Bettina's arm, drawing her mind back to him.

"It was a good fight," he bit out. "And a clever move. No wonder the people chant his name now."

How difficult that must be for Cas to say. His childhood had been miserable among the Deathly Ones, yet over the course of the last week, they'd begun to sing his praises.

But the kingdom was fickle. Much of the attention

he'd been enjoying had shifted to the vampire, his own people clamoring for Daciano.

She wanted Cas to have acclaim as well. She wanted him to have demonesses worshipping him and throwing garters and squeezing his muscles—

Her breath left her in a rush. With that thought, she knew the truth and accepted it: her feelings for Cas weren't as she'd supposed them. . . .

Cheers reverberated even louder when Daciano folded the fire back into the staff, dousing it, controlling the weapon of an enemy with absolute surety.

Morgana murmured, "Now *that* is an accessory I must acquire."

Bettina quickly asked, "Do you think you could use it to get my sorcery back?"

"If only it were so simple, freakling. It's merely a channeling device, a conduit, to upload powers to their storage vault. But still, for a Sorceri to possess a scythe of the Vrekeners? How it would gall them! How it would rally us!"

Instead of acknowledging all the crowd's praise, Daciano kept his eyes on the prize, staring up at Bettina with that dark, arresting gaze.

At the end of each match in the past, his expression had said: *I'm fighting for you. Soon you'll be mine.*

Now his expression said: *I'm coming for you. You* are *mine.*

Ah, gods, he looked fierce. She swallowed. And not a little scary.

Morgana registered the vampire's expression and advised, "Be wary, freakling. As I said before, Lorean males become very brutish after fighting over a woman. They need to thrust at things. To *rut,* if you will. They lose their higher faculties."

"Morgana!" she cried, trying to wrap her mind around everything that had happened. It fully sank in that Daciano lived. Which meant that it fully sank in that he would fight Cas. She gazed up at him, recognizing him for what he was: her guide, her lifeline, her mentor.

Her best friend. "I don't know what to say, Cas."

"Enjoy tonight with the vampire, Bettina," he grated. "It's his last." Cas traced away.

The certainty in his words gave her chills. A week ago his statement would have delighted her. Now . . . ?

She couldn't lose *either* of them.

Morgana grabbed her hand. "Off we go. You must get ready."

"For what?"

"The Prince of Shadow will be coming for you," she said, ushering Bettina away from the ring, Inferi trailing. "To stake his claim."

"Morgana, please, I'm in no mood for this."

"This was *the* battle," she insisted. "Killing Caspion tomorrow is just a formality."

"Stop talking like that!" The male she was falling for had lived, and the gut-wrenching fear she'd felt for him had momentarily dissolved. But on the heels of her relief, dread rebounded.

"Your demon is simply too young, with too few kills under his belt. He doesn't stand a chance against that vampire." As Morgana whisked her back to the castle, she said, "The Prince of Shadow is no longer a prince, dear. He's as good as king of this realm."

38

Three onerous hours had passed since Bettina had returned to her spire, with no sign of Daciano.

She'd spent the time with Morgana and Salem in her room. The two were convinced that Bettina and the Prince of Shadow would consummate their relationship tonight, so they'd decided to wait, hold vigil with her—and give her pointers.

Bettina was *not* convinced this was happening. *I just want to talk to him, to ask his opinion.* She knew exactly what she would say: "Okay, you were right, vampire. Cas *is* just a friend, but he's my best and oldest one. I can't lose him. Having sex for the first time—with the male who's going to behead my best friend—is a difficult concept to wrap my mind around. Suggestions? Comments?"

Now Bettina crossed her arms over her chest. "I thought you said he was coming."

"So eager to be bedded by the vamp?" Morgana

asked, reclining over the foot of Bettina's bed, wine-glass in hand. She looked tipsy, relaxed, and happier than Bettina remembered seeing her in, well, *ever*.

Salem had been hanging out in her headdress, thrumming comfortably.

"You shan't go to him—it would scream of desperation," Morgana said. "He'll be along."

Bettina's eyes went wide at a sudden thought. Oh, gods, what if Daciano's injuries had been worse than she'd supposed? She hopped from the bed to her feet.

"Salem here will bar the doors. Won't you, Salem?"

"Right you are, Morgana." He was all but purring.

With a glare at both of them, Bettina grudgingly sat back down. When did they get to be so chummy?

"Besides, we haven't finished our chat," Morgana said. A birds-and-bees lecture. "I'm just getting to the good parts."

Bettina knew that no matter how hard she mentally scrubbed her brain, the sorceress's words of "wisdom" would never be forgotten. Nor Salem's *commentary*.

Among other things, she'd learned about . . .

—An immortal male's refractory period: "A vamp in his prime? We're talkin' seconds, chit."

—A sorceress's infrequent fertile seasons: "No ankle biters for a while, then? Actually, Princess, vampire spawn *will* bite your ankles. You'll be knees up, doin' a lively jig."

—And some mortal named Gräfenberg: "Now, that's the spot!"

Though Bettina had barely digested this information, she supposed listening to them beat waiting for Daciano alone to the sound of the clock ticking. "You two are just assuming I'm going to sleep with the vampire?"

"Like it or not, he's coming for you," Salem said. "Probably just getting hisself cleaned up. Letting his wounds heal a bit."

Morgana grinned. "Ah, the spirit is willing, but the flesh is weak?"

He chuckled.

Bettina narrowed her gaze. "You're both *happy,* celebratory."

In a deadpan tone, Morgana said, "Yes, goddaughter. We are pleased that you don't have to wed a giant toadlike creature." They *both* chuckled.

"I'm going to lose someone tomorrow," Bettina said gravely. "I'm going to have to watch him die."

In a harsh tone, Salem said, "Cas is a big boy. If he wants to live, he'll bloody figure out how to win. I've faced worse odds."

At times like this, Bettina recognized that Salem was harder—and colder—than she'd initially supposed. He could be playful and teasing, but beneath that front, a calloused phantom warrior lurked. She parted her lips to ask him about his curse—

Without warning, Daciano traced into the room. Bettina scrambled to her feet again.

The vampire wasted no time, telling Morgana, "I have much to discuss with my queen in private, and you are in our rooms."

Our rooms?

"Ordering me about? Deference would serve you well just now," Morgana said, all earlier signs of relaxation replaced with ire as she rose. "It's one thing for me to tease Bettina that you're as good as king of Abaddon, it's another for you to act like it. For now, you're merely the king of foregone conclusions."

"What do you want?"

"It seems that I stand between you and something you desire"—she waved at Bettina wide-eyed by the bed—"I can put your *discussion* on hold indefinitely."

"You try to keep me from what's mine, and I will end you, Morgana."

Bettina gawked at his tone. Morgana allowed Raum to get away with his blustering, because that was all it would ever be. But this quiet menace coming from the vampire was something else entirely.

"Though I've put you on your knees before and could easily do it again, I'm feeling magnanimous. Let's bargain, shall we? I'll turn a blind eye toward this little liaison. But I want the scythe."

The accessory Morgana "must possess."

"What purpose would that serve?"

"I'm sentimental that way. Hand it over and"—again she indicated Bettina—"enjoy."

Bettina was appalled. "You can't just *trade* me! I'm not a bargaining chip."

"In fact, that's exactly what you are, freakling."

While Bettina sputtered for a reply, Daciano disappeared. An instant later, he returned, brusquely tossing the staff to Morgana.

"Wise choice." She caught it in one hand, twirling it like a baton. "Just my size!" Turning toward the door, she said over her shoulder, "Don't do anything I wouldn't do. Which means naught in the definitive sense."

And then she was gone.

Daciano started for Bettina, only to pause and narrow his eyes. "Phantom."

Salem had remained?

"I discovered a way to kill an unkillable being tonight," the vampire said. "Watch my queen bathe again, and next I'll discover how to gut a sylph. Now, *begone*."

"Right you are, Your Kingness," Salem said with a chuckle, but then he did disappear.

Leaving her alone with Daciano. "There's nothing like being bartered for a weapon to make one feel like chattel," she snapped. "You're just as bad as she is."

"I want you as my wife, my queen. But I want you freely given." He began advancing on her with the same dark look of hunger that he'd had in the folly. *I can see where I would kill to be. . . .*

With a swallow, she started retreating.

"I gave up something very valuable for the *chance* to convince you that you are mine."

"I-I can't be with you. Not like this."

He stalked her around the bed. "The first time I was in this bed with you, I believed I was about to make love to you. The last time we were together here, you dreamed of me taking you. Why would you deny us?"

Trehan's eyes narrowed with realization. "It's because of *him*, isn't it?" Earlier, instead of cheering for Trehan after his match, Bettina had slipped her gaze up to Caspion, her wide eyes full of sadness.

Then she'd hastened away from the ring without a word, without any acknowledgment.

Trehan had barely registered his victory, or even his injuries—until they'd continued to bleed. He'd ordered his squire to bandage his chest, then forced himself to wait for enough regeneration to stem the blood loss.

Trehan had felt no pain, the need to mate overwhelming him. Now that he could claim her without repercussions, nothing would stand in his way.

Nothing. Least of all Caspion the Tracker.

"Be careful, female. One day I will reach my limit. One day you will convince me you want him above all others." After last night, Trehan had thought they'd come to an understanding.

Maybe he'd only imagined how agonized she'd been during his battle, wanting something so badly he'd conjured it in his own mind. Would he *never* win her?

Perhaps not her affections—but after tonight's victory, she was his by right. *I've as good as won this tournament.*

"It isn't like that," Bettina said. "I've told you why I feel this way. I can't make love to the male who will murder my best friend."

Best friend? Could it possibly be . . . ?

"I barely made it through tonight," she said, her voice despairing. "I can't take another round of this!" She rubbed her forehead, sending her mask askew, and with it, his traitorous heart.

Damn it! Exhaling a breath, he asked, "What if I told you there was a way for both Caspion and me to survive tomorrow?"

She stopped backing away. "How? Is it possible?"

"Would you yield to me tonight?"

She rushed up to him. "Tell me how!"

"I've found an escape clause in the rules. But I must explain it later—my need is great, and my control is slipping. Do you trust me?"

"Can you vow to me that you'll both live?"

"I vow it."

"You and Cas will both survive?"

"Yes. Now do you yield—"

She leapt into his arms, wrapping her arms around him, kissing his face. Her clasped hands knocked against his injured neck, her breasts against his bandaged chest; yet he felt nothing but pleasure.

For the first time since this nightmarish tournament had begun, Bettina felt hope.

Daciano had told her that both he and Caspion would survive. He never lied. "I believe you, vampire. I trust you."

When he traced her to the bed, she laughed against his lips.

His curled in turn. "My merry sorceress. All will be well." He removed her mask, slipping it into his pocket.

"You're so good to me, Daciano."

"Call me Trehan."

She brushed a dark lock of hair from his forehead, well aware that she was gazing up at him dreamily. "Trehan."

"I will protect you, Bett. No queen will be more treasured than mine." Even as he said these tender promises, tension radiated from his body. "Tomorrow, I wed you. Tonight, I claim you forever. *Eternitate*." He slanted his mouth over hers, fiercely taking her lips.

I'm truly about to make love? Her introduction to passion had only whetted her curiosity.

As she met his fierce kiss, she recalled how his shaft had pulsated against her tongue. Would it do that inside her? She replayed feeling his hot seed on her hand—and watching it arc thickly over his torso. Now, with her tongue twining his, she imagined his semen flooding deep into her body, filling her.

Her sex dampened from the mere idea.

His kisses grew more demanding, scattering her thoughts. Between his sensuous forays at her mouth, he began undressing her. She eagerly assisted.

Arching her back as he removed her shirt. Arms raised as he bared her breasts. Hips up as he tore free her panties.

When he broke away to remove his own clothes, she opened her eyes, realizing he'd stripped her of everything but her jewelry.

Yet once he'd returned to bed, she noticed the injuries marring his mighty warrior's body. He had a swath of bandage tied tightly around his chest. "How badly were you hurt?"

"I feel little pain." His voice was roughened, his jaw now clenched. That tension rolled off him. His eyes were fully black as his gaze raked over her naked body.

Bettina's excitement dimmed; his control *was* slipping. He looked like he was about to launch himself at her.

Her human friends had spoken about losing their virginity, had described the pain they'd felt—and they hadn't mated a thousand-year-old vampire who was strong enough to defeat a primordial!

Then his eyes dropped to the pulse she could feel fluttering in her neck. This time he didn't stare at it with mere lust; he looked *ravenous*.

She'd accepted that lovemaking would hurt at first. But did she have to get bitten as well? To experience so many milestones at one time—after the night she'd had—seemed . . . excessive.

Still, when he caught her gaze and laid his palm between her breasts, she found herself easing back under the firm press of his hand.

"Open for me, love."

She hesitantly spread her legs. He knelt between them, his erection jutting hungrily between his narrow hips. The head was bulbous, daubed with seed. When he planted a fist on either side of her head and leaned over her on straightened arms, his thick shaft bobbed above her belly.

She couldn't help but note that it appeared even more swollen than it had the night before.

His onyx eyes again landed on her pulse. "Tell me I can do anything to you."

If a vampire's exceedingly thirsty or inexperienced . . . "Um, wait, Daciano." All the desire she'd felt began to evaporate, replaced by apprehension. "I *can't* say that."

39

"Some big steps can come later, right?" she asked Trehan. "Like maybe in the near future. But *not* tonight."

His Bride was supposed to yield! Yet now she was about to tell him that she didn't want him inside her. *Denying my claim?*

She was glorious beneath him with her shining braids spreading over her pillow, her pert breasts taunting him to touch, her lustrous eyes gazing up at him. Bettina was *his* treasure. *Comoara mea.* But now she seemed distant.

He wanted them connected completely; she felt a thousand miles away.

There could be only one reason for her hesitation. "Big steps," he said in a toneless voice. Again and again he'd surrendered his exquisite prize.

Not tonight.

"I mean, maybe we could just . . ."

She can't even say the words. She knows better than to say them!

"Can we just make love?" she said in a rush.

His weakened arms began to shake, forcing him to sink down on his forearms. "You've lost me, Bett. What big step were you musing about?"

Looking anywhere but at his face, she said, "Um, bite play."

"Pardon?"

"Losing my . . . virginity is, well, a big step for me. And maybe we could save your first bite for later. I'm not saying never, just not everything at once."

Relief soughed through him. "*Bite play,* is it?" Even in the midst of his body's craven need . . . even though he was wounded . . . he had to stifle a grin, not wanting to embarrass her.

"Maybe we could experiment with those kinds of things later?"

My virgin Bride is naked beneath me, talking about experimenting. *How will I last?*

"I want you to make love to me." Her cheeks and throat flushed with blood, tempting him to take a nip. But he wouldn't have, even before she'd voiced her concerns. "I-I *really* want you to. But I just need to take other things slowly."

Now that he understood what she was talking about, he could recognize the new tension in her body, the blunted desire. She wasn't nervous—she was afraid.

"Look at me, love." When she did, he said, "I can't drink from you anyway." *What I do tonight affects us eternally.*

"You can't?"

"I have to keep control to make this good for you, *perfect* for you." He wanted to make love to her till dawn, to give her memories to last an immortal's lifetime—and to coax more of her affections. *Capitalize on her passion . . .*

If it proved perfect, she would fall for him. He had to believe that. "Remember when I told you how often I've envisioned this? I never once considered biting you during your first time."

"You don't think about it?"

A humorless laugh. "Ah, Bettina, it's a fevered fantasy of mine. And it will remain so for now." Because *perfect* would be hard won tonight.

Already his injuries would hamper him. With both his cock and fangs deep in her body, he'd probably come in an instant, and he feared that once he emptied himself inside her, he'd weaken even more.

She cast him a brilliant smile. "Then you do understand?" He could feel her relaxing beneath him. "My human friends told me that there'd be pain—and they'd only been with mortal males."

"I'll do everything I can to spare you hurt," he said, drawing back to sit up. "Come." When he held out his hand, she rose up on her knees and climbed over to him, her sweet breasts quivering.

Pulling her sideways across his lap, he leaned back against the headboard, hissing in a breath from the pain in his wounded neck—and from the pleasure of her bottom gliding over his engorged shaft.

Once he had his arms around her, he brought his forehead against hers. "I'm going to touch you inside, make you ready for me." He cupped a possessive hand between her legs, massaging her there.

Eyes languid, she nodded. *So trusting. So innocent.*

With teasing caresses, he rubbed the pad of his forefinger over her clitoris. When he felt the little bud swell, he dipped his finger to her opening, just inside her core, stirring her. "Do you like that?" Her first time to be penetrated . . .

"Yes!"

"Deeper?"

In answer, she eased her thighs open for more.

He began sliding his finger farther inside, stunned by the snug heat that gloved it. She was already slick—but so tight. His cock jerked beneath her. *Like me, it's hungry for the virgin flesh I'm exploring.*

When his finger moved deep inside her, she gasped. "Oh! That feels . . . good." Her lids were growing heavy, her breaths shallow. Her irises sparkled.

"Another finger?" he grated.

She bit her lip and nodded.

He gingerly wedged a second one inside her, then delved the pair into her glistening sheath. With his thumb, he rubbed her clitoris until her head lolled.

Once he began slowly thrusting, she arched her back over his arm, jutting her breasts, beckoning his mouth. Had her little nipples ever been so stiff? He nuzzled them, licked at them, then latched on to one, suckling the peak hard.

She worked her hips, brazenly meeting each thrust. Her ass grinding over his aching shaft nearly robbed him of his seed.

No! Must make this perfect. My Bride, my prize.

Once he'd taken her to the very edge, when she was whispering, *"Please, please, please,"* he slipped his fingers from her. Laying her back down, he knelt between her spread legs.

No silk to bar my way.

She reached for him with outstretched arms. Her lashes lowered over her glittering eyes as her soft palms swept across his chest. The utter hunger in her gaze rocked him, humbled him, made him want to roar with satisfaction.

With a shaking hand, he tilted his length down—

Slick heat greeted the crown; when his shaft pulsed in reaction, the tip grazed up and down her cleft, as if stroking it, *kissing* it.

Where I would kill to be . . . The instinct to thrust was nigh undeniable. Cock throbbing for that kiss of wetness, he just prevented his hips from slamming home. *Want inside!*

No, control, Trehan!

Restraint took its toll. His body quaked; sweat beaded his skin. And still he shuddered with abject pleasure as he eased forward to her maidenhead.

Fixed tight. Silken folds hug the head. Don't hurt her tender little sheath—

"Trehan, I need . . . I need you." She began to undulate on the tip.

His frenzied gaze pinned hers. *"Eşti a mea! Eternitate."* *You are mine! Forever.* With a shallow pump of his hips, he claimed his Bride.

Bettina's eyes watered from the tugging pinch. Then came the sensation of being filled beyond her limit.

She was stretched so tightly around his penis that she *could* feel it pulsating inside her.

His every muscle bulged with strain, his face tense. He gazed down at her with a tormented look. She flashed him one of her own.

Before, pleasure. Now, pain.

He eased back, withdrawing; unexpected tingles radiated inside her, drowning out some of the twinges.

"More, Bett?" His voice was almost unrecognizable.

"Um . . . okay?"

As he slowly fed his shaft back inside her, she held her breath, trying to determine whether she liked this. *Undecided.*

Another withdrawal. "Love, I'm going . . . to do it . . . harder."

When she reluctantly nodded, he groaned and thrust; she didn't know whether to expect pain or . . .

Pleasure! This time his shaft brought heat, fullness, friction. Her hands flew to his shoulders, nails digging in. In a strangled tone, she cried, "I-I *love* that!"

Whatever she was saying or doing made his tortured look deepen. "Waited a thousand years for this. Want to last the night through." He withdrew once more, taking his hardness away. So she followed his hips, raising her own.

"*Dragă*, still!" He gripped her waist, holding her down. "You must not move!"

She froze.

Luckily, *he* didn't. He kept rocking his penis in and out until she was panting, "More, vampire!"

He gave more.

"Ah, *deeper*."

"Like this?" He sank himself as deep as he could, grinding against her clitoris with the most exquisite pressure. "Tell me what you need, love," he rasped, his accent as thick as she'd heard it. His body was bowstring taut, muscles rigid beneath her nails. "I will give it to you—I swear."

"That! Keep doing *that* . . ." Her clitoris ached for even more stimulation; he *did* give it to her, circling his hips, moving his body like a sinful dream.

So much delicious stimulation. Her head thrashed, her legs locking around his waist.

"I told you, Bett . . . that you'd have me as deep"— circling those hips—"and as hard as you need me."

She couldn't answer his words—because pleasure gathered right at that spot in a sudden blinding wave.

As if from a distance she heard herself scream his name. Mindless, she writhed beneath him, clutching his hair, rubbing her nipples against his sweating skin.

Was that her throaty voice, shamelessly begging him? *Don't stop, don't stop, don't stop.*

"Never!"

With a wet rush, she orgasmed around his erection, spasms so strong he had to feel them, tugging his length deeper, *deeper*—the connection unending. . . .

Control fraying. *No, don't follow her!*

Keep your seed, keep your seed, Trehan's mind chanted. Must make it last.

But what male on earth could withstand that irresistible clench? *A better male than I.*

And then her abandon? *She screamed my name as she thrashed on my shaft!*

Somehow, *somehow,* he'd steeled himself against her wanton response as her release subsided.

Wide-eyed, breathless, she asked, "Could you . . . could you feel me do it?"

She's asking me if I felt her orgasm. He shuddered.

Her innocent question, posed in that sultry voice . . . "Ah, gods, Bett, yes! Yes, I could feel you very well."

And now the slippery heat of her climax beckoned him to plunge deeper, to revel in it.

He might have succeeded in keeping his seed for now, but he was paying for it. Urges began to spur him, primal drives that he'd never contended with before.

When a bead of sweat dripped from his forehead to her neck, sliding down, his gaze followed the track—then fixed once more on her pulse. He was not only battling his need to take her blood—he was denying the overwhelming drive to plant his semen deep inside his woman.

Both instincts screamed inside him.

Mark her neck, claim her! Pound between her thighs. Give her everything—your bite, your come, her female pleasure.

Until she surrenders completely.

He gaped down, stunned to find he'd collected her wrists, locking them over her head. *Pin her, possess her. Master her!* He felt very little like a Dacian, and very much like a savage vampire.

And it felt . . . *good.*

"Trehan?"

No! He wasn't some common Horde vampire. He could control these impulses!

So why did he feel like he was denying them both something critical?

Dimly, he bargained with himself: *Just a taste, a graze of your fang as you spend.* The fantasy from his youth finally come true—

"Y-you said you wouldn't hurt me."

She fears me? He remembered her heartbroken

plea the first time they'd been together. Somehow he gathered the ragged tatters of his restraint, forcing his predator's gaze from her neck—to focus on her shimmering eyes. "*Never* hurt you." He released her wrists, then twined his fingers with hers. As he began to move inside her once more, her eyes anchored him. *"Better?"*

She answered by going soft beneath him, opening up, meeting his thrusts. A plaintive moan escaped her lips.

Another bargain with himself, one he accepted: *When she comes again, you join her.*

To this end, he used his body to work hers, pumping his hips while she writhed on his pistoning cock.

Her eyes widened once more. "*A-again,* vampire?"

Between his gnashed teeth, he commanded her, "Ah, gods, *again,* my sweet."

Even before she screamed, he felt the telltale squeeze around his shaft. The pressure of his rising seed mounted; his muscles tensed in readiness, his mind blanking.

"You—are—*mine!*" he roared as the clench of her orgasm milked him to perfection. No longer could he resist its demand. *"Eşti a mea!"*

Pleasure wracked him, made him throw back his head and bellow her name as he began to ejaculate deep inside his woman. Scorching jets of semen bathed her womb . . . over and over . . . until his voice was hoarse, his body emptied.

Never letting you go, female. Never!

With a dazed groan, he collapsed over her. Between breaths, he rasped, *"Bettina, eternitate."*

40

The next morning, rain poured outside, the wind whipping Bettina's tower, lightning flashing all around.

But she was cozy inside her workshop, humming as she polished the most important piece of jewelry she'd ever created.

A wedding ring for tonight's ceremony.

She'd started on it as soon as Daciano had left her at dawn. In the hours before that, they'd laughed, touched, and explored each other's bodies in her bed. Actually, it was now *their* bed, in *their* rooms. He'd claimed them as well.

With Daciano in her life, suddenly her spire didn't feel like a cloistered prison, but a hideaway for them from the world.

"I dunno what tune you're hummin'," Salem said as he appeared beside her, "but I'll bet the lyrics go like this: *'I—love—sex.'*"

Bettina shrugged mysteriously, deciding not to be one to kiss and tell. But, yes, she did in fact now *love* sex. She had decided this after the first time, then *enthusiastically* confirmed it on the second and third.

She and Daciano probably would have enjoyed a fourth, but he'd been hindered by his healing wounds.

Just before he'd traced away this morning, he'd tucked her into bed. His hair had been tousled over his forehead, his eyes devilish. "I have some things I have to take care of today. But I await more of this tonight."

She'd been wide-eyed and not a little awed by her vampire lover. As he'd pressed a kiss to her hair, he'd murmured, "Last night, I made you my Bride; tonight, I'll make you my wife."

Bettina Daciano? Instead of the constant crushing loss she'd come to expect in this tournament, now all she felt was excitement. To be his wife? To have an immortal lifetime of nights like the last, of losing herself in his onyx gaze . . . ?

There'd been no sleep for her; she'd rushed to her workshop and started on a gold band for him. It was simple in design to suit his taste.

And now, she understood the symbolism of an unending circle more than she ever had.

"Oh, and by the way, right thanks to you for the proverbial sock on the doorknob, flatmate," Salem said, occupying the backboard. "I had nowhere to go."

"I'm surprised you didn't return to my room, you peeping phanTom."

"*Of course* I returned. Would've stayed too. But last night, you and the vamp were so loving—and yet oh, so *durty*—it messed wiv me mind." He made a shuddering sound. "Seems you got over Cas quickly enough. R.I.P. tonight, demon. Hookers the worlds over will go into mourning."

She rolled her eyes. "*Nothing* is going to happen to Cas. Daciano found an escape clause in the rules because he's *brilliant*. Bottom line: both of them are going to live." She tucked the polished band into a velvet pouch for safe keeping.

Instead of sharing her happiness, Salem merely said, "Sounds a little too good to be true."

"The vampire can't lie, and he said they'd both survive." But Salem's comment got her thinking. The outcome might be as she wanted it, but the crowd's reaction might not be.

If there was a draw at the end, the rowdy and drunken Abaddonae might riot. Some entourages of fallen contestants still lingered—would they accuse Rune of fixing the tournament?

Thinking like a queen? Perhaps she should institute some precautions. She could assign soldiers to trail the entourages, then station even more guards at the ready for crowd control.

Should she ration the demon brew? No, that'd be wildly unpopular. She tapped her chin. But free baked goods would soak it up! She began scribbling her decrees for tonight.

"So you think this 'draw' is going to make everything just peachy?" Salem asked.

She stilled. "Maybe I do."

"And what about the tension between the vamp and Caspion? Daciano's still an assassin—what's to keep him from offing Cas directly after the tournament?"

"*Me.* He knows I could never forgive him for that." She'd told Daciano as much in the folly.

Salem shimmered from the backboard into a nearby drill bit. "All right, say the leech actually gives the demon a pass. You can't be thinking that the two of them'll just live here and be chums. Two swinging-dick alphas like that? You're deluded if you believe they won't be at each other's throats."

"It won't happen. I won't *allow* it to happen," Bettina said, as if she were used to getting her way. Perhaps she hadn't been in the past, but in the future—

"Don't be a git. Daciano's going to run Cas out of this kingdom—and your life—at the earliest."

"They'll *both* be in my life, Salem. My husband and my best friend. Eventually I'll bring them around."

"Lemme know how that goes for you, dovey. . . ."

She sensed Morgana arriving then. "Godmother's here." She'd wondered when the sorceress would show up to gossip.

Bettina and Salem were waiting in the sitting room when the doors to the spire whooshed open.

"Wine! Details!" Morgana looked different this morning. She always had a glow about her, but now she seemed *cheery*. . . .

They took their wine on her settee, Salem returning to his perch in Morgana's headdress.

Instead of providing the salacious account Morgana expected, Bettina revealed the new development: that both males would survive tonight.

Yet the sorceress didn't seem overly surprised by the information. "That's *interesting*," she said as she examined the end of a braid. "Alert me when we're about to get to the good parts."

"Fine! I was with the vampire, and it was *wonderful*, okay?"

She peered at Bettina's neck. "He didn't bite you?"

"No, I asked him to wait—and he did."

"Interesting," Morgana repeated.

"Oh, she had that leech in a right state," Salem explained. "She could've asked him to slam a sun shooter, and he'd have demanded seconds. Seems the chit's got some upskirt action we hadn't suspected—"

"In any case," Bettina interrupted firmly, talking over her blush, "I have a lot of stuff to do. I need to make sure we're prepared for any reaction the crowd might have."

"Oh, is this a bad time? It sounds like you're a very important freakling now. Kind of a big deal. Huh?"

"One night o' sex, and she thinks she's Madonna," Salem quipped.

"You're obviously busy." Morgana rose. "I guess I can wait till a more convenient time to talk to you about your power."

"P-power?"

"The tides have turned. This Accession, the Sorceri will rise once more. Thanks to the scythe."

"How? What does that mean? Y-you said you couldn't get my sorcery back from the weapon. That it was just a conduit to get powers up to the vault."

"I lied. I wasn't sure if this was possible at the time, and my style is to under-promise and over-deliver. But I've used my unparalleled abilities and the full force of my sorcery to—how do I put this?—reverse the flow. Only two virgins and a basket of puppies had to be sacrificed for the ritual."

Bettina swallowed, hoping she was kidding. "You've stolen back *all* the Sorceri powers?"

"Naturally I've collected a few abilities for my own—a kind of tax on my subjects, as it were, for our defense. But most powers will be returned to their rightful owners."

Bettina's heart began to pound. *Like* this *rightful owner?*

"Incidentally, after I downloaded all those powers, I *uploaded* a nasty little spell for our Vrekener foes."

"What kind of spell?"

"Let's put it this way: the mighty? Oh, how they will fall. And that's all I'll say on the subject."

Bettina didn't care, her mind focused on one thing. "Am I to get my power back?"

"There's something you must agree to first."

She was about to cry, "Anything!" But then Bettina realized she was no longer that girl—the one who'd begged, the one who'd agreed to the tournament in the first place. "Tell me, Morgana."

"You must never use this power against the Valkyries. At least not until after the Accession."

"What? Why?"

"That Valkyrie soothsayer was the one who predicted the scythe would come into play in this tournament. She provided Raum and myself with inside information," Morgana said, adding dryly, "though she neglected to mention that she was divining for both of us."

A *Valkyrie* had been turning the crank? "The raven-haired one? But you hate the Valkyries."

"Hate? Just because I secretly wanted them all dead? It was never *personal*." She waved a hand, as if at a buzzing fly. "It seems the Sept of Sorceri are now siding with the good guys. Apparently, Team Vertas doesn't mind that I'm evil. Once you're queen of Abaddon, I suggest you align your kingdom accordingly, so my new Valkyrie besties and I don't have to annihilate you."

"Team Vertas," Bettina repeatedly dumbly. She supposed it could be worse. The great Sabine and her new husband were allying with those "good guy" factions. "I agree to your condition."

"Good. And now that we've taken care of the fine print"—Morgana's hand started to emit light—"would you like to be made whole?"

Mouth gone dry, Bettina nodded. She wished Daciano were here to see this moment. She wished Cas were by her side. And Raum.

She gazed in Salem's direction.

"Go on, Princess, get your heart-stopping on!"

As Bettina crossed to her, Morgana raised her hand, and more light boiled up from her palm. Heated air began to flutter around the sorceress's body, her gold jewelry vibrating.

At once, a rare wind blew, rocking the spire, bursting open the balcony doors. Rain pelted the interior. The flame chandeliers hissed and died. The wind twisted inside the round room like a tornado, scattering sodden papers and silks.

"Are you ready?" Morgana queried over the din.

The air was heavy with magic; it pricked at Bettina's skin. Her hair tossed in the wind. "I'm ready!" She inhaled deeply—

Morgana's hand suddenly went dark. The wind died, the sorcery dissipated. "You know, I just remembered how you doubted me. It seems this tournament has been wonderful for you. But you complained incessantly about the minor details, like the countless deaths. Bitch, bitch, bitch—"

"Morgana!"

"Who's your favorite godmother? Who's the best sorceress in the entire Lore? Say it."

With a roll of her eyes, Bettina muttered, "Morgana's the best sorceress in the entire Lore."

Mollified, her godmother said, "Then enjoy." She shoved her palm against Bettina's forehead. Fire seemed to leap from the sorceress's hand. The wind howled once more.

Bettina's body seized, her back arching, her limbs twisting. But Morgana held her aloft, pouring sorcery into her, as if into an empty vessel.

"Almost done, freakling. Almost . . ."

Levitating. Heat rushing. Bettina's muscles knotted until she thought they would snap—

"There!" Morgana finished, releasing her at last.

Gasping breaths, Bettina clutched her godmother's shoulder for balance. *Is it back? Am I whole?*

Salem laughed. "That was bloody brilliant, ladies! And oddly arousing. If I had a body, I'd be cock-up right now."

Amber light filled Bettina's palms. The excruciating emptiness she'd suffered had disappeared. Happiness bloomed, manifesting itself in swirls of sorcery all around her. "Oh, my gold. It's . . . *back*." She staggered before she found her footing.

Perhaps I have finally *found my footing?*

"Consider that a wedding gift." Morgana smoothed her hair. "Now. What shall you wear for your nuptials tonight?"

Though hours had passed since Morgana had left, and the day's storm had long abated, the vampire still hadn't appeared.

Even after her shocking turn of fortunes, Bettina grew apprehensive. *No, think of something else. Like your wedding!*

Tonight, after the final round, she would return here and change, then Raum would escort her to court.

She gazed over the bridal ensemble laid out across her bed. It had been Eleara's. The skirt consisted of tulle layers with an ivory silk overlay and a train. Gloves cut to match. The top was an elegant bustier, forged of—what else?—white gold.

Morgana had used her sorcery to update a couple of touches and freshen the fabrics. Then she'd tossed a glamour over her own face to disguise her misting eyes. The afternoon had been wonderful; even Morgana had said, "I think we just bonded. Is this bonding?"

So why was Bettina laden with this apprehension? Why hadn't Daciano checked in? What if his plan was being derailed right at this moment? What if Cas *wasn't* safe?

At the very least, she needed to be privy to the vampire's plan—so she could take the news to Raum, the de facto referee.

Decided, she donned her cloak, readying to set out for Daciano's tent. On her way out, she passed Salem, reading mags.

"Oi! You need an escort?" he asked.

"I'm okay," she said. *I think. We'll see.*

"I'm supposing you will be, now that you're the Queen of Hearts again."

She frowned. Cas assumed she was braver because the Vrekeners had perished. Salem thought she'd been emboldened by her power.

Sure, these things hadn't hurt matters. But Cas and Salem didn't understand—even without those developments, Bettina still would've made this walk.

After the last two nights with the vampire, something had shifted with her thinking. Not simply because a strong, sexy vampire had told her *greatness resides in you*—but because she'd begun to see that he might just have a point. . . .

"I'll be back soon," she told Salem.

Out on the street, the buildings didn't loom so large. Maybe the more she pushed herself, the easier it would be?

The easier for this mouse to twitch her tail at the sky.

When she reached Daciano's tent, she ducked under the flaps, careful not to let even the setting sunlight in. She found him alone, looking as if he'd just stopped himself midsentence.

She peered around. "They were just here, weren't they? Your cousins?"

"Yes. They congratulated me on my success, on winning you and this realm's crown." His appearance startled her.

Whereas she was refreshed and invigorated, he looked distracted and weary, so different from how he'd been just hours before. Now his face was pale and dark circles marred the skin under his eyes. He looked like he'd lost weight over the day, his tailored clothing hanging looser on his frame. And why not? Much of his blood stained the clay ground of the Iron Ring. If he wasn't drinking to replenish it . . .

"They also brought word of Lothaire. It seems he has found the way to make his Bride immortal. They are bonded."

"That's amazing."

"It's been a long time coming. We have voted to install them as regents. Or at least, my cousins have."

She went to him, laying her hands on his chest. "That must be bittersweet for you."

"There is much to . . . take in. Over a span of mere days, I've been blooded, surrendered one kingdom to become king of another, and forsaken the Realm of Blood and Mist for Abaddon, the land of my Bride."

I will make you happy here, vampire. You won't regret it. "When was the last time you slept through a day?" A brutal tension seemed to be grinding inside him. This close she could perceive it.

"Weeks." His lips curled, but the smile didn't quite reach his eyes. "I've had much to do with the tournament and with my last duties to Dacia. In any case, I'll sleep once I've made you my wife. We won't leave our bed for days."

Though that sounded heavenly, she still worried about his health. "You aren't drinking either?"

His gaze strayed to her pulse again. The idea of his weakness and thirst brought on a pang of worry.

Maybe I should have let him bite me. He'd made everything else wonderful for her; why should that prove any different? Tonight, she would bare her neck for him.

For now, she went to his sideboard and poured a goblet of blood from a crystal carafe. In the past, she might have found it distasteful, but now it was literally her vampire's lifeblood. "Here, Trehan. Drink."

He groused—like a typical male—but he did take the glass, downing it with a grimace. "All other blood is foul after I've tasted yours." Then he frowned. "Why are you here? Is something wrong?"

Maybe she could tell him about her power later. He seemed to have a little *too* much on his mind just now. "I need to know more about your plan for tonight."

"Why?"

"For one, it *involves me*. And I don't walk blindly into situations like this anymore."

He tilted his head appraisingly. "Very well." He traced to the heavy contract scroll, hefting it in one hand. "I read every minuscule handwritten word of text in this, every rule."

"But isn't it written in old Demonish?"

"Correct. Which proved time-consuming to translate—another reason I'm fatigued." He shrugged. "Though the language is Demonish, the rules are based on ancient Sorceri law, from a time when your kind valued gallantry. There's a mercy clause."

"What does that mean?"

"If one competitor is facing certain death, the prize female can bestow a favor upon him, removing him from the tournament, but saving his life. When I have Caspion at the point of my sword, you'll plead mercy. And then the tournament will be ended."

Mercy? "But I thought there was some way for it to be a draw between you and Cas."

"Then you were mistaken. There must be a victor."

"I have no idea what Cas will do. Vampire, he's very proud. He was a foundling, has had to work his way up in the world. This plea might be intolerable for him. He could lash out."

And Cas had been getting stronger with each kill. Though she was under no illusion that he could defeat the vampire, Cas might not be easy to subdue without hurting himself in the process.

"All will be well," Daciano said. "I have this under control."

If she'd known this information a little sooner, she could have sat Cas down and tried to explain the situation to him, to persuade him to accept it. Now she'd be lucky if she found him before the match at all. "There's absolutely no way to have a tie?"

Daciano shoved his fingers through his disheveled hair. Voice growing louder with each word, he asked, "I've found a way to save his life, and that's not *good enough for you?*"

"I-I just wish I had known." He'd never raised his voice to her.

"Why? What would have changed?" His eyes flashed black with fury. "Last night in your bed?"

She swallowed. "I-I know you've been under a lot of pressure. And I don't want to fight with you. I should probably let you rest."

"You're going to find Caspion then!"

She thought about lying, considering all avenues to smooth this over. But she refused to be browbeaten. If this vampire wanted to share her life, then he'd best understand that Cas would always have a place in it. "First I'm going to see Raum—so he'll know to end the fight when he hears the plea. But then, I *am* going to talk to Cas, to explain this to him. Otherwise, he might do something hotheaded and charge you. I just want to make sure that you'll *both* come out of this unharmed."

Menace rolled off the vampire. "You don't trust me to control what happens in the ring against a whelp like him?"

"Whelp?" His condescension rankled.

"I've told you to trust me, Bettina."

Her chin shot up. "And I've told you I need to take this to my friend, out of caution."

His fangs sharpened, glinting in the firelight. "Always you think of Caspion!"

Perhaps she *had* been deluded to think she could bridge the distance between Daciano and Cas. "Please, just calm down—"

"Calm down? Do you know how many times that phrase has been uttered to me? *Never.* You've got me on the razor's edge, Princess!" He gave a bitter laugh, and she thought he muttered, *"Backsliding."*

If she'd ever wondered what a blood-starved, exhausted, jealous Dacian would look like . . . *behold.* She'd try one more attempt at reason. "Trehan, I *am* grateful for what you've done. I should have told you that. Like I said, I don't want to argue with you. But there are other things to consider. I'm just trying to prepare everyone involved. I know better than anyone the danger of being unprepared."

At that, he inhaled deeply, clearly making an effort to rein in his temper. "*I* will speak to Raum. Afterward, I'll escort you to the ring."

"No, that wouldn't be right. This round might be a formality, but—"

"*Eşti a mea, Bettina!*" He gripped her shoulders, bringing her face close to his. "You are already mine. Forever, you belong *to me!*"

She remembered something else Salem had said: *The cold ones go big.* "Vampire, be practical. The people might take cues from me and back you more than they already do." No one to cheer for Caspion? He'd fought hard to advance this far in the tournament, risking his life repeatedly—he'd *earned* some consideration.

And he's about to lose so much.

"Your people *should* take cues from you."

"What I mean is that everyone will think I'm siding with you over Cas." *Perception is reality.*

"You are!"

She shook her head. "It's not that simple."

"It is! Then you're *not* choosing me over him?"

The vampire's already driving the wedge! "Don't put it like that! And don't put my back against the wall over this!" Bettina would be damned if they set this precedent. *With your actions, you train others how to treat you.* "Cas will have a place in my future—resign yourself."

"Do you or don't you choose me?"

"You're not being fair to me, and you're not *hearing* me!" He seemed to interpret everything she said as: *I want Cas.* "I choose *both* of you—for different things. Trehan, I can't turn my back on him just because of how I feel about you—"

"Not good enough!" he snapped. In a softer tone, he added, "There will be only one male in your life—me. Tonight in the ring, I will *explain* this to Caspion. By the time his bones mend, he'll fear ever to look at you again."

"Enough!" she cried. "What is wrong with you?" *Where is my tender, gentle vampire from last night?* "You're about to get *everything*—this victory, your Bride, the entire kingdom. Cas gets nothing! And now you want to grind him under your boot? In front of our people? I won't have it! Show some compassion!"

"You feel that for him!" The vampire grasped her nape, studying her face with eyes gone black as pitch. "What other feelings linger?"

"Of course I feel compassion for him! We've shared years of friendship."

"It's *my* right to win this night!"

"Yes, it is—but that doesn't mean you have to crush my best friend to do it."

"One day, Bettina, I will reach my limit with this." He brushed her hair back, then straightened her mask. His touch was tender even as his words were harsh: "You'd best make your plea ring out, lest I rip him apart with these hands." Then he traced away.

41

Still shaken by Daciano's behavior, Bettina had found Raum and hastily explained the clause. He'd been bemused but accepting, deferring to her in everything—as if she were already queen.

As if he couldn't wait to have another rule. It was a little unnerving.

Next, Bettina set out to find Cas, locating him near the entrance to the sanctum. His rowdy friends were pumping him up, punching his torso as they yelled encouragement: "Gut that fucking leech!" "A pair of fangs to start your collection!" They rammed his horns, spurring his aggression, his instinctive need for a fresh kill.

"I have to talk to you, Cas."

He traced over. "What is it? I'm about to go in."

There was no easy way to put this. "What if I told you there was a mercy clause in the rules, an out for one of the contestants?"

"What are you talking about?"

"If Daciano gets you at sword point, then I can plead mercy, sparing your life. But it will disqualify you from the tournament."

Cas's eyes went wild. "Don't you dare use that for me!"

"Just wait—"

"Do you think I have no honor?"

"It isn't like that!"

Gripping her arm, he traced her out of earshot of his friends. "I was born with *nothing*—I've worked so damned hard to get where I am, risking my life again and again. Would you cut me down just when I'm at my highest? You would humiliate me like that?"

"You're my best friend. I can't let you die."

"Don't do this." He pinched his forehead. "I think . . . I think I would grow to hate you."

"Hate? Do you really want this to be the end of your life? To die at twenty-five? For a female you're not even in love with?"

"Tina, I know you've gotten attached to the vampire. Dear gods, I can scent him on you."

She flushed, averting her gaze.

"But I would rather die with honor than lose that way."

"I won't let that happen. I have watched round after round, sitting helpless on the sidelines while you and the vampire risked your lives. At last I can do something to help you."

"Help me—against *him* of all people? Daciano?"

Yes, Salem, apparently I was *deluding myself about them.* She'd never known two males who hated each other so bitterly—and who had so little reason to.

"Worry more for him, sorceress!" Cas snapped, angrier than she'd ever seen him. "I will take him out. I *cannot* lose."

Where was this confidence coming from? "Did you not witness the vampire against the primordial? Be realistic. Daciano has so many years on you."

"That won't matter, not when I use his weakness against him."

"What weakness? He doesn't have any."

"*Everyone* has a weakness," Cas insisted. "You must let this play out! I'm a death demon fighting for my honor—I'm going to prove myself to all of them!"

"He's a thousand-year-old Dacian fighting for his fated Bride. I got you into this, Cas. I'm going to do what I have to in order to get you out of it." With that, she left him to his friends, a pack of demons yelling for Cas to slay a vampire.

Trehan had regretted his harsh words almost as soon as he'd said them. He'd returned to the tent, but Bettina had already gone.

She'd accused him of not hearing her, and she was likely right. Just the mention of that demon's name had sent him into a rage.

He exhaled a long breath. He should have explained his situation to her:

I am exhausted, Bettina, drained of blood, and my mind is not well. Today, I've learned that Dacia will definitely have a new king, and for the first time in a millennium, I am certain it won't be me. I've made sacrifices to have a life with you, and so I unreasonably expected you to bow to my will without question.

He would tell her this tonight before the ceremony, smoothing things over. And once they were wed, he would take her repeatedly, savoring more of the bliss she'd given him last night. At the memory of her abandon, even his blood-starved body stirred for more.

Except for her hesitation over his bite, she'd surrendered herself fully, satisfying him in untold ways. The final time he'd taken her, he'd gazed down at her face and a truth had struck him: *Bettina este viață.*

Bettina is life. He could never go back to the way he was before.

Tonight, after he'd claimed his wife, he would force himself to drink and sleep, and then finally his thoughts would clear. *They can't get worse.*

Nothing made sense today. His temper lay ever at the ready, his mood foul. His body was weakened, his head dizzy. *Something is* off *with me.*

Was it because he hadn't marked her? According to the physiology book, a vampire needed to pierce his mate.

But he wasn't just a vampire. He was still *Dacian.*

Right now, he wished he wasn't. Trehan never would have thought that he'd envy a maddened red-eyed vampire like Lothaire, one who'd apparently taken his Bride's neck as he'd claimed her.

Binding her to him. Lothaire obeyed instinct; Trehan resisted it.

The Enemy of Old was healing; *I'm backsliding.*

Trehan felt . . . ill. His throat burned, and his tongue seemed thick, sticking to the roof of his mouth. His lightheadedness was turning into a pounding headache, even as numbness spread through his limbs.

Just get this fight over with. Everything he desired, everything that belonged to him, was there for the taking. He was so godsdamned close, only needed to go seize it.

He gazed in the direction of the ring. *My prize awaits with widened eyes.*

Ready for his match, Trehan squared his shoulders, the movement sending him atilt.

He realized something was definitely wrong . . . when he traced to the sanctum . . . and collided face-first into a wall.

42

"One doesn't have to be a sorceress to sense the night's portentous atmosphere," Morgana murmured from her seat on the dais.

Bettina agreed. As Raum greeted the crowd, she gazed over the arena. The rain today had left the ring a red-clay mire. Coils of fog slithered around the cage, oozing from the ground and weaving through the bars.

The full moon riddled the haze with wavering spears of light.

When Raum announced the competitors, the crowd cheered, but their reaction was muted, as if they sensed the ominous air as well.

Caspion and Daciano entered the ring then, tracing over the mud. At this point, she just wanted the two to be safe. She'd deal with the fallout later.

While Raum continued his announcements—about the midnight wedding ceremony, the forthcoming kingdomwide holidays to celebrate, and so on—Bettina studied the vampire.

In each round, he'd been the picture of coldness. Eyes intent, expression focused. A male bent on a single task.

Now sweat dotted his brow and tracked down his temples. His pupils were dilated, and the finest lines of blood streaked from the corners of his eyes.

When he shook his head hard, nearly losing his balance, Bettina's hand shot to Morgana's arm. "Look at the vampire!"

"What is it?"

"Look at his eyes."

She squinted. "Oh, for the love of gold! You have to be kidding me."

"He's been poisoned!" Bettina hissed. She knew the symptoms as well as the next Sorceress.

Morgana gave an astonished laugh. "Your wastrel got clever."

"No! Cas wouldn't have done this," she said, even as she recalled his unwarranted confidence.

Tomorrow night's his last. . . . I cannot lose. . . . I'll use his weakness against him. . . .

"Perhaps Caspion and another planned this?" Morgana sliced her gaze over to Raum.

Cheating is rampant. Was that what the two of them had been talking about last night? Poisoning wasn't outside of the rules.

Then comprehension dawned. It had to be Daciano's cousins who'd done this! He'd told her that all of them were forever trying to kill each other, and they'd been in his tent earlier.

"Your vampire's been given something very potent," Morgana observed. "On a scale from one to five—five being the rare toxin that could actually kill an immortal—I'd put him at four."

"*Four?* What do I do? What *can* I do?"

"Hope he can rebound from such a strong dose."

In an obvious bid to do just that, he shook his head again. He nearly reeled before he regained his balance. He seemed confused, his feet sluggish in the thick mud.

He's getting worse.

She turned to Cas. He was seething, his horns ramrod straight, his fangs swollen. He unsheathed his sword, gripping it tightly, his arm muscles bulging. His friends in the stands yelled, antagonizing him even more.

Daciano ran his sleeve over his eyes, then again, as if his sight had been dimmed. When he drew his own weapon, he staggered once more.

The gate clanged shut for the last time. Before Bettina could say a word, Raum gave his signal. And she was helpless yet again as the horn sounded its final blare—

Cas attacked immediately, his sword flashing out. Daciano could barely deflect the hit in time. Their swords clanged loudly, the metallic pitch ringing out in the night.

Cas struck again; Daciano managed a lethargic block. The vampire's reflexes were deteriorating even more, while Cas was faster, stronger, than she could have imagined—

With a sudden lunge, Cas thrust his sword straight out, like an extension of his brawny arm. Too late, Daciano reared his head back; the blade tip caught his cheek, flaying the skin open.

At that moment, moonlight hit the vampire's face, illuminating ghostly white bone before blood welled.

Daciano evinced no expression—no pain, anger, confusion—just vacantness as blood flowed down his face.

Cas followed that parry with another lightning fast strike; a deep laceration appeared on the vampire's sword arm.

As Bettina gaped at this turn of events, Morgana calmly observed, "Only a matter of time now, freakling."

"No, no, the vampire will shake this off!" she said, feigning confidence she didn't feel. Daciano looked like he could barely control his heavy eyelids—much less what was happening in the ring. "Y-you know how strong he is."

With a mindblowing ferocity, Cas swung his sword high, using both hands to deliver a brutal strike; Daciano lifted his sword overhead to defend.

Again their blades clanged, metal scraping metal. Sparks rained down over Daciano's head, highlighting his sweating, bloody countenance.

Pressing his advantage, Cas whaled hit after hit, as if swinging an ax at a chopping block.

The spate of furious blows drove Daciano down . . . down. . . .

When the vampire's knees sank into the mire and confusion registered on his proud face, Bettina realized two things.

She was in love with him.

And she'd do anything to save him.

Sword quaking in my hands, metal pealing in my ears, mud sucking me down.
Caspion hammering at me.

"Know defeat, vampire! Delivered unto you—by a demon!"

Must shake this weakness! Yet nothing could pierce Trehan's stupor. His peripheral vision was still obscured by blood, his equilibrium wrecked.

His disordered mind finally accepted the truth: he'd been . . . poisoned. Likely by the coward who was even now striving to take his head.

But how could Caspion have dosed him before the round? Trehan had only been around his cousins and Bettina.

The hits . . . ceased? Like a blur, the demon began tracing around him, cleverly keeping to his blind spots. Trehan struggled to rise. For her, he would fight on. *Everything I desire is here for the taking—*

Suddenly, steel pressed against his throat. From behind, Caspion had him dead to rights.

Or so the demon thinks.

At last, adrenaline began spiking throughout Trehan's veins to burn away the toxin. Power flowed into his muscles, his body rebounding with the strength of the Daci.

Now you've irritated me, whelp. Trehan bared his fangs. *Gods, I'm going to enjoy teaching you a lesson.* "The fight's not over, boy. You forget what I am—"

"I plead mercy!" Bettina cried.

What? *Too soon, Bett!* The crowd grew hushed. He twisted his head around to glimpse her face.

"*I plead mercy for the Prince of Shadow.*"

Trehan's breath left him. She'd just invoked the clause . . .

For me? *Disqualifying* me *from the tournament?* No, no, he'd misheard. His mind was unclear. She had *not* just taken herself out of his reach forever.

After the night they'd shared? After all he'd sacrificed? *A mea!* She wouldn't do this. *She knows how much I want her.*

Caspion leaned down to sneer, "I didn't forget what you are. You're a loser, *disqualified* from the tournament. I told you she'd never be your wife!"

Now she would be this demon's?

Caspion laughed. "Go back to your lonely home in the ground, old man."

I have no fucking home! Gave up everything for her! And she was *always* going to be with Caspion.

Were they in league together—

Realization struck him like a mace to the throat. Bettina had handed him a goblet of blood less than half an hour ago. *Here, Trehan. Drink.* She possessed an extensive arsenal of poisons.

Not Bettina. It couldn't be her.

Who else, you fool? His cousins would never stoop so low. Even Stelian had too much honor for that. And hadn't Bettina been wearing her customary poison ring earlier? He'd thought the taste of the blood was off, thought yet again that he'd been ruined by the ambrosia flowing through her veins.

The ambrosia she'd denied him last night.

His fangs shot longer, gone sharp as razors. All the aggression Trehan had vigilantly harnessed over ages came howling to life inside him—a ravening beast rising for carnage.

With a bellow, he gripped the end of Caspion's sword. The blade sliced his hand, blood gushing as he snatched it away from the stunned demon. Tracing to his feet, Trehan hurled the weapon to the far edge of the ring.

As the demon gawked, Trehan sheathed his own

sword, wanting to deal this death personally. *To feel bone breaking and skin rending between my fingers.*

· Even as the toxin was seared away, his thoughts grew even more jumbled, a tangled snarl in his mind. *She will never be mine, will always want the male before me.*

He threw back his head and roared, fists clenched until his arm and chest muscles knotted. As the sound died in his throat, he gazed at Bettina, at her pale face. *You want Caspion so badly? I'll give you his fucking head!*

When he turned to face his prey, a bloodred haze covered Trehan's vision. *Kill.*

For the first time in his long, wearying existence, he fully gave himself over to rage.

43

Daciano had become a creature possessed, with more fury even than the Lykae—and far less reason.

He told me he'd rip Cas apart with his bare hands.

Already the vampire had fractured Cas's right arm and pummeled his head and face with bone-shattering hits. Cas's visage was unrecognizable, his left eye a swollen pulp; blood streamed from his mouth.

In a desperate bid to retrieve his sword, Cas lunged into a clumsy trace, diving for it; Daciano predicted his move—and backhanded him across the ring.

Cas went flying, crashing into the mud, sending a wave of it up and over the first row of spectators.

The vampire followed, snatching Cas by a horn, dragging him to his knees to deliver more vicious blows.

"Oh, dear gods," Bettina muttered. "This isn't happening." She'd thought Cas could recover, or that

Daciano would see reason. "Please stop them, Morgana!" Her godmother ignored her, leaning forward, riveted by the battle.

"Raum!" Bettina cried.

"What do the rules state about this, m'girl?" he said. "You've called mercy—what more can we do?"

"I don't know!"

As Cas struggled to free himself, delivering futile hits to Daciano's body, the vampire bared his fangs, stark white against his bloody face. A chilling predator's smile.

He's reached his limit.

Obviously Bettina had screwed up; she'd thought she was saving his life, never imagining that he could shake off such a severe dose.

When she'd pled mercy, Daciano's expression of stunned realization had transformed into one of pure hatred. The savagery in his onyx eyes . . . He must believe that she'd cheated him out of the tournament win—in favor of the demon before him.

She'd only wanted to protect Daciano. And now Cas was going to pay for her mistake if she didn't intervene.

"I have rarely in all my long years seen a being dominate a match like this," Raum said to Morgana. "It calls to mind the legends. Does it not?"

"Indeed. Lachlain, Demestriu, Furie, the Enemy of Old."

Agreeing with each other? In a conversational tone? What was happening here—why was no one else freaking out?

Daciano picked Cas up bodily, launching him across the cage like a missile. When Cas connected with the bars, one of the spikes embedded itself into the base of his skull, *breaking off inside it.*

Bettina gave a sob as Cas moaned mindlessly, swinging wildly—the spike had . . . blinded him? Still, he struggled to defend himself as Daciano snatched his matted hair.

The vampire's fist smashed Cas's face with another series of crushing blows, over and over, as Bettina begged, *"No, no, no!"*

Then came the final hit. She heard the crack of bone. Mud splashed up Cas's body when he collapsed to his back. Limp.

Sprawled in the mud, broken, Cas didn't move again.

The vampire loomed over him and unsheathed his sword. She could never reach the ring in time—

"You're about to lose both of them," Morgana said. "One dead—and one never to be forgiven." To Raum, she suggested, "Do send in the guards, demon. They might be able to keep the vampire busy long enough to smuggle Caspion's body away."

Raum glanced at Bettina. When she gave a desperate nod, he signaled the troop at the ready.

At once, they traced into the ring, swords drawn, surrounding Daciano.

Like an animal guarding a kill, the vampire positioned himself in front of Cas. His fangs dripped blood, his muscles rippling with raw power.

When the guards charged as one, he reared up with a deafening roar. The sound reverberated like thunder, shaking the arena, the very city.

Demons in the crowd held their ears.

With ungodly strength and speed, he batted the

guards away, felling them one by one—until each was left crawling or unconscious in the filth.

"There went that plan!" Morgana said with a shrug. "Freakling, only one person can stop this now."

"Who?!"

The sorceress smiled widely, taking a deep, dramatic breath. "The Queen of Hearts."

Me? Bettina's lips parted. Could she use her power against the male she loved? The vampire who'd claimed her body—less than twenty-four hours ago?

I made his heart beat, and now I'm to stop it? Even if briefly?

"Vampire, don't do this!" she cried, desperate not to hurt him. "Please, *no*!"

He bared his fangs at her, gave a bloody hiss, then turned back to his prey, so clearly wanting to murder Cas.

If she didn't act, Bettina *would* lose both of them. "You leave me no choice," she said, raising her hands. Power amplified inside her like a building storm. Tears poured down her face as she aimed it at the vampire, unleashing utter agony—

He recoiled as if lightning struck. Then he lurched, clutching his chest.

When he swung his head around at her, his hair whipped over his bloody cheek. She could see comprehension dawning on his ghastly face, accusation in his rage-black eyes.

He cast her a look so murderous that she flinched.

Resisting her hold over him, the vampire yelled to the crowd, "Mark me, and listen well! I've won this tournament. . . . No one here can deny my victory. . . . I've won this crown"—he pointed his bloodied sword at her—"and Bettina as my wife." Claws digging into his chest, lungs failing, he bellowed, *I forsake you both!*"

Trehan held her gaze, scorned her tears, withstood the blistering pain in his chest.

In his *heart*.

Somehow she had her sorcery back. And she was using it against *him*. Her male. Her fucking male!

Her gaze was uncanny. Those bright pinpoints that sparked in her eyes were now tinged amber. Her hands glowed with more amber light.

The sound of his heartbeat dimmed. A thousand years ago, his heart had stopped. But now—because of her—he needed it to live.

Only seconds remain before my other organs follow.

A fresh wave of torment erupted inside him. *Must escape her hold.*

"You've gotten what you've always wanted, sorceress," he grated. "Now live with your regret!"

With the last of his strength, he traced back to his tent, out of her power's range. At once, the pain faded. His heartbeat resumed, his body recovering. But his mind . . .

Chaos!

She'd cried for the one she truly loved; she'd stopped Trehan's newly beating heart. Nothing could be more telling. And she'd done far worse before that.

He lunged for the goblet she'd handed him, scenting it.

Poisoned. *Here, Trehan. Drink.* So guileless, so lovely.

Such treachery!

Like a flash, he recalled the night he'd sat with her on the grandstand. When he'd asked Bettina if she'd planned to poison anyone, she'd looked him dead in the eye and answered, "One leech is making the short list."

How prophetic. With a deranged roar, he crushed the goblet. She and Caspion had *played* him.

And now Trehan had nothing! As he stabbed his sword into its scabbard, he remembered how his father had counseled him to accept his lot.

But with Bettina, Trehan had thought he'd found his family, friend, mistress, the grand love of his life.

Gone.

"Be an example, Son." All these ages later, Trehan had failed utterly. *"I have nothing!"*

Nowhere even to fucking go.

"NOTHING!" he roared, tearing at his blood-stained hair. *I want her, hate her. Go kill the demon. Can't.*

In the ring, Trehan had realized that his vows bound him; like a fool he'd told Bettina that both he and Caspion would survive. *Can't kill . . .*

"Trehan!" Viktor appeared in the tent, with Mirceo and Stelian behind him.

Maddened with rage, with loss, Trehan swung around, hungering to fight, didn't matter against who.

Mirceo raised his brows at Trehan's appearance. "Our apologies for the interruption, Uncle. Your wedding night will have to wait—"

"What do you three want now?" Trehan thundered. *There is no fucking wedding night!* His prize, forever gone. "Gods damn it, I thought you were done with me! Why've you returned?"

Stelian said, "He's as frothing at the mouth as you usually are, Viktor. You must field this one."

"Give me credit," Viktor snapped. "I've been doing much better." To Trehan, he said, "What the hell has happened to you?"

"I won; I fucking lost everything!" he spat the words. "I am not who I was!"

"What does that mean, Trey? There's no way you lost the tournament to *Caspion*."

"I defeated him. I won, but I lost the prize!" Trehan clasped his forehead, squeezing until his skull threatened to shatter. "Tell me what you're doing here or leave!"

"You need to calm yourself, Cousin."

His head whipped up. "Fucking *leave*!"

"I'll tell you then," Mirceo said. "The situation with Lothaire has reached a crisis. He's been attacked, nearly decapitated. We can't breach his apartment because of his barrier spell, and his Bride is missing. We must locate her."

Trehan gave a crazed laugh. "Must you, then?"

Stelian said, "Yet again, there's a catch."

All three hesitated before Viktor said, "Elizabeth was likely the one who brandished the sword."

Lothaire's Bride had struck out against him? *I feel your pain, brother.* "I will help him," Trehan finally bit out. "I will do my godsdamned duty to Dacia!" He leveled his gaze on each of them. "But I want back in. . . ."

44

WEEKS LATER

"W e've come full circle, haven't we?" Caspion said quietly. He and Bettina had taken their drinks out on the balcony, just as they had the night before the tournament had started.

From here, they could see the tops of the giant trees. Bats jagged in front of the waxing moon. But tonight the scene wasn't romantic. Instead it was somber.

Seeing those moonraker trees reminded her of the folly she'd shared with Daciano, of perfect acceptance and pleasure. He'd been the ideal male for her. Until suddenly, he *wasn't*.

Still, she missed that vampire—with his eyes like the forest, eyes that could turn onyx with desire.

Or with rage.

Now that she'd known true love—hurting, raw, stunning, spectacular love—Bettina wondered how she'd ever thought Cas was the one for her. . . .

She drank deep from her goblet of wine. "It might not feel like it, but I've got to believe we're better off than we were then. Even though we're both heartsore."

"Better off?" Cas said. "I suppose. That night before the tournament, I was convinced I was about to die, and you were convinced you were about to wed a Cerunno." He faced her, his handsome face grave. "But, Tina, things *are* bad for me here now."

Her people worshipped strength and battle prowess; they hadn't been keen on the loser of the match becoming the winner of the tournament. Especially not due to an ancient *Sorceri* technicality. Especially not when there were rumors of a poisoning.

Strongest equaled greatest. *Might maketh right.* The Deathly Ones considered the Prince of Shadow to be their king.

Once Cas had healed, he'd gone along with the tournament "win" long enough to accept Bettina's summoning medallion and the king's crown of Abaddon. Then he'd turned both of them over to her—along with any claim he had on the throne.

The medallion hung from a lead on her neck, right beside a plain gold wedding band.

She was queen alone in her own right. But her crown, which she'd forged to look like demon horns, sat heavily on her head. . . .

The vampire's poisoning had rocked the kingdom, with almost everyone suspecting Cas. Though she'd blamed Daciano's cousins, she'd felt obligated to ask Cas and Raum if they'd had anything to do with it. When they'd denied it, she'd asked Cas, "Then what was his weakness you were going to exploit?"

"His arrogance, Bettina. His overconfidence. I

wanted to use his cold-bloodedness against him. I had no idea he'd turn into an animal."

Just as Morgana had once predicted, Daciano had turned into an unthinking, savage brute.

Salem hinted around that he was on the trail of the real poison culprit: "Update at eleven." But the sylph could look all he wanted to—he would never reach Dacia. No one could.

Cas said, "You know I can't stay in Abaddon any longer."

She admitted, "I thought this is what you wanted to talk about." From the moment he'd arrived tonight, she'd sensed he was soon to leave. "But I need you here, Cas. You're one of the few people I can completely trust." He was part of the ragtag family she'd assembled, along with Raum, Morgana, and even Salem.

"You don't need me. You're doing an amazing job."

"What if we're to go to war?"

Cas gazed up at the sky. "Do you think the Vrekeners will ever attack?"

She didn't know. Surely, they would have by now. "In any event, I need a general by my side." Raum had declined the position, telling her, "I'll get you settled in, m'girl, but then I want to retire. Maybe learn *golf*!"

"A general?" Cas scoffed. "They won't *follow* me, Bettina. But they'll follow you."

Though she had been accepted as queen, in the beginning the reception had been *chilly*. Basically, her entire populace believed she'd been spurned by *two* suitors.

Morgana hadn't been here to advise—the sorceress had disappeared, leaving only a message: "La Dorada risen. Happy Accession." So Bettina had followed Morgana's example, holding floor shows every night.

Raum had been instrumental in helping her organize the drunken festivities. Though he hadn't spoken to her about her situation—other than to offer a few gruff but well-meaning platitudes—he'd devoted himself to rehabilitating her image.

He'd taken care of all the heavy lifting with the extravaganzas, leaving her to provide the final touches and Sorceri flair. Gold plus color plus spectacle equaled dazzled demons.

Now when she passed people in the street, they smiled and called her "Good Queen Bett."

Each day, Bettina grew more comfortable in her role as regent, exerting power more confidently. The days of Bettina the Pushover had disappeared, replaced by Queen Bettina, a bold(ish) sorceress. Like Morgana and Patroness, Bettina got what she wanted.

The situation hadn't improved for Cas, though.

"Tina, believe me, I'd rather not go. I hate leaving you after he . . . after Daciano . . . after you lost the male you thought to marry."

The vampire had humiliated her and her oldest friend, but she still missed him to an aching degree. She'd been up and down—cursing Daciano, then yearning for him.

Tonight, I'll make you my wife, he'd said. *Bettina eternitate,* he'd assured her.

How could the vampire just leave her behind?

Directly before he'd traced away, he'd said: "You've gotten what you've always wanted, sorceress." Had he thought she still wanted Caspion over him? After she'd given the vampire her virginity? After the night they'd shared?

Perhaps the poison had muddled his thoughts?

But then, even before the finals, Daciano had seemed unwell—besieged by that grinding tension. . . .

So many things in the kingdom reminded her of him. She thought of Daciano every time she practiced with her power, or worked in her shop, or simply walked by herself around town.

Merely lying in her bed made her crave him to a staggering degree. She tossed and turned, waiting for him to appear.

It had been *their* bed—at least for one amazing night.

She had so many feelings bottled up inside her, with no outlet. What she wouldn't give for a chance to talk to him!

Bettina knew exactly what she'd say: *Trehan Daciano, I screwed up. I thought you were going to die, and I acted to save you. Clearly, I was too hasty. Sometimes I do foolish things, especially if my entire life is off kilter, and I'm struggling with emotions I've never felt before.*

But you . . . your behavior . . . how could you turn into a nightmare?

Sadly she wasn't expecting a sit-down with him anytime soon. He could be anywhere in the worlds.

Now Cas pointed out, "You'll have Salem to keep you company when I leave."

Though Bettina couldn't turn Salem back into a regular phantom, she'd revoked his servitude to her, melted down his copper bell, and made him a partner. He was a full-fledged businessman, even now out negotiating her next commission. "Where will you go, Cas?"

"The Plane of Lost Years."

That plane was a hell dimension of continual wars where time moved even more slowly than in

Abaddon—because days stretched on endlessly in hell. "You wouldn't go there. You can't."

Cas could experience years and years there, then return a day later.

"I need to go work this off. And get stronger." Many Abaddonae went there to make kills and harvest power.

"I understand, but does it have to be there?"

His hand tightened on his mug. "I will do anything—*anything*—so that I may never know defeat like that again."

"Please, just give this some time," she said, but she knew he couldn't continue on as he'd been doing.

"The people don't accept me. *I* don't accept me." He wasn't exaggerating; when Cas passed Abaddonae, they . . . *spat* in his path.

"Once we find the real poisoner, they'll come around."

"I'm sorry, Tina, I have to go."

There was no changing his mind. At that realization, her eyes began to water. "When will you return?"

"Centuries, if that's what it takes. So maybe a year in this time." He forced a smile. "Wish me luck, friend."

Sniffling, she whispered, "Good luck, Cas."

He pressed a warm kiss to her forehead for long moments, then disappeared.

Caspion was venturing into hell, to risk his life repeatedly, all because of Daciano—the reserved, patient vampire who had turned madman.

Though she'd been expecting Cas to leave, it still hurt. And now she was all alone.

Alone on the balcony, up so high—*in the dark*? With an "imperfect" barrier spell?

She shrugged and took another drink. Since Daciano had left, she'd mastered her anxiety even more. She challenged herself constantly, and its hold on her continued to wane. Plus, she'd begun to *believe* in her ability to defeat it.

Greatness *did* reside in her, after all. But there was one other factor.

She was too heartbroken to feel much of anything besides sadness—least of all fear.

Trehan Daciano had broken her heart when he'd left her behind, to live a life without her in it.

After that, she just didn't particularly care what happened to her.

Yes, these days Queen Bettina got what she wanted. Except for what she wanted most.

My vampire.

45

Though Trehan sat in his favorite chair with a book in hand, he couldn't read it.

So he stared into the flames.

Just as before, he took pleasure in nothing. A shade with a stupefying existence. Over the last several weeks, his pain had proved so unflagging and pervasive that it had grown into a raw sort of numbness. . . .

For his service in helping to save Lothaire's life, Trehan had been allowed back into Dacia. Perhaps he oughtn't to have bothered. Away from Bettina, his mind had only gotten worse—concentration nil, reason and logic absent.

But his body had eventually recovered, and it hungered for hers without cease.

The whispers among the Daci resumed. Everyone knew he'd left their realm, found his otherlander Bride—only to be betrayed in some way by her—then returned.

Those whispers held that he was even worse of a shade than before. And they were right. About all of it.

"Take another female," Viktor had advised, which just confirmed that he had *not* been blooded. Or else he'd know how ridiculous that sounded.

Bettina had awakened Trehan to experiences he never would have known. She'd given him life.

His body was hers, his seed was hers. He could never give either to another female.

They'd already been claimed. *He* had already been claimed. Then discarded.

Which left him alone, with a book in his lap, staring at the flames. . . .

"Good gloaming, Uncle!" Kosmina said as she traced into his sitting room. "I bring a message from Lothaire."

The newly crowned—and completely unhinged—king of Dacia.

Lothaire had turned out to be a ruthless dictator, prone to rages, with alternating bouts of lunacy and lucidity—more of the latter now that he'd reconciled with his Bride. Indeed she had nearly decapitated Lothaire, by *accident*.

It'd taken Lothaire weeks to realize that. Before that epiphany, when he'd been separated from his Bride, he'd lashed out at his cousins, Trehan included.

At one point, Lothaire had clawed his own heart out of his chest and sent it to Elizabeth in a box.

Trehan laid his book aside and rose. "What does he want now?"

Of all the cousins, Trehan understood Lothaire best—*because I'm dancing at the edge of sanity myself.* Kosmina, however, *liked* Lothaire best. She thought he was exciting and misunderstood and believed his love affair with Elizabeth was the stuff of legend. "He's summoned you to court."

"Has he, then?" *Like some common subject.* It rankled. Twice over, Trehan could have been a king. Now he regretted not seizing this throne.

Kosmina nodded brightly. "I told him I'd bring you straight away."

Straight away? Suddenly Trehan found himself in the mood for a leisurely stroll.

"You're walking?" she asked. "May I go with you?"

"I don't think I'm good company, but I don't object."

Once they'd exited the library and started along a misty cobblestone street, Kosmina said, "Wait till you see the castle, Uncle. Queen Elizabeth has been busy!" His niece was delighted by all the changes in their realm. As she'd told Trehan, "We don't have to hate each other anymore! I can visit you without worrying if my brother will try to kill you for it."

For eons, the great black castle had lain empty with echoing halls. No longer. Ever since Lothaire and Elizabeth had reconciled and begun their new rule, it had been in a continual state of upheaval.

As soon as Trehan and Kosmina made their way through the castle's towering gold doors, they were met with chaos.

Servants flitted all around them, tracing furniture and decorations. Some mongrel-looking canine chased them, baying with impatience. A vividly decorated Christmas tree stood in each alcove.

"Elizabeth said we'll have 'Christmas' year-round and decorate with only the choicest adornments!" Kosmina explained. "I don't know what Cracker Barrel is, but its wares are of great importance to our queen."

As Trehan took in the mayhem surrounding him, he wondered how Bettina would view the scene. *What would she see? What could her beautiful eyes alone descry?*

There was no higher sensibility inside Trehan—he'd needed her for that.

"You grieve for her," Kosmina said softly.

He stiffened. "I've told you I don't want to discuss this with you."

She and Elizabeth had been haranguing him to return for his Bride.

He hadn't been able tell them that Bettina loved another, had found it impossible to utter the words: *My Bride chose a demon over me. My Bride nearly broke me with her duplicity. My mind is not well, and I don't know how to fix it.*

In a wry tone, Kosmina said, "I'd tell you I won't bring it up again, Uncle, but it would be a lie."

"The situation's complicated. One day I'll explain it." *When you're three hundred years old.* Changing the subject, he said, "Any idea what Lothaire wants?"

"None. But he's lucid today," she said happily.

The last time Lothaire had appeared even remotely so, Trehan had attempted to give the king an overview of the family and the houses, outlining the last three millennia of their secret history.

"*Five* houses?" Lothaire had sneered, cutting Trehan off. "You all live under one roof now. Mine. Because I'm the king of the castle." Then his red eyes had grown vacant, and he'd begun muttering about "Lizvetta's lingerie."

Trehan had been . . . *underwhelmed* by the Enemy of Old's attention span.

Now Trehan said to Kosmina, "Even when he's lucid, Lothaire doesn't exactly personify the traits of his house." He was descended from the king's line, the most ancient one, known for its wisdom.

Wisdom? Lothaire couldn't be bothered even to hear about his vaunted house.

"Every day he gets better, Uncle! And guess what else. Lothaire and Elizabeth want me to journey . . . outside."

"Pardon?"

"He wants me to undertake a mission for the kingdom."

"What kind of mission?"

"To infiltrate a covey of nymphs in a place called Louisiana!" she said in a breathless voice. "I don't know exactly why. He just said the task would be 'eye-opening' for someone like me."

Infiltrate a covey? Over my dead body. Kosmina would perish of shock before the plague ever touched her.

In addition to all his faults, their new king had a twisted sense of humor. "We'll discuss this *later*." *Again, when you're three hundred.* His voice must have been harsh because she paled.

Anger always at the ready, Trehan? Striving for an even tone, he said, "There's no need to rush into these things, Kosmina. One change at a time, then?"

"Oh. Of course, Uncle." Wisely, she didn't press the subject.

At the great entrance to the court, she gave him an encouraging nod, then traced away.

When Trehan entered the enormous space, Lothaire was sitting in his throne with Elizabeth upon his lap—she rarely sat in her own, a feminine version of Lothaire's.

The new king had scrapped the ancient and revered thrones of their forebears and designed new ones. Each was decorated with gold-dipped skulls, only Elizabeth's skulls were "daintier."

The two regents were sickeningly in love. As usual, they were deep in conversation, taking little notice of the world around them; Lothaire stroked her bottom lip with his thumb, while she brushed his light hair from his forehead.

Can't touch each other enough. Trehan had been that way with Bettina.

Though Lothaire had proved difficult, Elizabeth was intelligent, amusing, and friendly. She was already learning Dacian and had taken her new immortality in stride. She also kept Lothaire in check.

Just yesterday he'd announced to the court that he would like to "go kill something. Anything!"

Running her forefinger over his chest, Elizabeth had purred in her mountain accent, "Let's go kill time, baby. In our bedroom."

Lothaire's eyes had flashed red, and he'd traced her away in an instant.

Now he told her, "The question remains . . . do we open the gates of Dacia?" He yearned to announce Dacia's presence to the Lore. In one of his bouts of madness, he'd railed, "A king of a kingdom no one fucking knows about! I'm the tree in the forest that silently falls—when no one is around to be crushed!"

Lothaire looped both arms around her, tucking her even closer to him. "I want your opinion, Lizvetta."

"You're only askin' 'cause you're afraid I'll cut off your head again."

"Just so. But I also like how your tricky mind works."

"I think we should have a soft opening," she said. "You know, like they do with fancy restaurants."

He tapped his chin with a black claw. "Soft opening. Yes."

"We could keep folks, I don't know, quarantined when they come in. Make sure that vampire plague doesn't hitch a ride inside."

In a move that would have pulverized Elizabeth as a mortal, Lothaire yanked her even tighter to his chest. "My wise little *hellbilly*."

"Shut it, Leo." She'd nicknamed him that, an acronym for his name. He was one of the most feared fiends in all the Lore—and yet she ribbed him with ease.

Lothaire, in turn, loved it.

They were about to kiss when Trehan cleared his throat.

"Ah, Cousin Trehan." Though Lothaire's red eyes were uncanny, today he looked rational—and very cunning.

"I'll let you two boys chat." Elizabeth extricated herself from his arms, earning a growl of displeasure. "And once you're done, Leo, come on up and see me." She winked and began sauntering toward the exit; like a male possessed, Lothaire rose to follow her.

Then, making a visible effort to restrain himself, he sat once more. "I know what you're thinking, Cousin. *Lothaire keeps a tight rein on her*," he said, looking immensely pleased with himself. "Indeed I do."

From the anteroom: "Oh, please! I've got you locked down tighter than a gopher's ass in flood season. And we both know it!"

Lothaire gazed with utter longing in Elizabeth's direction before turning to Trehan. "She'll pay for that comment later."

"Brang it, Leo."

"Let's be quick about this, Trehan, because I'm about to—as my beloved Bride likes to put it—get laid." Steepling his fingers, he began, "Your occupation for centuries has been to track Dacian fugitives as the official royal killer, or some such. Know that if we open the kingdom, your position will be downsized."

As if Trehan gave a damn about that.

"It's a new economy here in the Realm of Blood and Mist. Some fortunes will rise, some will fall. Perhaps you should reconsider your lead on that Abaddon job?"

"I have no interest in this topic," Trehan said stonily, wondering how Lothaire had found out about Abaddon. Probably Stelian. "Is there anything else you wanted to discuss?"

"Yes, there's another matter. You are related to me by blood and, like me, are a Dacian royal."

"So?"

"So that means your ridiculous behavior reflects upon me."

"What are you talking about? *My* ridiculous behavior?"

In the short time Lothaire had been king, he'd already lost a soothsayer within the realm, destroyed the council room, and lashed out against all the cousins, crushing Viktor's skull in a vicious attack. Viktor still railed over the insult.

And earlier, one of Trehan's assassins had brought word that Lothaire might have secretly abducted the Forbearer vampire king, to settle some age-old vendetta.

Gods help us. "I've done *nothing* to warrant this summoning, Lothaire. I keep to my library—and to myself."

"Exactly. You sit in your room and stroke off to memories of your Bride."

Trehan ground his teeth, unable to deny this. "And you've been spying *on me*?"

"Of course. I spy on everyone. Why would you be any different?" he asked in all seriousness. "Not that I needed to in order to know what you're going through. I've been there. You're weak in body and spirit, as if the most insidious illness festers inside you. You can't drink, can't sleep. Your chest aches as if it'd been gouged to the spine. And when you envision the future without your Bride, all you see is a great yawning *nothingness*."

"Yes," Trehan rasped in surprise. "Yes, that is it precisely."

Lothaire truly was the scion of his house, the one of wisdom and history. The House of Old.

"Ah, Cousin, there was a reason I clawed out my heart and sent it to Elizabeth." Gazing past Trehan, Lothaire said, more to himself, "It hurt less outside my chest." He returned his attention to the conversation. "So I'll pass on some advice I received. Perhaps it will help you as well."

"I'm listening," Trehan said quickly. Anything to end this anguish—

"Stop being a pussy, and go retrieve her."

So much for *wise*! Trehan's fangs sharpened. "You don't understand the dynamics of my situation!"

"Explain them," Lothaire demanded, beginning to lose his temper as well. "How bad can it be? As your king, I command you to answer. And you vowed an oath of fealty to me."

Trehan had no choice but to respond. "My Bride poisoned me so that I would lose a match against the demon male shc loves."

Lothaire hiked his shoulders. "So?"

"Did you not hear me? She dumped toxins into a goblet of blood, then handed it to me, urging me to drink. Then she disqualified me from a tournament I was sure to win. She removed herself from my reach forever. To add insult to injury, she wielded her Sorceri power—against *me*—to protect the demon."

And even now Trehan craved her. *Comoara mea.* Gone.

"Lizvetta nearly decapitated me. And look how happy we are."

"Queen Elizabeth *accidentally* struck against you with her new immortal strength. My Bride deliberately tricked me."

"Who doesn't have petty spats during courtship? So fucking what?"

"So she doesn't fucking *want* me!" There. The words said out loud.

Lothaire roared back, "She doesn't get a gods-damned say in the matter!"

Trehan's brows drew together. "What are you advising—that I abduct her? As you recently did the For-bearer king? And your Bride before him?"

Lothaire snapped his fingers. "Exactly!"

He doesn't deny capturing the king? In the past, this news would have jarred Trehan. Now he could think of naught else but Bettina. "What's your interest in my life anyway? You couldn't care less about the rest of your family."

"Your Bride is a princess of Dacia. Are you going

to allow a demon to rut betwixt her thighs? Not to be borne! If you won't put your house in order, I vow to you I will!"

House? Had Lothaire meant that in a general sense? *Or has he actually been listening?* Then his other words sunk in. "You push too far, Enemy of Old! Bloodlust has enfeebled your brain—"

"Look in the mirror, Cousin. Look at your pale face and your eyes black with wrath. What amazes me is that you actually wonder *why* your mind's declining. I'll bet you didn't mark your Bride's neck when you claimed her. Denied your instinct, did you? Then prepare for punishment."

Trehan fell back on an old argument. "Dacians don't drink from the flesh. We don't pierce other creatures!" No matter how seductive Bettina's flesh had been, Trehan had withstood its call.

No matter how *wrong* it had felt to deny himself and his Bride—as if he were letting them both down.

"You're a blooded Dacian in his prime, but you believe yourself above the most natural drives a vampire can have?" Lothaire smirked. "Above such 'savage' urges? It's laughable that you Daci shun a vampire's most basic need."

That need *had* felt basic and natural—*and savage*—all at the same time. "Should I become red-eyed like you?"

"As if you could! Do you know how many Loreans I had to tap to get like this? The sheer variety and quantity would astound you. Merely tippling from your toothsome Bride isn't going to do it." Lothaire rolled those red eyes. "Fool, you are *supposed* to mark her! You are *supposed* to drink from her!"

I know this, I felt this!

"If I have to instruct each of my cousins how to truly live as vampires, then I will." Lothaire steepled his fingers once again, his eyes swirling with crimson. "I'm the Enemy of Old, from the *House of Old*," he added with a sneer, "and my kinsmen each have lessons to learn from me."

So much for his underwhelming attention span.

"Mark my words, Trehan. You will *all* learn from me—though you won't like how I deliver my teachings. Now put your house in order!" Without a final look in Trehan's direction, he traced away.

Breaths shallowing, mind in turmoil, Trehan returned to the library, standing before his lonely fire.

Maybe Caspion had pressured Bettina into tainting the blood. Perhaps she hadn't *wanted* to betray him.

Not logical. She possessed the poison, she'd handed him the goblet, she'd bidden Trehan to drink. *She doesn't want* me.

Which is too bad. He withdrew his scry talisman. *Since she doesn't get a godsdamned say.*

No longer would Trehan deny himself what he desired—no longer would his savage hunger go unsated. He'd rise up from the ground like a true shade and seize the female who haunted him. . . .

46

"Two Sorceri and a sylph walk into a bar," Bettina muttered as she peeked through a cracked window pane into Erol's, a Lore watering hole.

Accompanying her this evening were Salem and Sabine: the Queen of Illusions, consort of the rage demon king, and Bettina's esteemed patroness. The three of them were just outside the entrance of this Louisiana shanty, preparing to go in.

Bettina squinted to see inside, but a valance of cobwebs dangled across the dirt-caked glass. The interior was filmy; smoke from cigars, opium pipes, and intoxibongs steeped the air. *No use.* She turned from the window.

Sabine flipped her magnificent mane of red curls over one pale shoulder, saying, "I've never been the subject of a joke that doesn't have ' . . . viscera!' as the punch line. But then, the night's still young." She ran one of her claw-tipped gauntlets down the bar's clapboard wall.

From Bettina's collar, Salem said, "First of all,

Salem doesn't walk. Second? I'd like to actually get into the bar sometime *tonight*. Third, I'd rather be the subject of a dirty limerick, preferably with the words *rising tunic, dick,* and *lick*."

"How do we even know we're in the right place?" Bettina asked. The two sorceresses were on a mission to find the soothsayer Nïx the Ever-Knowing, who'd disappeared from Abaddon without a whisper. Salem was tagging along to meet with someone from his phantom network of spies—about a lead on the poisoning case.

The three had just been traced here by one of Rune's guards, their designated demon for the night. He awaited them in the oyster-shell parking lot, smoking with other drivers.

Behind her wicked leather mask, Sabine rolled her tawny eyes. "Of course, we're in the right place. Nïx is leading the Vertas, and this is one of their haunts." She lifted her face and delicately sniffed. "Can you not *smell* the self-righteousness of all those do-gooders inside?"

Sabine had joined the Vertas because of her adoring demon husband, King Rydstrom the Good; didn't mean she had to be happy about it.

"How do I look?" Bettina asked. Knowing she might meet new allies, she'd taken care with her dress, wearing a slinky bandeau top of gold thread, a jade mask, and matching sarong. A pair of strappy gold sandals with blades in the heels—a new line!—completed the outfit.

For jewelry, she wore her crown, a collar, two armlets, a thighlet, and an anklet—all doubling as weapons.

This was her first return to the mortal realm, and she was prepared for anything, her heart-stopping power at the ready. . . .

Like a fool, Bettina also wore that necklace with Daciano's wedding ring tucked down in her top. But, alas, her summoning medallion had gone the way of Salem's copper bell, melted down, its control over her ending forever.

Chin raised imperiously, Sabine said, "You look passable—though not nearly as good as me." Bettina's great patroness wore a black miniskirt that matched her thigh-high boots and her mask. Atop her fiery red locks sat a blue-gold crown studded with gems, a present from Rydstrom. Sabine's solid-gold bustier was engraved to look like dragon scales.

Not bad work, if I say so myself. Well, except for a minor nip slip or two. *Or four.*

Sabine narrowed her eyes. "Though I am the fairest, you really are wearing the better jewels. Is it wise to outshine your patroness, Queen of Hearts?" Shimmying, she tugged up her bustier. "And you two price-gouged me with this piece."

"None doin', Trixie." Salem took his partnership in the biz *very* seriously. "We gave you a bang-up deal."

"I suppose. If you like nip slips." Sabine sighed, "And, let's face it, I *do*."

Salem said, "While you birds are arguing over who's the fairest of them all, just know this: I am. Me and me swingin' dick would put you two to shame. So if you ladies are done tarting yourselves up . . . ?"

"You're fortunate that I like you," Sabine began solemnly, "you price-gouging, foul-mouthed, sylphic man-slut. Ah, yes, I like these things about you indeed." With that, she opened the door.

As they entered, all eyes turned to them: two former Pravus sympathizers in full Sorceri regalia and an invisible sylph.

Conversations halted midsentence. Even the old-fashioned jukebox ran out of quarters at that moment.

Crickets.

Haughty Sabine traipsed deeper inside; Bettina put her shoulders back and followed.

Once conversations and the music resumed, Bettina said, "Do you always get this reaction here?"

"Of course, it's one of the reasons I continue to return," Sabine said over one shoulder. "I think of it this way: they stare because fear; they fear because they respect."

Bettina gazed around the place, supposing Erol's had a certain charm. Other Loreans seemed to be enjoying themselves. In the back, a foursome of fey threw darts from a good thirty feet away, aiming for a board the diameter of a tankard.

At the bar, several twenty-something Lykae chugged whiskey. Their clothes were stained with mud and blood, and they tossed around a dirty rugby ball. A handsome, slightly older Lykae broke up any roughhousing with a threatening growl.

That jukebox didn't play the music Bettina normally enjoyed, but at least she was out of the castle for a spell—away from things that reminded her of Daciano.

Such as, oh, *everything*.

When they passed a table full of nymphs, Salem took notice; Bettina's collar started to thrum. "Been so long since I got laid, I'm goin' to be revirginized," he muttered.

She'd been trying to glean more about his predicament from the secretive sylph. From his offhanded comments, she'd begun to suspect that the phantom had either gotten caught stealing something very valuable—or that he'd scorned a very powerful female.

Still vibrating for the nymphs, he said, "If I didn't have business to tend to, I'd just pop off for a spot of thigh diving and cleavage nesting. But then, that would be wrong. *Wrong*. Depraved, even. Immoral . . ."

Stifling a grin, Bettina scouted for the raven-haired Valkyrie. "I don't see Nïx."

"We can at least get a lead on her whereabouts," Sabine answered, her eyes alight with purpose. She was desperate to save her sister Melanthe from the Vrekeners. To that end, the sorceress was determined to find the soothsayer, so she could find . . . Daciano.

Gossip had spread among the Sorceri about the Prince of Shadow, the "Forbearer" who hunted Vrekeners "for fun" and jaunted to Skye Hall "at his leisure." When Sabine plotted rescue scenarios, they always included Trehan.

Bettina sought the Valkyrie for more selfish reasons. If that pointy-eared creature had already been meddling in her life, and Abaddon's affairs, then Bettina wanted to know why she'd . . . stopped.

I'd been so close to a life with Daciano.

"Someone here must know where Nïx got to," Sabine said. "If they're reluctant to share, we can field-test our weapons." She flashed the last one Bettina had made: a collapsible wand infused with a jolt of heart-stopping power.

"Oh, no, no. You need to be on your best behavior. If your husband finds out you're here . . ." Bettina reminded her, adjusting her mask.

Sabine wasn't listening. She'd stopped in front of a table with her brows raised, telling its demon occupants, "I'm curious as to why you're sitting at *my* table."

If Morgana was like a mesmerizing serpent, a giant king cobra of unfathomable power, then Sabine was like a sleek jungle cat, entrancing but deadly. And she'd just swished her tail.

The demons were burly, each wearing a black jacket embossed with NOLA GHOUL DISPOSAL—obviously a tough and hazardous job; still they fought each other in a beer-tossed wrangle to get away from Sabine.

As the Queen of Illusions, her power was matched only by her lethal reputation.

Salem politely used telekinesis to brush peanut shells off the table. "Ladies . . ."

As they sat, Sabine said, "Rydstrom won't even know I'm gone. He's shoring up a damaged dam today, selflessly rescuing demon lives."

How wonderful that must be—to have a hot, adoring king at home who was busily involved in public works. Bettina had learned that being a single ruler was challenging; now that Abaddon was a hopping, new Lore-ist destination, life could get crazy around the kingdom in a hurry.

It'd be nice to have a partner. . . .

"And besides," Sabine continued with a glare, "I wouldn't have to be here if you hadn't chased off the one mysterious vampire who knows the way to Skye Hall."

Bettina would never live this down. When she'd told Sabine—who knew much about vampires—the overview of her relationship with Trehan, the sorceress had been incredulous. "You allowed him to claim you, but then you denied him his vampire bite?"

Daciano had been so bent on pleasuring Bettina, on soothing her fears, that he'd agreed to wait until she was ready.

Sabine had gone on to explain, "Do you remember how empty you felt without your power? Well, imagine you'd suffered that lack for lifetimes, but at last you could get it back, little by little—from your mate's neck. Regrettably, he just didn't feel like putting out." Then she'd added the coup de grâce: "His denying his instinct to bite would be like you denying your need to create. No wonder he lost his mind and ditched you."

Now that Bettina understood more about his kind, her guilt had mounted—even as she'd felt a spark of hope about their future.

Then she'd remembered that she still couldn't *find* him.

A shifter waitress sauntered up to the table then. "What'll you two have?"

"Clearly, we're Sorceri." Sabine gestured at her resplendent self. "Ergo, we'd enjoy some Sorceri wine."

"Don't got it."

Sabine quirked a red brow. "Do you not? Check with Erol, shifter. He'll have an emergency bottle for me—because whenever I arrive, it's *an emergency*." She rapped her claws together. As the shifter scurried off, Sabine advised her, "And never naysay me again."

Back to business, Sabine asked Bettina, "You still have no reason to expect your vampire to return?"

"I don't know." *No reason at all.* "Maybe?" *Never.*

Salem snorted. "The vamp basically told her, 'I'm in a weird place in me life right now, and I need some space.' Of course he told her that by pointing a bloody sword at her whilst bellowing, 'I forsake you!' in front of the entire kingdom."

Bettina glared down at her collar. But then she admitted, "I think I kind of . . . broke him." Reflecting over that week, she'd begun to compare Daciano to metal under strain. Lack of blood and sleep had been applied pressure and heat. Apparently, denying his instinct to bite her had been corrosion.

Her plea of mercy? The blow of a smith's hammer. *Broken.*

At Bettina's stricken look, Sabine said, "Listen, Rydstrom and I had a few bumps in the road. Our initial romance consisted of me chaining him in a dungeon and sexually tormenting him. And yet we worked past it."

"Don't they make cards for that?" Salem chuckled.

"But Rydstrom wouldn't let you out of his sight until you were bonded," Bettina pointed out. "I can't even *locate* my male to work things out."

The waitress returned then with a bottle of wine and fine crystal glasses. Her hand shook as she poured. "Erol s-says this is on the house."

Sabine blinked at her. "Any reason it wouldn't be?" Before fleeing headlong, the female backed away three steps, as one would to royalty—which Sabine was.

"And speaking of *on the house,*" Sabine said, raising her glass, "all my jewels are going to be *free* until my sister is *free.*"

"Do you want our fledgling enterprise to go tits-up?" Salem sputtered. "It's called *cost,* sorceress. . . ." He trailed off. "Oi! I see my contact. I'll just go have a quick chin-wag, then."

Before Bettina could ask more, he'd ghosted away.

"I do like your phantom's greedy bent," Sabine said without a thread of sarcasm. "Such a pleasantly mercenary fellow." She scanned the room once again, meeting eyes with that older wolf at the bar.

The Lykae cast his boisterous companions a warning look, then started wending through the crowd toward her.

Not surprising. Sabine was magnetic.

But a couple of those younger Lykae even raised

their glasses to Bettina. She waved and smiled, musing, *Why couldn't I have fallen for a hot young Scot?*

An uncomplicated pup who liked to fetch rugby balls?

When the Lykae reached their table and sank his towering frame into a chair beside Sabine, the sorceress barely quirked an eyebrow. "Munro MacRieve, as I live and breathe."

She knew this gorgeous wolf? He was darkly attractive, with overtly masculine features and molten amber eyes. But his expression was severe. He looked as troubled as Cas had the day he'd left Rune.

Munro inclined his head to Sabine. "Sorceress." Then he indicated Bettina with a sexy lift of his chin. "And you are?"

"Queen Bettina of the Deathly Ones." That would *never* get old.

Munro gave her a nod, then turned to Sabine. "You've still no' found your sister?" he asked with a marked Scottish accent.

Yes, Bettina needed a hot young Scot *with a brogue.* And soon. The unfortunate part about discovering sex?

Craving it constantly, even when there was no chance of having any.

She decided that if she ever got over Daciano, she was going to put some feelers out.

Sabine gave a curt shake of her head. "My sister's still missing," she said with a pointed glare at Bettina. "We're hoping for an assist from Nïx."

"All the best with that. I've been hunting her up and down this realm. Heard there's a bluidy mile-long sign-up sheet for her. No, really, it's supposed to be over five thousand feet long."

"You seek help with your twin?" Sabine asked. *A*

male that handsome has a twin? "From what I heard, Uilleam's not exactly rebounding from his torture."

An expression of pain flashed over the Lykae's face, his amber eyes flickering the lightest blue. "No, Will has no' yet recovered."

Bettina knew that an order of evil humans had abducted and experimented on hundreds of immortals before all their prisoners had escaped. Had Sabine's sister Melanthe been tortured as well?

Sabine and Munro began speaking in more hushed tones about their siblings. Feeling like an eavesdropper, Bettina turned her chair to survey the denizens of the bar, members of the great Vertas army. There were so many interesting species inside, so much color and spectacle.

But her attention was unerringly drawn to the back, where couples necked on myriad couches. A demon and a nymph were getting particularly busy with wandering hands and long, wet kisses.

Daciano had been an incredible kisser, those firm lips of his so talented. She sighed. Who was she kidding? She was never getting over him.

She'd cleaved.

As ever, she wondered what he was doing. Would he have tried to return to his homeland? Or would he strike out and start a new life altogether?

Nothing was stopping him from finding another female, from *wedding* another. If she'd thought she'd been jealous over Caspion, the idea of Daciano making love to some gorgeous vampiress made her power flare uncontrollably.

Before Bettina could rein it in, her hands lit up. Her own *rattle rattle*. Great. Unintentional sorcery use on the mortal plane. "Sabine, we need to start wrapping up here." Bettina might be prepared to face down

Vrekeners if push came to shove, but she'd rather avoid it. "I've got to get back to Abaddon."

Even Sabine, who'd warred with the Vrekeners for centuries, gave them a wide berth. Or at least she had, before Lanthe had been taken.

Munro turned to Bettina with a narrowed gaze and a flash of recognition. "Did you say *Abaddon?*"

Oh, boy, I can guess where this is going. It seemed like everyone in the Lore had heard about the tournament. "I did."

At once, his irises glowed that eerie blue. "My clan's heard tales of what goes on in your demonarchy," he grated. "One of our own was beheaded there, no? One newly turned?"

"Yes," Bettina said simply, a habit learned by a vampire.

"Turned human or no, he possessed the Instinct. That made him our brother."

With a pang, Bettina recalled that Lykae's last word: *Brother.*

Munro bit out, "Any reason we shouldn't retaliate against Abaddon?"

"That male was entered into an irrevocable blood contract," Bettina said in a steady tone, her palms beginning to glow under the table, power at the ready; Munro dashed a hand over his chest, no doubt wondering why his heart had stuttered. "After that, there was nothing we could do."

Sabine was watching this exchange like a demon at a kobold toss.

"Who entered him?" Munro demanded.

"A sect of warlocks called Those Best Forgotten. I couldn't get them out of my kingdom fast enough."

"Warlocks." His lips curled in disgust, revealing

lengthening fangs. It was no secret that the Lykae distrusted all things magical.

"As a show of goodwill between my kingdom and yours," Bettina said, "I will give you information we gathered on them. Seems they're making many more of your kind, turning humans, then using them as slaves. We've also got their location."

"Slaves?" Munro's dark claws punctured the table. "My clan knows how to find the Forgotten."

"Good. Then you can 'retaliate' against those that *deserve* it. And that's all I'll say on the matter," she added, just because she could.

"Happy hunting," Sabine said as Munro levered himself to his feet, his chair clattering behind him as he charged off.

To his crew at the bar, he snapped rough words in Gaelic. They sounded like marching orders.

Each of the young Lykae reacted with aggression, his eyes turning, an image of a wolven creature flashing over him.

When the pack plowed out of the bar, Bettina thought, *I could almost feel sorry for Those Best Forgotten. . . .*

Sabine faced her with a raised brow. "Oh, Munro just called from the parking lot, mentioned something about wanting his testicles back. What's gotten into you?"

Bettina shrugged.

"You have all this new confidence, and you don't fear me anymore. Which begs the question"—Sabine peered intently at her—"am I losing my touch? Or are you *finally* finding yours?"

"Maybe I am." *I totally am.* She felt more comfortable in her own skin, more confident with her rule.

But the aching emptiness she'd felt after losing her power had only been replaced by losing the vampire.

He was her first real love. He would be her last.

Why couldn't Trehan Daciano be her devotedly hot king, involving himself with public works and demon lifesaving—

Right before her eyes, the bar's haze of smoke seemed to transform, changing consistency all around them. Loreans grew uneasy. More than one group shuffled, flew, or scampered toward the exit.

"What's happening?" Sabine demanded.

Bettina could no longer see the sorceress through the haze. She glanced down at her now glittering skin. *Speak of the vampire.* "He's . . . here." She shot to her feet, whirling around.

Daciano!

His skin was even paler now, his build rangier than the last time she'd seen him. He was dressed all in black, like a reaper in a long leather coat. His lips were thinned, his eyes black with emotion.

Rage? Vampiric hunger? Lust?

All she knew was that he was absolutely about to seize her. A male vampire in his prime had come for his Bride.

He disappeared. *No, wait—*

His strong arms wrapped around her from behind, enveloping her with his scent and heat. At her ear, he rasped, *"Miss me, Bride?"*

Through the mist, Trehan had gazed at her, a vision in her bold silks and jewels. A demonic-looking crown perched atop shining braids. A dark green mask high-lighted her eyes.

He grudgingly admitted that she was even more beautiful than when he'd last seen her.

Life with Caspion must be agreeing with her.

At the thought, Trehan squeezed her tighter. *Now she is warm and trembling in* my *arms. Where she will remain.*

Just before he traced her back to Dacia, he glanced over his shoulder at her Sorceri companion. The female darted her eyes blindly, unable to see through the mist, but she looked delighted. "Have fun, Bettina! You two meet me back here in an hour. . . ."

Trehan frowned, then forced his Bride back to his home.

Inside his suite, Bettina staggered back from him. By the way she was staring at his eyes, he knew they were still black.

"Where have you taken me?" She peered around his home with an expression of dawning horror, then rushed to the opened balcony. As she gazed out over the city, she rocked on her feet. "I-I'm in Dacia."

"Yes."

Without turning back, she cried, *"Why?"*

"I've been accepted back in. My Bride as well."

"H-how dare you take me to this place!"

For the thousandth time, he pictured the look on her face as she'd handed him that goblet. "I dare easily." He traced behind her, inhaling her scent. "You belong to me. And it was time to collect my belongings."

47

In the confusion of the bar, the vampire had been able to snare Bettina so easily, plucking her like gold from a rushing stream, then taking her to . . . Dacia.

A place where outsiders could check in, but could *never* check out. Yes, she'd wanted to talk to him—but not at the expense of her freedom!

Barely tamping down her rising shock, she'd hastened across the spacious, gilded room to a balcony. At the railing, she'd gazed out in bewilderment, seeing everything Daciano had described of his home.

Soaring caverns, wisps of mist, carved-stone buildings. A giant crystal above all twinkled with prismed light. A haunting black castle stood sentinel not far away.

The vampire had truly ferried her to the land of the legendary Daci.

Bristling, she pivoted around, finding herself eye level with his chest. He was scant inches away, so close that she had to crane her head up to meet his gaze.

Close enough that she could take in his addictive scent. It *still* scrambled her thought processes.

He opened his mouth to speak, then closed it, looking as confused and miserable as she'd been feeling for weeks.

Were his thoughts scrambled as well?

Part of her was outraged by his behavior; part of her was stunned that they were together. *I'm with him; he's just here.*

No, he'd *abducted* her. Sure, deep down she'd wanted him to come for her—but she'd never imagined a reunion like this. Why couldn't he have shown up, proverbial hat in hand, asking for another chance with her? Not even hat in hand—how about just looking at her with a steady gaze as he admitted they had some things to work out?

How quickly she would've folded. But nooo, he had to kidnap her with a crazed gleam in his eye! And he'd taken her to this one-way realm? Just when she was getting the hang of ruling her own kingdom? "If you think I'm going to be stuck down here, think again. You trace me back or I'll . . ." She trailed off, catching sight of a metallic sparkle out of the corner of her eye. His vast weapons collection! "Or I'll . . ."

. . . take every single one of those with me?

Lances, maces, axes, long swords, shields, blades. Arms classed in groups, divided by epochs. Shining. Flawlessly curated in gold cases. *Like a monument to tissue disruption.* It would take her days to investigate all the items.

When she could drag her gaze from the collection, she peeked around him to survey the rest of his home. A solitary chair with books stacked around it sat in front of a great hearth. A lazy fire burned, illuminating a luxe interior. Artwork lined the walls; she thought she recognized a few . . . from infamous heists?

One corridor branched off from this sitting area, opening up into a wing with scores of bookshelves. Through another corridor, she glimpsed a bedroom— with a bed of furs low to the ground.

A vampire's library lair.

"Investigate all you like," he told her in a rough voice. "Familiarize yourself with your new surroundings. We have all the time in the world. . . ."

Even in the midst of his turmoil, Trehan felt pride over his home, over the luxuries that his sorceress so obviously appreciated.

He stood taller, knowing she was impressed. Before, he'd brought nothing to their union—other than a coveted crystal and one family sword. Going forward, they would enjoy the wealth that *he* provided.

Now that he'd abducted her, this plan struck him as brilliant. *Strange that it took a mad vampire like Lothaire to teach me that I need to* be *a vampire.* Dimly, he wondered, *What else are we Dacianos to be taught?*

"So are you and I going to talk about what happened during that fight or not?" Bettina demanded, tossing her long hair back, as if preparing to spar. "You have to know why I did what I did."

"You made that abundantly clear!"

"I never imagined that you would shake off the poison so quickly."

His jaw slackened. Brazenly admitting it?

"But if I were in the same situation, I'd do it all over again!"

"*What?*" he roared, punching the closest wall. The building rocked.

Strangely, she didn't flinch, just took his measure with glittering eyes. "Obviously you're still unwell. I'm not going to fare any better with you now than I did the last time we talked. You need to take me home, Trehan."

"I'm not done with you, Bride." *Will* never *be done with you.* "As you once told me: resign yourself."

"I won't be kept here against my will."

He raised his brows. "And what will you do to stop me?"

"You forget I have my power back." Light glowed from her raised palms.

"How could I *ever* forget that?" He stalked to her, looming over her. "Do it, sorceress!" He bowed his chest against her hands. "At least my heart will feel altered from its current wretched state." *Stopped heart, lost heart.* What did it matter?

Chin raised, she shoved at him with both hands. He felt heat rising from them and tensed against the coming pain.

But she didn't go through with it, dropping her hands with a frustrated sound.

"You hesitate to use your power to help yourself? Yet you wielded it so readily to protect that demon."

"Of course I protected him! I always will if I can."

Fangs gone sharp, Trehan vowed, "He can't want you like I do—no one can! Even if you do worse than you already have, I'll still come for you."

∽

Before Bettina could even react to his baffling words, Daciano had clamped her around the waist and traced her. An instant later, she perceived furs beneath her. He'd taken her to his bed?

"Vampire, stop! Just think about what you're doing!"

Without slowing, he followed her down, pinning her arms above her head, stretching his body over hers.

When he grazed the side of his face against hers, seeming to breathe her in, she peered past him at the vaulted ceiling.

His own scent called to her—his skin, his *need*—and she found herself responding to him. Gods, she'd missed him so much! "I-I don't understand what's happening." Maybe if she had more experience with relationships, or with his kind in general, she'd be able to decipher his words, his wild emotions. "I don't understand *any* of this."

"All you need to understand is that I'm never letting you go."

Some weak part of her thrilled at his words. But . . . "You can't just keep me here. I have a kingdom to rule."

"Can't I? Maybe I wouldn't have done so back when I had honor. But you've stripped me down to the bone, woman. Until I'm nothing but pain and need. A shade."

"Did you bring me here to punish me?"

"Yes! *No.*" He worked his hips between her thighs, rucking her skirt up to her waist. "I'll figure this all out when I'm inside you."

Just like that night in his tent, she could feel his rigid erection pressing against her panties. Against her will, her sex readied for that hardness, growing damp. "I don't want you—not like *this.*"

He drew back above her, but he kept her wrists pinned. "Damn you, Bettina!" With his free hand, he clutched the back of her head, searching her expression. "Choose *me* over him! Want *me*."

Over *Cas*? *I did!*

But before she could work up a scathing retort, the vampire yelled, "What do I have to do? Fucking tell me!" He jostled her mask, partly obscuring her vision.

"Let my hands go!" When he didn't, she rubbed her shoulder against the corner of the mask to right it.

At once, a change seemed to come over him. With his irises flickering from black to green and back, he released her, tenderly straightening it for her.

Then, with a groan of misery, he buried his face against her neck, punching the pallet again and again. "I can't hurt you," he rasped. "Even now, I can't."

"But clearly you *wish* you could?" she sputtered. She didn't deserve this from him! Yet he didn't seem to be listening to her whatsoever.

Against her ear, he murmured, "Before you, I was a male of little emotion." As if he couldn't help himself, he lifted his head up to brush his lips over her cheek. "Now with you? I've never struggled against such lust. I've never felt such wrath." He punctuated his harsh words with a gentle kiss to her temple. "I've never hurt so deeply." A kiss to the corner of her lips. "Or loved so hard."

"Love?" Daciano had talked about fate and bloodings and Brides. But he'd never mentioned love!

His eyes were mesmerizing as they caught hers. "I hate what you did. And still I love you." With a bitter curse, as if he'd said too much, he drew away from her. Turning to sit at the edge of the pallet, he dropped his head into his hands. "I won't let you go, *dragă*. You'll stay in this underworld with me until your other life is but a memory."

"Stay with you?" She righted her clothing with snappish movements. "After how you've treated me!" He'd abandoned her, then abducted her—never explaining his actions, nor allowing Bettina to explain hers.

His head swung up. "*You* are angry at *me*? You betrayed me repeatedly! And then, on top of everything, you used your power on me—on *me*. Apparently I was the *last* to know you'd recovered it!"

"I had no choice but to use it. And what about your actions? You humiliated me in front of my people! Not to mention what you did to Caspion."

"You *dare* utter his name in my home?" A chilling malice laced his tone. "I blame him for your treachery. He talked you into it. You wouldn't have betrayed me on your own."

"He had nothing to do with it! I didn't know what else to do! I was terrified for you."

Double take. "So you *poisoned* me?"

"I had to— Wait. What?"

"You handed me that fucking goblet of blood, the one *spiked with poison* from the ring you always wore."

She gasped. "Vampire, you believe *I* did that?"

48

When Trehan registered her dumbfounded expression, hope bloomed in his chest.

Then logic reminded him that she and Caspion had the means, the motive, the opportunity. *You reach, because you want her so badly.* "If not you and the demon, then who would dare?"

She cried, "How about *your cousins*? The ones who are always trying to kill you!"

"They would never do something so dishonorable."

"But you think *I* would?"

In a singsong tone, Salem said at his ear: "You're both wrong."

"Sylph! You followed Bettina here?" *And remained? When I was about to take her?*

"I'd morphed wiv her collar a split second before your mist came. Then I figured you were goin' to nab her, so I tagged along to make sure you wouldn't hurt her." The being shimmered around the room as if excited. "Do you know how long I've been wantin' to come here?"

Bettina looked as mystified as Trehan felt. "Salem, how are we both wrong? Who did it?"

"The vampire's squire! Not twenty minutes ago, another phantom told me he'd heard the young vamp brag about mickeying Daciano's carafe of blood." Salem addressed Trehan as he said, "Seems the Horde lord you killed in the melee was his sire. The little bugger couldn't murder you outside the ring, but he could hamstring you before a match so Caspion could take your head."

The bloody squire *poisoned me?* That soon-to-be-dead vampire?

Not Bettina, then.

Trehan's eyes widened, and his heart began to thud. *Not* Bettina! "This news is . . . welcome," he choked out in utter understatement. "Now, begone from here."

Salem chuckled. "Right you are, Your Kingness. Commencing me tour of the Realm of Blood and Mist—"

"I didn't mean *into the kingdom!*"

Salem was already gone. And Trehan couldn't stay angry, not with all the relief he felt.

In a quiet voice, Bettina said, "You truly thought I could do something like that to you?"

He traced to the edge of the bed, sitting beside her, just preventing himself from dragging her over his lap. "Bettina, I am sorry. I thought the demon had influenced you."

She pulled her knees to her chest and turned away. "Cas *wanted* to defeat you on his own. He believed he could, until you went crazy."

She will never forgive this. "I . . . didn't know."

"That night, I had just realized that I was feeling something deeper for you than I'd ever felt before," she said softly, *sadly*—as if she was speaking about something long lost, never to be found again. "I saw that you had been poisoned, and I thought I was saving your life." She gave a humorless laugh. "I believed I was *finally* going to be able to help."

She'd wanted only to save me? He tried to speak past the lump in his throat. Couldn't.

"I'd recognized that Cas was nothing more than my best friend—one I will always treasure. I'd accepted that what I felt for you was completely different. But then you turned around and humiliated both Cas and me."

So we'd gotten past the demon at last, and I *fucked my chances?*

She continued, "I'd pointed out that you were about to get *everything* and asked you not to hurt him. But I guess consideration for us went out the window when you suspected me of poisoning you."

He flinched.

"My coronation was a misery. Everyone had accepted you as their king, so when you forsook me, they thought there must've been a good reason!"

She'd already felt like an imposter in Abaddon, and he'd made it that much worse for her. "Bettina . . ." How to explain what had been going on in his mind? When even now he could hardly think? Instinct was riding him hard.

"I've been able to 'rehabilitate' my image, but Cas wasn't so fortunate. He was shunned, forced to leave. He's gone to the Plane of Lost Years."

Then he'd gone to hell. *I have* definitely *fucked my chances with her.* How to make amends? How to—

Gaze narrowing, Trehan reached for the crystal around his neck, yanking it free. "This will be his."

She faced him. "Pardon?"

"Caspion is a tracker? Consider this amends."

"You'd do that?" She tilted her head. "When it's been passed down through your house?" Trehan took her hand and placed the crystal in her palm, closing her delicate fingers over it.

Bettina stared down at the crystal, then up at Daciano. She had never seen a male look so anguished, as if he'd been gutted and was slowly expiring. "Vampire, I appreciate the gesture, but I can't accept this," she said, returning it to him. "Please put it back on."

Brows drawn, he reluctantly did, his bemusement seeming to deepen—as if she'd rejected him anew.

"I'm only saying that you should think about a decision like this."

"Think? Bettina, I *can't* think. Since my blooding, logic and reason have vanished. As I said, all I can do is feel. And I've very little experience . . . feeling."

"What happened between the morning after we made love and that twilight in the tent?"

"I don't know how to explain myself, or even if it's possible."

"Try."

"During the tournament, there'd been much . . . pressure," he began haltingly. "It continued to build."

"What kind of pressure?"

"Over that week, I experienced your attack first-hand, and it filled me with unimaginable wrath. And yet I could only murder and torture your foes *once*. I was expected to slay Goürlav—but not to injure him. I'd believed that I would fight Caspion to the death—and that I would lose you if I survived. Then, when we made love, I denied . . . instincts."

His instinct to bite. Just as Sabine had said.

"I'd lost blood against the primordial and continued to deteriorate over the day. Then you appeared, and you showed such concern for Caspion. I thought I'd been doing everything right to win you from him—denying myself, toiling for the future, trying to earn your affection."

She was aware of how hard he had worked and all the miraculous feats he'd accomplished in such a short time. He'd been under enough pressure to make twenty Dacians snap. Even now he wasn't physically well, obviously hadn't been drinking enough to sustain himself.

"The jealousy maddened me. You were right—I wasn't hearing you. I can see that now. Even the mere mention of his name enraged me."

"Why? I thought I made it clear that he was my friend. And I . . . I made love to *you*, Trehan. Surely you understood how I felt about you. I believed we were getting *married* in hours."

"I see it now, but gods, I couldn't then! The jealousy . . . Always I remembered our first night together. Always I could see how you would be with Caspion, could see *exactly* what he would enjoy if you ever went to him. It made me crazed. . . ." He trailed off, clenching his jaw.

She tried to imagine what he'd gone through. How would she feel if Trehan had welcomed her into his bed, yet then she discovered that his every touch and kiss had been intended for another?

Jealousy scalded her at the mere thought.

"Then, in the fight, when I realized I'd been poisoned, I remembered that you'd handed me that goblet. I concluded that you were in league with Caspion." He clasped his forehead. "I believed that you would wed him and that I'd lost you forever. I wanted to punish him for winning you. I couldn't handle the idea of not having you," he said, adding in a mutter, "any better than I can now."

"If I'd let you drink from me, would you have reacted differently?"

"This is *in no way* your fault. It was mine."

"But would you have suffered that confusion and aggression?"

"No matter my condition, how could I have suspected *you*?"

How? She sighed. *Probably because I had a poison ring, a poison arsenal, a smoking-gun goblet in my hand, and my best friend in the ring with you.*

Suddenly his hand shot out, palm gripping the back of her neck. "Bettina, I thought . . . I truly thought that I was doing everything *right*. I want only to do right by you."

And with those laden words, Bettina recognized that this wasn't over between them. Her grief from losing him started to evaporate.

She began to view their circumstances in a completely new light. Cas was alive, Bettina was a free queen in her own right, empowered in more ways than one—and this gorgeous, sexy Dacian looked as if he was barely restraining himself from pulling her beneath him and kissing her until she decided to keep him.

And she *would* keep him.

I want him above all things. These days, Bettina of Abaddon got what she wanted.

49

Grabbing her, Trehan? Snatching her nape?

With an inward curse, he released her, turning away to try to reason this out. To calm his frenetic thoughts.

Merely looking at her face made instinct *scream* inside him. Much less the siren's call of her sexy, little pulse-point.

"I can't stay mad at you for suspecting me." She touched his back, the contact jolting him with anticipation. "Just as you doubted me, I doubted both Cas and Raum." He heard her exhale.

He didn't breathe.

"I'm not blameless, Trehan. I'd do things differently if I could." Over his shoulder, she dangled a chain, threaded through with . . .

A male's gold ring.

His eyes slid shut as he clasped it in his fist. "You made this?" Voice gone hoarse, he said, "For me?" He yanked it off the chain, couldn't shove it on his finger fast enough.

"Yes. The morning after we made love."

He twisted around to face her. "Then you can forgive me." Everything he desired—family, friend, mistress, grand love of his life—was so godsdamned close. *My love awaits with widened eyes.* . . .

"Vampire, you were a certain way with me in the beginning, and then you changed. It hurt so badly, like I lost you twice. I could never go through something like that again."

He clenched his fists to keep from grabbing her once more. "I vow to you—and I vow to the Lore—that I will never treat you that way again. I'll spend the rest of my life showing the Abaddonae how much I adore you, if you give me another chance."

"Then it's given, Trehan. Because you *did* try to do everything right. You *did* work hard and you gave so much. If not for the squire's actions, we'd be in our bed right now."

He frowned. "No, Bettina, even without the poison, I still . . ." He shoved his fingers through his hair. "My mind, it isn't well." How exactly was he supposed to present his dilemma to her? *I need to sink my fangs in your neck while I'm inside you.* "Vampire males . . . we need . . ." He eased closer to her, his fangs sharpening.

She had to notice them, but didn't pull away.

"We need to drink. I can't deny what I am."

She *nodded*? "I'd decided to give you my blood on our wedding night. I'd regretted not trusting you to make a bite wonderful. I shouldn't have denied you before."

Again, she'd shocked him. Again, he moved nearer. Had she sidled closer as well?

If she could accept him, then *nothing* would stand in their way. Which meant his heart would be whole, his mind eased. He would use both to cherish her, and all would be well.

"You can accept my nature?"

She blinked at him. "I already *have*."

"Wed me, Bett! As soon as possible. I want you to be my queen. I want us to rule together."

"You'd truly come back to Abaddon? Give up Dacia again?"

"To have you? *Anything*. But Dacia will likely open its gates, so visiting is not out of the question."

By now, their lips were inches apart. "We could come back and play with all your weapons?" She looked bold and breathless—and happy. Heated air whorled around her body, her sorcery mirroring her emotions.

"*Our* weapons." He removed her mask. "As you wish to, my merry sorceress."

"Then take me home, Trehan, to our bed."

How those words affected him! He traced her directly there, easing her back across the silk.

Cradling her face, he bent to her lips, taking them beneath his own. With all the fervor he felt inside, he kissed her.

Only this time, no gallows awaited.

As their tongues twined, he and Bettina began ridding each other of clothes in a mad rush, hands colliding in their haste to touch bared skin.

Once he had his Bride naked, he drew back to simply gaze down at her. Swirls of light emanated from her supple skin, her eyes so lustrous. Magic heated her very palms as she reached for him, her fingertips sizzling when she swept them over his chest.

A sorceress desirous of her male.

Dipping his head, he nuzzled his lips all around one nipple, then the other, as his hand grazed up her thighs, higher . . .

She swiftly spread them, as if impatient for his touch.

With a reverent groan, he cupped her dewy sex, caressing it, demonstrating how much he adored her with every lingering stroke—

"Trehan," she began in a breathless voice, "can you . . . can you really *wait* for this much longer?"

Against her breast, he grated, "Gods, I love your questions, female!" Like a shot, he rose above her. When he was poised at her wet entrance, she laid her soft palms on his face.

Holding his gaze, she murmured, "You know you can do *anything* to me, Trehan. I'm yours, only yours. I always will be."

At last! Words from a dream—

She pulled her shining hair over her shoulder, baring the lovely column of her neck. "Anything, vampire."

His fangs throbbed for that skin. "If you knew how badly I've craved this . . . I don't want to hurt you."

"You won't."

"It's more than thirst, *dragă*. I hunger for your *lifeblood*. I need it mingling with my own forever."

"Then take it."

I'm truly to pierce her? She wanted *him,* had accepted him in all ways. And he would spend eternity proving to her why she was right to.

Must make it pleasurable.

Though he quaked with eagerness, he painstakingly fed his length inside her tight sex—with a slow, hot, wet glide to the hilt. He yelled out from the shock of pleasure, savoring her throaty moan.

Seated so deep inside her, he lowered his head, bringing his mouth to the tender skin where her neck and shoulder met. He licked her there, preparing her.

To take her blood while claiming her body. After centuries of waiting, fantasy would be made flesh. "Bett?" he rasped against her, still disbelieving.

"Now, Trehan. Now!"

As he opened his jaw wider, his fangs lengthened even more. He pressed the tips against her pulse. . . .

His bite breached the surface of her skin—again, with a slow, hot, wet glide. Her sweet flesh enveloped his aching fangs—a tight seal that made him shudder above her. So tight that no blood welled.

He had to *suck* her, and the feel of it was . . .

So fucking perfect.

He gave a wretched groan as her blood touched his tongue. With that first contact, Trehan lost his mind.

Or found it.

Under his fangs, she writhed, her pale throat working as she screamed, "Trehan! Ah, gods, yes!"

His hips began to rock between her thighs as he drew her essence into him—a swift, scorching infusion that coursed through his every vein.

With each drop, his weeks-long grief ebbed, his ages of loneliness faded.

His female tasted of magic and heat and mystery. Sorcery steeped her blood, now dancing in his, enlivening him body and mind. *Bettina este viață.*

His lids slid shut with bliss as he thrust wildly, drank deeply. *Better than fantasy!*

But his eyes flashed open as he felt her body readying to come, those beginning tremors like strokes around his shaft. . . .

When the vampire had eased his fangs into her flesh, Bettina had trembled with shock.

Like brands, they'd scalded her with white-hot pleasure. Like brands, they'd changed her irrevocably.

His bite *was* ruinous, pleasuring her so thoroughly she knew she would crave it forever.

As he sucked her blood with rumbling growls, ecstasy welled up inside her. Each of his draws magnified it. A cry escaped her lips, making him snarl into his bite.

Her body tightened beneath his—twisting, rocking, spiraling—rapture about to overtake her. "Vampire! *More!*"

Though his mouth and bite were gentle, his hips began to surge between her legs, pounding his thick shaft inside her, just as she needed him to.

His hands covered her breasts, kneading possessively, sending her closer to the edge. She arched into his palms, rubbing her achy nipples against his callused skin.

Friction. Pressure. His *fangs*—

"Trehan, I'm coming!" Her climax engulfed her. In turn, he drew harder from her, intensifying the spasms until they ripped through her like an electric current.

He kept thrusting, plunging into the wetness of her orgasm as it continued on and on.

She was still coming when he drove his erection as deep as it'd go. Fangs and shaft buried inside her body, he joined her release, beginning to pump his semen into her womb.

She gloried in that first searing jet of seed. But then he had to relinquish her neck, his back bowing from the intensity of his spend.

He bared his fangs as he roared to the ceiling, *"Bettina!"* Muscles wracked, he thrashed atop her . . . again and again, filling her with copious heat. "You were made . . . for me alone. *A mea, eternitate!"*

Another frenzied thrust . . . and another . . .

With a final dazed groan, he collapsed over her, mouth back at her neck to kiss the bite, as if in thanks. When his hoarse exhalations fanned over his mark, she shivered anew, her lips curling. "Could you feel me, Trehan?"

"Ah, love, I could feel you very well," he said, easing to his back, with her enfolded in his arms. "And you liked my bite." Could he possibly sound any prouder?

"You *know* I did. So, is bite play something we can do daily? Or more like, hourly?"

"I love your questions, Bett."

She raised her head, laying her elbows across his still heaving chest and surveyed her vampire. The change in him was immediate—and profound.

She noted the color tingeing his high cheekbones, the swelling of his muscles as her lifeblood became his, the clearness of his eyes.

Green like Abaddon's forest.

And when he smiled at her, with his black hair tousled over his forehead and his eyes dancing, he took her breath. That grinding tension . . . had *disappeared*.

He brushed a braid from her cheek. Sounding very

much like a well-pleasured male, he rasped, "I love you, *dragă mea*."

"I love you too." She sighed like a sap, knowing she was gazing at him with a dreamy expression. *"Bad."*

He cast her a double-take, then his grin deepened. Satisfaction rolling off him in waves, he held up his warrior's hand to view his ring. "Will any spikes pop out of this, I wonder."

"Only if you try to take it off."

A laugh rumbled from his chest. "No chance of that. I'd get you a ring as well, but I'd never find one equal to what you can create."

"If you wear my ring, I'll wear your bite."

He brushed her hair from her neck. "Already it fades."

"I guess you'll just have to give me another one." She felt his shaft pulse at her words.

"Delightedly," he said in a husky tone. "But first, I meant what I said, Bett. I want to wed you as soon as possible. Today."

"Okay! It counts as *two* boons. . . ." Yet then her excitement dimmed somewhat.

"What is it?"

She bit her bottom lip. "Do you recall the woman who was with me in the bar? She's my patroness, Sabine. She's been searching for you." At his quizzical glance, Bettina said, "Her sister has been taken by Vrekeners, and she's very interested to learn how you reached Skye Hall."

"I see. Do you want me to help her find her sister?"

"I . . . maybe? In any event, I feel like I should warn you—the more I look at my life, the more complicated it seems. Are you sure you want to sign on?"